THE TIME ROADS

TOR BOOKS
BY BETH BERNOBICH

Passion Play
Queen's Hunt
Allegiance
The Time Roads

THE
TIME
ROADS

BETH BERNOBICH

TOR®

A TOM DOHERTY ASSOCIATES BOOK
NEW YORK

THE TIME ROADS

Copyright © 2014 by Beth Bernobich

A Tor Book
Published by Tom Doherty Associates, LLC
175 Fifth Avenue
New York, NY 10010

www.tor-forge.com

Tor® is a registered trademark of Tom Doherty Associates, LLC.

The Library of Congress Cataloging-in-Publication Data is available upon request.

ISBN 978-0-7653-3125-0 (trade paperback)
ISBN 978-1-4299-5209-5 (e-book)

Tor books may be purchased for educational, business, or promotional use. For information on bulk purchases, please contact Macmillan Corporate and Premium Sales Department at 1-800-221-7945, extension 5442, or write specialmarkets@macmillan.com.

First Edition: October 2014

Printed in the United States of America

0 9 8 7 6 5 4 3 2 1

To Dr. James E. Scanlon,
for making history class magical

ACKNOWLEDGMENTS

Twelve years ago, I sat down to write a story about mathematics and murder and time. One story soon turned into three, with the hope of someday writing the fourth and final chapter of this braided tale.

The list of friends and editors who helped me along the way numbers close to infinite. My thanks go out to Greg Feeley for his thorough and uncompromising critique of the first story. To Lois Tilton, for her comments on matters of prose and alternate history. To Mark Hünken, for feedback on the German as well as the story, and to Liz Bourke and Jenn Vhrin, for their patient help with the Irish. And to all my friends on Livejournal and Absolutewrite, for the critiques and suggestions and epiphanies over the years, a huge round of thanks and appreciation. Your encouragement has been invaluable.

I also owe a great debt to Sheila Williams and Nick Gevers for publishing the first three installments about my alternate Éire; to my agent, Vaughne Hansen, for her tireless work on my behalf; and to Claire Eddy for giving me the opportunity to bring all four stories together into the single book I envisioned all those years ago.

And finally, to Dr. Scanlon, who taught the world's best alternate-history class: thank you. You are an amazing teacher.

THE TIME ROADS

THE GOLDEN OCTOPUS

NOVEMBER 1897

I first met Breandan Reid Ó Cuilinn in my father's Court, in Cill Cannig, on a bright, cold November day. I was seventeen, a Princess Royal and heir to the throne. He, I knew from reports assembled by the King's Constabulary, was the son of a country gentleman, thirty years old, with degrees from Awveline University in physics and philosophy.

He never even noticed me.

To be sure, he was there to impress my father—the king—and the many astrologers, scientists, and councilors who made up the king's Court in those days, not a young woman watching from the shadows. But I'm rambling on without purpose. Let me tell you what happened that day.

It was late November, as I said. We were all gathered in the smallest of my father's audience chambers, the one where he liked to hold such demonstrations. (*Miscellaneous Scientific Inquiries, Etc.*, is how the steward labeled them.) Sunlight poured through the high square windows; an early morning rain shower had spattered droplets over the panes, which cast a hundred tiny rainbows upon the gray marble floor. A raised platform ran around three sides of the room, with a series of recessed alcoves. I sat in my usual place, the middle alcove, which gave me the best view of my father and Ó Cuilinn both.

"Tell me," my father said, "what you hope to discover."

Breandan Ó Cuilinn—excuse me, Doctor Ó Cuilinn—said, "I cannot tell yet. I can only report on what I have achieved."

The old astrologers, who had served my grandfather and great-grandfather since the middle of the century, nodded. They recognized temporizing, no matter what form it took. "True, true," one old man mumbled. "We can chart the moon and all the stars of heaven, but there are subtleties beyond even the most learned of the cloud diviners."

The Court scientists and mage-mathematicians, whose philosophies belonged to both the old and the modern schools, merely shrugged and stared hard at the strange machine Ó Cuilinn had brought, which now sat upon a large battered worktable, evidently provided by the steward from the palace attics.

He was not a rich man, this Doctor Ó Cuilinn. He had arrived in a hired van, with no servants, no assistants, and had transported the five large crates to the interview chamber himself using a freight trolley. He must have assembled the machine as well. That would account for the oil stain on the sleeve of his frock coat, and the dusty knees of his trousers.

The machine itself gleamed in brass and silver splendor upon the table. It was as large as a man's torso and shaped like an octopus, with shining glass tubes writhing about the massive central orb. Wires ran through the tubes, like thin black veins; more wires snaked over the table and connected the device to a crate of batteries sitting on the floor. The metals themselves, however beautiful, were likely chosen for their properties, I thought, remembering the man's initial letter. And it required a great deal of electricity. But what were those strange knobs and dials for?

With a practiced gesture, Ó Cuilinn drew a small metal bar from his pocket. It was just a few inches long, made of some dull silvery material. He pressed a spot on the side of the octopus's body. A section of the front slid open—as though the octopus had opened its mouth into a rectangular yawn. Ó Cuilinn placed the metal bar inside. The mouth closed again; this time, I could see the thin lines marking its edges.

"What kind of metal is that?" my father asked.

"An iron-chromium alloy, Your Majesty," Ó Cuilinn replied. "It proves less reactive than pure iron."

If he doubted my father's ability to understand the answer, he made no sign of it. But one question led to a barrage of others from the Court scientists. Those batteries, what were they, and what charge did they produce? Was it purely electricity his device used? If so, what role did those glass tubes perform? A modified Leclanché cell, Ó Cuilinn replied. Ammonium chloride mixed with plaster of paris, sealed in a zinc shell, each of which produced 1.5 volts. He was corresponding with a collective of scientists from Sweden and the Dietsch Empire, concerning a rechargeable battery with nickel and cadmium electrodes in a potassium-hydroxide solution. Yes, the results would certainly prove more reliable. Also, more expensive. (Here the councilors muttered something about how these research men always demanded more money.) As for the role of the batteries, they were purely to start the necessary reactions. He would rather not discuss the further details until His Majesty and the gentlemen had observed the machine's performance.

Turning away from his audience, Ó Cuilinn began to manipulate a series of switches and dials along the lower edge of the machine. The scientists and mathematicians fell silent, absorbed in watching his work. The astrologers were less entranced, and one old man continued to mumble about the stars and their effect upon the Earth's magnetic currents. Ó Cuilinn ignored them all. His long slim fingers moved deftly over the octopus's face. Gradually I became aware of a soft buzzing between my ears. The skin along my arms itched. Just as I reached up to rub them, a loud crack echoed from the device.

The audience gasped. I started, then found myself unable to move.

Gas inside the tubes ignited into gaudy colors. Smoke roiled around the device, and there was a distinct burning odor, as though lightning had struck inside the palace. The astrologers and other philosophers were all whispering. The scientists frowned. My father too was frowning, but in concentration.

Ó Cuilinn alone seemed unperturbed. He leaned down and touched the device. Again the octopus yawned. I stared, uncertain what I might see inside its mouth.

I saw nothing.

More muttering broke out, louder than before.

"Where has it gone?" my father asked.

"The future," Doctor Ó Cuilinn replied.

An uncomfortable silence followed that pronouncement.

Less assured than before, Ó Cuilinn said, "Please understand that I've not yet calibrated the time frame. So I cannot predict when it will reappear."

"Meaning, it might be anywhere," one mathematician said.

"Or any *when*," another quipped.

One of the courtiers smothered a laugh. Ó Cuilinn's eyes narrowed—his irritation was plain to see—and I thought he was about to say something regrettable when my father said, "Your application states you are on the point of proving that time travel is possible."

"I have proved it," Ó Cuilinn said, a bit heatedly.

My father smiled. It was a kindly smile, but his obvious sympathy clearly irritated this young son of a country doctor just as much as the open disbelief from the scientists. "I have proved it," he repeated. "Even if I cannot predict precisely when into the future my machine sends these objects. And, well, there are certain difficulties. But to overcome them, I need money. It is a crass plea, Your Majesty. I know that. But I swear you shall not regret offering me and my work your patronage."

My father gazed at him steadily, no trace of kindness on his face now. "What use do you see for such a machine, Doctor Ó Cuilinn?"

"That is not for me to say, Your Majesty. But if you were to ask—"

"I just did, young man."

A brief embarrassed smile flickered over Ó Cuilinn's face. "So you did, Your Majesty. Very well. I would say the uses are infinite, just as time is. You could send artifacts forward, for future historians. And if once we find the means to travel into the future, surely it follows that the reverse is possible. Think of that, speaking with the future and hearing its reply."

One of the astrologers objected. "Impossible. If the future is immutable, our descendants cannot interfere by offering us assistance, in any form."

"How, immutable?" said one of the philosophers. "If the future has not happened yet, we are free to change it."

"But change implies existence—"

"It implies nothing of the sort. You can change a man's potential after all. The future is nothing more than potential until it becomes our past—"

The argument broke out, louder and more strident than be-fore. Ó Cuilinn scowled. My father shook his head, but made no effort to quash the debate. He beckoned Ó Cuilinn to one side. They stood within a half dozen steps from my alcove. One glance upward, and the man would see me, or at least my dim outline, but his attention was wholly upon my father.

"Tell me truthfully," my father said, "how you believe to breach the walls of time." And as Ó Cuilinn looked about to launch into a longer speech, he held up a hand. "In simple terms, please. I have dabbled in science in my youth, but I am no scholar."

Ó Cuilinn offered my father a polite bow. "You undervalue yourself, Your Majesty. I know your reputation. Well, then, my research and my methods depend on time fractures. These are—"

"I know what time fractures are. Most scholars believe them to be a myth."

"They are not. Or rather, I have uncovered certain historical documents that support their existence. My theory is that they cluster around specific events. If you provide me with funding, I can map the largest of these clusters and use them to send for-ward items. Of course I would also need to refine my calibrations for how far into the future . . ."

My father nodded, his expression noncommittal. By now, the noisy debate had died off. Clearly the demonstration was over. My father spoke a few final words to Ó Cuilinn, so softly I could not make them out. Then with a signal, he and his Court departed.

From my alcove, I watched Ó Cuilinn disassemble his ma-chine into pieces and pack them into the same five crates. Though I knew he must be frustrated, or angry, he worked without hurry, carefully wrapping each item into paper sleeves, then packing them into straw and cotton. His were strong, deft hands, pale and beautiful in the fading November sunlight. A faint flush lingered on his cheeks. Now that I had the leisure, I could examine him freely. He was long limbed and graceful. His complexion was fair, his hair the color of pale straw, and fine. His eyes were of a blue so dark, they reminded me of thunderclouds. Not precisely handsome, but pleasing to look upon. I wondered if he had had many lovers.

Doubtful, I thought. A man like that—a scientist—could have only one obsession in his life, and usually that was his craft, not a woman.

He had done with his packing. Still he had not detected my presence, but then I had placed myself outside of anyone's casual notice. It was a trick my mother had taught me, back when I was a young child. *Watch first*, she said, *and then you will know how to act.*

One by one, the crates vanished from the room—no doubt going back to the same hired van. Ó Cuilinn returned a final time and scanned the empty chamber, as though checking for forgotten items. The sunlight fell across his face, but his expression was hard to read. Discouraged? Or merely preoccupied?

The door swung shut. I counted to ten before I left my hiding place.

Only a half hour had passed since Ó Cuilinn had begun his demonstration, and yet the sun already dipped below the windows. The fire burned low; the air felt chill. Soon servants would come to sweep the floor and carry away the worktable. Soon my father would send for me, to ask me my impressions. Still, I lingered. I made a slow circuit of the room, sniffing. The burning odor had faded, but traces of it remained. The closer I approached the table, the stronger the traces were. The prickling sensation returned, as though tiny pins ran over my arms and neck.

Intrigued, I held my hands a few inches above the table. Where the octopus had sat, the wood felt pleasantly warm.

His demonstration was exactly like that of an illusionist. One moment, you saw the apple on his palm, the next it had disappeared. Hardly proof of a scientific discovery.

But he was so certain. And I am certain he could not lie, even if it meant his death.

Then I saw it—a shadow on the table. A clear, dark shadow, in spite of the fading afternoon light. I bent closer. Not a shadow, but a thin layer of ashes on the tabletop. Exactly where the bar had sat inside the machine.

My pulse beating faster, I touched a fingertip to the shadow. A film of dust clung to my skin. I tasted it. (A rash move, since several of my recent ancestors had been poisoned.)

The dust had the texture of fine grit, and a sour metallic flavor. Was it rust?

Cold washed over my skin as I realized what I had consumed. This was not mere rust, but the remnants of a metal bar, corroded.

Very quietly, I brushed the iron flakes into my palm and closed my fingers around them. I felt as though I held the future.

A year and a month passed before I saw Doctor Ó Cuilinn's name again.

My father had approved a grant for his research, and from time to time the King's Constabulary sent reports on his work, but these went directly to my father. My own days had lately been consumed with preparations for my formal presentation to the Congress of Éire. I had appeared before them five years ago, after my elder brother had died, and my father named me the presumptive heir—more a formality than any real change in status. Now that I was eighteen, almost nineteen, this ceremony signaled I would take my place at my father's side in ruling the kingdom.

This morning, however, one of those reports lay on top of the stack of documents handed to me by my father's secretary. Memory shivered through me as I scanned the first page. Only after a moment did I understand its import.

"He has given up his post," I said. "I wonder why?"

"Who has?" my father said.

We sat at the breakfast table, both of us reading feverishly in preparation for another long day. Lately, my father spent more time reading than consuming his breakfast, which worried me, and his face had taken on a gaunt and harried look. He seemed older—much older—than his fifty-seven years. One could almost see the shadow of bones beneath his skin.

He has outlived three children and his wife.

Hurriedly, I put that thought aside. "Doctor Ó Cuilinn," I said, in answer to his question. "The man who invented the time machine."

"Hardly invented," my father murmured. "There were and remain several significant obstacles to such a device."

"The corrosion of materials?" I guessed.

"Among others. According to the Constabulary, our doctor made slow but regular progress for the first six months. Lately, however, his laboratory assistants admit they do little more than sweep the floors while Doctor Ó Cuilinn scribbles notes and formulas in his journal."

"You set spies upon him."

My father laid his papers aside and regarded me with mild eyes. "I set spies upon everyone, my love. It is necessary, and you know it."

I did. I remembered the assassination attempts from my childhood, and the investigations after my mother's and brother's deaths, when my father stalked the corridors of the palace, suspecting every councilor and courtier of plotting against the throne. My mother and brother had died of fever, and nothing more. But the assassination attempts—those were real.

"Back to Doctor Ó Cuilinn," my father said. "Yes, I knew he had resigned his post. He gave no concrete reason to the university, but if I were to guess, I would say he believes himself close to discovery. He wants no distractions."

"But the reports—"

"Are accurate, but they can only record his outward activities. Not his secret thoughts."

Or his soul, I thought. I had only observed the man for a scant half hour. Still, he had impressed me as someone who did not give up very easily. The word *obsessed* came back to me. "Will you extend his grant, then?"

"Possibly. Certain members of our Congress believe the device will have practical applications, and my scholars agree Doctor Ó Cuilinn's theory about time fractures is . . . plausible."

His gaze turned inward a moment, as though he surveyed a scene far different from this elegant breakfast room, the warm yellow gaslight glinting off the silver tea urns. Was he pondering the implications of time fractures? (The idea alone made me queasy.) Or was he perhaps remembering my mother?

Then he gave himself a shake. "Enough speculation. We both have a busy schedule this morning. Let us finish our breakfast and set to work."

It was Tuesday, a day set aside for private interviews with delegations from other nations. Today, my father would meet with the Prussian ambassador, a stiff-necked, belligerent man, who matched his king's personality well. It would not be a pleasant hour. The Prussian Alliance was seeking to expand their territory, and while their activities did not affect Éire directly, they did affect our closest ally, Frankonia.

Mine was the less taxing morning. An informal meeting with the newly appointed representative from the Papal States. Another with a group of Egyptian scholars, who wished to organize an exchange between their universities and ours. A much longer session with an ambassador from the Turkish States, listening demurely as the man droned on, and his interpreter murmured in my ear.

The noon bells chimed. The Turkish ambassador and I rose and went through all the formalities of leave-taking. It had been an especially tedious hour, and later events should have erased this insignificant moment from my memory, but a scattering of images and impressions remained. The man's watery green eyes, almost ghostly in his brown face. The soothing lilt of his voice, which was echoed by the woman who translated his words. How faint lines and the mottling of his skin belied his otherwise youthful appearance. The scent of coriander and rose that hung about his person.

One of the senior runners escorted the ambassador and his interpreter from the room. I closed my eyes and breathed deeply. I had a moment of respite before my next engagement, an intimate luncheon with my father and a coterie of influential representatives from Éire's Congress.

Then, a door swung open.

I heard it first, a deep, grating noise that penetrated to my bones.

Even when I opened my eyes, I could not quite take in what I saw.

It was not the unobtrusive side door, used by servants and runners. Nor the ordinary ones used by visitors, such as the Turkish ambassador. No, these were the doors used only for the most formal state affairs. Each panel measured six feet by sixteen, and was carved from a single tree imported from the western continent. I had only seen the portals opened once during my lifetime, and that was when my mother had died.

An old man in livery marched into the room and stepped to one side.

Next came a silver-haired lord with the ribbon and chain of office draped over his raven-black coat. It was Lord Mac Gioll, the oldest of my father's councilors. He had served as an officer, then as my grandfather's personal adviser, when my father was but a young man. Old, so very old, his thin white hair like a veil over his skull. He walked with a stiff limp, but he held his chin high, and I saw there were tears in his pale gray eyes.

He stopped six paces away. "Your Majesty."

"What are you saying?" I whispered.

Lord Mac Gioll knelt before me and bent his head. "My Queen. I have the great misfortune to report that your father . . ."

I heard nothing past that, only a roaring in my ears, but I knew what he was saying. My father was dead. *Impossible,* cried a voice within. *He was well not three hours ago. He—*

". . . the first to pledge my honor, my loyalty, my blood, and my self to your throne . . ."

As Lord Mac Gioll recited the vows of lord to queen, a part of me recalled that he had recited those same vows to my father, twenty-five years before, when he had lost *his* father to an attack by Anglian revolutionaries. It was important that I face the news with as much strength and composure as my father had. And so, when Lord Mac Gioll finished his speech, I held out my hands to receive his kiss upon my rings. With great difficulty (I knew better than to make any move to assist him), Lord Mac Gioll rose and gave way to the next man just entering the room.

Later, much later, I sat alone in my private chambers and laid my head upon my hands. Firelight jumped and flickered against the walls. No gas lamps burned here. Only a single candle guttered on the table. Its orange-scented perfume overlaid the wood smoke and pervasive sourness of my own fear.

I was Áine Lasairíona Devereaux, the seventeenth of my house to take the throne, the thirty-first ruler of Éire.

I do not want this, I thought.

———

I did not want it, but I could not turn away from my duties.

And so I let tradition carry me through the next six weeks. When I looked back upon them, I remembered nothing in particular, just a weight against my heart, a curious and lasting numbness. The funeral itself proceeded without any misstep. A hundred ambassadors passed before my father's coffin; thousands more—from Éire, from Alba, from a dozen or more nations of Europe and beyond—paused to bow and whisper a prayer, before making way for the press of mourners behind them.

And I, I stood dry eyed upon the podium, flanked by guards.

I have no tears, I thought. *No grief.* Or had grief been burnt entirely away?

There was no one who could answer that question. Or at least, no one I trusted.

Afterward, I met with my father's ministers and other members of Éire's Congress. I held innumerable interviews with representatives from the Continent and farther abroad, those who came to express their condolences, and to reassure themselves that an alliance with Éire would continue to be to their advantage.

I also met with the royal physicians and ordered an autopsy on my father's body. They soon reported he had died of a seizure of the heart. There were no signs of poisoning, nor that the seizure had been induced by artificial means. I thanked them for their thoroughness, wondering all the while when my grief would break free.

Ten days later came the coronation—a hurried affair, but my ministers agreed I should take control of the throne as soon as possible. Once crowned, others would find it more difficult to dislodge me. And there were those who would attempt it. I knew that from my own history.

The day began with a stuttering of snow—a typical late-January morning. The skies were flecked with clouds, and the sun, when it finally consented to rise, cast an uncertain light over Cill Cannig and the nearby city of Osraighe. Cold nipped at my skin as I darted from the palace into the waiting carriage.

The kings and queens of Éire had lived in Cill Cannig and the Royal Enclosure for six centuries. Tradition, however, proclaimed they would receive their crowns in the ancient cathedral of Osraighe. And so I rode alone in the royal carriage, shivering in my finery, in a slow, creeping procession from the palace, through intervening fields, and into the city. The clocks were just chiming ten as I arrived at the cathedral. There Lord Ó Cadhla took hold of the lead horse's reins, while Lord Mac Gioll flung open the carriage doors to greet me with a long ceremonious speech. A cold dank wind blew against my face. I paused upon the step to listen, as the ritual required.

It was there the assassin took his chance.

A shot rang out. Fire exploded inside my shoulder, as though a white-hot spear had pierced me. I gasped and fell backward, reaching for that spear and thinking confusedly that if I could pluck the damned thing out, the agony would stop.

After that, I had difficulty remembering. Pain and more pain. The strong stink of blood. Lord Mac Gioll's creaking shout, then Lord Ó Cadhla's stronger voice calling for the Queen's Guard. And me, retching all over my grand expensive gown, and weeping at last, weeping so hard and furiously that I retched more and finally collapsed onto the ground.

The wound proved painful, but not dangerous. Once the physicians removed the ball and bandaged my shoulder, they allowed themselves to be herded away by Lords Mac Gioll and Ó Cadhla.

"Your Majesty," said Lord Mac Gioll.

I turned my head away.

"Áine," said Lord Ó Cadhla.

That nearly caused me to look around. I stopped myself, but not before I glimpsed a smile on Lord Ó Cadhla's grim face.

"You are not dead," he said quietly. "Nor so badly wounded we can put off this interview."

He was right, of course. I sighed and waved a hand to show my assent.

That, apparently, was not good enough.

"Stop grieving for yourself," Lord Ó Cadhla said crisply. "You have lost your father. Well, and so have I. Lord Mac Gioll here lost a brother and two sons in the last Anglian Uprising. I understand. But you must postpone your mourning for a more propitious time."

"When I am nearly dead myself," I muttered.

"That would be more convenient."

His words brought a puff of laughter to my lips. "Speak," I told him. "You will anyway."

"So I will," Ó Cadhla said. "First, you must have a more competent bodyguard. Lord Ultach and his staff have vetted all the members of the Queen's Constabulary deemed fit to protect you. And they are fit. But they are not quite so . . . thorough as the man I would propose."

"A bodyguard," I repeated. "Who . . ."

"Commander Aidrean Ó Deághaidh," Ó Cadhla said. "He served as a covert agent in Austria and that region for six years. More recently, at my recommendation, he enlisted in your father's Constabulary to acquire experience at home. I have always found him reliable."

"You mean he is one of yours."

He nodded. "One of mine."

Someone outside Court, but inside our circle of trust.

Though I disliked the necessity, I understood Lord Ó Cadhla's reasoning.

"Very well," I said. "Have him come tomorrow for an interview. Surely the Constabulary can protect me until then?"

They left me with a thick packet of reports, which I set aside for later. My shoulder ached, and I had little appetite for reading reams of bureaucratic paragraphs. It was easier to lie motionless, hoping that the drugs the physicians gave me would send me to sleep.

I spent a restless, fruitless hour in search of that sleep. Finally I abandoned the attempt and stared upward at the patterned ceiling, awash in moonlight. I briefly considered summoning the physicians for another sleeping draught, then abandoned the thought. It was not sleep I needed, but a sense of purpose.

He knew it, I thought, as I maneuvered myself painfully onto my good shoulder. *He knew I would get bored.*

Whatever their faults in predicting the assassination attempt, my Constabulary had worked quickly to discover those at fault. The attempt had been led by members of two key political groups with ties to certain influential members of Congress. With a sense of dread and irritation, I read the name of a cousin who had allowed himself to become the nominal leader of this movement.

You, I thought, *have made a grave mistake.*

More reports listed the names of lesser conspirators and the probable extent of their schemes. My difficulties would not end with one attack. Many in Éire's government believed me too young to rule. Some wanted a regency. Some worked to shift power from the queen to Congress.

And there were the Anglians. Always the Anglians.

We shall never rid ourselves of the danger, my father once said, *until we cut their chains and help them build a new nation of their own. Several new nations. They are not a monolith, after all.* He had meant to accomplish that in his own reign. . . .

The tears burned in my eyes. I swiped them away and read past the further details of plots and political maneuvers, to the details about this man, Ó Deághaidh.

Commander Aidrean Conaill Ó Deághaidh. He had taken an undergraduate degree in mathematics from Awveline University, then begun his graduate studies in Austria. Those same studies were broken off within the year, for reasons unknown. Fluent in German, French, Russian, and Czech, with smatterings of others. He had spent two years wandering through Europe and the Near East, during which time he'd come to the notice of Lord Ó Cadhla's people, who recruited him for his ability with languages and his understanding of political matters. I saw nothing to suggest he would make a good bodyguard, but I knew Lord Ó Cadhla. My father had trusted him. I began to think I might as well.

"Commander Ó Deághaidh."

"Your Majesty."

It was three days after my near assassination. I chose for this meeting the smallest of my parlors, an intimate room with knotted silk rugs and cloth chairs gathering around the fireplace.

Commander Ó Deághaidh, however, remained as formal as if we were met in Cill Cannig's grandest audience chamber. He stood at attention, his hands clasped behind his back: a tall man, as lean as a shadow and nearly as dark. Warm brown eyes. Dark hair cut short and swept back in the newest fashion. The reports said he was thirty-four. He appeared younger, except for the faint lines around his eyes.

"Why did you quit your studies?" I asked.

"Let us say I allowed myself to be distracted by the larger world."

A reply that had a practiced quality, as if he had often had to answer this same question.

"Is that the truth?" I said.

His eyes narrowed with humor. "As I know it, yes, Your Majesty. However, I find in certain cases the truth depends upon perspective."

I laughed. Aidrean Ó Deághaidh's mouth quirked into a smile—a brief flicker of shared amusement. It changed his expression entirely. That intrigued me.

"So tell me," I went on, "how you would protect me better than my own guards."

At my insistence, he took the chair opposite me. We leaned toward the fire, heads close together, as he described his own impressions of the political situation. A part of me absorbed everything he said, to be reviewed later when I was alone. Another part took in details of the man himself. How his mouth was fuller than I would have expected for someone with such an angular face. How his voice had started off so cool and official, only to drop to a warmer lilting tone. He wore a pleasing scent, too—another surprise. From Lord Ó Cadhla's initial description, I had expected Ó Deághaidh to be more the automaton. Instead I found myself intently aware of him as a handsome man, clever and so very competent.

"So you believe the conspiracy to be widespread."

He paused. "I believe the number of opportunists is greater than expected."

"There is a difference?"

He spread his hands, palms outward. "Given Éire's history, I would say no, not ordinarily. But with your father's sudden death, your inexperience, and the uneasiness on the Continent, there are many more these days who will be tempted to grasp power for themselves, while in other times they would refrain. Your father and grandfather often chose to mete out lesser sentences for those who strayed into treason, especially those duped by others. However, my recommendation to you is that we make no difference between the opportunists and the true conspirators. Call it a message to those who watch your reign."

I nodded and felt a flutter of hope in my chest. "Do you want the position?"

He tilted his head, observed me for a moment—a long assessing look, as though he were measuring me, not as his queen, but as another human being. "Surely the question is yours to decide," he said at last. "But since you ask, I say, yes, Your Majesty. Yes, I do."

And so we talked and planned and argued about the coronation and how to keep me alive and whole, while giving the people a spectacle they could remember all their lives. For, as Lords Ó Cadhla and Mac Gioll and others in the Queen's Council reminded me, this ceremony was meant to imbue me with the authority of history and tradition. Aidrean Ó Deághaidh himself simply shook his head, and took their recommendations into account. He had neatly insinuated himself into the ongoing investigation of the conspiracy. When he found the time, I had no idea. His absences from my side were few.

As for myself, I kept to my private chambers, visited only by my closest advisers and my physicians. The official reports said I needed time to recuperate. I suppose I did. I hated it, nevertheless. *Kings and queens do not hide,* I thought. *They act. Just like my father did. And our ancestors before him.*

The physician's last visit had left me aching and breathless. In between, there were other indignities. Nurses to wash the wounds and apply fresh ointment. Formal inquiries from the Congress about my recovery. Uncharacteristically, Aidrean Ó Deághaidh had vanished a few hours before. He returned just as the Court astrologers departed.

"Where have you been?" I demanded.

He smiled, as though to a fractious child. That only worsened my temper. The astrologers had made long and noisy protests over the new date for my coronation. They had calculated to a fine degree the position and phase of the moon—never mind those of the stars—and wanted another month to assure me of a propitious day. Now I pressed the heels of my hands against my eyes.

"You are tired, Your Majesty."

"I know that," I snapped.

Ó Deághaidh shifted his glance toward the fire. I saw his fleeting grimace.

"I'm sorry," I said. "I . . . I am impatient. I dislike being caged." And before he could reply, I hastened to add, "That is hardly an excuse, I know. Merely an explanation."

He acknowledged the apology and the explanation with a wordless gesture. There were bruises underneath those brown eyes, and a web of lines radiating outward. He must have spent half his nights in ceaseless work on my behalf. I felt a stab of shame.

"I'm sorry, Aidrean."

A flinch, nothing more, at his given name.

I had forgotten—just for the moment—that we were queen and servant, not two friends. There was no possibility of apologizing. That would only exacerbate my offense.

But truly, I did not mean to offend. I meant only . . .

Better not to think what I meant.

"Can we manage it?" I asked hurriedly. "The coronation, I mean. In just two weeks."

He nodded. "Most of the guests have remained in the city. The others could arrive by airship. What about the astrologers?"

"Let them determine the hour. Within reason," I added.

His smile, edged by firelight, caused the last of my bad temper to leach away. "It shall be exactly as you wish, Your Majesty."

It was.

Telegraphs went out the next morning to all the nations of Europe and beyond. Within a day the first balloons arrived—scarlet, silver, the royal blue and purple of the Austrian Empire, the golden lilies of Frankonia, the red lion of Alba, and pale blue dragons of Denmark. More and more filled the skies over the next ten days, from as far away as the Mexica States and the Japanese Empire, as though my guests had anticipated my plans and only awaited a word to set off for our shores.

My coronation was set for the second Monday in February—a cold bleak day, the skies mottled with cinder-black clouds that spat snow and frozen rain over the bare fields. Once more I rose at dawn and gave myself over to the maids and ladies of the Court. Once more I donned the layers of silk and cloth-of-gold—all new stitched because the old gown was burnt and stained. My shoulder ached in memory of that other day, but then Aidrean Ó Deághaidh appeared at my side to escort me to the waiting carriage.

I rode alone in my carriage through the gates, my guards on horseback at points ahead and behind. It was like an echo of that previous journey—the same and yet so different. My nerves felt raw and exposed. The ticking of sleet against the cobblestones sounded loud. And my heart, my heart danced fast and light. I thought I could feel an answering pulse from Aidrean Ó Deághaidh's hand as he assisted me from the carriage, even through all the layers of cloth. I paused, just as before, and listened to Lord Mac Gioll's studied speech. I gazed over the crowds of onlookers. I felt so removed from my surroundings, from the event itself, that it was not until I stepped into the cathedral's shadowed entryway it struck me fully I was to be queen.

I paused a moment to recover myself. Then, with a signal to my guards, I continued forward into the pale yellow light of the cathedral's vast body. Step, step, step, my guards keeping time with me. Then they too fell away and I walked alone the last distance, there to kneel before the archbishop.

She stood upon the steps leading up to the nave of the church. Her silver crown flared like a circle of flames around her seamed face, reminding me of ancient portraits of the saints.

"May the blood of our mothers and fathers bless you," she said.

"May the flesh of our Lord and our ancestors guard us," I replied.

So we continued, giving challenge and response. Behind me, I heard the low chant of the priests, smelled the rich rank scent of blood in the air. When the acolytes approached, one bearing a bowl and one a silver flagon, the archbishop dipped her fingers into the bowl and smeared the lamb's blood over my brow.

"Let this symbolize our dedication to the mother and the father, to oak and stream and the Lamb of God."

She offered me the silver flagon, also filled with blood. I drank it all.

Thereafter, memories scattered into fragments. I remembered the clouds of incense, impossibly thick, rising toward the ceiling with its portraits of saints and gods. The archbishop's fingers brushing my temples as she set the crown upon my head. The warmth and weight of gold pressing against my forehead, like the weight of centuries. The ritual words intoned in Latin and old Éireann and the chants from the choir. Then a bell rang out, and I felt a pang within my heart.

I was Queen of Éire.

The archbishop offered me a flagon of cold water to wash the taste of blood from my mouth. More rituals and rites followed, first in the cathedral and then upon my return to Cill Cannig. A stream of festivities crowded every moment through the rest of the morning and into evening. My maids kept busy, helping me from one formal gown to the next. That night I dined with visiting kings and queens and ambassadors.

On and on and on. Until at last I sat in my rooms, swathed in a warm robe and drinking a soothing infusion of tea. It was past midnight. Outside, I heard the crackle and boom of fireworks. The skies were clear and spangled with stars. Aidrean Ó Deághaidh lingered by the windows, though both of us knew he had no official reason to be here.

"Did you know my father?" I asked him.

He paused, longer perhaps than the question warranted. "Only from afar." Then he answered the true question, the one I had not dared to ask. "I thought him a good king. I believe you will make a good queen."

"Ah." I smiled, more pleased by his good opinion than I had expected.

A log broke. Aidrean turned toward the fire, alert. The shower of sparks sent up a spray of golden light that limned his profile. I don't know how long we stayed thus—just a heartbeat—but it seemed I had all the time to study his face. The lines running in angles, the shadow black of his hair edging his dark face, the curve of his lips. His expression was pensive, as though he were searching the fire's red-gold heart for answers.

Then he chanced to look around. My glance caught his. There, no mistake, a flash of ardor in those warm brown eyes.

My cheeks burned. I turned away.

Aidrean—Commander Ó Deághaidh—did nothing. How could he? He was my servant. I was his queen. It was all fraught with impossibility.

Later, much later, I lay in bed, sifting through my emotions. Oh, and sure, I was the queen. Oh, and sure, my predecessors, almost all of them, had taken favorites. But I was young, newly come to my throne, and my authority not yet proved. I could not follow my desires as I wished.

With a sigh, I closed my eyes and felt the beat of my pulse against my eyelids.

Surely, if I reached out now, my hands would meet the bars around me.

He effaced himself after that.

Of course. He thinks you wanted a dalliance.

I paused in reading correspondence and pressed my hands

against my eyes. Luckily, I was alone. My secretary was occupied in the outer offices, sorting through invitations and handling the many impromptu visitors from Court. Aidrean—*You must not think of him that way*, I told myself—Commander Ó Deághaidh spent less time in the Royal Enclosure than before. These days, he oversaw the entire branch of the Queen's Constabulary assigned to Cill Cannig. We met each morning, but these interviews consisted of mostly perfunctory exchanges. Commander Ó Deághaidh handed me a detailed written report, including his current assessment of security, as well as summaries of the most important reports from the Queen's Constabulary. If I had questions, I might ask, but he had made them so thorough and complete that I never needed to.

And so I sat alone, weeping like a child.

Furious, I thumped a fist against my desk. *I am not a child. I am the queen.*

So be one.

The words came to me in my father's voice.

I wiped the tears from my eyes and pulled the closest stack of papers toward me. These were applications and petitions my secretary had reviewed and sorted according to their urgency. The first few I scanned automatically: a petition from a county in the north, requesting a temporary reduction in their taxes; a long rambling paper setting forth grievances between two major guilds; yet another polemic concerning Anglian liberty; demand upon demand for monies to support this or that worthy cause . . .

. . . a request from Doctor Breandan Reid Ó Cuilinn, asking for an extension to his grant.

I stopped. Flicked away the other papers and concentrated on his alone.

He was no politician, I thought, reading closely. He stated without apology or preamble that he had quit his position at

Awveline University, though they had offered him a higher sal-
ary and the rank of senior professor.

> . . . I have discovered, through painful experience, that I
> cannot do proper research when I am distracted by other
> obligations. My blessed father died the year before and left
> me a small inheritance—enough to live off, but not enough
> to afford a laboratory and materials for any substantial
> endeavor. Your father's generosity enabled me to accomplish
> a great deal, but—and here I apologize to you, just as I did
> to your father, for such blatant beggary—I must have
> another year's funding if I am to transform my theories
> into reality . . .

He believes in his cause, I thought. *So do they all.*

And yet, I remembered that handful of iron dust, the electric tension in the air when Ó Cuilinn's golden octopus worked its magic.

It was not golden, but brass, I reminded myself. And he used
science, not magic.

Nevertheless, I found myself transported back to that cold sunlit room, watching a shabbily dressed scientist perform a miracle
before my father and his Court.

At least I can do some good here, I thought as I called for my secretary.

"Doctor Ó Cuilinn."

"Your Majesty. Thank you for inviting me to Cill Cannig."

He had changed little in the past year and a half, but those few
differences revealed much—his fine golden hair lay thin over his
skull, a tracery of lines marked his pale complexion. And though
his eyes were just as dark and brilliant, the gaze as direct, I thought

I detected a new uncertainty in his manner. Not a good sign, for my purposes.

I gestured toward the waiting chairs. "Please. Let us be comfortable. I invited you because I wanted to discuss your research."

There was the briefest hesitation, an even briefer glint of wariness, before he smiled and bowed and followed me to the comfortable grouping of stuffed chairs set around a low table. Beside us, tall windows overlooked one of the palace courtyards, now rife with lilies and roses and the last sweet-smelling blossoms dripping from the apple trees. Spring rains had given way to the tenuous summer sun.

Servants silently poured tea into porcelain cups etched with falling leaves. At my glance, they withdrew. Ó Cuilinn watched them throughout their work. Only when we were alone did he glance back in my direction. Expectant.

"I was not entirely truthful," I told him. "I want you to move your laboratory here, into the palace, and—"

"You cannot purchase me," he said abruptly. Then added, "Your Majesty."

So he had not entirely lost his arrogance. Good.

I nodded. "I do not intend to. But you see, I believe in your work. I have ever since I observed your demonstration to my father two years ago."

His eyes widened as I opened a drawer and withdrew a handkerchief wrapped many times around. I set the handkerchief on the table. Its contents shifted slightly. Was it only in my imagination, or could one hear the hiss of iron dust, smell the faint metallic scent, old and stale?

Breandan Ó Cuilinn stared at the handkerchief. "What is that?"

"Your metal bar," I told him. "The one you sent forward in time, when you last were here."

"How did you—"

"I waited." Never mind that I had not known what to expect,

or when. The essence was true. "Not long after you departed, the bar reappeared. Or rather, its remains did."

I untied the handkerchief and carefully unfolded the cloth. There in the center lay the handful of iron dust, somewhat diminished. Ó Cuilinn stretched out a hand, plucked it back. He glanced up at me. "What do you want?"

He spoke as one equal to another, not a servant to his queen.

"I want you to continue your research," I said. "I am willing to allot you substantial funds. However, I would find it simpler if we could eliminate the layers of letter writers and secretaries and other middlemen."

A flush edged his cheeks. He had freckles, I noticed.

"I believe I understand. But Your Majesty, if you truly want me to continue my work—and dedicate myself to it entirely, not in piecemeal fashion as I have over the years—then I will require a great deal of equipment. And money."

"I understand," I said. "Please, tell me what you've discovered so far. And what you hope to accomplish in the future."

My early education in the sciences allowed me to follow the shape, if not the details, of his account. In between careless sips of tea, he spoke about using carbon-free chromium objects, which resulted in less corrosion. His most recent experiments with the material had yielded larger flakes of dust, along with fragments of the bar itself. But that alone, he told me, was useless—merely a device for proving the concept. What he needed to do was reduce the effect of time travel itself. In fact—and here his gaze went diffuse, obviously following this thought along all its permutations—he ought to search for ways to shield objects inside the chamber. A combination of the two branches of research . . .

"What about the past?" I asked.

"What about the past?" His eyes narrowed as he regarded me with obvious suspicion. "Is this a scheme you have for some political end?"

"I do not mean that. I only mean—"

"What everyone else means," he said bitterly.

"If you think I will make any preconditions on you, you are mistaken," I replied, my tone equally sharp.

"No. I did not think that—"

"You did," I said. "But never mind. I am sure we can come to some agreement. You want money. I want to continue my father's legacy with scientific progress."

A smile twitched at his mouth. "I see. Yes. Yes, Your Majesty, I believe we can meet both our goals."

Orders, however easily spoken, were not so lightly carried out. Doctor Ó Cuilinn had no outstanding obligations to any landlord or university, but he did have an enormous quantity of records and equipment to transfer from Awveline City to Cill Cannig. A month went simply to negotiating what quarters he required for his work. Two more passed in transferring his belongings to the palace, and arranging them to his satisfaction. I had once thought his arrogance a worthy quality, but I found myself hissing whenever my steward or secretary mentioned Ó Cuilinn's name.

That, unfortunately, was not the end of my worries.

"You say this fellow—"

"Scientist," I said.

"This scientist holds the keys to time?"

Seven months had passed since Doctor Ó Cuilinn had taken up residence in Cill Cannig. I was breakfasting with Lord Fitzpatrick, a senior member of the Éireann Congress and an elderly man, used to the perquisites of age and rank. Others were present, but they all deferred to him.

"He investigates them," I said patiently.

Apparently my patience was too transparent.

"He walks the time roads," Fitzpatrick said.

A shiver went through me, in spite of knowing he only used the terms from legends past.

"He is a scientist," I said. "He researches possibilities."

"At a considerable cost," another said. I recognized him— Lord Ó Bruicléigh, newly arrived in Congress after his father's death. An ambitious man, with a reputation for cleverness. He had attached himself to the Committee for Economic Affairs.

"Explain yourself," I said.

The other members of Congress flinched at my tone, but Ó Bruicléigh himself was oblivious. "The monies spent on Doctor Ó Cuilinn's research are a matter of public record, Your Majesty. The committee has studied those records. We wish merely to express our concern about spending so freely—"

"We are hardly in danger of ruin." It took a great effort to keep my voice calm.

"No, but as you know, Your Majesty, there are troubling rumors from the Continent, echoed by troubling rumors within our own borders. We need an advantage, be it economic or political or . . ." Here he offered me an edged smile. "Or an advantage both scientific and concrete."

"You mean a weapon," I said.

He shrugged. "Whatever you wish to call it, Your Majesty."

I studied the man before me with growing anger. His threat was plain enough—if I did not give him the assurances he wanted, he and the committee would work to undermine Ó Cuilinn's project. Though I had established a measure of authority over the past year, I could not afford to insult or ignore these men, however badly I wished to.

You must make concessions, my father's voice added. *He holds a portion of influence, and has the means and determination to increase it.*

That night, in a rare private conference with Aidrean Ó Deághaidh, I reopened the matter. Though he knew all about the invitation, and Ó Cuilinn himself, I recounted everything, from Ó Cuilinn's first visit, almost three years before, to Ó Bruicléigh's speech.

"They want reassurance," Ó Deághaidh said.

"I know that," I said. "I only wished to know your opinion about the matter. As a friend," I added in an undertone.

His expression did not change, nor did he glance in my direction, but I thought that his pulse had jumped at my words, and the tension around his mouth eased momentarily—faint clues that I nearly missed, despite the ubiquitous gaslight.

"If you wish my opinion," he said, "then I will give it. Spend the money for his research, if you believe it necessary and right for Éire. For you. But do not promise anything to your Congress. Otherwise you break the promise you made to him."

No need to ask how he knew. He knew everything.

"Thank you," I said.

"No need to thank me, Your Majesty."

The odd inflection caught my attention. I started to speak—it would have been easy to breach the strangeness between us, I thought—but Aidrean Ó Deághaidh was already rising and bowing, a deep graceful bow expressing loyalty and obedience and all the qualities I loved in him.

You have spoiled me forever, Aidrean Ó Deághaidh.

Alone, I considered the problem. The difficulty was that Ó Bruicléigh did have a point. Our alliance with Frankonia, sealed with treaties and blood ties, had assured us security for decades. But now Frankonia's king was failing, and the electors were voicing disagreement about his successor. The Turkish States were embroiled in another succession battle. Our few dependencies across the Atlantic had broken free, only to find themselves at war with the Iroquois and Delaware nations. The Prussian Alliance and Dietsch Empire pressed upon our colonial borders in Palestine and in Southeast Asia, and the Austrian

Empire, failing for decades now, proved no less dangerous in its dying throes.

"I will not renege on my promises," I told Doctor Ó Cuilinn at our next meeting.

He seemed unsurprised by the rumors I told him.

"It has always been the case," he said. "They are politicians. They think scientists are nothing but servants to war."

And, as if I had not mentioned any difficulties at all, he went on to talk about his latest discoveries. He had made great progress in mapping out the time fractures. Indeed, they seemed to be multiplying, though he could not yet determine why. The largest cluster centered over Awveline City; others had appeared in the neighborhood of Osraighe and the northern provinces, and he was corresponding with scientists on the Continent to determine if they had discovered any. Whatever their origin, he said, they represented a weakness in the fabric of time. If his theories were correct, he could use them as avenues between the years.

"A road between times?" I said.

"Possibly. I cannot guarantee anything yet."

Of course, I thought.

There were no guarantees in science, I knew. None at all in politics. Nevertheless, I found myself reviewing Doctor Ó Cuilinn's reports with greater eagerness than I knew was wholesome. And though I hated the necessity, I played the conciliator to Lord Ó Bruicléigh and his faction. But to what end?

Uncertainty nibbled at me. In turn, I asked each of my advisers their opinion.

"Remember your father," Lord Mac Gioll said.

"Remember the longest road," Lord Ó Cadhla told me.

And from my closest friend, "Remember what you wish others to remember of you."

"Is that how you make decisions?" I asked Aidrean Ó Deághaidh.

He never answered me; I never pressed him.

By summer of the following year, I had several answers, none of which satisfied me.

"Tell me again," I said to Breandan Ó Cuilinn, "what you have accomplished."

We stared at one another a few moments. He disliked being questioned—I could see that at once—but then, I disliked excuses and obfuscations.

At last he bowed his head.

"We have made progress, Your Majesty."

"How much?"

"A great deal."

"Show me."

Now his anger was unmistakable. "Why? Because you want a good return on your investment?"

I met his glare with one of my own. "Why not? Or are you so gifted by God and Mhuire and Gaia that I dare not to question you?"

At that he gave a snorting laugh. "I should have known." Then, before my anger could flare hotter, he added, "Your Majesty, I have been a thankless, arrogant creature. My apologies. Let me show you what you have bought with your generosity."

He led me from the interview chamber through a series of ever-narrower corridors into an unused wing of the palace. Nearly unused, I thought, taking in the many recent renovations. Surely my secretary had cleared all these beforehand. Or no. I remembered saying once, *Do whatever it takes.*

We came into a vast, brightly lit laboratory, lined with shelves and cabinets. Several assistants sat at workbenches. At our entrance, they glanced up and made as if to stand, but I signaled them to remain at their work. Ó Cuilinn trailed me as I advanced into the room. Bins of supplies, all of them neatly labeled, took up most of the shelves, but others held books and folders, half-finished replicas of that original machine, and several strange devices I could not identify. More shelves and more cabinets crowded the far end; in front of them stood a long, broad worktable, with neatly arranged stacks of journal books and tools set out in ordered rows.

All of these paled before the machine that Ó Cuilinn wheeled out before me.

The octopus, I thought.

But this octopus overshadowed everything else.

It was three times the size of a man, golden and polished and wrapped all around with gleaming glass tubes. A vast crate of batteries, or who knew what, crouched under the workbench, and there were other, larger cubes sheathed in lead off to one side, connected with an umbilical cord of wires. The air in the room felt close and stale and charged with electricity.

Ó Cuilinn crouched down, tugged open a drawer.

"I meant to show you this earlier, but . . ."

Without finishing his explanation, he extracted a small object from the drawer. It was a balloon and its basket, worked in the finest gold and silver. An artist's rendering, a craftsman's masterpiece. As if inspired, Ó Cuilinn picked up one of the journal books from his worktable. He pressed a button, and the octopus's mouth stretched wide. He placed both objects inside, pressed the same button again, and took a hasty step backward.

The octopus closed its mouth.

"Wait," he said, before I could speak.

The air went taut. A note rang through the laboratory, as though someone had plucked a gigantic string. My pulse thrummed inside me, and I felt an answering vibration from Breandan's hand pressed against mine.

"What is that?" I whispered.

"I sent them forward in time," he answered, just as softly.

"To when? To where?"

"Here. And twelve months from now."

"Why so long?"

"To prove myself. To everyone. To you."

We were both breathing fast in excitement. Afterward, I could not tell who turned first toward the other. All I remember is that our lips met in a fleeting kiss. Pressed again and did not part for an impossibly long interval. Only when we paused to breathe, I realized I did not wish to stop. Belatedly I remembered we were not alone. I did not care. My hand snaked around his neck and I pulled him into another kiss that lingered on. Time and time uninterrupted, and none of it satisfied me.

At last, he pulled back. His face was flushed, his eyes so dark, they appeared black.

"I have taken too many liberties."

His voice was husking and low.

"Not nearly enough," I said.

Even in my bed, in the midst of kissing me, he could not refrain from speaking about his research. "There must be a way," he said, as he ran his fingertips along my hip. His hands were cool and raised a trail of goose bumps; the rest of him was like a winter's fire.

"A way for what?" I asked when he did not continue.

"To send a person ahead in time, like a courier to the future."

I noticed that he was tracing a pattern on my skin. A mathematical formula, a schematic for a new octopus, a pathway through time for his imaginary courier. Laughter fluttered in my belly. When he kissed me again, I had no doubt his attention was focused entirely upon me, and the laughter changed to a new and sharper sensation.

"What is wrong?" he whispered.

"Nothing. Nothing at all. Tell me about these couriers."

His breath tickled my cheek. "They would be like runners in the old empire. But traveling through time instead of ordinary roads."

"The time fractures? But what if they close?"

He paused. I could sense his attention withdraw to some secret citadel within. I waited.

"It depends on the nature of the fracture," he said at last. "If my theories are correct, they might be stranded in the future, or past, in the wherever and whenever of their destination. But others suggest that time fractures indicate parallel histories. It's possible my couriers would be stranded in a different *now*."

As he spoke, he rose and absentmindedly pulled on his clothing. He paused only to kiss me, then he was gliding through the doors. I sighed. Obsession. And yet, we were much alike. Already it occurred to me that I should discuss these possibilities with my ministers. Not as a weapon, but surely a way to maintain our predominance, as Lord Ó Bruicléigh so delicately phrased it.

As I exited my private chambers, I stopped.

Aidrean Ó Deághaidh stood in the parlor outside. The hour was late, and the room lay in shadows. But I hardly needed sunlight or lamplight to read his expression, which was cold and remote, like the trees of winter.

In my memories of those days—memories blurred and splintered by later events—it seemed I did nothing but lie in bed with Breandan Ó Cuilinn, the two of us absorbed in carnal pleasure as we talked about mathematics and the properties of time. In truth, I spent the chief of my hours as I always had, doing the work of a queen, while Breandan pored over countless treatises and monographs ordered from universities throughout the civilized world, from Sweden to Iran to the Mayan Empire. When he came to me, saying that certain theories pointed toward signs of time fractures at high altitudes, I hired engineers to construct a special balloon with heavyweight baskets for Breandan's equipment. As the months passed, Breandan studied balloons as he studied everything else. Soon others began to call him the expert.

They said he was my favorite, which was true.

I told myself he was a friend as well.

"Your Majesty."

Aidrean Ó Deághaidh had arrived for our daily conference. Since the day I encountered him outside my private chambers, we had confined ourselves purely to the business of Court and Éire. There were no more private conferences, no sudden access of intimacy, on either part. We were as two strangers.

Aidrean Ó Deághaidh silently handed over his neatly typed report. Just as silently, I accepted it.

On every other day, he would repeat the same formula—that he hoped the report was satisfactory, but if I had any questions, I had but to ask.

Today, however, he paused. "Your Majesty . . ."

I waited. "Yes, Commander?"

Whatever I expected, it was not these next words.

"There has been a murder. At Awveline University."

"A murder?" My skin went cold.

"Several," he answered, then added quickly, "No one connected with Court."

Only then did I remember that several of my ministers and members of Congress had children studying at the university. "Who then?"

"Four students, all of them in studies for advanced degrees, in mathematics or the sciences. The local Garda has found the case to be a difficult one. They tell me they can find no motive for these killings. The city is panicking, and I fear this panic will spread into the surrounding countryside." He paused and glanced to one side. "The murders were bloody and . . . peculiar."

In a flat voice, he recited the particulars. All four victims hacked into bloody pieces, the bodies left exposed. Rumors were already spreading. Some claimed it was the work of a gang. Some whispered about a larger conspiracy. There was talk about dissidents from Anglia or another of the Dependencies, hoping to create confusion, or even agents from abroad. All nonsense, of course, but panic and rumors did not always yield to reason.

"I want you to monitor the investigation," I said, interrupting him. "Assign an officer from the Queen's Constabulary to work with the local Garda—someone you trust. Have them send regular reports on their progress. Let the newspapers know as well."

Aidrean Ó Deághaidh's glance met mine. For just that moment, the remoteness vanished from his expression. We were friends and allies once more.

Before I could speak, however, a mask dropped over his face. He nodded stiffly and turned away, saying, "Very well, Your Majesty. I will carry out your orders at once."

He left me startled and not a little irritated. Then I heard a rustling behind me and a hand descended on my shoulder.

"Áine."

It was Breandan, clad in rumpled clothes from the day before, his mouth tilted in a warm smile. I turned into his embrace, grateful for the warmth of this man.

"There've been murders at Awveline University," I said.

"And so you sent your commander to solve the mystery."

"Not exactly. He . . ."

But when I glanced up, I could see that Breandan's gaze had

traveled past me, to an unseen point in the distance. I knew that look. Most likely a sudden insight into his machine had distracted him. I wanted to shake him, yank his attention back from that inward world to the present. But I did not. My first impression, from all those years ago, was the true one. A man like Breandan Ó Cuilinn could have only one obsession in his life. Everything else was a temporary diversion.

And you are much the same way. He is your favorite. No, not even that. A dalliance.

That is not true, I insisted. *He is my friend.*

You cannot afford to have friends.

Words recalled from a long-ago lecture from my father, the king. I had confronted him about his new favorite, an acclaimed poetess invited to Cill Cannig because of her work, and who had stayed because my father desired her company. I had been angry with him for months.

I miss him.

With a twitch, I shrugged away from Breandan's arms. "I'm sorry," I said. "I didn't sleep well. And I have a great deal of work. Commander Ó Deághaidh's report awaits me."

"Yes," Breandan said softly. "I believe I understand."

Our love changed after that. Or perhaps, I saw things more clearly. Oh and sure, he kissed me just as tenderly. And sure, I invited him to my bed as often as before. But our first heedless passion had ebbed. Breandan spent longer hours in his laboratory; I buried myself in my work.

My ministers approved of the change. None of them had openly objected—the tradition of kings and queens taking lovers was older than Éire itself—but now I caught Lord Ó Cadhla nodding in agreement during our Council sessions, and Lord Ó Breislin no longer had the air of someone barely tolerating my opinion. Lord Ultach, it was true, had a perpetually dreamy manner. He took opium, and the habit had grown worse since my father's death. Soon I would have to replace him.

As for Commander Ó Deághaidh . . . He remained the proper officer of the Queen's Constabulary, but his manner eased enough that our interviews were no longer so painfully stiff.

So the summer passed. Reports from the Constabulary about the murders in Awveline City were neither good nor bad: the murders had ceased, but the Garda in Awveline City suspended their inquiries for lack of evidence. Frankonia's king died, and now the electors were locked in a room until they voted in his successor. Another heir in the Turkish States had been assassinated. But negotiations with the Dietsch Empire were proving worthwhile, and it was possible we could create a new alliance to balance against the Prussian menace.

Meanwhile Breandan scarcely mentioned his research. It was from the official reports, and not himself, that I knew he was writing a treatise about time fractures in the upper atmosphere. He had commissioned a new balloon using the latest technology for his experiments—a navigable balloon with an enclosed carriage and compressed oxygen contained in iron storage flasks.

"If I could fly to the stars, I would," he told me, in one of our rare moments of intimacy.

"But would you fly back?" I said, more to myself than to Breandan.

He shifted around and grasped my face with both hands. "Yes," he breathed. "Yes, I would."

To my shame and regret, I could not find the words to reply.

He must have read my thoughts from my face, because he smiled unhappily, gave me a hurried kiss, and rose to begin his day. By the time I had bathed and dressed, he had disappeared into his laboratory. The servants brought me fresh tea and warm bread, while I reviewed my schedule, but my thoughts were scattered between my obligations as queen and those last moments with Breandan Ó Cuilinn, and in the end, I pushed aside my breakfast only half consumed.

(He loves me. I had not expected that.)

(And you do not love him in return.)

A loud rapping at the door broke into my thoughts. Even as I rose to my feet, Aidrean Ó Deághaidh burst into the room. He stopped, one hand braced against the door frame. He stared at me, his face so blank of emotion that I was immediately afraid. "Your Majesty. There's been another murder. In Awveline City. Lord Ó Cadhla's daughter."

I dropped back into my chair. "Lord Ó Cadhla's daughter. When? How?"

"Word came just half an hour ago," he said. "By telegraph from the Garda in Awveline City. They believe it is the same murderer as before." In a softer voice, he added, "A groundskeeper found her body at dawn, near the commons. The report is . . . ugly."

My stomach gave a sickening lurch. I had read the detailed reports of those earlier murders. "Where is Lord Ó Cadhla?"

"In his rooms."

With Aidrean following close behind, I ran to Lord Ó Cadhla's rooms. Though it was a warm September day, servants had lit a fire and drawn the curtains. Only a single gaslight burned here, its pale yellow light hardly penetrating the gloom. Lord Ó Cadhla sat limply in one chair, his chin against his chest, his arms flung to either side.

Like a dead man, I thought.

I knelt at Lord Ó Cadhla's feet. A pang of relief shot through me when I saw the shallow rise and fall of his chest.

And yet, there was death in the room.

"Lord Ó Cadhla," I said.

No response.

"Lord Ó Cadhla," I said again. "Whatever it takes to find that murderer, I swear I shall order it done. By Christ's mercy, by the blood I drank upon my coronation. Do you hear me? I am sending Commander Ó Deághaidh to lead the investigation."

Lord Ó Cadhla raised his head slowly. "Your Majesty," he whispered. With an obvious effort, he lifted his gaze to Aidrean Ó Deághaidh. "They tell me a lunatic murdered my daughter, Commander Ó Deághaidh," he said. "A madman." Then he gave himself a shake, and I saw a shadow of his old self. His eyes narrowed. "Find him, Commander. Find him and bring him to justice."

"I promise, my lord."

Aidrean Ó Deághaidh left at once. I canceled all my other appointments that I might stay with Lord Ó Cadhla until his wife and other children arrived from their estates. Later, my secretary and I wrote carefully worded announcements about the tragedy, making certain to emphasize that a senior officer of the Queen's Constabulary would oversee the case until it was solved and justice achieved. Thereafter followed a dozen or more meetings with my other councilors and ministers—with Lord Ó Breislin to discuss who would handle Lord Ó Cadhla's responsibilities in the interim, with Lord Ultach's senior aide, Lord Alastar De Paor, to discuss the possibility of a terrorist connection.

Hours later, exhausted, I returned to my chambers and sank into the nearest chair. Servants had left a tray of covered dishes on the table with bread and soup. A carafe held chilled water flavored with crushed mint. I poured a glass of water and drank it off. Though I had no appetite, I forced myself to eat. The day was not even close to ending.

I drank more water, then cup after cup of hot tea, until my head cleared. Only then did I notice the bells ringing noon. Odd, surely it had to be almost sunset by now. But no, the sun hung high in the sky, a blurred disc behind a veil of clouds. Nothing had changed in this room—not the elegant furnishings, nor the scent of roses and autumn wildflowers—and yet, the taint of death had invaded here, as well.

I wish Aidrean were here.

But he was not. He was already in Awveline City, by my command, searching for Maeve Ní Cadhla's murderer.

My hand fumbled for the bell—I thought Breandan might spare an hour from his work, and I badly wanted his company. For once, his inattention to state matters would prove a relief. The movement dislodged an envelope left upon the table. I saw Breandan's handwriting and my name. I snatched it up.

> *Áine, my love. Do not be surprised by my seeming disappearance today. If all goes well with my experiment, you will see the firmest, finest proof of my long research within the week . . .*

I hardly comprehended the rest of his letter. Something about the roads of time, of braving the perils before all the other scientists. Of gratitude. Of love. I knew not what else, because I dropped the letter onto the floor and raced toward the windows. Only now did I remember his talking about the appearance of new time fractures between Awveline City and Osraighe, and the last fine day of the year.

His balloon, I thought. It was large enough to carry his machine. "Breandan!"

I flung open the windows. The golden towers and spires of Cill Cannig spread out before me, below a green garden bordered by summer roses. My gaze took that all in, then snapped upward to the skies. Yes, there, between the tallest towers was an expanse of gray clouds. And against that expanse, a bright red sphere, glorious and huge.

Already the sphere was shrinking as the balloon climbed

higher into the skies. I could not move, could hardly breathe. Higher. Higher. Now the sphere was little more than a dot, wreathed in clouds and nearly invisible, and yet I could not look away.

Breandan, I hope—

The dot vanished. A bright flare of fire burst out, smearing my vision. I blinked.

The skies were empty. In the distance a plume of smoke rose up from the hills.

There is little to tell about the next few weeks—or rather, very little of those weeks remains true.

That sounds mad, I know. Let me attempt to explain.

It took several days to recover all the wreckage from Breandan's balloon. The fall had shattered the carriage into pieces, which were strewn over the countryside. From what the Queen's Constabulary could determine, the fire came first, then the explosion of the oxygen tanks. Nothing remained of Breandan's golden octopus but a charred ruin. And of Breandan himself, nothing at all.

The Constabulary and Garda searched for ten days; they found no sign of body or bones.

That night I called for two bottles of wine and dismissed all my servants early. I drank until the fire burned low and cold nipped at my skin through the layers of my woolen robes. Once, around midnight, I nearly summoned my secretary, so that he might send a telegraph to Aidrean Ó Deághaidh. But that, I knew, would have been a terrible mistake. Aidrean would refuse to abandon his murder investigation simply to comfort me. He had his pride, and his sense of duty.

As had I.

And so I left off drinking and retreated to bed, where I fell into a restless slumber. My dreams consisted of scattered images of the past five years—of my first interview with Aidrean Ó Deághaidh, of the golden octopus and its leavings of iron dust, of Breandan's face, illuminated with joy as he placed the miniature balloon into his new gigantic machine. Of Lord Ó Cadhla, as limp as a puppet, after hearing of his daughter's brutal murder.

I woke just before dawn to the rattle of wind against my windows. It was a cold gray October morning. The skies wept with rain. One of the maids had left a window partially open, and a current of air blew through the room, carrying with it the scent of moldering leaves. My head aching from the wine, I stumbled toward the window to shut it. I paused and blinked to clear my vision. Below me, Cill Cannig looked as it always did in autumn. Copper-brown leaves whirled about. The trees stood stark and black against the dull gray skies. All around, I had the sense of a world, dying, dying into winter.

(Though all our gods and saints taught us that resurrection was our right.)

Now. I have attempted to describe in writing the next moments several times over. None of them fit what I remember. Though "remember" itself is a tenuous concept.

So. Let me just tell the story.

It was a cold, wet October dawn. I was standing by the window, as I said. This early in the day, the world seemed empty of human life, except for a few curls of smoke rising from a nearby chimney. And I, I was wishing I could undo parts of the last few weeks. Or months. Or years.

Then, of a sudden, a wrenching pain took me. My vision wavered and blurred. *The wine,* I thought confusedly, gripping the windowsill to keep my balance.

But it was not the wine. By will alone, I stared until my stomach calmed and the landscape steadied before me. It was an ordinary dawn, with smudges of saffron and indigo against the dull dark sky, the thin scarlet line running across the horizon. Ordinary, but unsettled, as though an earthquake shook my perception. I stared harder. There, in the distance, the clouds roiled. Again my stomach lurched, as though I stood aboard a plunging airship. The clouds narrowed into a funnel that raced toward me. . . .

Hours later, I came to, lying on the floor of my bedchamber. All I could remember was a terrible dream about the world tipping into chaos. A bruise over my left eye told me I'd fallen, but when my maid arrived, they could not remember anything of that eerie dawn. Indeed, they had difficulty pinning down memories of the previous day or even the week before.

More strangeness followed. Lord Ó Cadhla appeared at midmorning to report a peculiar incident. Commander Aidrean Ó Deághaidh had collapsed in Awveline City in a fit of madness. Of course the Garda there had taken custody of the man, and had him sequestered at once in Aonach Sanitarium, but it was odd that neither I nor Lord Ó Cadhla could remember why I had sent him away from Court.

If I had.

Part of me remembered a terrible tragedy, but the details refused to come into focus. Another part remembered a different tragedy, but that one too eluded remembrance. As the days melted away, I stopped struggling to recall anything from the past six months. It was enough to ensure that Commander Ó Deághaidh received the best care, and to plan his eventual return to the Queen's Constabulary. (Though, to be sure, the doctors at Aonach Sanitarium were not sanguine.)

Those were the days of confusion, as I called them.

Now to explain how I remembered what had never been.

(Or rather it had been. Once. In a different world.)

It was a bright, cold November day. For once, I had an hour of leisure from my duties. A restlessness overtook me, and so, trailed by my guards, I wandered far from my usual paths, away from the public galleries and audience halls, through a series of ever-narrower corridors into an unused wing of the palace, and to a pair of high metal doors, with a heavy bar across them. My curiosity piqued, I ordered my guards to remove the bar. Leaving them behind, I entered the vast chamber that lay beyond.

Inside, it was dark and empty. A puff of stale air met my face, laden with the scent of something old and forgotten. Memory pricked at me.

We had lately added electric illumination to the palace. I pressed the switch, and light flooded the room.

It was empty—a cavern filled with dust and shadows. But my skin itched, and I took another few steps forward. My first impression was not entirely correct. Off to one side, empty shelves stretched from floor to ceiling. And there, in the nearest corner, a few scraps of crumpled paper, also coated with dust, were scattered about, as though someone had tossed them aside years before. Ahead of me, however, the room stretched unimpeded by any obstacles. It was amazing, I thought, that such an enormous space could exist within Cill Cannig without me knowing it. . . .

It was then I saw a pale square of light, as though someone had focused a lantern onto the tiled floor. I bent down to inspect it.

The air shimmered. Startled, I plucked back my hand.

And stopped.

There, in the center of that patch of light, lay a miniature balloon and a pile of loose papers. The balloon had once been an exquisite work of art, I saw at once, constructed of gold and silver and set with tiny ruby and emerald jewels on the jet-black basket and over the perfect red sphere of the balloon itself. But the wires connecting the balloon to its basket were bent, and the carriage itself was misshapen, as though someone had set the object too close to a hot fire.

I set the balloon aside and took up the papers, which were even stranger. They looked as though they had been sewn into a book, but the edges near the binding were torn, and the rest had turned brown, obscuring the rows and rows of neat handwriting. Curious, I picked up the top page.

June 18th, 1900. Cill Cannig, Osraighe. To Áine Lasairíona Devereaux, Queen of Éire, and my patron and benefactress in these investigations into the nature of the future . . .

An electric shock traveled through me. I snatched up another page. Here were formulas and schematics for a strange machine, one that resembled nothing I had ever seen before.

Except I had.

I read on, with each paragraph offering another of those electric shocks. The pages were from a journal, written by a scientist detailing his research. It was all fantastic, and yet, not entirely so. As I read about balloons and time travel, about batteries and energy sources based upon work from scientists in Mexica and the Dietsch Empire, I recognized terms from my father's discourses about philosophy, about a certain young scientist with theories about time fractures and travel between the present and the future. . . .

Time fractures.

I released a long-held breath.

And remembered.

Breandan. Breandan, what have you done?

Except I knew. Or thought I knew.

My hands shook as I set aside the paper. I glanced upward to the darkened ceiling, half expecting a rain of papers to descend upon me, describing an unknown past and future. Memory pricked at my brain, reminding me of days and months I had forgotten.

(Forgot. Or never lived.)

I took up a second page from the middle of the set. Glanced over a description of a failed experiment. Once more the name Breandan Ó Cuilinn made my brain ache with half-remembered events. He had demonstrated a machine to my father. That much I was certain. But the rest . . . a balloon, a diary of experiments conducted here, at Cill Cannig?

I took the balloon and the papers back to my private chambers. It was strange, but their presence gave me a stability I lacked and had longed for this past month. Over the next few weeks, I compared Breandan's journals against papers from other nations and other universities concerning recent findings about time fractures. I also pored over newspapers, searching for more clues about inconsistencies in present times. The more I investigated, the more I remembered from that other time, that other past. Someone had closed the fractures over Osraighe and Awveline City. Murders were undone, the past rewritten. Because of that, Lord Ó Cadhla's daughter lived, and Breandan had died.

(Perhaps. Or if he lived, it was in a different time. In a different world from the Éire I knew.)

And what if I could travel into the past, forbid Breandan to make his fateful journey? Would he listen to me, a stranger? Or would he nevertheless press onward, to be the first of all scientists to breach the walls of time?

He would go. No matter what the risk.

I knew that because he had done so already. He had launched himself forward to a future that had vanished. No, not vanished. According to the many treatises I had read, his future had jumped to a different path, severed from mine.

Now I understood the choices my father had faced when my mother died. It was not merely an acceptance of death. It was the knowledge that our duties and our path lay with Éire, not with any other person who happened to share our lives.

I picked up the miniature balloon and ran my fingers over its delicate tracery of wires, over the perfect sphere, now marred and blunted by its impossible passage through time. I would keep it, and its companion record of the vanished past. Ah, but that was all.

Wherever you are, Breandan Ó Cuilinn, I thought. *Wherever you travel. Fare thee well.*

A FLIGHT OF NUMBERS
FANTASTIQUE STRANGE

SEPTEMBER 1902

Like every other visitation room in Aonach Sanitarium—and Síomón Madóc knew them all—this one was painfully bare. No chairs. No carpet. The plaster walls scrubbed clean of any character, their blank expanse interrupted only by a single metal door and a row of narrow windows. In spite of the brilliant sunlight, a rare thing this September day, the air felt chilled, as though the thick glass had leached away the sun's vitality, and a faint astringent smell lingered, a hospital smell that Síomón associated with having his tonsils removed when he was twelve. He shivered and wished he had kept his frock coat with him.

Across the room, his sister sat cross-legged on the floor, her gaze fixed upon a corner of the ceiling. "141955329," she said. "Times two. Exponent 25267. Add one."

Gwen spoke slowly, enunciating each syllable with painful care. Even so, her voice sounded furry—a side effect of the drugs, Síomón knew.

"1031980281. Times two. Exponent 25625. Subtract one." She paused a heartbeat and her normally tense mouth relaxed, as if savoring the number, before she started the next.

The bleating of a motorcar horn filtered through the windows from the avenues bordering the sanitarium grounds. Síomón rubbed his forehead, trying to massage away an incipient headache. When his sister had first begun these litanies, he had immediately recognized the numbers for simple primes. As the months and years passed, however, the numbers had swelled to fantastical lengths, surpassing all the known tables. Síomón could only guess, but he suspected these were primes as well.

Gwen Madóc. Twenty-three. Her age too was a prime number, as was his.

Sit quietly with her, the doctors had advised. *Your presence serves to heal.*

He saw no sign of it, however. Four years had passed since Gwen first came to this sanitarium in Awveline City. Four years of weekly visits, in between his studies at the university. He could barely remember Gwen outside this whitewashed room, where even the floors were sanded to eliminate splinters. Formerly, they had allowed him a stool, but one day his sister had seized the stool and flung it at Síomón's head.

"1031980281. Times two exponent 25625 add one, Síomón. Add one."

Síomón snapped up his head. Had she really said his name?

"353665707. Times two. 25814. Minus 1. 353665707*225814+1. 1958349*231415−1. 1958349*231415+1."

The numbers poured out so fast that Síomón could barely distinguish between them.

"1958349 times two exponent—"

Gwen broke off, her face stricken as she groped for the next number. A moment's hush followed, so profound Síomón could almost hear the sunlight beating against the windows.

"Gwen?" he whispered, hoping she might hear him today.

His sister's eyes went blank, and she began to rock back and forth, keening. That too fit the pattern of their visits—numbers, confusion, grief, then anger.

Still keening, Gwen lifted her hands toward the barred windows, which cast blue shadows over the floor. In the sunlight, the silvery scars on her wrists and palms stood out against her pale skin. There was a theory associating particular numbers with certain colors. So far there were no practical applications, but several recent papers from Lîvod University in Eastern Europe claimed to support the theory—

Without warning, Gwen launched herself at Síomón. They crashed against the wall and rolled over, he grappling for her wrists while she tore at his face with her fingernails, shrieking, "Síomón Síomón Síomón Síomón."

The door banged open, and five attendants burst into the room. Four of them dragged Gwen away. The fifth helped Síomón to his feet, murmuring in concern, "You've taken a cut, sir."

He dabbed at Síomón's forehead with a cloth, but Síomón pushed the man's hand away. "It's nothing. Just a scratch. No need to trouble yourself about me."

"It's no trouble at all, sir."

Meanwhile, Gwen shrieked and cursed and sobbed as the other attendants wrestled her into submission. Her pale blonde hair fell in snarls over her face, ugly red blotches stained her cheeks, and her mouth looked swollen. Síomón could not tell if one of the attendants had struck her, or if she had injured herself in the fight.

I was right here. I should have heard a slap.

Before Síomón could say anything, the four attendants bundled Gwen out the door. The remaining man gave one last dab to

Síomón's forehead before he too departed. Síomón drew a long breath. He flexed his hands, which ached as though he'd been clenching them.

"Mr. Madóc."

Doctor Loisg stood in the doorway. Unlike the other doctors, he wore a plain tweed suit and not the white jacket they so often favored. His placid gaze took in Síomón's bleeding forehead and rumpled clothes. "A difficult session," he observed. "But not unexpected."

"I should not have come. We were too optimistic."

"Hardly too optimistic. Hopeful. Yes, we had a setback today, but I would urge you to continue your visits. Minz and Gerhardt speak of the soothing effect of familiar faces, and their latest research shows great promise."

"Of course," Síomón said, but his thoughts were still on Gwen. Had she sounded more desperate today? And, yet, she had remembered his name. That had to be a positive sign.

Still distracted by that possibility, Síomón only half listened as Loisg escorted him through the sanitarium's broad and well-lit halls, speaking in general terms about Gwen's condition. It was a familiar topic, this discourse on madness and obsession, and how a brilliant mind often shattered under unbearable pressure, only to seek refuge in that which had driven it mad.

For Gwen was mad, mad from too many numbers, and the damage appeared irreversible. However, they were trying kindness, as far as that went, and with Síomón's permission, they employed some of the more exotic cures—combinations of music and drugs, the newest electrical therapy, and other techniques Síomón didn't want to examine too closely. Loisg spoke of finding the root cause, as though Gwen were a complex number whose illness they could calculate.

They came at last to the staircase that wound down to the sanitarium's foyer, a grand airy room decorated with opulent couches and rugs, and hung about with enormous paintings from masters in the previous century. Bowls of fresh-cut roses were placed about on marble stands, giving off a sweet scent. Several visitors clustered about the windows, waiting their own turn to speak with the doctors. Síomón recognized their look of painful expectation as he and Loisg came down the stairs. A lone man occupied a couch by the empty fireplace, apparently absorbed in a book. As Doctor Loisg took his leave from Síomón, the man stood and approached.

"Pardon me," he said. "I'm told you might be Mr. Síomón Madóc."

He was a tall man, with a lean tanned face that certain women might call handsome. His eyes were warm and brown, his gaze direct. He wore a well-cut black frock coat and silk vest. Obviously an educated man, though his accent was hard to place. There were traces of shadows underneath his eyes, as though he had slept badly, and an air of tension beneath that polite expression.

"I am Síomón Madóc," Síomón said slowly. "But you have the advantage of me, sir."

The man smiled, one that vanished as soon as it arrived. "Perhaps I should start over. My name is Aidrean Ó Deághaidh. I'd like a few words with you, if I might."

He spoke politely enough, but there was something in his manner that told Síomón the question was a perfunctory one. "Concerning what?"

Another of those ghostlike smiles made its appearance. "Let us talk outside, Mr. Madóc. There's a park nearby, and a pathway along the Blackwater, if you would be so kind as to indulge me."

At once the clues shifted—Ó Deághaidh's manner, the way his gaze absorbed every detail—and though the man had not mentioned any official title, Síomón knew why Ó Deághaidh had sought him out. *He's come about the murders.*

He studied Ó Deághaidh with greater wariness. "I'm happy to

assist you in whatever way possible, but if you've come with questions about the cases from last spring, I've remembered nothing new."

"I didn't say you had, Mr. Madóc. Please. Come with me."

Síomón consulted his watch. An hour until his next lecture remained. Unless this man Ó Deághaidh wanted more than a few answers—and Síomón had none to give—he could easily make the university grounds with time to spare. He nodded his agreement.

They exited the foyer and set off along the sanitarium's pathways, winding down the sloping lawn toward the gates below. Síomón had expected Ó Deághaidh to begin his questions at once, but Ó Deághaidh remained silent, glancing from side to side as they passed the masses of late-blooming lilies, their rich scent hanging heavy in the warm air. Though it was still early afternoon, the grounds were nearly empty, the lawns rolling in smooth emerald waves, with stands of ancient oaks here and there, and a thicker wall of shrubbery and trees that concealed the iron gates. From certain angles, Síomón could almost imagine himself at home at Gleanntara, up north in County Laingford. It was for that reason, as well as its reputable doctors, that he had chosen Aonach Sanitarium for Gwen's confinement.

"You are a man of impressive wealth," Ó Deághaidh said.

Recalled abruptly from his reverie, Síomón nearly stumbled. "And you are a man of abrupt turns, Mr. Ó Deághaidh. Or do you have a title I should use?"

Ó Deághaidh shrugged. "My title is Commander Ó Deághaidh, if you prefer a more formal address," he said. "And I apologize for trespassing into your private concerns."

"Of course," Síomón said automatically. He felt an immediate spark of irritation, then, at himself and Ó Deághaidh both, and added, "But then, trespassing on private concerns is your trade, is it not?"

It was a direct jab. Rude, even, but Ó Deághaidh seemed unperturbed by the comment. "It is, sadly. We come to our jobs with a natural curiosity about the world, and our work encourages it. You might say the same for you and your fellow students, no?"

So the commander came well armed and ready to use his weapons. Síomón covered his reaction with a shrug of his own. "So they tell me. As the poet once said, 'The tools of mathematics are a curious set—the eye, the hand, the pen, the brain. It is with these instruments, we cast our net. And bring to earth a flight of numbers fantastique strange.'"

Ó Deághaidh nodded in recognition. "Henry Donne. The famously obscure Anglian poet of the late sixteenth century."

"An obscurity he earned," Síomón replied. "And yet, worth studying. His meter falters, but I find his sentiments ring true."

They had come to the outer gates, which opened onto Tulach Mhór Street, a broad avenue filled with carriages and the occasional motorcar. With Ó Deághaidh leading, they crossed between the horses and cars to the farther side, then into the park, where a series of well-tended footpaths soon brought them to the Blackwater, a dark and sluggish river that wound through Awveline City's heart. The sun shone like a diamond in the September sky, bright against a lacework of silvery clouds, and other pedestrians strolled the walkways—women in silk-lined pelisses, their faces hidden beneath sweeping hats; men in high-collared shirts and bowlers. The air was summer-warm, but then a gust of wind rattled the trees, sending down a shower of brown and crimson leaves.

"As you've guessed, I've come about the murders last spring."

Ó Deághaidh's voice was curiously light, as ethereal as sunlight. Síomón's skin prickled at the sound. "I thought the Garda gave up its investigation for lack of evidence."

"The department merely suspended their inquiries. They did not close the case."

"And now?"

"And now we have reopened it. Or rather, the murderer has."

Síomón stopped abruptly. "What do you mean?"

"We've had another death, Mr. Madóc. A young woman named Maeve Ní Cadhla."

The news struck Síomón like a physical blow. He'd talked to Maeve just yesterday afternoon. She had answered the last arguments from her adviser, and meant to start writing her thesis the following semester. It was to be a paper concerning a simpler proof for the prime number theorem. . . .

"When?" he whispered. "How?"

"Last night," Ó Deághaidh said. "A groundskeeper found her body at dawn, near the commons."

Síomón stared at Ó Deághaidh, still unable to comprehend the news. All around them, the autumn day continued, serene and lovely. A half-dozen balloons drifted across the skies, their motors silent at this distance. Blue messenger craft and grand air-yachts, heading across the Éireann Sea to the island of Albion—some to the kingdom of Alba in the north, or beyond to Denmark's territories, others for the various districts of the Anglian Dependencies— Manx or Wight or Cymru or to Anglia itself, who gave the region its name. Above them all, a single red balloon floated between the pale gray clouds.

"We've notified Lord Ó Cadhla about his daughter," Ó Deághaidh continued in that soft strange tone. "And we are talking to certain people who might have useful information. However, I would appreciate your silence until we make our formal announcement of the crime."

With an effort, Síomón recovered himself. "How do you know it's the same murderer?"

"The evidence so far supports our theory."

He could be speaking of mathematical theorems and their proofs, not of a young woman slaughtered by a madman. Dislike sparked inside Síomón, and he had to struggle to keep that reaction from his voice. "And you want it kept a secret. Why?"

"Several reasons, but the chief among them is that your provost pleaded strongly for discretion. He plans on making a general announcement tomorrow. You knew the young woman, did you not?"

"Of course I knew her!"

The words burst out of him, loud enough to startle a passerby. Síomón wiped his forehead and tried to calm himself. "Of course I knew her," he repeated quietly.

A gifted young woman, who had discarded all the trappings of wealth and privilege when she entered the university, much to her family's dismay. The family had become reconciled, then proud of her achievements. Síomón recalled how Maeve's cheeks flushed with the passion of numbers when she argued a theory. It was hard to accept that she was dead.

A breeze ruffled the Blackwater's surface, drawing silvery lines over the dark waters—waters that had cradled the murderer's first victim. The season had been early spring, the soft twilight air filled with newly blooming flowers.

"Did you like her?" Ó Deághaidh asked.

Síomón thrust his hands into his pockets to still their trembling. "I—I respected her greatly, Commander Ó Deághaidh."

"What about the others?"

"Are you asking if I liked them, or respected them?"

"Both. I'm sorry to disturb you with these questions, when you've surely answered them before."

You know I have not, Síomón thought. When they interviewed him five months ago, the gardaí had merely requested an accounting of his activities for every night the murderer struck. No one had asked Síomón about personal matters, nor had they requested his opinion of his fellow students' abilities. He suspected the provost had used his political influence to shield the students, and thus protected the university against further scandal.

But Ó Deághaidh was evidently waiting for some kind of response. "I knew them all," Síomón said. "In some cases, I knew more than I liked. It's a large university, but a small department—the graduate department, that is."

Ó Deághaidh nodded. "The Queen's Constabulary is much like that."

Síomón's pulse gave a sudden painful leap. The Queen's Constabulary of Éire normally concerned itself with only royal affairs. But then he remembered Maeve's family. Lord Ó Cadhla was a high-ranking minister in Éire's government and adviser to the queen. It was his influence, no doubt, that had brought Commander Ó Deághaidh to Awveline City.

"You look unsettled, Mr. Madóc."

Síomón ran his hand over his face. "I am more than unsettled. I am distressed. It's a hard thing, to hear that a friend has died."

And you gave me that news without warning. Then watched to see how I acted.

But he knew better than to say so to a stranger, much less a member of the Queen's Constabulary.

Ó Deághaidh himself appeared unmoved by Síomón's outburst. He motioned toward the path. "I understand your distress," he said. "But come, let us keep walking."

After a moment's hesitation, Síomón continued down the path. Ó Deághaidh kept pace with him with long, easy strides. They had come to a section where young ash trees bent over the path, making a leafy tunnel of green and gold. Close by, the Blackwater murmured and a dank, muddy scent filled the air. Most of the pedestrians had turned aside to the upper walkways, and they were truly alone.

Síomón waited for the questions to continue, but once more

Ó Deághaidh surprised him. "I've read the latest mathematical papers," he said. "Some of the theories from Mexica are intriguing, if somewhat whimsical. Those from the West African scholars, from the Nri Republic in particular, appear more practical."

This time it was obvious the abrupt shifts in subject were deliberate. "You mean the theory of numbers in relationship to the production of energy?" Síomón asked.

"Yes, those. But also the ones concerning electrical properties of certain equations."

He went on to explain which properties he meant, and in far greater detail than Síomón would have expected from any garda or even an officer of the Queen's Constabulary. Indeed, Ó Deághaidh seemed unusually well informed about recent controversies and debates in the field, even about the exotic corner of number theory Síomón had chosen for his doctoral thesis.

"How numbers affect dreams," Ó Deághaidh said. "Is that a fair description?"

His musing tone lulled Síomón into speaking as he would with a fellow student. "Not quite," he said. "My theory depends upon the concept that numbers have both abstract and tangible qualities. That is, we use numbers to measure and quantify, but we also use them to express theories completely divorced from the physical realm. I believe we might take that concept one more step—that they have a spiritual quality as well."

"Some might call that numerology."

Ó Deághaidh spoke softly, almost indifferently, but Síomón's face flushed. "You are hardly a mathematician, Commander Ó Deághaidh. How would you know?"

"Because I studied the subject myself. I never completed my degree, which I sometimes regret. However, I read the journals still."

Síomón exhaled softly. So and so. The commander was a failed mathematician. That would explain much. "My apologies," he said, with as much sincerity as he could muster. "I've had many arguments about my thesis. I've become somewhat sensitive on the topic."

"Sure and we all have our prickly moments, Mr. Madóc. No need to apologize. But speaking of mathematics, I understand your sister also intended to study at Awveline University. I spoke with your adviser, Professor Ó Dónaill, this morning, and he mentioned her name. He said she had begun work on prime numbers before."

Síomón stopped and wheeled about. "What does that have to do with your investigation, Commander? Or do you like to distress everyone you question, the guilty and innocent alike?"

He had spoken out loud, hardly caring who overheard them. Ó Deághaidh regarded him without any expression on that lean brown face.

"Once more I apologize," he said. "I was merely expressing my sympathy, however clumsily."

They had exited the tunnel of trees. Here a set of granite steps led up the bank to Mac Iomaire Avenue, which now crossed the river into the city's financial district. Síomón was vaguely aware of foot traffic on the pavement above, but no one paid any attention to them. It was just as Ó Deághaidh had suggested back in Aonach Sanitarium, though now Síomón suspected the privacy was for Ó Deághaidh's benefit, not his.

"Have you any more questions, Commander?" he asked.

Ó Deághaidh tilted his head and studied Síomón a moment before answering. "None for today, Mr. Madóc. The official investigation begins tomorrow after Doctor Ó Néill makes his announcement. I'll send someone by your quarters to take your formal statement." He smiled, and this time it seemed genuine. "I thank you, Mr. Madóc, for your company and your patience."

He held out his hand. Síomón shook it, noting the strength in his grip. "Good day then, Commander."

"Good day to you, Mr. Madóc."

Ó Deághaidh climbed the stairs and turned onto the bridge, where he soon blended into the crowd of clerks and messengers. Síomón lingered a moment longer by the riverbanks, taking in for the first time the fragile sunlight upon the autumn leaves, shimmering like so many raindrops. His gaze returned to the river and he shuddered. Paul Keller's body had been discovered not far from this bridge, his throat slashed and his face hacked into a purpled bloody mass.

Before the university had recovered, other murders had followed. Li Cheng. Úna Toíbín. Nicolás Ó Cionnaith. All of them graduate students—three in the mathematics department. The newspapers had focused immediately on that fact. They dwelt in loving detail upon university politics, the youth of the victims, and any irregularities in their pasts. That the murderer had mutilated his victims with a knife only heightened the titillation.

A madman, said the newspapers.

Surely not one of us, said the provost, thinking first of his reputation, so entwined with the university's.

The Garda had made no public statements, preferring to ask their questions in private. In the end they had run out of questions, and the cases remained on hold.

Until now.

Síomón glanced up. Above the city, the skies arced, empty of balloons for the moment. Then he glimpsed a swiftly moving speck—the red balloon from earlier, rising higher and higher toward the sky's limit.

In spite of his best efforts, Síomón could not find a cab until he had jogged halfway back to the center of Awveline's Old City. He arrived at the mathematics quadrant just moments before the clock tower struck three o'clock. Síomón galloped up the steps and into the building for mathematical studies, then around the stairs to the back of the lecture hall. A quick survey of the room showed him that Professor Ó Dónaill had not yet made his appearance. Even better, Evan and Susanna had saved him a seat a few rows down from where he stood. He sidled along the row and sank into the chair between them.

"Late," Evan whispered.

"Within reasonable deviation," Síomón replied.

"Certain combinations do prove to be predictable," Susanna murmured.

Síomón managed a smile at the familiar exchange, which had hardly varied over the four years they had known one another. They had first met in the library, in a furious argument over a rare volume of mathematical theory. The argument had led to a debate, which led in turn to a lasting friendship. Susanna, dark and neat and practical, came from a wealthy family who had immigrated to Éire from Gujarat several generations ago. Evan was the son of a north county family that traced its antecedents back to the first Anglian Wars. He was tall and fair and angular, with looks so much like Síomón's that many mistook them for brothers.

"How was Gwen?" Evan asked.

Síomón had to draw a breath before he could answer calmly. "The same as always."

Susanna laid a hand on his arm, lightly. Evan glanced around, then leaned close to Síomón. "An officer, from the Garda I believe, came by the library this morning. A man named Ó Deághaidh. I told him where he might find you. I hope that was right."

Síomón made a show of arranging his pens and books. "He's with the Garda, Evan. Of course you did right."

He ought to tell them about Maeve, in spite of Ó Deághaidh's orders, but he could not think how to phrase it without sounding trite. *Did you hear the news? Maeve died last night. They say she was murdered by a lunatic.*

To his great relief, a door swung open at the front of the lecture hall. Professor Ó Dónaill, the senior lecturer in the graduate department for mathematics, stalked to his podium, his white hair floating behind him in an unruly halo. The next moment, a side door banged open. Seán Blácach, a third-year graduate student, darted through and made for an empty seat behind Síomón. Papers spilled from his books, and he had a hurried, disheveled look.

"I'm sure someone robbed the city of all its cabs," he muttered.

Síomón shrugged, conscious of Evan's sidelong glance and how Susanna had pursed her lips in obvious distaste. Blácach ordinarily did not speak to them, except in passing before exams. He was a student of the fringes, dabbling at his studies in between gambling and other questionable pursuits. His family had little money, and Síomón often wondered how he could afford to stay at university.

Now Blácach leaned over his desk, between Evan and Síomón. "No luck today," he whispered to them. "But I can try again tomorrow. Will that do?"

His breath smelled sour, as though he'd been drinking already. Susanna shifted uncomfortably. Evan bent over his books, clearly unwilling to acknowledge Blácach. Reluctantly, Síomón glanced over his shoulder. "What are you talking about?" he whispered.

Blácach smirked. "Oh, how very chaste we are today. I thought you two might not dare—"

He broke off, and Síomón was abruptly aware of a thick silence in the lecture hall, and Professor Ó Dónaill gazing fixedly at them. "My apologies for being tardy," Ó Dónaill said. "Please do not let it overset you, Mr. Madóc, Mr. Blácach."

Síomón pretended an overwhelming interest in his pens and papers. Blácach muttered something unintelligible, but sat down.

Ó Dónaill nodded. "Today's lecture," he rapped out. "Electrical impulses and higher-order numbers. Mathematics? Numerology? Or gin fantasy?"

Someone in the back row barked out a laugh. Ó Dónaill gazed steadily at the culprit, one eyebrow lifted. "Perhaps someone experimented with these theorems last night," he said drily. "Indeed, that might explain *your* appearance, Mr. Blácach."

Evan coughed. Susanna, more discreet, covered her smile with her hand. The rest of the students settled into quiet, and with a last glance around the hall, Professor Ó Dónaill launched into the day's lecture.

The first incident took place during the winter holidays, shortly after their nineteenth birthday. Síomón had attended his first semester at university, having bypassed the usual courses for several advanced classes. Gwen had elected to remain at Gleanntara with their aunt and uncle, pursuing her private research.

When he arrived home from the train station, Síomón learned that Gwen had not yet returned from her walk. He would find her in the gardens, his aunt said, or perhaps rambling about the fields. There was an odd note of reserve in his aunt's voice, as if she wished to say more. Another quarrel, he thought. Gwen had written about their aunt's increasing attempts to transform her into a proper young woman.

He set off in search of his sister. It was a chill February afternoon, with the sunlight fading into dusk. Snow had fallen overnight, blanketing path and field. After casting about, Síomón soon found her trail. Footprints led him through the topiary, past the sunken garden with its pool lying silvery and quiescent beneath the gray skies. Once or twice, he thought he saw a flickering movement between the evergreen shrubs, but when he called out Gwen's name, no one answered.

More anxious now, he entered the woods beyond. All the day's light had leaked away from the sky, and dull gray shadows masked the trees and other familiar landmarks. Once, he smelled a fox's musky scent, then a strange coppery tang, which sent his pulse racing in dread. "Gwen," he called out. Only to hear the high shrill call of the fox, and the whispering of snow over snow.

He found her, at last, huddled under a thornbush near the gamekeeper's old hut. She was barefoot, dressed only in a thin shift. The tatters from her winter frock hung from one of the bushes; her cloak and her boots were discarded to one side. Gwen herself was like a pale gray stone.

Síomón knelt beside his sister. "Gwen?" he said softly. "Gwen, what happened?"

Gwen looked around vaguely. She must have been here for hours, Síomón thought. Her skin was red, her lips chapped, and tears gleamed in her eyes. It was a miracle she was not dead from the cold. She reached out, and he caught her hand. The touch of another human must have recalled her from that daydream, because she shuddered, and her gaze sharpened with sudden clarity.

"It was a number, Síomón. I followed it. . . ."

Her voice trailed off, and she frowned, as though confused.

Síomón touched her arm gently. "Gwen," he said. "Did someone hurt you?"

Her eyes went wide and blank. Her mouth worked, as though she would speak.

Then she screamed.

I was a coward. I said I was fetching my uncle, but in truth I was running away.

Síomón tapped his pencil against his palm in an irregular rhythm. A blank sheet of paper faced him, one edge darkened where he'd rubbed his thumb absentmindedly. Unable to face or-dinary conversation with Evan and Susanna, he'd sequestered himself in the library, leaving only to take supper at a nearby tavern. Now the mutton lay heavily in his stomach, and the over-cooked vegetables had left an unpleasant taste in his mouth.

Maeve was dead. The phrase echoed inside his head. Strange, he still could not quite take in that she was gone.

He glanced out the window. A harvest moon hung low in the sky, its orange disc sharply drawn against the black night. He and his uncle had called the doctors that same day; within a week, they had removed Gwen from Gleanntara to the hospital in Awveline City in the far south of Éire. *Only the best for her,* he thought now. *The best drugs. The best treatment—*

The floorboards creaked behind him. Síomón twisted around to see Evan De Mora standing quite close. Evan's face was drawn tight; his eyes were like blue moons against the whites of his eyes.

"Why didn't you tell me about Maeve?" he said.

Síomón hesitated, not certain how to reply. Evan must have mistaken his silence for a refusal to answer, because his mouth twitched into a grimace. "Confused, Síomón? That's not like you."

"No, I—"

"That's why that officer wanted you, isn't it? He told you about Maeve."

"He did. He asked me not to say anything until tomorrow. Who told you?"

"Her sister." Evan pressed both hands against his cheeks, as though to suppress an ache. "I thought it peculiar when I heard about Ó Néill's assembly tomorrow," he said in a muffled voice. "Even when I didn't see Maeve at her afternoon lectures, I didn't think anything amiss. I knew she was spending extra time with her advisers, and that I'd see her at supper. It wasn't until she didn't show that I—"

His voice broke. Síomón started to speak, but Evan waved for him to stay silent. He soon mastered himself. "I went to her rooms. Her sister was there with a crowd of servants, packing Maeve's belongings. She told me what happened."

His cheeks were wet with tears. Síomón touched Evan's arm and felt him trembling beneath the apparent control. "Evan, I'm sorry."

His friend drew a shuddering breath. "Thank you. Whatever that means. I was so angry. Not with you. With—"

"I understand," Síomón said softly. "Come. It's nearly ten. We'll go back to my rooms for coffee."

Evan wiped a hand over his eyes. "I would like that."

Síomón collected his books from his desk, and together they retrieved their gowns and coats from the closet on the first floor. The college bells were ringing ten o'clock as they bid good night to the porter.

Outside, the wind had picked up, damp and raw with the promise of rain. Clouds raced across the moon's face, and the green was nothing more than a black expanse, with the library at their backs, and the several junior dormitories lining either side. At the far end of the quad lay Begley Hall and a cluster of smaller buildings for Anglian Studies. Síomón and Evan buttoned their overcoats and turned up their collars before venturing from the portico's shelter.

Evan shivered. "Last week I boiled in the lecture halls."

"It's the turning point of seasons," Síomón said. The sound of the wind sifting through leaves recalled Gwen's voice, reciting her numbers, and he had the unsettling impression of memories blurring together, like photographs of dancers whirling across the stage. He shook his head to dispel the sensation.

They set a fast pace across the empty green, while leaves whirled about them. Few students were about at this hour, and though most of the upper floors of the dormitories were alight, the grounds themselves were nothing more than shadows. Síomón could taste rain in the air. Soon frost would silver the pathways, the winds would strip the trees completely, and the world would become like an ink sketch, with sharp black lines and shades of gray.

A harder gust caught him full in the face. Síomón ducked his head, blinking away tears. Ahead, he heard Evan's footsteps slow, then come to a stop.

"Síomón."

Síomón looked up to see Evan pointing toward a spot farther ahead. Squinting against the wind, he made out a dark mass sprawled upon the brick walkway. Whatever it was lay motionless, except for a fluttering edge of cloth, as though a blanket or cloak had worked loose from the body's weight.

His skin prickled. *We don't know it's a body.*

Evan retreated a few steps and took hold of Síomón's hand. "How cold you are. Can you manage? We cannot go without seeing what has happened."

Síomón gripped Evan hard. The warmth of his friend's hand revived him, and together they approached the thing on the walkway. No, not a thing. A man. Síomón could make out the head, resting on the grass. One arm was invisible beneath the cloak, the other extended, as though reaching for something in the last moments of life.

Evan knelt and pulled back the cloak, exposing the face. "It's David Levi."

Síomón couldn't make sense out of his words at first. David? Dead? Numb with disbelief, he knelt beside Evan and touched David's face, which looked gray and stark beneath the strong moonlight. Blood trickled from the slack mouth, painting a black trail over David's cheek and onto his collar. Síomón jerked back his hand.

"We must find a garda," Evan said.

"Shouldn't we call a doctor first?"

"He's dead, Síomón. A doctor cannot help him."

Evan's voice sounded muffled and strange. The wind, Síomón thought, or was it the pounding in his temples that distorted his friend's voice? He stumbled to his feet, then fell down, sprawling to avoid David's body.

"Síomón, what's wrong?"

"Nothing. I—"

Evan gripped his arm and pulled him upright. "It's the body," he said. "You're faint because of the blood. Am I right?"

Síomón shook his head. "I don't know." He gulped down a lungful of cold air. Another. He was about to say he felt better, when he saw a shadow among the trees, not ten feet away. At first, he thought it was just branches, swaying in the wind, but then the moon broke through the clouds, and he distinctly saw the figure of a man.

"Evan, look," he whispered.

Evan straightened up. "What do you see?"

The stranger spun around and darted into the ink-black divide between Begley Hall and the nearest dormitory.

"Stop!" Síomón called out. He sprinted after the man, ignoring Evan's shout. The man dove into an alleyway behind the next building. MacAuliffe, it was. The lane led directly to the front of the college, Síomón remembered. Once the murderer was clear of that, he could vault over the iron fence and vanish into a maze of streets. Síomón paused, breathing hard. *I must not fail. Not now. Not so close.*

Before he could take that next step, however, Evan yanked him to the ground.

"Are you mad?" Evan wheezed, falling to his knees beside Síomón. "What were you doing?"

"Didn't you see him?" A cramp took hold of Síomón. He doubled over, retching.

"Who? I see that you're sick. Here, let me wipe your face."

Evan took out a handkerchief and cleaned away the mud and vomit.

Síomón pushed Evan's hand away. "There. Can't you see him? There!"

He pointed frantically toward the lane. A shaft of moonlight illuminated the space between the two buildings, plainly showing the man at the far end, but just as Evan turned, the stranger vanished around the corner.

"Tell me where you spent the afternoon, Mr. Madóc."

Síomón pressed both hands against his eyes. Hours had passed since he and Evan had tracked down the night sentries and led them to David's body. By now he wished only for the solitude of his rooms.

"I was in the library," he said, "writing up notes from Professor Ó Dónaill's lecture. I—how much do you want to hear?"

"Everything. Do not worry about boring us, Mr. Madóc."

"Yes. I see. Well then." Síomón massaged his face. Though he had scrubbed his face and hands in the Garda lavatory, he could still smell the blood and vomit on his skin. "I spent some hours writing my notes. Around seven o'clock I went out to supper, then returned directly to the library. May I have a glass of water?"

Ó Deághaidh signaled the nearest uniformed garda, a sergeant, who fetched a tin cup filled to the brim. Síomón drank half the cup in one swallow, grimacing at its metallic taste. Once he and Evan had notified the college patrols, the city's gardaí had arrived promptly and hurried them off to a station on the north side of Awveline City. He had not seen Evan since they entered the building. Indeed, he'd had no other company besides Commander Ó Deághaidh and his three gardaí. For all he could tell, it was nearly morning, but his own internal clock said an hour past midnight.

Ó Deághaidh waited patiently until Síomón set the cup down. "You attended Professor Ó Dónaill's lecture after we parted," he continued. "Is that correct?"

"Yes. Evan De Mora can tell you that I was there. Susanna Patel can as well—"

"And if I need confirmation, I shall surely ask them. This moment, I wish to hear your account. Did you walk to the university or ride?"

"I took a cab."

"Directly to the lecture?"

"No, not directly. Cabs aren't permitted on the grounds. In any case, my rooms are in the square opposite the East Gates. I stopped by to fetch my gown and notebooks for the lecture."

"Anything else?"

"Nothing. No, wait. I had promised a book for Susanna."

"Did you encounter anyone, talk to anyone, between your rooms and the lecture hall?"

Síomón shook his head. "No. No one."

Ó Deághaidh studied him a moment. His eyes, which had appeared so warm that afternoon, had turned hard and glittering in his weathered face. It was, Síomón thought, as though Ó Deághaidh had stripped away every superfluous quality, leaving behind only that relentless curiosity.

"Very well," Ó Deághaidh said. "What next? You came to the lecture hall. Whom did you first see?"

They covered Síomón's activities from when he and Ó Deághaidh parted by the Blackwater, to when the gardaí arrived at the murder scene. Throughout, Ó Deághaidh's voice remained calm, his manner detached, but his attention to detail was meticulous. In the background, Síomón could hear the scratch of pens moving over paper. Two gardaí were taking notes in parallel, as though Ó Deághaidh did not trust the account to a single chronicler. Another, the one who had fetched him the tin of water, simply waited and listened.

Eventually they reached the point when Evan De Mora approached Síomón in the library.

"What was the hour?" Ó Deághaidh asked.

"Near ten. I remember the hour bell ringing just as we left the library."

"And how would you say Mr. De Mora appeared?"

Síomón paused, the tin cup in hand. "Upset, of course."

"At you?"

"No!" Síomón slammed the cup onto the tabletop, sloshing water over the sides. Hands shaking, he mopped up the spill with his handkerchief. "I apologize for my outburst, Commander. It's been a long day."

"To be sure, Mr. Madóc. We are all a bit weary and shaken. Tell me, if you can, exactly how Mr. De Mora appeared. Upset, you said. Did he seem angry? Grieving? Nervous?"

His mouth tasted like cotton, but Síomón resisted the urge to request more water. "Do you suspect him? Surely not?"

Aidrean Ó Deághaidh's expression remained bland. "I suspect everyone, Mr. Madóc. Did you know David Levi?"

The sudden shift in topic caught Síomón off guard, and, for a moment, he couldn't collect his thoughts into an answer. "Yes, I knew him. Not as well as Evan does—did. But David attended a number of mathematics lectures, so we talked from time to time."

"About electrical impulses in numbers?"

Was that mockery in Ó Deághaidh's voice? Some sly reference to Síomón's own discredited theories? He could not tell. Suppressing his urge to shout, he answered, "Yes."

"But you were not friends."

"No. Colleagues."

"Respected colleagues, you might say. I understand. Do you

know if he formed any closer ties with the other mathematics students?"

So far he'd answered freely, but now Síomón began to mistrust the shape of Ó Deághaidh's questioning, which seemed designed to draw out his opinions in dangerous ways. "Not that I know of."

Ó Deághaidh favored him with another thoughtful look, but apparently he had no further interest in David Levi, because he went back to the step-by-step questions, asking Síomón about his departure with Evan De Mora from the library, what they saw from the portico and walk, who first noticed the body, and when Síomón observed the unknown fugitive.

"Man or woman?" Ó Deághaidh asked.

"A man. At least, I believe so."

A pause. "Tell us exactly what you saw."

Síomón considered how to phrase it. "First I only saw a movement. I thought it was the wind, moving the tree branches, but then I clearly saw a . . . a shape or shadow amongst the trees. I'm sorry I cannot be more clear. When I pointed them out to Evan, whoever it was started running."

"A shape or shadow. That does not sound so certain."

"I wasn't at first, but now I am."

"So. You saw a man amongst the trees. He ran, and you gave chase. Very foolhardy of you, Mr. Madóc."

"I know. I wasn't thinking very clearly. Evan shouted for me to stop, but all I could think was I had to catch the murderer before he escaped."

Ó Deághaidh nodded. "I see. Go on."

Síomón licked his dry lips. Without a word, the same sergeant refilled his cup. Síomón drank the water down in one swallow, trying to ignore how Ó Deághaidh watched him. "I chased him across the green," he said, "and around Begley Hall and into the alleys behind. I had stopped to catch my breath. Before I could go on, Evan caught up and tackled me to the ground. By that time, the stranger got away. But before he did, I had a clear look at him in the moonlight."

"You saw his face?"

"No." Síomón closed his eyes, trying to recall exactly what he had seen. Mist and shadows. The knife-cold wind blurring his vision. The hiss of leaves sliding over leaves. A figure outlined against the stone wall of the dormitory.

"He wore a strange squashed hat and a loose coat. I could not make out his face. But it was a man."

"Are you certain of what you saw? Mr. De Mora says you took ill by the body."

"I am quite certain," Síomón said evenly. "I knew by his height and his clothes and the way he stood."

"Just so." Ó Deághaidh exchanged a glance with one of the gardaí. "Mr. Madóc, I should tell you that we've spoken with Mr. De Mora. He does not recall any stranger, man or woman."

"Impossible. Evan ran after me. He threw me to the ground and said I was a fool to chase the man."

"Mr. Madóc, your friend was quite clear about that point. *I saw no one,* he told us, *but with the clouds over the moon, I'm not surprised.*"

Síomón shook his head. "I cannot believe he said that. Sure there were clouds, but the moon was bright enough to see by."

Ó Deághaidh's expression did not change, but his gaze shifted momentarily from Síomón to the other men in the room, then back. "Tell me about your meeting yesterday with Seán Blácach," he said.

"I had no meeting with Seán Blácach."

"Do not lie to me, Mr. Madóc, else things will go badly."

Síomón reached for his water cup, then remembered it was empty. In a level voice he said, "There was no meeting, Commander. Not yesterday. Not ever. No matter what he said—"

"Seán Blácach said nothing, Mr. Madóc. My sources are other witnesses. Three students have reported they saw two men outside the dining halls near dusk. One was Seán Blácach. The other was a tall fair-haired man, well dressed. Normally they would have thought nothing, except that the fair-haired man seemed quite agitated."

"Any number of men could fit that description."

"No, sir. No, they could not. We have a list of those in Awveline and the university who match this description. You are on that list. So are three others, including your friend Evan De Mora. Do you deny meeting with Seán Blácach?"

"I do." His voice came out as a whisper. Louder, he repeated, "I do deny it, no matter what anyone else claims."

A short interlude followed, with Ó Deághaidh consulting with the gardaí. One exited the room, only to return within moments with a stack of scribbled notes. Ó Deághaidh pressed his lips together, as if annoyed, then his countenance cleared.

Síomón thought the interview done, but Ó Deághaidh launched into another series of questions about Síomón's activities for the previous week—every lecture, every session in the library, every person who spoke to him, or who could confirm his whereabouts. "We are not singling you out, Mr. Madóc," Ó Deághaidh said, during a pause. "We are asking everyone the same questions. Mr. De Mora sits in another room in this same building, and Mr. Blácach in another yet. Tomorrow we shall interview Miss Patel. I cannot expect you to like our methods, but I do expect your cooperation."

"I am cooperating," Síomón said wearily.

"Yes, you are." But to Síomón's ear, Ó Deághaidh's tone sounded ambiguous. "Tell me," he went on, "about the arrangements you have with your uncle. He manages your estates of Gleanntara, in County Laingford, does he not?"

"He manages *our* estates," Síomón said, with a slight emphasis. "My sister and I own the property jointly. Why do you need to know this?"

"To complete my understanding of your circumstances, Mr.

Madóc. Your parents left everything—land and money—to you without division, is that not so?"

"Yes. We had talked earlier about dividing the estate—the will allowed us to alter the arrangement once we came of age— but then my sister took ill."

"And so you kept things as they were."

Síomón nodded, but his mind had wandered. He was seeing Gwen's face, chapped by hours in the cold, and hearing her sing-song voice as she talked about following a number. *There will be nothing like it was,* he thought. *Not unless we wind ourselves backward through time a half dozen years.*

To his relief, the interview ended at last. Síomón stood and shook hands with Ó Deághaidh. The gestures and the words came to him automatically, even in such a strange situation, and he did not begrudge them this time.

"I've ordered a cab for you," Ó Deághaidh said. "Remember that we might need to speak with you again tomorrow."

A sergeant escorted Síomón from the building and helped him into the waiting carriage. Once inside, Síomón collapsed into the corner. His entire body ached, as though he had worked every muscle from his scalp to his toes. He wanted nothing more than to sleep, but when he closed his eyes, he kept seeing David's pale face, his outstretched hand, as though he had tried to grasp something in those last moments of life. Then there was Ó Deághaidh and his endless questions, seemingly random but by now Síomón knew that Ó Deághaidh never spoke or acted without purpose.

At last the cab stopped before the house where Síomón rented a suite of rooms. He climbed down stiffly and was grateful when his valet met him at the door. Kevin Garret removed Síomón's muddy coat without comment and handed him a hot drink.

Síomón drank down the tea in one long swallow. "Thank you, Kevin. No need for you to stay up. I'll take myself to bed."

"As you wish, sir."

Síomón stumbled into his bedroom and closed the door. His hands were shaking again, and he nearly called Garret back to help him unbutton his shirt. It was then he noticed the stain on his sleeve. Blood, he realized, suddenly queasy. David's blood, still damp to the touch.

Their guardians invited Professor Glasfryn to visit the spring after Síomón and Gwen turned thirteen. Glasfryn was a retired professor, Uncle Liam told them, and had taught mathematics at Éire's largest university, in Awveline City. He was man of considerable reputation, their Aunt Eilín added, in a tone that suggested they would show respect for once.

"What do you know about him?" Síomón asked Gwen.

"Nothing," Gwen replied, a little too quickly. Then, "Enough to know he's worth listening to."

They had retreated to the attic above their bedrooms. Their aunt called it their schoolroom, but for Síomón and Gwen, it represented a refuge from the ordinary. Not even their most recent tutor, a man they both liked, ever ventured into this space. Síomón wanted to ask Gwen what she meant by *worth listening to,* but her expression had already closed. He took up the nearest book and pretended to study a diagram of numerical theory.

Glasfryn arrived in midafternoon. Now stationed in the parlor, at their aunt's command, Síomón and Gwen watched the liveried footman help the old man disembark from the carriage. He looked nothing like Síomón had imagined. Old, yes. But with a face so brown and seamed, it was as though he'd spent his years laboring in the sun, not confined to lecture halls. Gwen stood with her hands clasped together, silent and demure, but Síomón could tell she was studying Glasfryn as intently as he was.

They took an early tea in the parlor while Aunt Eilín fussed over their guest, and Uncle Liam explained at tedious length about the twins' schooling. Glasfryn stirred his tea and nibbled at the scones, but it was clear to Síomón that he was ignoring their uncle.

"Let me talk to them," he said, interrupting Aunt Eilín's third inquiry about his health.

Their aunt bit her lips, clearly irritated. Their uncle started to make excuses why he ought to remain present, but when Professor Glasfryn waved them away absently, Uncle Liam rose and motioned for Aunt Eilín to come with him.

"But Liam," she said softly. She glanced toward Gwen with an anxious expression, but then she shook her head and excused herself.

Glasfryn waited until the door closed. "Now then," he said. "Let us speak openly."

He began with straightforward questions about their lessons. They answered dutifully, just as they did with their tutors. Without their uncle to explain and repeat himself, the interview lasted only a quarter hour.

Glasfryn fell silent and studied them a few moments through rheumy brown eyes. "What do you think about numbers?" he asked abruptly.

Síomón and Gwen blinked. "What do you mean?" Síomón asked.

"The ancient Greeks thought numbers were dead. Myself, I wonder if they were right. Maybe mathematics is like so much lumber. Take the sticks and build a house."

Gwen's cheeks flushed pink. "What about Pythagoras?"

"Answer my question first."

His tone was blunt, but Gwen smiled, unflustered. "If you view numbers as dead, then you imply a dead house, and one that invites termites. Besides, the premise is wrong."

Síomón caught his breath at her words, but Glasfryn's mouth widened into a slow pleased smile. "How so, young miss?"

"You assume a universal quality of men, just as your statement assumes a universal quality of mathematics, or even of numbers themselves."

"Does it follow, then, that you believe numbers exist apart from mathematics?"

A slight hesitation. "I do."

Another pause, while Glasfryn drank down his cold tea. When he spoke again, it was to ask Gwen more questions. She answered—tersely at first, then with growing volubility. Glasfryn eventually turned his attention to Síomón and, in the same way, drew out more and more of what the twins had worked at in mathematics, their private research as well as their formal lessons.

Questions soon gave way to discussion. With the professor leading, they spoke of topics ranging from the mundane to the bizarre—of the origins of mathematics, of whether numbers had undiscovered properties invisible to the ordinary mind, and the newest theories from Egypt and Mauritania. Twice their aunt pleaded they stop for dinner. Both times, the professor waved her away. After another interval, a troop of servants brought in trays of covered plates and pots of tea, leaving them on the sideboard. Síomón didn't remember eating, but he assumed they did, because later the servants retrieved the piles of dirty dishes.

The bells were ringing midnight when the professor rose and held out his hands to them both. "We must have you at Awveline, and soon," he said. "I shall speak with your uncle tomorrow."

Glasfryn rose late the next day, and departed for Awveline shortly after luncheon. Síomón and Gwen watched from their attic refuge as their visitor exchanged a few final words with Uncle Liam. Once the carriage exited through the gates, Gwen took Síomón's hand. "Come with me," she said, leading him down the back stairs and through the service quarters to the garden and beyond.

Síomón retained only vague impressions from that walk. The

sunlight upon Gwen's hair. The crunch of autumn leaves. The woodland scents of pines and damp earth. The warmth from his sister's hand as she led him deeper into the wilderness.

The next morning, it took three cups of strong tea to clear his mind. With Garret's help, Síomón dressed in his best black suit, then walked the four streets over to Evan's rooms. Yesterday's sunshine had vanished behind a mass of gray clouds, and the dank breeze, with its taste of frost, brought him fully awake. It also reminded him uncomfortably of the previous night and the abiding cold he felt when he had touched David Levi's face.

Susanna had arrived at Evan's flat already, and the two of them were drinking tea. Susanna's eyes had a dull bruised look, as though she had been weeping for hours.

"Evan told you about David and Maeve?" Síomón said.

She gave a short nod. "I knew last night. Evan came by my rooms to tell me."

Evan himself seemed distracted. He gathered his and Susanna's cups and set them on the sideboard. "It's not an hour to the assembly. We should hurry."

They set a brisk pace through the streets to the nearby gates, and across the grounds to the assembly hall. Even so, they found nearly every seat claimed. Síomón recognized only a handful of the students, and those were from the mathematics department. *Voyeurs,* he thought, angrily, glaring at the strangers.

Susanna laid a hand on his arm. He glanced down, surprised to see a smile on her face.

"They are frightened," she said softly. "So are we."

Síomón let the breath trickle from his lips and nodded. He even managed a smile in return. When the priests spoke of God and Mhuire and Gaia, he could take comfort from the familiar words. Other priests from other churches and temples made their appearance—rabbis from the Hebrew temple that David Levi had attended, a Protestant minister, a Vedic priest, and even the lone Muslim cleric. But then came the Provost with a long unctuous speech, and his mood soured. David and Maeve deserved better.

More speeches followed. When the last official gave way once more to the priests and rabbis, Síomón released a silent exhalation of relief.

Requiem Aeternam dona eis, Domine et Gaia.

Baruch dayan emet.

Assalaamu 'alaykum wa rahmatu-Allah.

On and on through the litany of faiths, but Síomón could bear these more easily than anything from Doctor Ó Néill and his minions. At last came the moment when the Provost dismissed them. Susanna took hold of Síomón's hand. She already had Evan's, or perhaps she had never let go.

"Outside," she said. "I can't bear the crowds."

She led them out of the building and onto the green, where a mass of students lingered. "We can go to my rooms," she said. "I've tea and coffee and stronger drink, if we like. Or would you rather something fancy?"

Evan made some reply that Síomón could not attend to. Through the mobs, he had caught sight of Seán Blácach. He glanced around, intending to make some excuse to escape the crowds and Blácach, only to spy Professor Ó Dónaill emerge from the assembly building. Ó Dónaill immediately started for Síomón. "Mr. Madóc," he called out. "I'm glad to find you here. Would you have time for a short talk? It's a question of your studies."

In truth, Síomón wanted nothing more than to retreat to his own rooms, but he suspected his friends would not allow it. He politely smiled. "Certainly, sir."

"We'll come by later," Susanna told him.

Síomón followed Ó Dónaill into the faculty quadrant, which proved to be nearly empty, and into the building occupied by the mathematics professors. Ó Dónaill ushered Síomón inside his office, then shut the door and turned the lock.

"I heard what happened with you and De Mora," Ó Dónaill said. "Terrible shock. Terrible. Come, sit." He indicated a chair in the corner.

Ó Dónaill kept his office in cheerful disorder, with stacks of books arranged on and around his desk. More books occupied a table off to one side, and these were mixed with loose papers, covered in calculations. Used cups and saucers were shoved up against the coffeepot and tins of spices, which bore Arabic lettering. Papers covered Ó Dónaill's desk as well.

Síomón edged around the stacks of books to the chair.

"Would you like a cup of tea?" Ó Dónaill said. "No, it seems I have none. Will coffee be acceptable? I brewed a pot not long ago."

He offered Síomón a cup of hot, bitter coffee, seasoned with cardamom and lightened by thick cream. Then he filled his own cup and busied himself with the spice tins a moment.

"You know about classes being suspended?" he said. "Good idea. I'm glad Ó Néill decided for it. As late as yesterday afternoon, he wanted to keep up the pretense, but after Levi died . . ." Ó Dónaill shook his head. "I'm babbling. My apologies. I am distressed about the murders, but talk will cure nothing. So then, let us be forthright. You should know that I'm taking a short sabbatical."

Síomón started. "Why, sir?"

"Let us call it a break in habit. Mathematics requires a suppleness of mind, and I hope to regain a certain flexibility, shall we say." He shot Síomón a sharp glance. "Are you worried about your studies?"

"I hardly know, sir."

Ó Dónaill nodded. "You are though. I can see it. However, do not fret. As I said, I'm taking a sabbatical, but I shan't disappear from the university."

He moved a heap of papers to one side of his desk. They contained rows and rows of calculations, Síomón noticed, as he glanced over them. Then his skin went cold as he recognized the complicated formulae. He had presented these same ones to Ó Dónaill the previous semester.

And he'd rejected them.

He glanced up to see Ó Dónaill studying him.

"How goes your research?" Ó Dónaill said.

"It goes . . . with difficulty, sir."

"I warned you about that."

"You did, sir."

Síomón took another sip of coffee. He wondered if Ó Dónaill would admit to reviewing Síomón's work, but the professor's next comment was about a new monograph from a Frankish mathematician that had caused a stir. They discussed the theory a while. When Síomón finished his coffee, Ó Dónaill offered him more, but Síomón politely declined.

"Then I must beg your indulgence and bid you good day," Ó Dónaill said. "I've stumbled upon an interesting line of research and would like to mark good progress before the day ends. But do come again, especially if you have questions concerning your research. I would not like it said that I abandoned my students. And speaking of that, I meant to ask before—how goes it with your sister?"

Síomón's stomach gave an uncomfortable lurch at this change in topic. "Not well, sir. But the doctors are hopeful."

Ó Dónaill shook his head. "Then we must hope, but it grieves me to see such promise lost."

Their interview trailed off into commonplace exchanges, and Ó Dónaill's repeated assurances that Síomón should not hesitate to come again if he had questions. Síomón descended the stairs, more dissatisfied with himself than before.

He took a footpath to the nearest gates, which opened onto Gúilidhe Square, a wide expanse paved with gray cobblestones, and fountains in each of the four corners. In the past two hours, the chill had vanished from the air, the sun had already burned away the fog, and the sky overhead had cleared to a pale blue, speckled with clouds. Here, outside the university grounds, motorcars and carriages choked the avenues bordering the plaza. The world in general appeared oblivious to the murders.

Síomón threaded his way directly across the square. He had just gained the northern edge, when a boy in a shabby coat thrust a newssheet at Síomón. "News! News of the day! Death in high places. Scandal in the capital." Then as Simon shook his head, he added, "Just ten penny, sir."

With a muttered curse for the boy's persistence, Síomón paid the boy and stuffed the newssheet into his pocket. He had to get away from the traffic and the noise. As soon as he could break free, he hailed a cab.

"To Aonach Sanitarium," he said, climbing inside the first one that approached.

"Right, sir."

The cabbie maneuvered his horses and cab into the thoroughfare leading away from the square. Síomón settled back and pulled the newssheet from his pocket.

SENSATION IN COURT, read the headlines. Doctor Breandan Reid Ó Cuilinn, a renowned scientist and the queen's favorite, had plunged to his death from a balloon during an experiment. The cause for the balloon's malfunction remained uncertain. The Queen's Constabulary was conducting a thorough examination of the incident.

The rest of the article disappeared into hyperbole and incoherent smudges. *This has nothing to do with me,* Síomón thought, but he found his pulse beating faster at the mention of the Queen's Constabulary. He crumpled the paper in his hand and looked out the cab's window. As though to confirm the news, a line of blue messenger balloons glided north toward the capital in Osraighe and Cill Cannig. Aidrean Ó Deághaidh. A strangely unsettling man. Why had he quit his studies in mathematics? Did he regret working on this case of Awveline's murdered students and not that of the queen's lover?

The cab stopped abruptly. The cabbie swore. Ahead, voices rose in complaint, and someone shouted about a blockage. Síomón leaned out the window and saw a long motorcade creeping through the intersection ahead. Small pennants lined one automobile's roof—the mark of a visiting dignitary.

Lord Ó Cadhla.

He drew back into the cab, feeling ill. Maeve's father must have arrived by train that morning. Death in high places, indeed.

The noon bells rang, and still the traffic did not move. Síomón glanced at the newssheet, but he no longer had any desire to read about Court gossip. He stuffed the paper into his jacket pocket and closed his eyes to wait. The closed cab smelled strongly of sweat, old leather, and horse—it reminded him of the stables at home. Soon he was dozing and hardly noticed when the last vehicles in the motorcade passed by, and the lines of traffic oozed into motion.

He stood on a high peak, his gaze turned upward. Night had fallen. Glittering digits, like pinpricks of fire, stippled the dark skies. Síomón tilted back his head, trying to take in the entire number . . .

"Aonach Sanitarium," bawled the cabbie, rapping against the cab's roof.

Síomón jolted awake. Still groggy, he paid the cabbie and dealt with the gate guards. By the time he reached the main building, his head had cleared.

His visit was unexpected, however, and there was a delay before Doctor Loisg arrived in the lobby. The man frowned, obviously unhappy to see Síomón.

"Mr. Madóc. I'm sorry to have kept you waiting, but today is not your regular day. I'm not certain we can accommodate you."

"I understand," Síomón replied. "However, you've said more than once my visits are helpful. Is there a reason why I should not see my sister?"

Loisg frowned again. "I did say that. But she spent a somewhat restless night. . . ."

"Indulge me this once," Síomón said. "I promise not to distress her."

The other man studied him a long moment, his round face uncharacteristically pensive. "Perhaps you are right," he said at last. "Come with me."

He dispatched a crew of orderlies to prepare Gwen Madóc for her visit, while he and Síomón followed at a much slower pace. He described the changes in Gwen's behavior over the past day. She had left off reciting numbers, he said, his voice curiously distressed. She either wept or sat in dull silence, and when Loisg attempted to soothe her, she had struck him.

"We've installed an observation window," Loisg told Síomón. "So that we can watch without your sister being aware. Just a precaution, you understand. Do you object?"

They had arrived at the third floor, to the visitation room itself. Síomón paused and searched Loisg's face, but found only a doctor's reasonable concern. "No. Not really."

Loisg unlocked the room. Síomón proceeded alone. As always, he felt a jump of panic when the door closed behind him, and he heard the audible click of the lock.

Gwen sat underneath the windows, hands circling through the air as she murmured her numbers. She wore a simple, loose-fitting dress today, instead of her usual hospital gown, and someone had brushed and plaited her long fair hair. She appeared content, or at least absorbed, with no sign of the violence Loisg had described.

He scanned the room, noting the small observation window at the far end. No doubt Loisg was already stationed there, along with his orderlies. Telling himself that he had nothing to hide, and certainly not from his sister's caretakers, Síomón eased around to a point opposite Gwen and lowered himself to the floor. Gwen seemed oblivious to his presence. She continued to gesture in those strange rhythmic patterns, her long fingers catching and stroking the air, as though weaving strands of light. "Seven," she whispered. "Seven and thirteen and seventeen."

She had returned to the early stages of her illness, when she recited only the simplest primes. He even recognized the old intensity in her whisper, as though her numbers represented words in a different language. . . .

Síomón's skin prickled as he made the connection at last.

"Seven," he said, when she paused. "That's when our parents died."

Gwen trembled, but did not look in his direction. "Thirteen. Seventeen."

He remembered thirteen, when their uncle arranged a meeting with Glasfryn from Awveline University. Seven and thirteen. These were dates burned into Gwen's memory, which even madness could not eradicate. But seventeen?

He glanced toward the observation window. *Witnesses be damned,* he thought and crossed the room to Gwen's side. Gwen stiffened, her jaw working in sudden alarm. Síomón stopped a few paces away and knelt so that his face was level with hers.

"Nineteen," he said softly.

Her eyes widened slightly. Síomón waited, hardly daring to breathe. His patience was rewarded when, at last, she whispered, "Twenty-nine."

Keeping his voice calm, he repeated the number.

Again, he had another long wait before Gwen spoke. "Thirty-one," she whispered. "Thirty-seven."

Síomón drew a pencil and the newssheet from his jacket pocket. Gwen immediately tensed. He waited, motionless, until she calmed.

This time, he initiated the exchange. "Seven."

"Thirteen."

"Seventeen."

They repeated the sequence, Síomón writing down each number in the margins and empty spaces.

". . . Thirty-seven. Forty-one. Forty-three."

The third time through the sequence, Gwen stirred restlessly, her gaze flickering from Síomón's paper to his face, as though she expected something more. He tried repeating the numbers, but she struck the pencil from his hands. Before he could soothe her, the attendants arrived and led an unusually pliant Gwen away.

Loisg escorted Síomón to the lobby in uncharacteristic silence. "You were right to come, sir," he said, when they arrived at the front doors. "Quite right. We have made true progress today, you and I and your sister. Kindness—that is the key to your sister's illness."

Only part of the solution, Síomón thought as he walked along the sanitarium's winding paths, between the stately trees and their rain of falling leaves. The true key was written on the sheet of newsprint in his pocket.

That night Síomón pored over Gwen's numbers. He started by working through a series of basic formulae, each designed to expose any underlying patterns. When these proved fruitless, he applied the newer analysis methods discussed in academic journals. No success. Finally, on a decision based midway between frustration and whimsy, he turned to more fantastical methods— Lîvod's color theories, Frankonia's exploration into the electrical properties of numbers, the latest research from Egypt, Iran, and the Gujarat Empire.

Seven. Thirteen. Seventeen. Nineteen. Twenty-nine. Thirty-one. Thirty-seven. Forty-one. Forty-three.

He found himself doodling numbers on his scrap paper—huge numbers interspersed with smaller ones. Their pattern echoed Gwen's patterns and recalled his dream of numbers burning like stars across the night. Numbers whose voices sang to him, the notes changing as he transformed them through calculations.

He had Garret brew a pot of strong tea, then requested privacy for the evening. Garret, ever deferential, withdrew to his own room.

Síomón pulled out a well-thumbed primer on mathematical history. He skimmed the sections on Pythagoras, with his belief in mystical properties; on Fermat and his seemingly logical theory on primes, which had proved false; on Fermat's correspondent, the monk-conjurer Mersenne, and Euclid, who had posited that the list of primes was infinite, and therefore led to immortality.

I wanted my name written in the same list, Síomón thought as he turned the page. An arrogant wish, but arrogance seemed a prerequisite for mathematicians, especially those who put forth unpopular theories, such as his own. Ó Deághaidh had mocked him. Ó Dónaill had tried to discourage him, but Síomón knew the proper sequence of numbers could transform lives. He distinctly remembered . . .

Cold washed over him. Slowly, he laid down his lead stick and stared at the open book on his desk. The scrap paper was gone— possibly now another crumpled ball upon the floor. Instead, the once-empty margins of his book were decorated with a tapestry of miniscule numbers. When had he written them?

He reached out to shut the book. Paper crackled inside his breast pocket. Síomón stopped, hand hovering over his desk. He'd emptied all his pockets before the assembly—he was certain of that. *Just another bit of foolscap,* he told himself. He was always storing bits of paper about his person. He'd simply forgotten about this one.

He was still making excuses as he felt inside the pocket. His fingers met a rigid square—completely unlike the usual crumpled note. Hands trembling, he plucked out the object and let it fall onto his desk.

It was a thin packet of stiff brown paper, its edges sealed and one flap folded over to make an envelope. Síomón examined it, searching for any kind of mark or label to indicate what hid inside. When he flipped it over, the contents hissed. Like sand or sugar, he thought. He tore off one corner and poured out the contents onto his desk.

White powder streamed out to make a perfect pyramid. He stared at it warily. Not sugar. Definitely not sand. The grains were too fine. Where had he seen its like before?

You remember. You and Evan . . .

He wet his forefinger and touched the substance, making a slight dent in the pyramid's smooth surface. After a moment's hesitation, he transferred a miniscule amount to his tongue.

A strange taste filled his mouth, bitter and sweet at the same time. Within a moment, his tongue went numb. Cocaine. He and Evan had experimented with the drug one night, after reading texts from the addict philosophers of the previous century—another of those laughably regrettable incidents from their first year at the university. Síomón had forgotten the episode until now.

He closed his eyes. He had no memory of acquiring this substance, and yet he must have. But when?

Certain symbols have a mystical significance, Pythagoras believed. Our reality is mathematical. Our souls can rise to union with the divine.

Discounted theories from a long-dead mathematician, sometimes remembered as a genius, persecuted in his own time, whose secret society ended in bloody and violent suppression.

Seven. Thirteen. Seventeen. Nineteen. Twenty-nine. Thirty-one. Thirty-seven. Forty-one. Forty-three.

Now I remember.

The summer they turned seven, an unusual heat wave muffled County Laingford. Every breeze had died off. Even the messenger balloons appeared stranded, and the buzz from their engines set the air vibrating, as though from gargantuan mosquitoes. Síomón and Gwen spent their hours in their playroom, or in subdued conversation with their aunt and uncle, who had come to supervise them while their parents traveled on holiday on the Continent.

The news came on a Monday. That day, the skies were empty of balloons; the sun was a dull smudge against the sheets of clouds. Síomón and Gwen had retreated to the mansion's cool cellars with boxes of colored chalk. Síomón drew a series of squares, then rectangles, then circles. Whatever came to mind.

Gwen worked more deliberately. She brushed the wall clear of grit, then laid out her pieces of chalk with care. Síomón paused from his drawing to watch as she sketched the gardens surrounding their house. It was more than just a picture—woven in between the lush foliage and graceful trees, he could pick out a three curling between the branches like a snake, a six that also looked like a ripple in the pond, a seven disguised as the gardener's scythe.

"Síomón. Gwen."

Gwen paused, her chalk poised above the next number. Síomón, always obedient, called back, "Down here, Bríghid."

Bríghid clattered down the stairs, her face pale and her eyes wet with tears. "Come quick, master and miss," was all she said. With gentle hands, she laid aside Gwen's chalk, brushed down their clothes, and smoothed their tousled hair. No time for washing their faces. It didn't matter, she said as she led them upstairs and into the grand front parlor, before retreating with a final whispered encouragement.

Their aunt and uncle sat on the magnificent sofa where their parents so often entertained guests. With a twinge of dread, Síomón took in his uncle's black suit, his aunt's black veil and dress, unrelieved by any jewels.

Uncle Liam stood and held out his arms. "Síomón. Gwen. Come here."

Síomón felt a sudden heaviness in his chest. He glanced to Gwen at his side. She too had turned immobile, and there was a frightened, frozen look on her face. Síomón fumbled for his sister's hand. She clasped him tightly, her fingers unnaturally cold in the summer heat.

Their uncle glanced at his wife, as though puzzled how to proceed. Aunt Eilín swept her veil to one side and knelt. "Síomón. Gwen, love. I have terrible news."

Their parents had died, she told them. The cause had been a freak accident—two balloons colliding in midair had scattered their wreckage over the train rails in the remote Italian countryside. Moments later, a train had rounded a curve, and despite the engineer's efforts, the engine had derailed and plunged into a ravine, taking all the passenger cars with it. There had been no survivors.

"You'll stay here, in your own home," Aunt Eilín said. "We'll take care of you, I promise. Your mama and papa made every provision for your upbringing."

Síomón tried to speak, but his throat and chest hurt too much. Gwen let go of his hand and took one step forward, her pale blue eyes bright with fury. "No," she whispered. "That's not true. Not true. Not true. Not—"

With a smothered sob, she turned and fled. That night, Síomón heard her whispering the same words as they both pretended to sleep.

Síomón flung the cocaine out the window and went to bed. He had no dreams, for which he was grateful, but when he awoke, a strange lethargy enveloped him. He washed his face, shaved, and ordered a hearty breakfast. Coffee and eggs revived him, and he set to work at once.

The greatest purification of all is disinterested science, Pythagoras said. The man who devotes himself to that cause is the true philosopher.

He worked from midmorning to midnight and later, drinking pot after pot of strong tea brewed by the faithful Garret, while searching for the key to Gwen's numbers. Seven, thirteen, seventeen, nineteen. So many of the clues seemed obvious, but when he applied his formulae, they led into a wilderness of confusion. Over and over, he scribbled down calculations, scratched them out, and started over fresh.

Late on the third morning, a loud knocking broke into his concentration. Síomón paused, his pencil poised to finish off an equation, expecting Garret to attend to the visitor.

But Garret did not appear, and another series of knocks rattled the door. "Síomón! Síomón! Open up, man."

Evan. He sounded panicked. Síomón rose, unsteady from sitting so long. He had the strange impression of doubled voices, and though the hour bells were just ringing, he was convinced they'd rung not five minutes ago. He smoothed back his hair, arranged his pencils, and hastily covered up his worksheets.

And stopped, his heart racing.

A snowy white pyramid, the size of his thumbnail, occupied the center of his desk.

"Síomón! Open the door, or I'll get the key from Mrs. Drogha."

Síomón covered his eyes with his palms, willing himself to see nothing but blackness. No cocaine. No numbers. No dizziness after which the day had mysteriously dissolved into night. Evan showered more knocks against his door, yanking him back to the present. "I hear you, Evan. Give me just a moment."

He swept the cocaine into an old envelope and shoved it into his desk drawer. With a damp rag, he wiped his desktop clean, then tossed the rag into the waste bin and stirred up the contents. A glance into the mirror showed that his face was pale but otherwise ordinary. He brushed his hands over his trousers, then opened the door.

Evan stood in the corridor, shoulders hunched, hands shoved into his coat pockets. Except for a stark white shirt collar, his clothes were entirely black. Síomón gestured for Evan to come inside, but Evan did not move. "They held David's wake yesterday," he said in a clipped voice. "Why didn't you come?"

"I—I didn't know."

"They sent a notice around."

A red haze washed over his vision, and his stomach roiled. He wished he'd not drunk quite so much tea the night before. "I haven't been well, Evan."

"So Garret told me," Evan said, in that same hard voice. "And Mrs. Drogha. So that is the excuse I gave Commander Ó Deághaidh, when we spoke at Maeve's funeral."

Pennants fluttering atop the long black motorcar. Lord Ó Cadhla, come to fetch his daughter's body home. Ó Deághaidh saying, We've had another death.

"Síomón!"

Síomón flinched. His gaze swung immediately to his desk. He

half expected to see the cocaine again, but the desk remained innocently clear.

Evan stared past him into the room. His expression softened to concern, looking more like his usual self. "What's wrong, Síomón? Can you tell me? Is it because of the murders?"

"Nothing." Síomón swallowed against the dryness clogging his throat and tried again. "Nothing that sleep and the right food won't cure."

An awkward pause. Evan shifted on his feet and glanced away. "I see. Well. The other reason I came was that we're holding a wake ourselves, a private one, for Maeve and David together. It's tonight, at Bantry's Pub. You should come."

"Bantry's," Síomón repeated. Then a shadow crossed his vision, and he distinctly heard Evan say, "I'm sorry you're too ill to come. Shall I stop by tomorrow?" and his own answer, "Yes. Please do."

When Evan had gone, Síomón closed the door and leaned against it, eyes squeezed shut. "It's nothing," he whispered. "I'm unsettled. My nerves strained. Nothing more."

He stumbled into his bedroom and lay down. Hours later, he woke with a start, sweating, his heart beating against his ribs. His rooms were dark, the air stale and cold. A rapping sounded at his door—a steady rhythm as though someone had been at it a while.

Evan.

Síomón rolled from the bed, calling out, "Just a moment."

He scrubbed his face with cold water and ran a comb through his hair. The cocaine had not mysteriously reappeared. Calmer now, he opened the door, ready to face Evan.

But it was Susanna who stood outside. Susanna with her plain black sari, her face serious. "Síomón," she said. "You must not do it."

He blinked, confused. "Do what?"

She gestured sharply, taking in his appearance and the cluttered room behind him. "Make yourself a recluse. I haven't seen you in three days. Evan tried calling on you yesterday, but you wouldn't answer the door. He said you were ill. Bollocks."

"Susanna . . ."

"Don't." Her voice scaled up, and she made an obvious effort to regain her control. "Don't lie to me, Síomón. I know you're grieving for Maeve and David. We all are. I just came to ask—to say that you should not hide from your friends."

With that, she turned and fled down the stairs.

Síomón closed the door and turned back to his rooms. Only a day had passed since Evan's morning visit, but a veneer of dust coated the floors, and his rooms had an odd neglected look. Where had Garret disappeared to?

Evan tried calling, but you wouldn't answer.

Síomón's gaze veered to his desk. The cocaine had returned.

He had trouble remembering much after that. Morning. Night. Afternoon. The hours flickered past his eyes like pages of a book. Once he found himself crouched over his wastebasket, retching. Another time, he massaged his cramped hands, studying a list of numbers. Moments later, he stood in his bedroom, drinking coffee, bemused to find himself dressed and shaved.

He was still gazing at his carpet when someone tapped at his door. Evan or Susanna, he thought. Or possibly the long-absent Garret.

But his visitor was Aidrean Ó Deághaidh, looking grim and weary. "You must come with me, sir."

"Why? More questions?"

"More questions than I like, sir. I cannot tell you more until we reach the Garda station."

"Am I under arrest?" Síomón demanded.

"No, Mr. Madóc. Not unless you give us reason."

Ó Deághaidh helped him into his overcoat and led him outside, where a cab with a sergeant waited. It was late in the afternoon, or early in the evening, Síomón could not tell which. The air felt damp and chill with impending rain, and Síomón huddled into a corner of the cab, glad for his heavy coat. Ó Deághaidh himself remained silent throughout the long uncomfortable drive to the Garda station. Fatigue lined his face, making him look much older than he had that first day, when they walked along the Blackwater. Síomón noted a scar below Ó Deághaidh's left temple and faint hatch marks beside his eyes. How many years had he served in the Queen's Constabulary? And why had his superiors assigned him to this obscure murder case?

They arrived just as the sun was sliding behind the Garda station, which stood on a prominence overlooking the Blackwater. Ó Deághaidh dismounted first and scanned the walkway. When Síomón climbed down, the commander took him by the elbow and hurried him inside.

Gardaí and their charges filled the outer rooms—tramps and beggars, a woman with gaudy makeup, a nervous man in evening dress explaining his possession of a gun. Ó Deághaidh guided Síomón up the nearest stairwell, along a deserted corridor, and into a waiting room. He closed the door and pointed to a chair. "Sit."

Síomón hesitated. He had expected the same scene as last time—the several uniformed sergeants standing along the walls, the gardaí writing notes, another of Ó Deághaidh's colleagues listening in. Instead, they were alone, and Ó Deághaidh himself remained silent, his narrowed gaze upon Síomón.

"The newest victim is Susanna Patel," Ó Deághaidh said abruptly.

For a moment, Síomón's mind went blank. Then the blood drained from his face and he sank into the chair. "Susanna? When? How?"

Ó Deághaidh studied him a moment before answering. "Last night. Very late, if our witnesses are telling the truth. The coroner is confirming their testimony."

Susanna. Dead.

Síomón leaned his head against his hands. "That's not possible," he whispered. "She visited me this afternoon. No, wait. She came by yesterday."

Ó Deághaidh gave no reaction, except that his features went more still than before. "Tell me everything you did this past week. Leave nothing out."

"I . . . I spent them in my rooms."

"The entire five days? Doing what?"

Five days? Another wave of vertigo passed over Síomón. He steadied himself against the tabletop and managed to meet Ó Deághaidh's eyes. "Research. Studying."

"For your thesis?"

"Yes. That and . . . something that concerns my sister."

Ó Deághaidh regarded him steadily. "Miss Patel was last seen in the mathematics library. She bid the librarian good night just as the clock struck ten. The librarian happened to look out the window and saw a man waiting underneath one of the lampposts. He accosted Miss Patel. They spoke a few moments, then walked off together. The librarian said he had only a glimpse of the man's face, but he swears it was you."

"Impossible," Síomón whispered. "I never went there. My manservant can testify—"

Ó Deághaidh stopped him with a gesture. "We spoke with Kevin Garret. You dismissed him two days ago, he claims. We also spoke with your landlady. Mrs. Drogha and the chambermaid both agree that you remained in your rooms throughout the day, but they cannot guarantee your whereabouts after sunset."

Síomón felt a trickle of sweat down his spine. "I did not leave my rooms, Commander. I—besides my studies, I was quite ill, Commander. Ask Evan De Mora. He came to my rooms."

Ó Deághaidh nodded. "We know. As did Miss Patel. She spoke

with Mr. De Mora yesterday morning. She was concerned, as was he, about your health. He did not say it outright, but Mr. De Mora thought you had had dealings with Mr. Blácach."

"That's a lie," Síomón burst out. He stood up hastily, knocking over the chair. Breathing heavily, he righted the chair. "I'm sorry. That was uncalled for. I can only say I'm upset. Any man would be with his friends dying and his sister—" But he would not speak of Gwen to this man. "Never mind about my sister. I've enough to upset me these past three days."

"Five," Ó Deághaidh said softly.

"Three or five or twenty-five. Does it matter? My friends are dead, and you accuse me of being their murderer."

"But I don't."

Síomón stopped. He had been circling the table, unaware that he did so. Now he faced Ó Deághaidh across the room. One of the windows had been opened a crack. A thin breeze filtered into the room, relieving the stifling heat. "You don't?"

"No." Ó Deághaidh watched him closely. His gaze was bright, disquieting in its intensity. "We have contradictory testimony, Mr. Madóc. We have other evidence I cannot share with you. Suffice to say that we do not have adequate proof to arrest you."

"Then why bring me here?"

"To question you. Someone murdered Susanna Patel. Someone who knew her quite well, and that is telling you more than I should."

Síomón rubbed his hand over his numb face. "I wish I could help you."

"So do I, Mr. Madóc. So do I. Now, please, sit. I have a few more questions."

A few questions turned into several dozen. Once more, Ó Deághaidh led Síomón through the past week. When had he entered his rooms? Who brought him meals? On which day did

Evan De Mora visit him? Had Mr. De Mora appeared distressed?
What about Miss Patel?

"Did you know that Mr. De Mora and Miss Patel had been
lovers?"

Síomón gripped the table's edge to steady himself. "Lovers?
No. I had no idea. I thought—" He eyed Ó Deághaidh, suddenly
suspicious. "Are you certain?"

"We are certain, Mr. Madóc. We have that information directly
from Mr. De Mora."

Síomón opened and closed his mouth, unable to respond to
this new information.

Ó Deághaidh watched him in silence. When he resumed his
questions, they seemed to come at random, skipping over the past
week, then leaping to years before, including his first meeting
with Evan De Mora. Gradually, as he answered questions about
Evan's recent behavior, Síomón's panic receded, replaced by a re-
alization that brought him no comfort.

They think Evan murdered Susanna.

At last, Ó Deághaidh let out a sigh. "Enough. We've had a long
day, you and I, Mr. Madóc."

"Am I free to go, then?"

"Yes. But remember, the investigation continues. I would prefer that you not leave Awveline City."

"Of course, Commander. I only meant that I was tired and
would be grateful for some sleep."

"That you may have, Mr. Madóc."

A garda called a cab for Síomón and escorted him home. The
ride back to his rooms remained a blurred series of images.
Moonlight alternating with clouds. Dusky purple skies. Faint
stars pricking the darkness. Long shadows stretching over the
roadway. He was vaguely aware of the garda helping him inside.
Even with the man's assistance, it took Síomón three tries to unlock his door, but at last he was inside. Safe and alone.

He scanned his rooms. Nothing extraordinary met his sight. Books, papers, and furniture all looked the same. Aside from Kevin Garret's strange absence, and the coating of dust, his rooms looked as though the past few days had not occurred.

Save that Susanna is dead, and the Garda suspects Evan.

He dropped into the chair by his desk. After a moment's hesitation, he yanked open the drawer and searched through its contents. Keys. Slips of paper with numbers scribbled upon them. An inkpot. A pair of dice he and Evan used to play statistics games. But no white packet of strange powder.

Síomón shoved the drawer closed and rested his head upon his hands. *I was upset. Confused. Nothing more.*

Work. He needed to work. To distract himself from the news about Susanna. He reached blindly for the nearest book: *Numerical Theories of the Syrians.*

For an hour, he was able to lose himself in reading and making notes. As one reference led him to another, he pulled out other books, until he had an untidy heap upon his desk. Metaphysical properties. Particles of thought. Time streams. The various theories hung in his mind, vivid and clear. It seemed that he had finally found the necessary strands to pull his theories together. . . .

The vision wavered. The brightly colored strands of his reasoning unraveled into a handful of nothing. "Damn," he whispered. "Damn. Damn to all eternity."

He pushed back his chair and stood. He'd go mad if he stayed alone much longer. He pulled on a hat, gloves, and overcoat as he walked out the door. There was no question of visiting Evan, not with Ó Deághaidh's oblique accusations fresh in his thoughts. But Ó Dónaill—Ó Dónaill had strongly suggested that Síomón come to him if he had any questions.

Questions about mathematics. Those aren't the questions you have. Those are the ones I can bear to ask.

The hour was later, and the streets much emptier, than he had expected. After a frustrating half hour, he flagged down a cab. Síomón gave the name of a street three blocks from Ó Dónaill's house. Mere precaution, he told himself, but the memory of Aidrean Ó Deághaidh's sharp, disquieting gaze seemed to follow him, even now.

The cab dropped him off at the agreed upon address. Síomón paid the fare and disembarked, to continue the last distance on foot. Ó Dónaill lived in a genteel neighborhood of aging gabled houses. Most of the windows were brightly lit, but the streets themselves were quiet and the sidewalks empty. A line of yellow halos marked the procession of streetlamps.

Ó Dónaill's house stood on a corner, somewhat apart from its neighbors and shielded by a high wall of bushes. Síomón paused at the edge of the property, where a brick walkway led up to the front porch. Lamplight glowed in one of the upper windows, but downstairs all was dark. He puffed out his breath in frustration and stamped his feet, suddenly aware how swiftly they'd grown numb.

A fool's errand, he thought. Ó Dónaill might be awake, but he certainly wasn't receiving visitors at this hour.

He turned away, thinking he ought to go directly home, but stopped when a light flared in the downstairs parlor window. A silhouette appeared before the curtains. Síomón recognized Ó Dónaill by the wispy halo of hair around his head. With a few moments, he had lit the parlor lamps.

Now a second, taller figure appeared by the window. Síomón drew a quick breath and advanced a few steps along the front walkway. Who else had chosen to rouse Ó Dónaill from his early evening? Another student? Commander Ó Deághaidh?

Too curious to resist, he dropped into a crouch and ventured closer to the parlor window. Light spilled through the glass, but he told himself that no one inside could see him in the darkness.

Luck was with him. Ó Dónaill had left the window open a crack, and he heard their voices clearly.

"Not possible," Ó Dónaill said.

"But sir, surely you've read the theories—"

"And just as surely I've read their refutations, Mr. De Mora."

Evan. Why had Evan come here? Ó Dónaill was not his adviser. And surely he would have remained at home, mourning Susanna's loss.

Síomón bent over double, his head spinning from the onslaught of suspicion. Here among the dying flowers and close-clipped bushes, the air felt colder, closer than before, and the scent of moldering leaves was strong. He swallowed against the bile rising in his throat and breathed through his nose until his stomach settled. Above him, the voices continued their conversation. They were arguing—something about formulae and the properties of numbers.

"Prime numbers," Evan said, his voice taking on that eager tone when he'd alighted upon a new and exciting idea. "You yourself wrote a paper on the subject."

"Years ago," Ó Dónaill said. "Others have since disproved the theory."

"True. But remember the new research from Lîvod and Tlatelolco—"

"Incomplete—"

"*Not* incomplete."

There was a heavy pause, and Síomón could picture the glower on Ó Dónaill's face. It was a look that intimidated less confident students. Evan himself apparently required a few moments before he could continue.

"Begging your pardon and your indulgence, sir, but the evidence is not incomplete. Here are the newest papers, delivered just this week from a community of Iranian scholars. Have you read them, sir?"

"Not yet, Mr. De Mora. I was engaged in my own research."

"As was I, sir. One very similar to your own, I would imagine."

Ó Dónaill snorted. "Indeed." But when he spoke again, his voice was oddly formal. "Mr. Madóc is your intimate friend, I believe."

"Mr. Madóc is my dear friend and a respected colleague, sir."

A longer silence followed, then Ó Dónaill cleared his throat. "I'm glad you paid me this visit, Mr. De Mora. Come with me, we shall go to my offices tonight. I have some papers to share—"

He broke off with an exclamation. What followed next, Síomón could not quite make out. Footsteps thudding across the wooden floor, a strange soft thump, as if a knife had been driven into a pillow, a garbled cry that robbed him of strength and sense. He doubled over, hands splayed in the cold mud outside that bright and terrible house. From afar, he heard a commotion, then a second, broken-off cry.

Síomón dragged himself upright and forced himself to look into the parlor.

It was empty, as far as he could see. Empty and bright and silent.

Without thinking, he raced to the front porch and flung the door open. A silent foyer met his eye. Cautiously he stepped inside, his heart beating hard against his chest. He heard a rustling from within the parlor and laid a hand on the latch.

The metal stuck at first. He pressed harder. The latch gave way with a loud click, and the door swung open. For a moment, he could not comprehend what he saw. A branch of candles on the mantel. The hearth itself giving off a glow from its banked fire. Several chairs overturned. And then, he saw what had not been visible from the window itself—two dark shapes lying motionless upon the carpet, one with fine white hair, one with blond, bleached to silver in the lamplight.

Evan. Ó Dónaill. But that means—

He heard a scrabbling. Before he could register what that signified, a man burst from behind the couch and ran full tilt into

Síomón. They both tumbled to the floor, arms and legs flailing as they wrestled. Síomón found himself pinned on his back, the stranger gripping his throat. Síomón dug his fingers into the stranger's wrist, broke free, and rolled to his feet. The next moment the stranger had done the same.

He was a tall man, with pale blond hair escaping from underneath a knitted cap, and his light blue eyes glittered in the moonlight. He could almost be Evan's brother. In his left hand, he held a butcher's knife, the point angled upward. Blood stained the blade.

Síomón's stomach lurched. He stumbled forward, hardly knowing what he did. To his surprise, the stranger gave a muffled cry and ran.

"Stop!" Síomón cried.

"Stop!" cried another voice.

Ó Deághaidh. In relief, he swung around. "Commander. Thank the Lord and Lady—"

Ó Deághaidh stepped over the threshold, his gun aimed at Síomón's chest. "Síomón Madóc, I order you to yield. Give me the knife, sir. I promise that it will go better if you cooperate. Come, lay the knife down. You know you have not a chance."

Síomón edged away. "What are you talking about? Didn't you see the man? He's the one who killed—"

With a shock, he realized he gripped a knife in his left hand.

He flung the knife away in horror. It clattered to the floor and bounced toward Ó Deághaidh, who dropped to one knee and fired. Síomón twisted away, but not in time. Pain blossomed in his shoulder. In panic, he stumbled down the hall and made it through the back door a few steps ahead of Ó Deághaidh.

A garda loomed to his right. Síomón swung a punch and connected. The pain in his shoulder nearly brought him to his knees. Ahead, he saw another figure darting through the gate and into the alley. Síomón drew a sobbing breath and ran.

Dawn came as a dark red haze.

Síomón pressed his hands against his eyes, trying to contain the pressure inside. He'd spent half the night chasing and being chased. Twice he had spotted the murderer, and twice Ó Deághaidh's men had nearly captured Síomón. Finally he'd taken refuge in a derelict stable, deep in Awveline's slums.

He tilted his head back and breathed in the dusty air. His shoulder ached fiercely where Ó Deághaidh had shot him, and dried blood pulled at his skin. It would be only a matter of hours before Ó Deághaidh and his patrols located Síomón. They would charge him with murder, try him, and execute him. And why not? The proof lay at his feet—the bloody knife that killed Evan and the professor—even though he clearly remembered dropping it inside Ó Dónaill's house. He also remembered a stranger fleeing with the same knife in his hand. Two memories, equally vivid. Which one was true?

"Seven," he whispered. "Thirteen. Seventeen." He paused and listened a moment. A pattering against the doors and broken shutters told him that rain was falling. A faint silver light seeped around the shutters. Day had arrived.

"Nineteen. Twenty-nine. Thirty-one—Fuck! Damnable fucking numbers!"

A coughing fit overtook him. Síomón fumbled in his jacket pocket for his handkerchief. His fingers met a square packet.

"No," he whispered. "That's not possible."

Síomón pulled out the packet and ripped off one corner. He poured the contents into his hand. After a moment's hesitation, he tipped back his head and poured the cocaine into his mouth.

A bittersweet taste filled his mouth. His stomach heaved in protest. Choking, he managed to force the powder down his throat.

His tongue went numb. Next came the tremors, which shook him so hard that his fist knocked against his teeth, and he tasted blood. His chest felt tight, as though a vise gripped him. Hard to breathe, hard to—

I had trouble finding you.

Midnight in the orchard. A bright half-moon illuminated the trees with clouds of light. Síomón held Gwen tight against his chest to quiet her trembling. Her hair smelled of new apple blossoms. Underneath, however, lay the distinct scent of fear.

What is wrong, Gwen? What happened?

I can't sleep, thinking about numbers. Remember what Pythagoras said, about numbers and the soul. What the mystics said about the paths our lives take.

One memory blurred into the next. Memories of comforting Gwen after her nightmares. Memories of rigorous arguments, where each delivered their reasoning in dispassionate tones. Memories of a life shared so completely that Síomón often wondered if their separate bodies were just an illusion.

Look, Síomón.

Images of the moonlit orchard overlaid those of the stable. Even as he watched, the silver-dappled leaves faded into stone, and the moonlight dulled to a rain-soaked dawn.

The murderer crouched opposite Síomón. His long hair hung in wet tangles over his face. Síomón scrambled to his feet and snatched up the knife. The man did not acknowledge him at all as he poured out a quantity of white powder onto his palm.

Breathless, Síomón watched him swallow the cocaine. The stranger wore his face, with all the differences age would make.

Silver threaded the fair golden hair. Lines radiated from his eyes and mouth. The flesh along his jaw drooped slightly. A handsome man just entering middle age.

Síomón laid a hand over his own shirt and felt the cocaine packet in his breast pocket. No longer surprised, he too took out the packet, poured out the entire contents, and swallowed them. When the stranger rose and walked out the door, so did he.

Outside, the slums had vanished into a haze. Síomón and his twin walked along a strange path lined with dense green foliage. Above, stars burned like digits of a never-ending number.

They came to an intersection, where a dozen paths curved toward the horizon. *Impossible,* Síomón thought. The Earth curved, certainly, but the unaided eye could not discern it. He glanced toward one of the branches.

They were nineteen. The hazy sunlight, falling through the leaves, cast green shadows upon Gwen's face, which had the luminescence of youth.

"The past is not immutable," she said.

"How?" Síomón demanded. "You've not proved your theories."

"I don't have to. We prove it by living. Our parents proved it by dying."

They stood by the sunken gardens, underneath a stand of ornamental trees. The late summer sun glittered upon the pool, and a brilliant haze filled the air, making the trees and foliage beyond appear indistinct. Síomón blinked to clear his vision. Paused. Gwen had gone silent, and he sensed a difference in the air. When he glanced back to his sister, he saw creases beside her eyes and strands of silver in her hair.

Thirty-seven.

David Levi bent over a workbench, delicately twining copper wires onto a perforated board. Maeve stood by a tall desk, writing out columns of numbers. . . .

Forty-one.

The same room, but a different day. He and Gwen stood over a worktable, which was hidden beneath an enormous sheet of paper. Lines covered the paper in a complex grid of red and black and blue. Green circles marked certain intersections; their distribution made a pattern that Síomón could not quite grasp.

Gwen was speaking in low urgent tones. "I thought Paul could manage. He and I discussed it. I judged the risk acceptable."

"You're letting emotion distort your judgment."

"Not this time," Gwen insisted. "Look. Forget the ordinary intersections. We've already identified the ones that matter. Here—" Her finger hovered above one of the green circles. "And here. And here."

Seven. Thirteen. Seventeen. Nineteen. Twenty-nine . . .

"I know that," Síomón said. "But we have not identified all the permutations of twenty-three. Until we do, the path remains incomplete, and we cannot risk making even one journey."

"141955329," Gwen said crisply. "Times two. Exponent 25267. Add one. Ó Dónaill confirmed the latest pair of primes yesterday. He said that true pioneers cannot always wait for absolute knowledge before testing their theories. You used to believe that yourself."

"In a different time line," Síomón said. "A safer one."

"This one *is* safe." She jabbed her finger at the intersection marked *twenty-three*. "David ran the new primes using the same formulae. The results looked promising. Take the route through this intersection, and we have a clear path to the day in question. Alter one conversation—just one—and that balloonist might have known about the high winds. He might have—" She stopped, drew a deep breath. "He would have chosen a different route and avoided the accident. Our parents would have lived."

"What about the permutations?" Síomón asked softly.

Gwen set her mouth into a thin line. "Close enough."

"Obviously not."

Tears brightened her eyes. "Obviously not. Síomón, we were so close, and when Paul volunteered . . ."

It was Paul Keller who first had the idea of using prime numbers in their work. Li Cheng and Úna Toíbín had researched the formulae they needed, and David Levi had designed and built calculators to speed their computations. Nicolás Ó Cionnaith had alighted upon the inspiration of linking the human brain with the machine. From there, Evan, Maeve, and Ó Dónaill had begun to map out a viable path through the past. But it was Gwen who deduced they could use a combination of numbers and drugs and electricity, just as the old mathematician-conjurors had claimed.

"We can start with cocaine," she told the others. "And test its effects on varying levels of current."

The results had proved terrifying. And effective.

We used our madness and our genius, Susanna used to say, *and from that we would benefit mankind.*

Síomón took his sister into his arms. "Hush, Gwen. We'll get Paul back and try again—after we check the numbers more thoroughly."

She made an involuntary noise. Warned, Síomón took a step backward and studied his sister's expression. "What? What else happened? Tell me."

Gwen opened and closed her mouth. "Time fractures," she said with obvious difficulty.

Síomón drew a sharp breath. He'd read about the theories and discounted them. And yet, the concept of time fractures was no more fantastical than his and Gwen's own theory that said time lines followed the curvature of space, bending gradually over vast distances and meeting themselves again at different points.

"I'll have to go back myself," he said.

Gwen's mouth tensed. She was speaking again, but Síomón

could not make out the words. Something about patterns over-laying other patterns and creating chaos in the time streams.

"Too late." Gwen's voice was a disembodied whisper. "We were too late to save them."

"How do you know?" Síomón asked.

Of their collaboration, only he, Gwen, Ó Dónaill, and Evan De Mora remained. Nicolás Ó Cionnaith had followed Paul Keller through the time lines, never to return. *Lost*, Síomón told himself. Reluctantly, he'd allowed Úna Toíbín and Li Cheng to launch an expedition to recover their colleagues, but, instead, they were the next to vanish—their existence blotted out when two time lines reconverged. At that, Síomón ordered the equipment locked up, and the experiment shut down. To his dismay, Maeve defied those orders, convinced she had the key to their problems. When Susanna, mad with grief, chased after her friend to prevent another death, she too died. Time had fractured, and the paths no longer ran true.

"We cannot do *nothing*," he said to Gwen. "I must go—"

"But Síomón—"

"I'll take the same path as Paul," he said, speaking over her. "I'll find him and do whatever is needed to remove the fracture."

Gwen pressed her hands against her cheeks. She made no objections, however, and when Síomón indicated for her to assist him in preparing their apparatus, she did so, albeit silently.

One moment of inspiration, Síomón thought, as he tapped the keys rapidly. Decades of necessary research and experimentation had followed, but it was that initial insight that counted most. Strange to think that that same moment intersected so many other time lines. It had taken the best minds in Éire's universities to invent the necessary formulae for traversing those lines, and more complicated formulae with ever higher primes to calculate all the factors involved in shifting those lines to alter the past.

Gwen injected the cocaine and counted until the drug penetrated his bloodstream. Síomón waited until she gave the signal
before he pressed the last digit and set the last control. His gaze
met Gwen's. She managed a smile, however unconvincing. Then
Síomón pressed the switch to connect the electrical current.

Darkness. The scent of raw earth and pine needles crushed
underfoot. He walked by instinct, having made a brief essay with
the machine before, when they had first tested its capabilities.
Even so, he found the lack of physical indicators unsettling. The
vivid scents, the cold prickling his face, the pinpoint stars, were
all trace memories, Professor Ó Dónaill claimed. Perhaps that
accounted for the sensation of being doubled, as though another
presence existed within his mind.

It did. It will. It does.

He paused and looked back the way he had come. A short distance behind him, the path split in two, each branch leading to a
different future. With a chill, Síomón could make out threadlike
strands beside each branch, signaling further confusion in time.

I'm not too late, he told himself. If he intercepted Paul before the
crisis, time would heal itself, or so Gwen had insisted. Even now,
the worst would be a blurring of the past. Events doubled. Contradictory memories. Nothing fatal.

His pulse beat an irregular rhythm. Down each strand of time,
another of his selves existed. He was doubled and tripled, each
self bound to the other through a tenuous connection. When he
glanced back, he could swear the strands grew more numerous.
Was time unraveling toward the future and Gwen?

He hurried on. With every step, the air turned thicker, pressing against his lungs. Voices whispered in the paths beside his.
No, it was a single voice, speaking different words, depending on
which direction Síomón tilted his head.

Time fractures.

He could reenter time at the next intersection. Ó Dónaill's calculations predicted a narrow crack, corresponding to the prime number pair. Twin primes, he called them.

But Ó Dónaill had stolen his theories. Borrowed them for his own research, he called it. Or had he simply refined the formulae and shared them with Síomón and Gwen? Síomón found it harder to remember which version was true. The voices distracted him, and the pressure had grown almost unbearable, drilling into his temples.

Panicked, he stumbled forward. He heard a roaring ahead, a cataract of time, spilling through the cracks into the world. If only he could reach it before he died from the agony. That was how Úna had died. And Paul. And . . .

He fell through the tunnel's diaphanous walls into a muddy clearing. A cold wind swept through his clothes. His hands stung from the fall. Strange noises and images assailed him. Raucous cries echoing overhead. Misshapen shadows blotting out the sun. Then, in the midst of strangeness, a human voice.

"Síomón? Is that you, Síomón?"

Síomón twitched and spun around. He saw her as a stranger might, a fair young woman, so lean that her bones seemed visible through her skin, her hair a tumble of gold, her eyes like the bluest of summer skies. She took another few steps toward him and spoke again, but all Síomón could think was that her skin must be warm to the touch. He wanted, needed that warmth, more than he could express. With an inarticulate cry, he rushed toward the young woman and tore at her clothes. She fought back, tearing at his face with her nails, but he was stronger than she was. . . .

Gwen. Oh dear God and Mhuire and Gaia. What have I done?

When he came to, he was stumbling along a muddy path. Stars winked overhead between the budding trees, and a heavy watery scent filled the air. He was cold. Hungry. Terrified and bruised. Someone had attacked him. Síomón had fought off the man and snatched away his knife. What came next was unclear. He only remembered that he came across a different man, walking alone by the river. Memory flickered. He recognized Paul Keller. Must stop Paul. Must.

He blinked and saw a knife flashing through the darkness. He blinked again, and a woman's shriek reverberated in his skull.

No!

He opened his eyes, the word still echoing in his ears. For a moment, he could not focus on his surroundings. Gradually he took in scattered details.

Crows taking flight overhead. The craggy trunks of the oak trees. The gamekeeper's hut. The scent of wood smoke and approaching snow. Leaves crackled in the distance. Someone was coming.

"Síomón? Is that you, Síomón?"

Gwen.

Lines radiated from the point where he stood, shimmering in the cold clear winter light. He saw himself walking toward Gwen, in three, four, a dozen directions. One future to invent a new machine so that he and others might travel through time. One to . . .

"One to heal," he whispered. He glanced up, and across the wavering lines of the future, he saw a solitary red balloon, gliding through the gray skies. Síomón's fingers closed over the knife hilt. He set the blade against his throat.

"One," he whispered. "Exponent one. Minus . . ." His hand shook. "Minus one."

A quick strong movement.

A spray of blood.

0

Síomón. Where are you, Síomón?

Here. Oh, Gwen, I nearly lost you. I nearly lost myself.

Hush. It's all right. I'm glad you came back from the university. I have some new equations to show you.

But Gwen, we have to be careful—

Yes, my love, I know that now. Come with me.

She took him by the hand and led him along the woodland path.

ARS MEMORIAE

APRIL 1904

Years ago, during his mathematical studies—studies broken off, or discarded, he no longer knew which—Aidrean Ó Deághaidh had proposed certain theories involving time and its equations. The modern scholars were wrong, he declared, when they talked about measuring time in discrete units. The ancient philosophers had touched closer to the truth when they described time as a continuous ether, its flow rising and falling like a river's current.

Ah, but I was wrong, too, he thought. Time was like sunlight pouring in all directions, susceptible to prisms and mirrors, or even a child's hand.

An automobile horn bleated in the streets below, penetrating the leaded windows of Doctor Loisg's private study. Off in one corner, a grandfather clock ticked away the seconds, its muffled rhythm a counterpoint to Loisg, who spoke in hushed tones about trauma and its effect upon memory. It was an old topic— one they had often discussed over the past year.

"Commander Ó Deághaidh? Are you well?"

Loisg was studying Ó Deághaidh closely, a look of mild concern on his fair round face.

"My apologies," Ó Deághaidh said with a smile. "My attention wandered. You were asking?"

"About your dreams, Commander. Specifically, the nightmares."

You asked about them last week, Ó Deághaidh thought. *And the week before.*

He was being unreasonable, he knew. Loisg was an expert in disorders of the mind. More important, Loisg had treated Ó Deághaidh since the beginning of his illness, when nightmares had consumed his life, and they had needed restraints and strong sedatives to conduct these sessions. Loisg did not repeat these questions from mere curiosity.

And so Ó Deághaidh dutifully answered him. Yes, the nightmares had stopped entirely. No more violent, bloody images broke his sleep, and he was no longer plagued by a sense of vertigo, as though reality had shifted beneath his feet. Throughout, the clock ticked on, dividing time into miniscule bits that dropped away into the past.

The clock's machinery whirred; chimes sounded the hour. Loisg finished off a last note and smiled. "Once more, we are at the end of our session, Commander Ó Deághaidh. Until next week?"

Ó Deághaidh stood and smoothed out his frock coat. "Until next week, certainly."

There must have been something amiss in his tone, because Loisg glanced up sharply. "And yet you do not sound so certain yourself. Is something wrong, Commander?"

Careful, Ó Deághaidh thought. *He is a clever man.* "Nothing, Doctor Loisg. Why?"

The doctor's pale eyes narrowed. He appeared about to ask him more, but then shook his head. "We can talk about it later," he said, half to himself. Ó Deághaidh did not disabuse him of the idea.

Outside, it was a brisk, cold day, and gusts of wind carried along the scents of wet earth and melting snow. A tall hedge screened the house and its gardens from the boulevard. A walkway led off to one side to a private lane, also sheltered from view. It was all very discreet, but then Doctor Loisg treated many wealthy patients in Awveline City.

Ó Deághaidh glanced at his pocket watch—ten o'clock. Over an hour remained until his train departed. He decided to walk to the station. As he emerged from the lane onto Tulach Mhór Street, his eye caught on Aonach Sanitarium, a high, handsome building, which stood on a rise overlooking the boulevard. Ó Deághaidh shuddered, remembering its stark corridors, the terror no amount of drugs or electricity could banish.

That was one set of memories. He also remembered the sanitarium from a different perspective, as a representative of the Queen's Constabulary seeking clues to a murder.

Both were true. Both were subject to time's distortions.

Why did I lie to Loisg? he wondered.

A profitless question. One might as well ask why he remembered a past that did not exist.

He crossed the boulevard, threading his way between the automobiles and horse-drawn carriages, to a pathway that led through a pleasant green park and down to the Blackwater River. It was against Loisg's warnings about indulging in false memories—it was against his own instincts—to walk beside that river.

I've changed, he thought, as he turned into the park.

———

Once more, he stood in the examining room. Once more, all the details were wrong. He clearly remembered the telegraph had come shortly after sunrise. He could not have arrived in Awveline City before midmorning, and yet before him lay a room washed in moonlight, all colors faded to black and gray.

A stark, silent room, bereft of scent and movement and life.

In the center of this emptiness stood a single, raised pallet, draped in a coarse white sheet. Ó Deághaidh drew the cloth back and felt an involuntary shock, like a fist thrust into his gut, even though he had known what to expect. The assailant had strangled his victim first, then slashed her face with a knife. The indentation of the man's fingers around her throat stood out livid against the young woman's gray skin.

"Her name was Maeve Ní Cadhla," the medical examiner said. "Lord Ó Cadhla's youngest daughter."

The concierge knocked on the compartment door. "Ten minutes to Osraighe Station, sir."

Ó Deághaidh drank down the last of his tea and glanced over the papers in his lap—reports from the Queen's Constabulary, which had arrived by royal courier the day before. They were incomplete, which piqued his curiosity. Or rather, they were carefully edited summaries of what had to be longer, more detailed accounts from agents in the field. Still, they proved a good introduction to the current situation throughout Europe, western Asia, and the Mediterranean colonies.

> *. . . Frankonia's king facing opposition within his council from those who favor a partnership with the Prussian Alliance . . .*

*. . . sources from the Turkish States confirm the official
heir's recent death was the latest in a series of assassinations conducted between Koptic and Muslim factions . . .*

*. . . Serbia appears to be maneuvering to take control
over the Balkan States. Austria still maintains its
sovereignty over Hungary, Slovakia, and portions of
Croatia, but we have reports of Serbian militia units
engaging with Austrian troops in the eastern provinces,
while Montenegro's Prince Danilo II continues to press for
kingship . . .*

Delicate times, Ó Deághaidh thought. Especially for a prominent nation like Éire, which had to negotiate a careful path between these many conflicts. He stowed the reports in the case at
his feet, then touched a hand to his coat to reassure himself, once
more, that the envelope was there. The queen's personal courier
had delivered the packet and letter to Ó Deághaidh late the night
before.

Do not fail me, Aidrean, she had added at the end.

But I have failed you before, he thought. *Or had he?*

Doubts continued to pursue him for the next hour, as he made
his way out of Osraighe's busy train station and summoned a cab
to the palace. It seemed, if he could trust his recollections, that
more guards patrolled the grounds outside Cill Cannig, and the
sentries examined his papers more closely. A pair of runners escorted him from the gates to a suite of rooms within the Royal
Enclosure. He noted that they glanced him over as soldiers might,
and that they carried weapons, some obvious and some hidden.

Servants had already fetched his trunks from the station and
laid out his clothes. There was a valet assigned to him, but
Ó Deághaidh dismissed the man. He wanted a few moments
alone before he faced his queen and her ministers.

He washed his face, changed into a new gray suit, and brushed his hair smooth. The mirror showed him a thin brown face, made sharper and thinner still from the events of the past eighteen months. Well, he could not help that.

The same runners waited outside to escort Ó Deághaidh to the audience chamber. It was one of the smaller rooms in this wing of the Enclosure, long and narrow, with windows set high in the walls. Below, a series of portraits alternated with centuries-old tapestries depicting Éire's rise from Roman colony to independent kingdom to empire. Ó Deághaidh recognized the queen's coronation portrait among those of her ancestors.

One person had arrived already and sat at the far end of the table—a middle-aged man in a dark blue suit, with iron-gray hair swept back in waves. Lord Ó Cadhla.

Ó Deághaidh paused.

Lord Ó Cadhla's eyes were like dark bruises against his paper-white skin. He had wept in private, of course. Like all the men of his generation, he would display his grief to no one outside his family. Perhaps not even to them.

They tell me a lunatic murdered my daughter, Commander Ó Deághaidh. Find him.

I promise, my lord.

Ó Deághaidh blew out a breath. There was no help for it. He would have to face these false memories as they came. "My Lord Ó Cadhla."

Ó Cadhla glanced up. For a moment, his face went still. Surprise? Dismay? The change in expression was so brief Ó Deághaidh could almost believe he'd imagined it, because the next moment, Ó Cadhla was on his feet. "Commander Ó Deághaidh. I had not heard you would be present at this meeting. I am . . . I am so *very* glad to see you."

And he was glad. Ó Deághaidh could hear it in his voice. At the same time, there was that moment of unmistakable surprise.

You did not tell anyone about me, did you, Your Majesty?

Another clue, which did nothing to lessen Ó Deághaidh's uneasiness.

Ó Cadhla was gesturing toward the chair next to him. "Come. Sit. The others should arrive momentarily—ah, and so they do. Mac Gioll, your watch runs in order these days."

Lord Mac Gioll, a bent old man, limped into the room. He nodded at Ó Deághaidh in passing and lowered himself into a chair. "That jest was a weak jest twenty years ago, Ó Cadhla. And time does not improve its quality. Nor my humor." He scowled. "I hope our beloved queen doesn't have a mind to keep us here all afternoon."

Mac Gioll's entrance must have signaled the servants, because six liveried men appeared with silver tea carafes, crystal water pitchers, glasses etched with falling leaves, and delicate porcelain cups painted in the Oriental fashion. Lord Mac Gioll continued to grumble until he held a teacup in his trembling hands. "Much better. Can't think when I'm soaked to the bones with cold."

"It's age," Ó Cadhla offered. "Comes to us all."

"Damn the age. I don't like it. Neither do you."

Ó Cadhla tilted his hand, as though to agree. "How does Lady Mhic Gioll?"

Ó Deághaidh took a seat several chairs down from the two men, grateful to be ignored as they chatted about family, their respective estates, the likelihood of good hunting come autumn. Two episodes within the day. Two moments revisiting a past that had never existed. Willing his hands to remain steady, he poured himself a cup of tea and drank, while Ó Cadhla went on to speak complacently about his daughter Maeve, who had just received a second degree with honors in mathematics.

"To what purpose?" Mac Gioll asked. "Damned fine accomplishment, to be sure, but what does she mean to do?"

Ó Cadhla for once appeared uncertain. "She hasn't said

definitely. She's spending the summer with the family, naturally. After that, she mentioned taking a position in some new institute, run by that Síomón Madóc fellow and his sister. There's talk about a new physics. New everything. I could not follow the subject, though it pains me to admit it."

More names from the past. Ó Deághaidh closed his eyes against the vertigo. Maeve Ní Cadhla had lived—lived and prospered. Why should that be such a terrible thought?

An influx of voices recalled him. Servants and pages swept into the room, followed immediately by three more lords, their secretaries and aides. Then the chaos subsided as the Queen of Éire entered and everyone rose to their feet.

Áine Lasairíona Devereaux.

Ó Deághaidh drew a sharp breath and felt his pulse beat fast and strong. She was unchanged from when he last saw her. And yet the years had transformed her entirely.

He remembered a young woman dressed in silks and jewels, her finery a symbol of her office, she had once told him. The woman today wore no gems except a narrow gold circlet for her crown. Her gown swept in straight lines to the floor; her blood-red hair was pulled back smooth and tight over her skull. She was not beautiful, not in the conventional sense—she had inherited her father's strong jaw and arched nose—but Ó Deághaidh thought her so. He saw traces of anxiety in her face, and the way her mouth tensed as she spoke to her secretary, before she turned to face her ministers.

"My lords. Commander Ó Deághaidh."

Lord Ó Cadhla bowed. "Your Majesty. We are at your service."

"Then let us begin."

She waited until the secretary had cleared the room and they were all settled. "You will have read the initial reports concerning the situation in Europe," the queen said. "I have invited Commander Ó Deághaidh to join us because I believe the affair is more complicated than we first suspected. One where Commander Ó Deághaidh's long and varied experience will prove useful to Éire."

Ó Deághaidh observed the reactions around the table. Polite. Wary. Interested. Understandable if they knew his recent past, and as members of Éire's Court and Council, they would. In turn he studied the men who now served as ministers to the queen. Mac Gioll, Ó Cadhla, and Ó Breislin had been appointed by the old king. Ó Deághaidh remembered them well. They were solid, experienced men. Lord Alastar De Paor and Lord Greagoir Ó Luain were relative newcomers; he knew them only by name and reputation. There were other ministers, other advisers, but these five men occupied the innermost council.

"So you believe the crisis is greater than we first thought, Your Majesty?" Mac Gioll said.

The queen nodded. "The Balkan situation grows more troublesome. To be sure, the Balkans are nothing but troublesome, but I've lately received reports of certain events that appear to concern us directly."

"How so?" said Lord De Paor. "And you say Commander Ó Deághaidh has experience in this region?"

"Indirectly," Ó Deághaidh said. "I spent two years at the University of Vienna. My field was mathematics, but I also dabbled in languages and politics—or rather, political science. One does, abroad. Afterward, I traveled throughout the region, before I returned to Éire."

"A most complete education," De Paor said. "I had not realized it."

There was the hint of a smile beneath the man's polite expression. Ó Deághaidh turned to the queen, whose face was more difficult to read. "Your Majesty. You honor me by inviting me to your council, but if I might be blunt, I do not see the reason for it."

"Nor do I," Lord Ó Cadhla said. "Unless you have new information which you have not shared with us."

The queen's gaze skipped from one minister to another, the silence broken only by the *scratch, scratch, scratch* of the secretary's pen. Did she trust no one? Ó Deághaidh wondered, as he studied her face. There were shadows beneath her eyes, clear signs of a sleepless night.

"I do," she said at last. "Three very disturbing reports arrived here last Friday. It appears the Austrians have arranged a meeting between their own prince and Montenegro's, as well as certain of his advisers."

"What of it?" De Paor said. "A local matter."

She smiled thinly. "Not so very long ago, I might have agreed with you. No, Austria alone poses no threat. They've lost too much territory and prestige in the past decade. Besides, Prussia keeps them busy in the north. It is Montenegro and its neighbors to the east that concern me, as you will see from this newest report."

At her signal, the queen's secretary handed around folders to all the men. Ó Deághaidh flipped open the blank cover to see a half dozen pages of closely written lines. It was another summary, not a firsthand account. His attention caught on the words *Montenegro* and *recent elections,* but it was the final paragraph that made him straighten up.

"Anglians?" he said.

The others had reached that same point. Ó Cadhla pursed his lips and leafed through the previous pages. His expression was more thoughtful than troubled, but Ó Breislin's eyes widened in an unguarded moment of surprise, and Ó Luain appeared openly dismayed. De Paor gave no other sign except to gaze steadily at the queen, as though waiting for further clues.

"Yes, Anglians," the queen said. "Montenegro's elections last summer brought Austrian sympathizers into the majority. Certain local political groups mistrust the Austrians' goodwill. Sensing an opportunity, our own Anglian nationalists have joined with the more outspoken of these organizations. If I can rely on these reports, they have entered a pact to further each other's revolution."

Ó Deághaidh released his breath slowly. Civil war in Éire. That *would* be a crisis.

"But you are not certain," Mac Gioll said.

"I am not. And we cannot make any intelligent decisions until we know more. That is why I summoned Commander Ó Deághaidh, to investigate the matter."

"You want a spy," Ó Deághaidh said.

The queen's gray eyes measured him coolly. She was no longer a young woman, ardent and impulsive in matters political and personal. Or perhaps her nature remained unchanged, but buried deep beneath this guise of the dispassionate ruler. The transformation might prove to Éire's advantage, but he wondered what it had cost her.

"Call it what you will," she said. "Spy. Scout. Trusted emissary. What I want, Commander, is a pair of eyes and ears, thinking eyes and ears, to observe the situation at hand."

"To watch, but not to act."

She hesitated. "Let us say I empower you to act as your discretion dictates."

"No restrictions?" That was Lord De Paor.

"We shall work out the details before the commander departs. Do you have any concerns about this assignment, Commander Ó Deághaidh?"

Now it was his turn to hesitate. It was a chance to reinstate himself—in Court, in the Constabulary, in the queen's trust. A flutter of doubt intruded. He suppressed it. "More questions than concerns, Your Majesty."

Her gaze dipped briefly. "A fair point. My lords, do you have reservations?"

Ó Luain and Mac Gioll exchanged glances. De Paor's expression had turned distinctly bland, in marked contrast to Ó Breislin, who scowled absentmindedly at the table. Ó Cadhla continued to study his copy of the report through slitted eyes, as though searching for more clues. He said nothing, however.

The queen nodded. "Very well, my lords. Then let us make our desires clear. We desire Commander Ó Deághaidh to meet privately with each of you. You will brief him thoroughly on your departments and answer all his questions." To Ó Deághaidh she said, "We shall have copies of all our reports sent to your quarters for your review. Let us know if you require more, but do it quickly. You will start for the Continent this Thursday."

She rose. The ministers filed past her, already murmuring amongst themselves. Ó Deághaidh waited until they had all departed. The queen had turned to confer with her secretary. The man caught Ó Deághaidh's glance and touched her arm, indicating his presence. She looked over her shoulder to Ó Deághaidh, and with the barest hesitation, nodded.

Once they were alone, she resumed her seat and folded her hands together.

"Speak, Aidrean. I know you want to."

How well had she read him over the years? Better than he had her, obviously.

"Why send for me?" he said. "Are you doing this from charity?"

Áine met his gaze directly but her color was high. "Not at all. The matter is too important, Aidrean. I thought you would recognize that."

Her tone was just as he remembered from their early days together. Irritated. Demanding. And there was that use of his given name, which implied a level of intimacy. . . .

She remembers. Or does she?

It did not matter, he realized. It had not mattered then, whichever *then* one chose.

"But why me?" he repeated. "You surely have others with equal experience."

"Because I need a man I can trust."

Not a friend, a trusted minion. He felt the old, familiar weight of disappointment. He thrust that disappointment aside. "You have my service, Your Majesty. But you should know that."

"I should, but—" She broke off with an unhappy smile. "My father once said a king did not issue absolute commands, he could only provoke loyalty and inspire obedience. I sometimes think I have proved a bad student in these matters. I did not wish to presume."

But she had.

"And if I had refused?" he asked.

Again that quick coloring, which faded to white. "But you did not."

Because I could not. And that you surely knew.

Did she remember those false days, when he and she had spoken freely with one another? Did she ever know that he had loved her, both as Queen of Éire, and a woman of unsurpassed strength and intelligence? Or did she know, and did she use that information to bind his allegiance to her?

He turned away, not wanting to know.

The chamber went still and silent for a long, long moment. Then Ó Deághaidh felt a touch upon his sleeve. So light, it was as though she tried to excuse herself for trespassing.

"I must," Áine said softly. "Not for you or for me. But for Éire."

Then he felt the air stir as the queen left and the door closed silently behind her.

The queen's own secretary waited outside Ó Deághaidh's rooms with the promised reports. More secrecy, more discretion, but by now Ó Deághaidh was no longer troubled, merely relieved the

queen took so many precautions. He thanked the secretary, then
sent off a runner with an order for an early supper to be delivered
to his rooms.

Alone, with the doors bolted, he opened the packet and
skimmed through the lot. Here were the detailed field reports behind the summaries he'd already seen. Reports from agents in
Austria, Prussia, Serbia, the Turkish States—all the relevant play-
ers he would have expected. One last page gave Ó Deághaidh's
schedule for the next two days.

He paused and felt a ping of surprise. *That is not what I expected.*

Of course he was to meet with Ó Cadhla, Mac Gioll, and
Ó Breislin. These were the men responsible for matters touching
the military or foreign affairs. (Though he wondered at Ó Cadhla's being placed later and not earlier in the schedule.) Even De
Paor's name did not entirely surprise him—De Paor oversaw matters of internal intelligence, which would encompass the Anglian
connection. But Ó Luain? Economics and finance? Clearly, the
situation involved more than a minor crisis in a distant country.

A note in the queen's hand added: *I want no questions in your
mind when you start for the Continent. If you find anything lacking—
anything, Aidrean—please apply directly to me.*

He set down the paper. Laid his fingertips lightly upon the
pages spread over the table, as though to read more from their
texture. Considered the circumstances, the small details of the
courier, these luxurious private rooms, the queen's private words
about trust, her public ones about his experience.

She wants someone who knows the Court, but who is outside it.

Someone skilled in delicate investigations.

Taking up the topmost report, he started to read in earnest.

He read past midnight, taking notes as he went. By sunrise, he
finished what little sleep came to him, and rose to prepare for his

day. Lord Greagoir Ó Luain's name came first on the agenda. At eight o'clock, Ó Deághaidh presented himself to Ó Luain's secretary, who escorted him into the minister's impeccable private office. It was a large pleasant room, lined by tall bookshelves and many cabinets. Ó Luain himself appeared hard at work. At Ó Deághaidh's appearance, he set aside his pen and dismissed the several clerks who had been taking notes at his dictation.

"Commander Ó Deághaidh. Welcome. Would you care for coffee? Tea? No? Well, then, let us settle to the business at hand. Though to be quite honest, I'm uncertain how I might assist you."

Ó Deághaidh smiled. "I believe the queen simply wishes to reacquaint me with her concerns, whether they touch directly upon this matter or not."

Ó Luain pursed his lips, as though uncertain. "If you believe I have information you require, of course, I shall do my best. . . ."

Over the next two hours, Ó Deághaidh's initial impression remained unchanged. The man appeared exactly as his reputation suggested—a conscientious servant of the Crown, and he answered all Ó Deághaidh's questions with unfailing politeness. Yes, a civil war would prove unhealthy for the treasury. Éire had stretched itself thin over the past few years by sending aid to its many allies. And yes, any internal crisis of that proportion would certainly endanger the international exchange rates. No, he had not received any reports of unusual activity with banks or investment firms to indicate funds moving from the Anglian Dependencies to points east.

"None that are regular," he added. "For the irregular kind, you must inquire of Lord De Paor."

"Indeed I will, my lord."

Their gazes met and held a moment, and Ó Deághaidh had the distinct sensation he was being studied as thoroughly as he had studied Ó Luain. Was he wrong about the man? Was his manner a disguise for something more sinister?

He was still pondering Lord Ó Luain's character as he walked to his next interview, which was with Lord Mac Gioll. Mac Gioll had served as an officer during the Anglian Uprising thirty years before, and now advised the queen on military matters. He expounded upon the topic with more vigor than Ó Deághaidh expected for such an old man. "The sticking point," Lord Mac Gioll said in his wheezing voice, "is when to signal the first shot."

"Surely the first question begins with if, not when," Ó Deághaidh said mildly.

Mac Gioll laughed softly. "You've not served in war, young man. However, I see your point. So then, let us return to the matter at hand. If the Anglians do succeed and bring their Balkan allies to these shores, here are the items that will govern our possible responses . . ."

He plunged into a detailed account of Éire's four military branches, one for each of four knobby fingers, while Ó Deághaidh attempted to keep notes of the main points. The navy came first. It had blossomed in the last century, and proved well enough to defend against minor incursions, but clearly could not hope to equal the Dietsch Empire's astonishing fleets.

"Hence our withdrawal from the Hindu and Judaic Protectorates, and the Far East," Mac Gioll said. He bent one finger down, grasped the next. The aerial corps was a minor organization, used chiefly for reconnaissance, with two divisions. The aeroplane was an experimental device, its efficacy as yet unproved. The motored balloon showed a more immediate advantage. The army used it for tracking troop movements, but there was talk among the engineers about improving the balloon's maneuverability. Some thought they might carry small cannons or firebombs.

"Soon?" Ó Deághaidh asked.

"Not before the next decade," Mac Gioll replied. "So you see it is our army and our militia who guarantee our security." Two more fingers bent over, as he went on to those branches. The army defended the kingdom and the neighboring Dependencies of Anglia, Manx, Wight, and Cymru; the militia concerned itself with internal matters. "Against disruptions. Uprisings."

"Rebellions," Ó Deághaidh said quietly.

Mac Gioll shot him a calculating glance. "Indeed. We've been fortunate these past few centuries, apart from the Revolt. My concern is that another uprising, combined with any significant crisis in Europe, would prove too much for us. It has been eight hundred years since Alba and Denmark came to our aid, to drive the Anglians from our shores. If we show ourselves weak, they might decide to abandon us. Indeed, Alba might elect to support its southern neighbor outright—they being citizens of one island, as the radicals like to remind us. We cannot afford that, not with the continent so uneasy."

"Is it so uneasy then, my lord?"

For the first time during their interview, the older man hesitated. "You understand, I speak now of my own impressions, nothing more. There are, let us say, more incidents. More bickering and maneuvering between neighboring kingdoms. My fear is that any crisis, even a seemingly insignificant one, might incite violence, which, in the present atmosphere, would spread as rapidly as fire through dry kindling."

Meaning war, of the kind Éire and the Continent had not witnessed for a hundred years or more.

They were all so circumspect, Ó Deághaidh thought, as he returned to his quarters for dinner. He had missed the clues in the first meeting, but clearly the queen's ministers were uneasy amongst themselves. Of course they feared the possibility of an all-consuming war, but they also knew the queen had not shared all her thoughts about this current matter. If only he could remain at Cill Cannig another week to study the state of affairs at Court. It made no sense to send him off so ill prepared—not if the true problem lay inside Éire.

He sighed and shuffled through the papers, looking for that newest report about Montenegrin elections. There had been several notations added in the margins, something about the prince and his advisers.

What is this?

He lifted a crumpled sheet from the stack of otherwise neat pages. Underneath it, he found two more. All three were nearly illegible—stained by rusty brown splotches and creased through and through. Even more puzzling, each paragraph looked as though a different person had written it. In one, the script lurched across the page, while the next consisted of neat cramped lines.

But it was the contents that intrigued him the most. This was not the usual field agent's report. One page contained a list of names and occupations. The names were Montenegrin or Serbian, he noted. Another, labeled *Meetings,* gave dates and locations. The third page contained only a few paragraphs, but Ó Deághaidh recognized what had to be drop points and exchange signals. Here the name Kiro Delchev was repeated several times, along with references to a larger group of Éireann sympathizers, which Delchev represented.

Again he felt an inward tilt, as if a godlike hand had unbalanced the world. But, no. This was no case of time misremembered. He knew he had not overlooked these papers the night before. He also knew he had locked his rooms before meeting with Ó Luain, and that he had found the packets exactly as he left them.

Someone wishes me to know about Montenegro and Kiro Delchev. And they do not wish to tell me openly.

So, it was with some curiosity he went to his next interview.

Lord Ó Breislin's office was crowded with books, exotic carvings, and framed samples of illuminated text. A scent of incense hung in the air, mingled with tobacco, reminders of his time abroad. He had spent his early years as a diplomat in the East, with posts ranging from the Turkish States, to the various king-doms in the Indian subcontinent, to the Chinese Empire. After running the embassy in Constantinople for six years, and estab-lishing a network of agents, he had returned to Court to serve as an adviser for those affairs. He greeted Ó Deághaidh with a firm handshake and an offer of coffee or whiskey.

"Coffee, if you please," Ó Deághaidh said. "I would like to keep my wits about me."

"Wise choice. Roibeárd, give us two cups and then you may go."

An aide poured two cups of thick black Turkish coffee and withdrew. Ó Breislin added a lump of sugar to his cup and stirred. "You would think I'd had enough of this goop, as Mac Gioll calls it, when I lived abroad, but it seems that familiarity has bred a great love and no contempt."

"You spent fifteen years in Constantinople, I understand, my lord."

Ó Breislin glanced at Ó Deághaidh from hooded eyes. "Near enough. Ten years rattling about Turkey. Six more in the em-bassy. If you know that much, you should know the rest."

Ó Deághaidh tilted his hand outward in recognition of the shot. "It comes from my background, my lord. It makes me inde-cently curious. Did you ever have cause to investigate the Bal-kans during that time?"

The other man raised his eyebrows. "As events required, yes."

"Did you ever come across a man named Kiro Delchev?"

"No." A pause. A sip from the cup. "Wait, I have. There was a Doctor Delchev in Montenegro. A professor at the old university in Cetinje sometimes called in to advise Prince Danilo on inter-national matters. I don't know anything more than the name, however. I'm sorry. You'll have to ask Ó Cadhla about the man."

Ó Deághaidh finished his coffee, but slowly, as he considered this reply. Either Ó Breislin truly did not know, or had prepared himself for direct questions. He turned the conversation to the

most recent succession wars in the Turkish States. There Ó Breislin showed no lack of opinions, and the next few hours passed
in animated discussion about the recent assassinations, and what
might ensue, once a particular faction took firm control of the
throne.

When Ó Deághaidh returned to his rooms that evening, after
a late supper with Ó Breislin and Ó Luain, he locked the door
and built up a fire before collapsing onto the sofa.

He could make nothing of the clues so far. Ó Luain was competent, if dull. (Though Ó Deághaidh had not forgotten that flash
of keenness at the last.) Ó Breislin and Mac Gioll appeared exactly
as one would expect—shrewd, practical men. Capable of advising
the queen well, equally capable of manufacturing a complex
scheme that could throw Éire into confusion. But to what end?

He sighed and poured himself a whiskey. He was reaching
conclusions ahead of his data. He had another day, and two more
interviews. No, three. He would surely see Áine one last time
before he departed.

"Of course, Commander. I will relay your wishes to the queen."

"Please do. I understand I am being irregular—"

"Not at all. The queen was quite explicit. We were to satisfy
you on all counts."

No doubt the queen's secretary had a large staff to carry
messages. Nevertheless, he had answered Ó Deághaidh's summons himself, despite the early hour, and assured Commander
Ó Deághaidh he would personally relay his messages to the queen
and her ministers at once.

"Oh, and please make certain these letters are delivered to
Lords Ó Luain, Mac Gioll, and Ó Breislin," Ó Deághaidh added,
handing over three sealed envelopes. Inside were messages, ask-

ing for clarifications on several points discussed during their interviews.

Again the secretary bowed. "You may be certain of it, Commander."

Within an hour, Ó Deághaidh had replies from all five members of the inner Council. He set aside those from Ó Luain, Ó Breislin, and Mac Gioll to examine later. The answers themselves were unimportant. However, he was curious how De Paor and Ó Cadhla might answer such a seemingly impetuous request to change the hour and order of their interviews.

As you wish, Ó Cadhla wrote. Short and matter-of-fact.

De Paor's reply was longer, but also expressed his willingness to accommodate Commander Ó Deághaidh.

Shortly after that came the queen's response. *Let us meet Thursday morning at nine.*

In his message, De Paor had also named the location for their meeting—one of the larger, more lavishly appointed audience rooms. Was it a desire to keep his domain private? Or did the man simply like a showier stage for this audience? It would be too easy, Ó Deághaidh reminded himself, to misjudge the man on such petty grounds.

"Good day, Commander," De Paor said. "I see you prefer early hours."

"I do, my lord. Thank you for being so understanding."

Tea and coffee were provided by servants, who discreetly withdrew. Ó Deághaidh stirred honey into his tea and studied his new subject with keen interest. A youngish man, with hazel eyes, and a fair complexion overspread with freckles. He wore his thinning hair swept back in the latest fashion. According to Ó Deághaidh's sources, the queen had appointed Lord De Paor to his position just a year ago, when old Lord Ultach died of drink, or opium, as rumors would have it.

"I've been thinking how best to assist you," De Paor said. "I have nothing to do with Montenegro, of course, but there is the matter of those Anglians."

Ó Deághaidh nodded, continued to drink his tea.

De Paor rested a hand on a stack of bound files. "Those Anglians," he repeated, somewhat at random. "It is a curious affair. If you think they would prove useful, I've collected our files on various organizations, suspected radicals and the like."

The files contained numerous reports and analyses for all four Districts of the Dependencies, not just Anglia itself. Another folder offered a summary of the political groups with connections to the more radical Anglian dissidents, including a particular Franco-Prussian group known for violence against Judaic communities, which had tentacles throughout Europe.

"Indeed, these might prove very helpful," Ó Deághaidh said as he leafed through the pages. "May I take these back to my rooms to study further?"

"Of course, Commander. If we are not safe in Cill Cannig, then we are safe nowhere. Do you feel you are making progress, then? I'm curious to learn if you've reached any conclusions about the queen's affair."

"If I have, my lord, I have set them aside for later."

"Spoken like a scientist," De Paor said. "Or a member of the Constabulary."

"Hopefully some of both," Ó Deághaidh said. "The queen has presented me with a tangled mystery."

He went on to ask his own questions about the Dependencies in general and the political associations in particular. Lord De Paor proved to be as knowledgeable and helpful as Ó Deághaidh wished. No, he'd no reports about the illegal or excessive transfer of funds to points east. Yes, there were always dissatisfied parties, but he thought the ordinary citizen of the Dependencies disliked upsets and rebellions.

Ó Deághaidh politely declined an invitation to dine with Lord De Paor, instead taking a meal of soup and bread in his rooms. Two hours remained until his interview with Lord Ó Cadhla. He glanced over his notes, but soon gave it up and took off on a tour of the older public halls, hoping to settle his thoughts and recover his concentration.

It was a good decision. He had forgotten how lovely it was here, the exquisite mosaics laid down by the early kings, the portraits in the halls, the grace and balance of the arched passageways. He ended up in a small interior courtyard and stood before a fountain, whose waters leapt and tumbled within a marble basin. Sunlight glanced from the droplets, reflecting a rainbow of colors over the surrounding tiles.

Of course he knew the reason for his distraction—Maeve Ní Cadhla. He had already known about her taking a second degree with honors. Against his better judgment, he had followed the careers of her and everyone else connected with the nonexistent murders that haunted his memory. He knew about Paul Keller's advances in electrical theory. He knew Evan De Mora had taken a position at Awveline University, only to leave after six months to join his friends Gwen Madóc and her brother at their institute. There was talk that their theories would transform how scientists viewed physics and the passage of time.

Aidrean Ó Deághaidh bent and touched the endless fall of water. The rhythm broke; the rainbow scattered. But when he removed his hand, the waterfall resumed as though nothing had happened. Very much like time itself, he thought. He could not say the same of his own life, interrupted so abruptly by madness. He wondered what Doctor Loisg would say to this train of thought.

He dried his hand on a handkerchief, then set off for his appointment with Lord Ó Cadhla.

Less than two days had passed since they had last spoken. In that time, the other man appeared to have aged remarkably. The lines and folds in his face had multiplied, and though Ó Cadhla's gaze was as keen as ever, there was a weary, restless air about him, as though he had spent the past few days searching for answers, and did not like what he had found.

"You are troubled, my lord," Ó Deághaidh said.

"So are you, Commander. I find that strangely reassuring. Have you given much thought to how to approach this assignment?"

"Only that it requires discretion, my lord."

Ó Cadhla gave a dry laugh. "You always did understate the matter. I have several suggestions in that direction, if you would care to hear them. Yes? Very well, let us take as given that your movements will be observed, even before you leave Cill Cannig and Osraighe. So. We cannot help that. However, we can provide you with a different, more innocuous reason for your visit to the Continent. I spoke with the queen, and she agrees you might act as a private courier to Frankonia's new king."

Ó Deághaidh listened attentively to Lord Ó Cadhla's proposal. He would spend a few days in Frankonia's Court, ostensibly on business for the queen. If he had the opportunity to visit on friendly terms with other members of Frankonia's Court, he should take it. The length and manner of his stay would be at his discretion. But on his return to the airfields outside Paris, he would slip into anonymity, taking care to mislead and misdirect those who watched.

"And they will watch," Ó Cadhla went on. "If only because you are well known, and on the queen's business. Just as we watch those who enter Éire."

His office would supply the necessary papers, he said, along with names of trusted agents in each country. Ó Deághaidh made no objections—Ó Cadhla's suggestions were sound ones—

and they spent the full afternoon and half the evening reviewing the first few weeks of Ó Deághaidh's proposed journey.

Not once did either mention the name Kiro Delchev.

That night, Ó Deághaidh set out the letters from the five ministers. Next to them he placed the three sheets that had appeared so mysteriously. Even if he considered a deliberate attempt to disguise their handwriting, he could find no similarities between the two sets. Ó Luain's handwriting was straight and even, much like the compact sample, but without its cramped quality. Mac Gioll's hand most closely resembled the sprawling segment, but he could never have managed the rest, especially those paragraphs with stiff straight lines marching across the page. De Paor's stood out with its strong verticals and the way he crossed his *T*s with a broad stroke cutting across the other letters. His hand was almost too distinctive, Ó Deághaidh thought as he compared pages. To be sure, the same problem existed for Ó Breislin and Ó Cadhla, who both used old-fashioned loops and underlines.

Someone had expected him to compare handwriting. Someone very clever.

The palace bells were ringing nine o'clock when the queen's senior runner escorted Aidrean Ó Deághaidh into the small sunlit parlor within the Royal Residence. The queen was presently closeted with Lord Ó Cadhla, the young man informed Ó Deághaidh, but she would arrive momentarily.

A sideboard held carafes with water, and silver urns of coffee and tea. Ignoring these refreshments, Ó Deághaidh made a circuit of the room, wondering why Áine had chosen this particular location for their final interview. There was none of the usual portraits and ancient statuary found throughout the audience rooms. Instead, the walls were lined with numerous shelves, displaying mechanical curiosities. Clocks built of precious gems that rang the hour in chords. Strange devices set with lamps and mirrors and prisms that transformed plain sunlight into rainbow-colored patterns. One glass exhibit held nothing but an extraordinary complication of copper wires. A brass plate indicated a switch off to one side. When Ó Deághaidh touched it, a small red balloon—crafted from jewels and fine metals—popped from a niche in the wall to swoop along the wires, as though in flight across the skies.

. . . *the world tipped beneath him. He glimpsed a fair-haired man, loose limbed and graceful. Breandan Reid Ó Cuilinn, renowned scientist and the queen's favorite, who had plunged to his death from a balloon. If Ó Deághaidh had been at Court, he would have led the inquiry into the accident, but the queen had already ordered him away to a very different kind of investigation . . .*

Ó Deághaidh closed his eyes, willing the false memories to subside. So many things that never were. They pressed upon his consciousness, like fingers around his throat. Was it his imagination, or had their presence grown more insistent, here in Cill Cannig? *You are a strong-minded man,* Doctor Loisg had said, during one session. *But mere strength cannot cure you.*

The vertigo faded, but he felt its lingering presence, and though the world froze once more beneath his feet, he could still sense the flaws and cracks below its surface.

"Commander Ó Deághaidh."

Startled, he turned to see the queen just entering the parlor, trailed by a stream of servants bearing trays of bread and pastries. The sunlight made her dark red hair burn like copper against her milk-white skin.

"Your Majesty," he said, more breathless than he liked.

She smiled at him, a warm smile that nevertheless woke all

his instincts. Here was his last opportunity to abandon this assignment. Did he want to? He could not tell.

Áine dismissed her servants and proceeded to pour tea for
them both, as though they were two intimate friends.

"So tell me," she said. "What have you learned these past two
days?"

Ó Deághaidh accepted his cup and took a seat nearest the
window. He allowed himself a moment of stirring honey into his
tea to collect a proper answer. An honest one. He owed her that
much.

"You have given me a rather difficult task," he said. "I find it
has certain complications that might prevent an easy resolution."

The queen smiled, pensively. "So I have deduced myself. I
don't ask for the impossible, Commander. Find the truth. Let me
decide from there." Her smile turned a shade more genuine.
"Not that I can guarantee you will like my decisions, but that is
my burden, not yours. For now, let us talk about your mission."

It was easier than he expected. They spoke in matter-of-fact
tones about the Balkans in general, and Montenegro in particular.
The queen agreed with Lord Ó Cadhla that Ó Deághaidh should
assume a new identity as soon as possible after leaving Frankonia,
if not before. "You have the names of several agents throughout
the region," she said. "But approach them only if necessary."

"Do you object to Lord Ó Cadhla's suggestion that I contact
his man in Vienna?"

She hesitated. "Lord Ó Cadhla has far greater experience in
these matters than I. So do you. I would only ask that you use
your best judgment." Then she met his gaze with bright gray
eyes. "But I meant what I said before. If you find yourself with
questions, or with answers you cannot trust to anyone else, apply
directly to me. And no, do not write down this information.
Memorize it, Aidrean. Can you do that?"

So many meanings behind that simple question.

He drew a deep breath. "Yes. I can."

She nodded. "Very good. Letters are best, but in emergencies do not hesitate to use the telegraph. Here are the name and address, and how you must word your message . . ."

High above Paris, the gigantic passenger balloon described a wide circle as it began its descent toward the landing fields. The air was frigid at this height, with beads of ice along the rigging, never mind the late spring season below. Pinpricks of white and golden light reflected from metal fastenings, and the massive ropes cast a web of shadows across the cabin, where Aidrean Ó Deághaidh looked down upon the city.

Lutetia, Parisii, La Ville-Lumière. A city more ancient than Awveline or Osraighe. He could tell its map by its colors—the dusky red and brown brickwork of the oldest districts. The newer structures built from gray marble. Here and there, spires of amber and gold, or bright green gardens, like tiny emeralds. And winding through the center, the silvery ribbon of the Seine.

The balloon's great engine whirred; the rigging hummed louder as the balloon swung around for the approach, and its pilots adjusted the rudders and vanes.

And here might God, our inhuman Divine, tread light upon this world of ours and mine.

Henry Donne's words echoed through Ó Deághaidh's thoughts as the balloon glided downward through the clear bright air, leaving behind the immense silence to reenter the noise-filled realm of man.

A motor carriage (fetched swiftly and unobtrusively) carried Ó Deághaidh to the embassy near the royal palace. He spent the evening alone in his finely appointed rooms and rose early to dress in his most formal black suit, arrayed with decorations from his service in the Royal Constabulary. Lord Ó Cadhla's script ensured that he passed smoothly through the many offices, from the king's gendarmerie, to the foreign minister, and finally to a small audience chamber, deep within the Palais Royal, set with guards at all the doors.

"Vôtre Majesté."

The Frankish king accepted the silk-wrapped packet Ó Deághaidh offered. "We are grateful to your queen," he said in unaccented Éireann.

He was an old man, his skin slack, his eyes sunk deep into his skull, and his complexion had an unhealthy pallor. The electors had chosen this man by a bare majority, and only after months of debate. Was that another mark of the discord within the Frankish parliament? A sign of that unrest that so troubled Mac Gioll and Ó Cadhla? Ó Deághaidh let none of these questions show as he knelt and kissed the cool hands, and spoke the familiar formula.

More ritual of diplomacy consumed the morning. He spent the afternoon with colleagues from Éire's embassy, drinking wine and parrying questions about doings at Court and the queen herself. There were more questions designed to tease out news about Ó Deághaidh as well. They were curious about his long absence, though rumor had supplied certain details, and more curious about his sudden reinstatement. Ó Deághaidh smiled and answered as vaguely as he dared.

In keeping with his role, he attended a supper with Frankish representatives. After that, freed from obligation, he set off on a late-night stroll alone by the moon-silvered Seine, past weathered brick and stone churches of Frankish and Éireann design. It was a pleasant evening. A few dark blue clouds scudded across the star-speckled skies. Hours later, he arrived, as he had known he would, in a district where a man might purchase the company of a woman, clean and smelling sweetly of perfumed soap, her hair running like a dark red river over her milk-white skin.

*. . . once I lived alone within my skin. I was Aidrean
Conall Ó Deághaidh, mathematics student turned spy
and a member of the Queen's Constabulary. Doctor Loisg
argues that our souls and our selves are seldom known to
their possessors, but I would state I knew myself—my
self—as well as I knew my body. Now I am not as certain.
My name, according to my latest passport, is Dietmar
Bergmann, a citizen of Berlin in the Prussian Alliance.
Before that, I called myself Jean-René Baptiste of
Frankonia, and before that, William Sharpe of the
Anglian Dependencies. With each change of papers, I
sensed a pang within, as though the once-continuous
essence of my self had cracked. But if I wish to be
honest—and here in these confessions, at least, I can
indulge in that—this sense of division, of a multiplicity of
lives, began two years ago, even before the queen ordered me
to investigate Maeve Ní Cadhla's murder. Oh, the signs were
few and doubtful—merely bits of memories misremembered,
or conversations doubled. Even then, I told myself it was
nothing more than overwork. But then came true dissolution.
That moment I remember perfectly. It was close upon
dawn. The sky wept with rain. I was walking toward a
stable on the east side of the city, where I knew Síomón
Madóc hid. Just as I laid a hand upon the latch . . .*

Aidrean Ó Deághaidh crumpled the sheet in his fist and glanced
out the train window. The conductor had already announced their
approach to Praterstern Station, and the few passengers in the carriage had gathered their luggage and were proceeding toward the
exit doors. The brakes squealed as the train slowed on its approach
to the bridge crossing the Danube. Now the forested countryside
vanished as the train plunged between the outer ring of Vienna's
ancient walls.

He waited until the final approach, then struck a match and burned the latest of his diary entries. He had begun these exercises under Doctor Loisg's supervision—a means for sorting through the false and true memories. The art of recollection, Loisg called it. Now, these writings had to remain an ephemeral record, one he destroyed within moments of its creation, but the act gave him such necessary relief that he had continued the practice.

No more. It didn't matter that he wrote in code, that few could make sense of his musings, even if they deciphered every word. Anything so personal would only provide hooks and claws to the enemy. Whoever that enemy might be.

Ó Deághaidh swept the ashes into his hand and deposited them in the nearest bin as he passed underneath the grand arches of the exit. In the square outside, he bought a grilled bockwurst and took a seat on a low wall surrounding a statue. Very little had changed since he last visited the city, at least on the surface. There were the usual crowds of blond, blue-eyed schoolboys. The carriages with Russian and Italian nobles. A company of Swiss mercenaries marching in formation. If anything, he counted more Turks and Moroccans, refugees from various civil wars. And pervading everything, a sense of threadbare opulence, of an empire that still dreamed of long-ago glory.

He finished off his wurst and wiped his face on his sleeve. The sun was sinking behind the tallest buildings. He would have to find a pension for the night, and soon. He recalled one from his previous travels, years ago. It was an ancient pile of brick and stone, surely as old as Vienna itself, but its beds were comfortable, and the breakfast generous.

Ó Deághaidh shifted his satchel to a more comfortable position and set off. A troupe of jugglers and magicians had staked out a largish space nearby, and the square had filled within the past ten minutes. He had to thread his way between the tourists and their children, who squealed in delight as two jugglers tossed glass balls into the air, sending showers of brilliantly colored sparks over the crowds.

The attack happened suddenly.

Just as Ó Deághaidh passed by the jugglers, one man snatched up two balls from the pile at his feet and hurled them at Ó Deághaidh. The balls hit the ground at his feet. The glass shattered into a firestorm. Ó Deághaidh leapt backward, but not quickly enough. A third ball struck him in the chest. He staggered and fell, choking from the acrid smoke. More flames, more smoke. A man flung his coat over Ó Deághaidh and pounded at the sparks. All around he heard an outcry, people calling for the police, others shouting to catch the villain before he escaped.

He was still trying to draw a breath when strong hands pulled him to his feet and bundled him away from the square. He tried to shake them off, explain he was not hurt, but his throat burned, and he could not stop coughing.

"Kämpfen Sie nicht so," they told him. "Wir bringen Sie gleich zur Apotheke."

His unwanted rescuers propelled him through a pair of doors, into a brightly lit shop. Down he went onto a cot. A pale doughy face, surrounded by an untidy fringe of hair, came into view. The stranger, a young man, muttered in a thick Austrian dialect as he speedily and professionally examined Ó Deághaidh. "Do not worry," he said. "Those men ran, but we've summoned the police. I will tend to your burns."

He gathered several vials of medicines, and a bowl of soapy water. But before he could attend to Ó Deághaidh, a voice, sharp and imperious, sounded from the next room. The apothecary glanced over his shoulder and scowled, but when the voice called out a second time, he hurried toward the front room. His appearance provoked a lengthy exchange. Ó Deághaidh recognized the young man's patient drawl, interrupted by a woman's shriller, more insistent voice as she described a constant ache of the teeth, and could he not prescribe a stronger medicine.

He checked his pockets. Nothing was missing. He still had his money. More important, he still had all the necessary papers to explain his presence in Vienna—passport, letters from a cousin in Wien, properly marked tickets. If they cared to look, the police would find nothing suspicious, and yet, Ó Deághaidh found a growing dislike for keeping to the identity Lord Ó Cadhla had provided him.

He eased to standing and made a cautious circuit of the room. A second door opened onto a short passageway with doors to either side, and one at the far end. There was a whiff of woodsmoke, and the stronger smell of stewing chicken and onions. Ó Deághaidh heard the sounds of splashing water, a child's laugh, a woman's reply.

He trod swiftly and softly to the door at the far end. Outside, wooden steps led down to a narrow alleyway lined with trash bins. Just then, the woman called out, "Na, Wilhelm. Kommst du endlich?" Then he was through the door and gliding down the alleyway to the open square beyond.

Five days later, Aidrean Ó Deághaidh entered the small Byzantine church of Sankt Barbara and dropped a few shilling coins into the offering box. He slid into the front row and bowed his head, taking a surreptitious glance of his surroundings as he did so. Most of the church remained in shadows, but sunlight poured through the stained-glass windows above, bathing the nave and communion rails in a rainbow of color. Two elderly women knelt before the youngish priest. The rest of the church remained empty, as he had expected.

Someone had penetrated Ó Deághaidh's disguise. Not the

woman in Paris—he'd told her nothing. Not the few obvious Frankonian agents who had tracked him from Paris into Catalonia. He knew he had eluded them. It had to be someone in the queen's confidence. Lord Ó Cadhla, who had so carefully scripted this expedition. Or Lord Ó Breislin, whose experience lay in these regions.

A flicker of light caught his attention. He glanced back to see a tall man in a voluminous coat sidle into the second-to-last row of benches. That would be his contact—a man named Rainer Groer, forty-eight years old, ostensibly a dealer in rare books and curiosities, an occupation that often took him on jaunts through the remnants of the Austrian Empire. Groer was a relatively minor agent, but knowledgeable about the local politics.

Ó Deághaidh waited until he was certain Groer found the note, then sauntered down the aisle and through the church's front doors. Outside, he hurried down the street and rounded the corner into the Barbaragasse, where he waited.

After the attack outside the train station, Ó Deághaidh had spent five days in a cheap pension, one he had never before visited, reviewing possible steps to take. No, recovering his nerve. Those men had not intended to kill him. Unbalance him, perhaps. Rattle him and make his judgment unreliable. He wanted to say they had failed, but the reoccurrence of his nightmares belied that.

So let us say I am stubborn.

Over the next few days, he had made his plans. He decided he would meet with Groer, extract whatever information he could, and sow his own carefully chosen clues for those who would surely question Groer afterward. Following Lord Ó Cadhla's instructions, he had posted a coded message to the standard address. The message stated that Groer would find further details in the church of Sankt Barbara off the Postgasse, in the usual location. The building lay tucked behind a larger Dominican cathedral and several small temples of various faiths—a place ideally suited to such business.

Groer hurried down the church steps. Ó Deághaidh waited another moment, then followed. Taking a parallel street to the next intersection, he intercepted Groer as he rounded the corner, pushed the other man against the wall, and shoved a gun to his ribs.

"Mensch, was ist—"

"Silence," Ó Deághaidh said in German. "I'm the man who wrote to you, Herr Groer. But I've received some chancy news, and I would like your reassurance that we can speak in true privacy. Nod if you agree."

The man jerked his head down and up.

"Very good," Ó Deághaidh said. "You understand I am nervous. I might be forced to act hastily if I find myself compromised. For example, if you had a friend watching you—"

"None, but—"

"Hush. Speak only when I tell you. So, there is no friend. Anything else I should hear?" When Groer hesitated, he added, "If you have anything to tell me, other than no, you may speak."

Groer shook his head. He was sweating, and his dirty blond hair was matted over his brow.

"Good. We shall walk together as good friends do." Ó Deághaidh entwined his left arm around Groer's and drew him close. He thrust his right hand with the gun through his pocket and toward Groer's stomach. "Do not cry out; do not attempt to escape me," he said softly. "Remember, I've had a desperate few days. I will gladly shoot you and never mind what comes next."

They crossed a boulevard and entered a patchwork of lanes. Ó Deághaidh steered Groer through several turnings into a small courtyard, empty except for a pair of dogs quarreling over some bones. Opposite stood the wineshop Lord Ó Cadhla had named as a safe rendezvous. Ó Deághaidh knew he took a risk using it, but there were certain advantages in appearing careless.

A man in a grubby apron came from behind the counter, as they entered. "Naja, was wollt ihr?"

"Ein Zimmer. Und ein Krug Rotwein," Ó Deághaidh said gruffly.

The man's eyes narrowed at the mention of a room, but he only shrugged. "Also, gut. Zehn Schilling, bitte."

Ó Deághaidh nudged Groer. "Come, my friend. You promised to pay this time."

With a show of reluctance, Groer handed over a ten-schilling note. The man peered at it and grunted. "Upstairs. Second door on the right. I'll send a girl with your wine."

The room upstairs turned out to be little more than a closet with a couple of stools and a stained mattress flung in one corner. There was no table, but a plank bolted to the wall served the same purpose. Ó Deághaidh and Groer were hardly inside before a black-eyed girl appeared with a jug of red wine and two glasses of doubtful cleanliness. "You want company?" she said, without much enthusiasm.

"Not yet," Ó Deághaidh said.

She scowled. "What's the matter? You only like boys? Or just each other?"

Ó Deághaidh met her gaze steadily until she flushed. "No. We don't like each other. Come back in half an hour, and we'll talk about whether we like you."

The door closed with a bang. Ó Deághaidh shoved Groer toward the stools. "Sit," he said in Éireann. "You and I must talk."

Groer dropped onto his seat. "You are taking too many chances," he whispered in German.

Ó Deághaidh hooked the second stool closer and sat, keeping his gun trained on his companion. He filled both glasses and pushed one toward Groer. "What chances? Speaking in Éireann? Or coming here with you, when this is a known meeting place for agents?"

"Do not—" Groer swallowed. "Do not talk about those matters out loud. That man downstairs—he knows nothing about why I come here from time to time. When I do, I stay below and talk with friends, associates, while we drink."

"Never upstairs?" Ó Cadhla had assured him it was not unusual.

"I used to," Groer said. "But I suspect that girl listens."

Ó Deághaidh nodded. "Very well. We talk quietly and drink our wine. That should not make anyone suspicious."

Groer shrugged but he clearly was unhappy. He gulped down some wine and grimaced at its taste. "What is wrong?" he said in Éireann. "You asked for a meeting in the usual way. And I had word from the right people to expect you." He paused and his lips twitched. "It *was* you, wasn't it? The one attacked outside the train station? I read about the affair in the newspapers."

Ó Deághaidh made a throwaway gesture. "If you know that, then you know why I'm taking extra precautions."

"*Verdammt* be these precautions. You must report to the embassy at once. You cannot proceed if you are compromised."

Ó Deághaidh laughed softly. "I do not intend to. But before I return to Éire, I want some information. For example, I would like to know more about the Anglians who are operating in this region. Specifically in Montenegro and the rest of the Balkans."

Groer's pale blue eyes narrowed. "I know nothing of any Anglians."

Ó Deághaidh suppressed an exclamation—*You knew this,* he thought. *You suspected it long before*—but his voice remained cool. "Ah, then I was mistaken."

His tone did not fool Groer. "What Anglians?" he demanded.

"It is not important, I tell you. Merely a supposition gone astray.

The chief thing, the reason I am here, is the matter of Austria and Montenegro. Do you have any word about the negotiations between them?"

But Groer was not to be distracted. "There are no Anglians. Nor any matter between the Austrians and Montenegro, unless you count that business with the Serbs—

"What business with the Serbs?"

"The Serbs. Surely you know . . . Well, it's just a rumor, and a new one at that." He tossed back the rest of his glass of wine and stared longingly at the jug.

Ó Deághaidh refilled the man's glass. "Go on."

Groer took a swallow and wiped his mouth on his sleeve. "They should have told you, but maybe there wasn't time. You see, I heard the rumor just a few weeks ago—that this whole business between the Austrians and Montenegro is a farce. The Serbs are behind it all. Or rather, they are hand-in-hand with the Austrians, who are hand-in-hand with their supporters in Montenegro. Prince Danilo believes he is getting support for his ascension to kingship. His parliament believes they get an ally against Greater Serbia. In reality—"

The clues shifted into place, and Ó Deághaidh had to check himself from leaning forward eagerly. "In reality," he said, "Serbia takes Montenegro, while Austria gains a bulwark against the Turks. I see." And he did. It was such a simple reversal of expectations. But it was the implication of this missing news that troubled him the most. "You sent this information to your superiors?"

"Of course. What do you think?"

Of course. He ought to have foreseen that, as well. Ó Deághaidh tossed back the bitter, sour wine and slammed the empty glass onto the board. "What do I think? To be honest, I think you are a stupid, foolish man. Nearly as stupid and foolish as I am."

He stood and flung the door open. The serving girl stepped

back quickly, red-faced and stammering. "It was more than half an hour," she said fiercely. "You said—"

"It was not close to half an hour," Ó Deághaidh said. "But I am glad to find you here."

He drew her close, caught a whiff of soap and yeast and sweat. The young woman's mouth softened into a seductive smile. Her face was dirty, but her breasts were plump, and she had an animal attraction Ó Deághaidh could not deny. Was she another snare set for him?

I have not become so desperate, he thought. *Not yet.*

"So, you like me?" she said.

"Alas, no," he said. "But I know my friend does."

He shoved her into the room. She stumbled against Groer, who instinctively caught her in his arms. Ó Deághaidh slammed the door closed on them and ran down the stairs.

. . . With every passing mile, I find myself shedding the accumulated years, until once more, I am come back to those months following my studies in Vienna. It was then I set off on my grand journey through Europe. I traveled by train, by wagon, on foot. Like any enthusiast, I wanted to take in everything—every tone or gesture that differentiated the native Austrian, the immigrant Serb, the well-traveled Russian or Czech. It was that ability to drop myself into a country and a language that the Constabulary first took advantage of. Later, it was the queen who remembered my mathematical studies and sent me to Awveline City. Now I have circled around to the end of that circle, which is itself a new beginning . . .

He had long ago abandoned his temporary journal, but he found he could not break off these silent entries as he tramped along the backcountry trails. Vienna and that miserable room above the wineshop seemed a thousand leagues away; Osraighe and Cill Cannig had taken on a dreamlike quality. The hills and mountains lay behind him now and he traveled along a dirt road that descended into the heart of Montenegro, a high rocky plateau with the broad Cetinje River winding down to the sea. It was late morning. The air had already turned warm and shimmered with dust. In the distance, a rare balloon glided past, the sun glinting off its wires.

A jingling broke his reverie. He turned to see a farmer in his wagon just topping the previous rise. Ó Deághaidh stepped aside to let them pass, but just as the wagon drew alongside, a black and gray brindled hound loped up through the fields and barked. The farmer reined his horses to a stop and peered at him through rheumy eyes. "I nearly thought you were a ghost," he said in a thick dialect of Štokavian. "Standing so still in the tall grass. Where are you bound, my friend?"

"To Budva," Ó Deághaidh answered in the same language. "To buy passage on a ship. But tonight I hoped to sleep in Cetinje."

"Eh. A traveler? But not from these hills or this valley. Are you Prussian?"

His tone was suspicious. Ó Deághaidh knew how he looked—unwashed and unshaved, his coat and trousers stained from weeks spent sleeping on the ground. He smiled and shook his head. "No, my friend. I was born in Austria, but my father came from the hills, from Tuzi. It was the Austrians who took him for their army."

"Ah-ah." The old man spat to one side. "God and Allah be thanked the Austrians cannot do that anymore. Though truthfully, I'd rather have them than the goddamned Prussians, who are like ants in the kitchen. Come, get you into my wagon. I can take you to Cetinje."

Ó Deághaidh threw his knapsack up first, then climbed onto the seat beside the farmer. With a flick of his reins, the old man set the wagon creaking into motion. "So," he said. "Your father hails from Tuzi."

"Near enough," Ó Deághaidh replied. "For eighteen years he knew but firs and sheep, and then . . ." He snapped his fingers.

The other man nodded. "So many tales like that I've heard."

Their conversation went on, haltingly at first. Whenever Ó Deághaidh found himself groping for the right words in Štokavian, he would try Russian or German. The old farmer spoke a little of both—learned from his goddaughter, he said proudly, who was a teacher in Cetinje.

As they approached the city, the wagon track joined a wider road, which continued through a pair of long-disused gates and to a large square bordered by taverns and shops. Montenegro's capital was not a large city by Ó Deághaidh's standards, but there were at least thirty or forty thousand souls here, and over the centuries it had expanded to cover the surrounding folds and hills. Towers from the old university peeked above the buildings west of the river. On a ridge to the east, Ó Deághaidh glimpsed tall, elegant mansions painted in greens and golds and pinks. Those would be the embassies and houses for visiting dignitaries.

The farmer drew his wagon to a halt by the fountain. "You might want to take a meal at Lazar Burgan's cookshop," he said. "They've good sausages, and the prices are not so dear. Are you heading on tomorrow?"

"It depends on how willing my feet are." Ó Deághaidh climbed down from the wagon and hoisted his knapsack over his shoulder. "Thank you for your company and the ride, my friend." He offered a coin to the old man, who squinted at him before he accepted it.

The first goal achieved, Ó Deághaidh thought, as he scanned his surroundings. Ten days in the wilderness had left him unused to cities and their noise. He wanted a quiet shelter where he could regain his bearings. He blew out a breath, considering his next few steps.

A meal first, he decided, then lodgings.

He found Burgan's cookshop, where he ate a plate of sausages, then asked for directions to a suitable inn near the university quarter. Once he arrived at the inn—and it took a remarkably long time to traverse the city through its tangle of streets—he inquired about a single room for the week. The innkeeper took his money and showed him into a tiny bedchamber, with a single window overlooking a series of red-tiled roofs. It was like the dozen or so other rooms he had hired in this journey, and he could almost predict the innkeeper's speech about when meals were served and how often he might expect the bed linens changed.

Alone, Ó Deághaidh sat down on the hard bed and ran his fingers through his hair. Three weeks had passed since Vienna. Groer had surely telegraphed Éire to report his encounter with Ó Deághaidh, as required. He or the other local agents must have discovered the crumpled train schedule for Vienna and Croatia left behind in Ó Deághaidh's room at the boardinghouse, along with a map of the coastal roads.

He had taken a different route of course, though his destination was the same. Using new papers purchased in Vienna, Ó Deághaidh had boarded a train into the Czech Republic under the name Ivo Fischer. Once well inside Serbia, he traveled by whatever means possible into the hills, walking the last long segment to avoid the border patrols, and finally crossing into Montenegro. It was a carefully constructed trail, filled with deliberate gaps and misleading clues, so that those tracking him would not guess he meant for them to follow.

Because they must know I am here, he thought. Because there could be no better way to discover the traitor than to offer himself as the perfect target.

He slept badly that night, from the stale, close air in his room, from the unaccustomed noises within and without the inn. Breakfast proved to be palatable, and the coffee blessedly strong and hot. Ó Deághaidh wanted nothing more than to launch himself into the next stage of his plans, but he crushed that urge at once. *Caution, care and caution,* he told himself, or he would be dead before nightfall.

He took the entire day to refurbish his appearance. A few extra coins ensured him a hot bath, where he soaked then scrubbed away the grime from his travels. After that, he visited a barber for a haircut and thorough shave. A clean jersey and newer boots, bought from a street vendor, completed his transformation from tramp to migrant laborer.

He also acquired a supply of paper, ink, and quills. That night, he mentally reviewed all the details for contacting Kiro Delchev. The signs and countersigns were simple—no intricate spy craft here. Ó Deághaidh wrote what appeared to be a grocery list of ordinary items. Certain words as the third, fifth, and seventh items established his identity. A scribbled reminder at the bottom about "Aunt Mirjana's birthday" requested a meeting.

Early the following morning, Ó Deághaidh took a meandering walk around the nearby square, where the cookshops and booksellers already did a brisk business. Just as the mysterious papers had described, there was a crooked lane next to a coffee shop. He followed the lane into a small courtyard, where he stuffed his message behind the expected drainpipe, then continued to the next street. If Delchev agreed to the meeting, the man would leave a thank-you note, the wording of which would indicate one of three predesignated meeting spots.

Throughout the rest of that anxious day, and half the next, Ó Deághaidh avoided the lane and the courtyard. Instead, he scouted the rest of the city, from the old university on the western bank of the Cetinje River, to the several prominent plazas, to the centuries-old taverns beside the river. In all the wineshops and taverns, he heard the same talk he'd heard from the old farmer, about Prussians and their recent conquests, debates about independence versus an alliance with Austria—even the relative advantages to joining with Serbia in a Greater Slovakian Alliance. No one seemed happy about these choices, however.

A second visit the following day showed his letter untouched. Ó Deághaidh told himself that Delchev was a professor, not a regular agent who checked his letterboxes daily. He spent the morning poking through the displays of various booksellers near the university, then retired to a nearby wineshop, where he divided his attention between a book and the old men playing chess. After the sun had set, however, he decided to make another pass.

Most of the shops were closed by this hour, and the lamplighters had just begun their rounds, but two old women were walking their dogs, and a group of Russian tourists crowded around their guide in the square. Off in the distance, Mount Lovćen loomed dark against the dusky skies, its uppermost peak illuminated by the last rays of an invisible sun.

Ó Deághaidh made a desultory tour of the square. No one appeared to notice him, and so he continued into the lane beside the coffeehouse.

Here it was dark and quiet. He heard nothing except his own footsteps, and the tick-tick-tick of water dripping onto stone. Still his skin prickled, and he hurried toward the faint glow that marked the courtyard's entrance at the opposite end of the lane.

Just as he passed a doorway, an arm snaked out. Ó Deághaidh flung himself away and blocked a blow purely by instinct. His attacker came after him again. He was a thickset fellow with a knitted cap pulled low over his forehead. When he swung the next punch, Ó Deághaidh caught the man's wrist and twisted away, sending his attacker to his knees. Ó Deághaidh struck him between the shoulders, driving the breath from the man's body. That would keep him occupied long enough, he thought. But as he turned to run, a movement off to his left caught his eye. He spun around—too late. The second assailant struck him on the elbow with a wooden club. Ó Deághaidh dropped to his knees in a shock of pain. The next moment, someone grabbed his hair, yanked his head back, and pressed a wet cloth over his face. A cloying smell filled his nose.

Ó Deághaidh jerked his head back, but it was too late. His head swam and his legs gave way beneath him. His last memory was of five shadows standing over him.

Awareness returned with a stabbing pain at his arm, and a rising wave of nausea. Ó Deághaidh clamped his mouth shut and swallowed. His head felt thick; his tongue lay heavy and dry in his mouth. Cool air whispered over his bare skin, and he shivered. Whoever had taken him prisoner had confiscated all his clothes except his trousers.

Gradually he took in his surroundings. He lay on his side, on a cold hard surface with his hands tied behind his back. A low fire threw off a little light and heat, but otherwise the room was left awash in twilight. A basement or underground room? Then, close by, he heard the ripple of water against stone. Smelled wet earth. Underground, then. Cautiously he twisted his wrists. The ropes did not give at all.

Ó Deághaidh breathed slowly until the nausea subsided. His attackers, whoever they were—Delchev and his friends, or another rival faction—had not killed him. Yet. They wanted to question him first. It had happened too fast, too easily. They had marked him as a dangerous person from just that one message. A shudder went through him.

They want to know who betrayed their secrets. Then they will have me killed, and not Éire or my queen will know.

His movements must have attracted someone's attention,

because a blurry shadow interposed itself between him and the firelight. "You are awake, yes?"

It was a woman's voice. She spoke in German, in a low contralto, her accent blurred. With the fire behind her, Ó Deághaidh could make out little of her features—just the tilt of her head, the whiff of sandalwood, the quiet and stillness of her attitude.

"Who are you?" he said with difficulty.

Before she could answer, a second figure approached—a tall, lanky man, who held his hands loose and ready at his sides. The man stared at Ó Deághaidh. His lips drew back, and the firelight glinted from his smile, reminding Ó Deághaidh of a hungry dog.

The man spoke to the woman in a rapid monotone, too quick and low for Ó Deághaidh understand. She shook her head. The man stabbed a finger toward Ó Deághaidh and spoke sharply—a clear threat, because the woman flinched. She turned back to Ó Deághaidh.

"Listen to me," she said. "You must talk. And you must tell the truth."

"And if I do not?"

"We know about you. You wrote a coded message to Kiro Delchev, which means you must be from Éire or one of its agents. But you have chosen a curious time to ask for a private meeting."

There were strange, contradictory signals here. The man, so ready with his threats, he understood, or thought he might. The woman, however, was not so easy to read. Nervous and afraid of her companion, and her tone seeming to imply more than the words themselves. "Are you friends with Kiro Delchev?" he asked. "Where is he?"

She hesitated. The man rapped out another question. The woman answered slowly, keeping her face turned away from her companion. Ó Deághaidh had the impression she was giving him a carefully edited version of their conversation.

Another long tirade from the man. Again she made the translation, though clearly an abbreviated one. "We can answer none of your questions. It is you who must tell us why you have come to Cetinje, and why now. Please," she added in a breathless whisper. "If you do not, he will hurt you. He says it will be faster."

"What about you?" Ó Deághaidh said. "What do you think?"

She made a brief, negative gesture. "I cannot stop him."

"Cannot or will not?"

The man interrupted with a question. She turned to answer, but he shoved her to one side, pushed Ó Deághaidh onto his stomach, and wrenched his arms up until the bones cracked. Ó Deághaidh gasped and bucked against the agony.

Then it was over, leaving Ó Deághaidh sweating and panting. Above the roar in his head, he heard the buzz of voices, then footsteps retreating. A warm hand brushed his forehead. Someone placed a water canteen to his lips and held his head steady as he drank. The water tasted of cool minerals, and helped to clear away the bitter aftertaste of the chloroform.

"He has gone to fetch a friend," the woman said softly. "Another man who watches for the patrols. He says that between them they will persuade you to talk."

"And if they cannot?"

"Then you will die."

"While you watch?"

"I'm sorry for you. But I can do nothing, nothing at all."

"How convenient." He had no need to pretend bitterness. His death would be the least of his failures.

The woman shook her head. "You do not understand. Ilja would—"

Ó Deághaidh drew a deep breath that eased the pain in his gut. "No, I do not understand. But I would like to." He let a soft groan escape that was not entirely feigned. If only he knew how long before the man would return. The woman appeared unarmed. If he could distract her a moment, he might take her by surprise. "More water," he whispered. "Please."

She frowned and glanced over her shoulder. The moment her attention turned from him, Ó Deághaidh rolled onto his knees and launched himself at her headfirst. They both crashed to the ground. Ó Deághaidh rolled free and lurched to his feet. The woman scrambled away and fumbled at her boot.

"Hej! Valerija—"

Two figures rushed into the cave. It was the man who had questioned him before—Ilja, she had called him—and his companion. *Damn, damn, damn.* Ó Deághaidh wanted to snarl and curse, but he had no time. Ilja had drawn a gun. Ó Deághaidh aimed a hard kick at the man's knee and connected. The man dropped with a strangled cry, his gun clattering to the ground. Meanwhile, the second man circled around, a knife in one hand. Ó Deághaidh backed away. A glance showed him the woman pressed against the wall on the far side of the cave. She too had a knife in her hand.

His opponent took advantage of Ó Deághaidh's momentary distraction, snatched up the gun, and fired twice. Ó Deághaidh threw himself to one side. His shoulder burned. A shot must have grazed him. He spotted a flash of firelight against metal—a knife spinning on the ground. With his hands behind his back, he had to scrabble to catch hold of the hilt. There, he had it, and just in time. Regaining his feet, he saw the man was reloading the gun. Ó Deághaidh kicked at the fire, scattering hot ashes into the man's face. The man let his gun fall and clawed at his face. Ó Deághaidh drove his shoulder into the man's chest and shoved him against the cave wall. Before the man could recover his breath, he spun around and rammed the knife into his gut.

A gasp. A gurgled cry. Warmth spilled over Ó Deághaidh's hands, and the stink of blood rolled through the air. Ó Deághaidh staggered to one side, trying to catch his breath, and the man slumped to the ground. A few coals from the scattered fire cast a red, uncertain light over the floor and ceiling. Except for the labored breathing of the man Ilja, it was quiet. Where was the woman? Had she gone for help?

Then, he heard the echo of gravel falling. The woman was making her escape. He stumbled through the dark toward the sound. A few false starts and he discovered the opening to a narrow tunnel that slanted upward. From above came the thudding of footsteps over hard-packed dirt, the scent of crushed pine needles, the kiss of air upon his cheek. That way, yes. He scrambled up the tunnel. Very soon he came into the open, a hillside dotted with pine trees and fields of grass and wildflowers. Lights from a city speckled the plateau below. Cetinje.

His breath puffed out in noiseless laughter. No shirt and no shoes, no papers or money, and any shelter miles away. At least the night was warm and dry. He set off down the rocky slope, away from the cave and toward the city below.

The hard stones cut his bare feet, and he stumbled more than once, but he did not pause until he reached a stand of pine trees. There he wedged the hilt of his knife into a split trunk, then sawed through the ropes binding his wrists. The blade pierced his skin several times during that long painful exercise. Afterward, he washed his wounds in a mountain freshet, and the shock of cold water jolted him awake as nothing else could. His belly shivering, he set off down the mountainside, gathering up droplets of strength from a source he had not realized existed within himself, exhilarated, laughing aloud at finding himself alive and free. It was not until he reached Cetinje, and the alleyway where he would spend the night, that despair overtook him. If he did not solve this mystery, he would truly have nothing at all. No honor. No kingdom. No future. He wept until his throat burned, then wept again, shaken by his sudden loss of control.

The rising sun pulled him back from the despair, but it could not restore his former sense of purpose entirely. He spent two days wandering Cetinje's poorest districts, begging from those marginally better off than he. Seeing his tearstained face, they called him a madman, but they were gentle with him nevertheless. A local wisewoman dressed his wounds and blisters. A butcher's apprentice fed him with bones and scraps of fat. He clothed himself from trash heaps—a soiled jersey, a pair of boots beyond repair, which he fastened with twine. At night, he wrapped himself in a stolen blanket and slept underneath the glittering stars, uncertain whether he played a role, or lived it.

"You are a curious man," said Natka, as she offered Ó Deághaidh a mugful of hot ale. She was an old woman, her hands like rough slabs from washing pots for a riverfront tavern. It was she who had supplied Ó Deághaidh with socks to pad his ill-fitting boots, and a ragged coat for nighttime, which sometimes turned cool in spite of the approaching summer. "But then, you are probably filling in the empty places."

Ó Deághaidh drank down the ale, wiped his mouth on the back of his sleeve. He had spent the day listening for any talk about foreigners, murdered men, or Kiro Delchev's whereabouts, with no success. "Nothing into nothing," he replied, slurring his words to cover his accent. "Hard to fill that up."

Natka regarded him with a look much keener than before. "Or maybe, too much all at once, and it makes for confusion." Then she laughed, and her eyes disappeared into the folds of her fleshy face. "Oh, no. We neither of us have too much, do we, my friend?"

She gave him a couple stale bread rolls for later, and an old woolen cap she claimed no longer fit her youngest grandson. "We have some wet days coming," she said, brushing away his thanks.

Ó Deághaidh shuffled away toward the upper streets, to a

market square that lay between the riverfront and the university district. No luck, none at all. It was as though these men had not existed. As though he had dreamed that episode in the cave.

You know you did not.

I'm not certain what I know.

He had the knife. That much was certain, and he kept it as a talisman. And when his confidence failed him, he chanted the names: Ó Cadhla, Mac Gioll, Ó Breislin, De Paor, and Ó Luain. One of them the traitor. One had betrayed him, first in Vienna and now here, in Cetinje. Mac Gioll or Ó Luain? He discarded those names and picked them up again, unable to decide their character. Ó Cadhla. The minister best situated for such deeds. But surely he was too clever to place himself under suspicion. Ó Breislin? He no longer knew. De Paor? There was ambition in that man's voice, but so there was with all the queen's ministers.

At the water pump, he rinsed his mouth and absentmindedly chewed one of the rolls. He ought to save them for later, but perhaps old Sima in the rag sellers' district might have a pot of stew cooking today. Sima always had the best gossip, though it paid to double-check anything he said.

He had put the roll away, reluctantly, when he saw the woman.

She was crossing the square, chin tucked down, a plain black scarf covering her head. She had a woven basket filled with books slung over her shoulder, and more books in her arms. A breeze caught at her skirts and she paused to untangle them. When she straightened up, her glance winged past Ó Deághaidh to some unseen distant point.

His heart beat faster. It *was* her. He was sure of it. He had not forgotten how she moved, nor that all-encompassing, dark-eyed gaze. Ó Deághaidh drank another handful of water before he pulled his new cap low over his forehead and slouched off in the same direction.

Two streets away from the square, the woman turned a corner. Ó Deághaidh hurried forward, only to confront the empty lane. He kept walking in case anyone watched from above. By now he had memorized all the back lanes and courtyards. He took a deliberately roundabout path to an alley across the river, where he spent the night. The next day, he wandered a district on the opposite side, following a drifting, rambling path, and ending up by seeming happenstance at Old Sima's, where he consumed leftover stew and listened to Sima's account of his grandson's latest folly.

It was late on the third day, after hours of fruitless scouting, that he sighted the woman in a run-down neighborhood by the water. He followed her at a distance, through the back lanes and winding streets, back to the university district, not far from where he had first taken rooms. A few streets later, she ascended a pair of low steps and entered a three-story brick building. He sank down to wait. She might be visiting a colleague, a sister, anyone. He dared not make any assumptions.

Within a few moments—as long as it would take a weary and distracted woman to climb the stairs—a lamp blazed on the second floor. No sooner than he registered that when a shadow appeared against the window. A woman's figure, slim and sharp. Almost at once the shadow vanished, as though she winced away from observation. Ó Deághaidh stared at the window with satisfaction.

I know you now, he thought.

Several days of watching and planning followed. The rain Natka predicted had arrived, and the days were gloomy, alternating between downpours and a heavy drizzle, and a thick warm fog rose up from the wet streets, reminding Ó Deághaidh of Éire's summer rains. He observed the woman from afar, as she walked to and from the university district. During the midday hours, he studied the face of every tenant, every visitor to the apartment building. The doors were locked at all times, he discovered. Tenants had keys. Visitors rang an electric bell to gain admittance. There was a door at the rear of the building, but the yard had no other exit than a path leading back to the main street. In between these sessions, he acquired rope, bandages, a lockpick, and a wrist sheath for his knife.

He chose an evening when the sun sank behind a veil of clouds and mist, so that twilight came unnaturally early. It was one of the days when the woman remained at the university until late. He would have ample time to break into her apartment, make a search, and prepare for her arrival. The weather worked to his advantage another way. There were few passersby, which meant few witnesses to his activities.

Ó Deághaidh loitered in an alleyway opposite the building until he sighted another tenant approaching. He waited until the man had unlocked the door before he crossed the street, as if bound for the next house down, and whistled softly to himself. Just as the other man entered, Ó Deághaidh doubled back and ran up the stairs to catch the door before it shut completely. He waited, breathless, until he heard the rattle of keys, then a second door within open and close, before he slipped inside.

He found himself in a small entry hall, dimly lit by the streetlamps outside. It was an older building, with cream-colored plaster walls and polished wood floors. A row of postboxes by the door carried apartment numbers but no names, and the boxes themselves held nothing of interest. Ó Deághaidh continued up the stairs to the second floor. Four apartments occupied the corners. There were nameplates beside all the doors. Ó Deághaidh checked those facing the street. One read Petrović, one Delchev.

He stopped and his skin prickled. Of course. Surely it was the mysterious Kiro Delchev who had betrayed him to the kidnappers. He stood there, juggling the lockpick in his hand, unhappy with this new complication.

Footsteps on the stairway startled him out of indecision. He ducked behind the stairwell, hefted the knife in his left hand, and waited.

A woman left the stairs and headed straight to the apartment door labeled Delchev. No sooner had she turned the key and pushed the door open, than Ó Deághaidh rushed up behind her. He propelled her into the apartment, and before she could do more than gasp, he kicked the door shut and pointed the knife-point at her exposed throat.

"Listen," he whispered in German. "You will drop your bag at your feet. When I let go, you will take two steps forward, then stand perfectly still. Do not scream. Do not call out. Do not look around. Understand?"

He relaxed his grip slightly. She gave an abbreviated nod.

"Excellent. Now do it."

The woman dropped her bag and stumbled forward two steps. Ó Deághaidh locked and bolted the door, then, keeping his attention divided between her and the handbag, he made a quick search. For the most part, it contained the usual miscellany— keys, pencils, a notebook filled with addresses, most of them in the university quarter. In a separate compartment, he found a small pistol—loaded. Interesting. He clicked off the safety and aimed it at the woman. "Turn around."

She had jumped at the click, but she did as he ordered. In the dim light, her eyes were dark smudges in her pale face. The rest of her was like a shadow—black dress and black shawl, long black hair pulled back in a loose coil that had already come undone. Her gaze flicked from the gun to his face. She said nothing, but she clearly recognized him.

"Where is he?" Ó Deághaidh said. "The name on the door says Delchev. Where is Kiro Delchev? He lives here, no?"

No answer except a flicker of tension at her mouth. Then, "Not any longer."

"Did you kill him?"

She drew a quick, audible breath. That one pricked the truth.

"You did murder him," he went on. "You and your friends. The same ones who betrayed me—"

A soft knock sounded at the door behind him. Immediately, the woman darted around Ó Deághaidh. Before she could turn the bolt, Ó Deághaidh shoved her against the wall and pressed his arm against her throat. Both of them were breathing fast.

Again a knock, more insistent. "Madame? Madame Professor?"

It was an elderly woman's voice, scratchy and faint. One of the neighbors. Ó Deághaidh pushed the gun under the woman's ribs. "You will speak calmly to her," he whispered. "You will reassure her that all is well."

"Or you will murder me?"

"Or I will murder her. Do it."

He stepped back and gestured toward the door.

The woman massaged her throat. She looked as though she wanted to refuse. Ó Deághaidh gestured toward the door again, and mouthed the word *now*. Reluctantly, she undid the bolt and opened the door a few inches. "Madame Petrović. Can I help you tonight?"

She spoke in a quick, strained voice—hardly in her natural tone—but the other woman evidently did not notice. "I'm so sorry to trouble you, Madame Delchev," she said. "It was only that I heard such a thump, and it made me afraid for you, especially with you alone now. And you look so pale."

Madame Delchev gave a wan smile. "It was nothing, Madame Petrović. I stumbled over the rug, and it gave me a scare. If you will excuse me, I think I will go lie down now. I have a terrible headache."

She closed the door firmly and leaned against it, her eyes closed. Ó Deághaidh waited until he heard another door close, then seized Madame Delchev's wrist and twisted her arm behind her back. She struggled, but he was stronger. "Do not make this difficult," he said, taking the cord from his coat pocket. "Remember your neighbor."

Quickly, he tied her wrists and gagged her with the cloth, then bundled her through another door, into what turned out to be the bedroom. He dumped her onto the bed and bound her hand and foot to the bedpost with the remaining cord. Remembering her boot sheath, he made a quick impersonal search of her clothes. He found the boot sheath, but it was empty. There were no other weapons.

Madame Delchev had stopped struggling, but her breath came fast. He lit a lamp and studied his prisoner. Her eyes were bright, her cheeks patched with red. She returned his gaze steadily. Wary, afraid even, but not entirely subdued by fear.

"You understand the necessity," he said to her.

Her eyes narrowed. He hesitated, turned away, dissatisfied with himself.

A thorough search of the apartment did not take him long. There were just four other small rooms—a front parlor, which overlooked the street below where he had watched. A tiny kitchen with its cabinets filled with clay pots and dishes, tins of coffee beans, and bundles of fresh spices. A corridor led to a small bathroom with a hip bath and water basin.

The last room was a small study overflowing with bookcases. Two desks faced each other in the center of the room, and a Turkish-style rug covered most of the floor. Here and there amongst the shelves, he noted a space occupied by a handmade puppet, or the brass pocketed figurine of two lovers, or some other knickknack clearly chosen for its beauty or its whimsy. There was a faint scent of wood polish and leather and ink.

Nothing here indicated wealth—just the opposite. The desks were old and worn. The rugs finely stitched but needing repair. This might be the office for any academic Ó Deághaidh had visited over the years. He scanned the bookshelves, noting the titles in Štokavian, Frankish, German—even a few in Éireann. Most dealt with history and economics, but there were several about mathematics and natural philosophy, which intrigued him. He rifled through five or six, but found nothing that indicated any connection to Éire.

He turned his attention next to the desks and their contents. The first was mostly empty except for a few crumpled envelopes bearing Kiro Delchev's name. So madame had cleaned out her husband's papers. Interesting. He wondered how long ago the man had died, or was killed. Had the traitor known when he planted those tempting clues amongst the reports in Ó Deághaidh's rooms? Once more he had the sense of contradictory signals, as though there might be two plots at work, and not always in co-operation with each other.

The next desk proved more fruitful. Three dozen letters, all addressed to Madame Doctor Valerija Delchev, filled the top drawer. Many came from government officials, others from universities abroad, and were written in languages and about topics as wide-ranging as the books on the walls. Reading through the letters, Ó Deághaidh realized his and Ó Breislin's mistake. It was she who was the noted political scholar and adviser, not her husband.

Ó Deághaidh returned to the bedroom. Valerija Delchev lay still, eyes closed, body held in tense readiness. When he sat beside her, her eyes blinked open and she went still. Waiting. Watching.

He set the lamp on the bedside table, so that it illuminated her face. He had been mistaken about the color of her hair. It was not black, but a rich dark dusky brown, the same color as her eyes. Several strands had fallen over her face. Ó Deághaidh brushed them aside. She recoiled, and he drew his hand back, wishing he could recall the gesture.

"I will take away your gag," he said. "And we shall talk. Quietly. Do you understand?"

She studied him a moment, nodded.

He removed the gag and tossed it aside. She worked her jaw, licked her lips, and grimaced.

"When did your husband die?" Ó Deághaidh said.

A tremor ran through the woman. "Ten months ago."

"Killed?"

Another pause, as though she had to consider how to answer. Then, "An accident."

"How deliberate an accident?"

No answer.

"Were you aware of his correspondence with people in Éire?"

A shake of her head. A nod.

"Are you saying you do not know? Or that those connections do not exist?"

She gave him no answer, just regarded him with those dark eyes. He had the impression of looking into a deep quiet pool of water. For a moment, the thought unsettled his resolve, but then he remembered the traitor in Éire, and the cave above Cetinje.

"Why did your friends attack me?" he asked. "Was it for the ransom? Or is it part of some political plot here, in Montenegro?"

No reaction except the pulse at her throat beat faster.

More confident now, he went on. "Let me speculate, then. Your husband was in contact with certain highly placed individuals in Éire's government. They corresponded by coded letters, some sent by post, some by courier and delivered to the same letter drop where I left mine. When your husband died, or was killed, you notified those individuals and then continued the correspondence yourself. Or rather, you and your friends did. Am I right?"

"Why are you asking me these questions? How do I even know you are from Éire?"

"Because that individual told you I would come here. A warning."

All the tension drained from her face, and she regarded him with a puzzled expression. "No. There was no warning. No letter at all. I thought—" She broke off. "No, I cannot say anything more."

He studied her a moment. There were secrets here, obviously, but they were not the ones he expected. He took out his knife and cut her bonds. (She flinched at first, until she saw what he was about.) Then he laid her gun within her reach and waited.

She picked up the gun and regarded him curiously. "You want me to trust you."

He shrugged. "I think we could help each other."

"I do not want your help."

"Even though you badly need it?"

Her mouth quirked in a sardonic smile. "So you say."

"Very well." Ó Deághaidh tucked his knife in its sheath and stood up.

"Where are you going?" she asked.

"To find someone else who can and will answer to my questions."

He made a cautious departure from the apartment. Madame Petrović did not open her door, and none of the other tenants marked his descent down the stairs. Outside, he took up his post in the same alleyway across the street. From here, he had a good view of the windows into Valerija Delchev's front parlor. A warm drizzle had begun to fall. He pulled his cap low over his eyes and settled in for a long wait.

The windows of her apartment remained lit another half hour, judging by the church bells—long enough for the rain to die off and the newly risen half-moon to emerge from behind the clouds. Ó Deághaidh took out his knife and ran the edge lightly over his callused thumb, turning over his conversation with Valerija Delchev in his mind. Delchev dead. His widow involved with murderers. And yet, he would wager his life she was no murderer herself. He remembered that calm assessing gaze.

But the question was not Valerija Delchev, it was her companions. Revolutionaries, most likely. He remembered the man in the cave, the way he stared so avidly at Ó Deághaidh. There had been patients in Aonach Sanitarium like that.

Shadows flitted past the windows several times as Madame Delchev paced around her parlor. Then, her lights blinked off. A few moments later, the apartment building's front door opened. Ó Deághaidh tucked his knife into his belt, ready to follow.

Valerija Delchev paused on the steps, illuminated by the streetlamps. She wore a coat over her dress and had covered her head with a dark patterned scarf. No handbag, but he had to assume she carried the gun. From this distance, he could not make out her expression, but he could easily read the tension in her stance, the quick movement of her hand as she brushed away a strand of hair from her cheek. She scanned the streets in both directions, her gaze skipping over Ó Deághaidh's hiding spot. Then she hurried down the steps and toward the left.

Ó Deághaidh counted to ten before he followed. By now true night had fallen. The streets were empty, gleaming wet from the fallen rain. He skirted the puddles and kept clear of the streetlamps. He almost didn't need to. Valerija Delchev hurried along without a single glance behind her, heading straight toward the river. Soon she led Ó Deághaidh into a run-down district, where she entered a low rambling structure along the waterfront.

He waited a few moments, then eased the door open.

A solitary lamp hung from the ceiling in the entryway, casting its light in a dim circle. Ahead, a narrow hallway lined with doors stretched out in a straight line, to disappear into shadow. There was no sign of his quarry. Ó Deághaidh glided inside and closed the door softly.

It was a typical boardinghouse for those who could afford little. Its halls smelled of boiled cabbage and grease and tallow. Its rooms had thin walls and even thinner doors, and as he passed by he could hear a couple arguing in one room, the scratchy cries of a baby, and, farther on, the distinct sounds of lovemaking. At the far end of the building, a more substantial door opened onto a bare yard with a chicken coop. A fence with a gate enclosed the yard. Not far off, he heard the sound of water slapping against wood, and smelled the rank muddy scent of the river. There were footprints in the yard, but none of them looked fresh. She had not come this way.

Back inside, he followed the hallway as it wound through the building. By the third turn, he was convinced she had somehow escaped him, when a door to his right burst open and Valerija Delchev ran against him. By instinct, he caught hold of her.

She struggled, then stared in wild-eyed recognition. "You did it. You."

"Did what? What is wrong?"

She wrenched free and ran. Ó Deághaidh hesitated only a moment, then cursing, he pushed the door open. No reaction from anyone inside. He hefted his knife in his hand and entered.

It was difficult to see much—the windows were papered over, dampening the moonlight, and there were no streetlamps visible from this direction. Even in the dimness, however, he could sense something wrong. As his sight adjusted, he made out a wooden chair overturned, glittering specks on the carpet, and the pale white of scattered papers. Moving cautiously, he took another few steps in. His foot encountered a soft, immovable mass.

Ó Deághaidh knelt and felt around carefully. A man lay on the bare floor. No pulse, and he'd been dead long enough that his skin had turned cold, but not long enough for the body to stiffen. Dried blood matted the hair on one side of the man's head, and Ó Deághaidh felt where the skull had been crushed.

My poor friend, Ó Deághaidh thought. *I was nearly with you, a few days ago.*

His sympathy mixed with rising excitement. Even a dead man would have clues to offer.

He lit a candle from a coal in the fireplace and scanned the room. A cot had been shoved in one corner, next to a table with a washbasin and stacks of dirty cups and saucers. The rest of the room was given over to a laboratory of sorts, with desk and workbench and bookshelves. Someone—the murderer? a later intruder?—had swept all those shelves clean, forced open the desk, and flung its drawers onto the mess. Kneeling on the floor, he found two or three textbooks among the heaps of broken glass and twisted wires. He lifted them up, avoiding the glass, to discover a broken frame and a certificate of degree from Awveline University. *Yes,* he thought. *Yes, of course.* Here were the links he sought. More swiftly and certainly now, he sorted through the few remaining papers, all of them written in Éireann, all soaked in bitter-smelling fluid.

"Stand up. Do not move too suddenly."

Valerija Delchev stood in the doorway, her gun pointed at him.

Ó Deághaidh slowly rose to his feet. He noted with abstract interest that she handled the gun easily. "One of your colleagues," he said, indicating the body. "I see he studied abroad, at Awveline's University—"

"Shut up," she hissed. "We are going to the police."

"Are you certain that's wise? They might want to question you about all the accidents your friends have caused."

That produced a slight waver of the gun. "You know nothing of what we do."

"But I do know your friend is the link between Éire and Montenegro. And whether you expected me or not, you have been accustomed to messages from Éire. Why?"

Valerija Delchev made no answer. Keeping her gun on Ó Deághaidh, she circled around the room, stopping once in a while to pick something from the trash. A short length of wire. Several fragments of circuit boards, their components stripped off. Once, a heavy metallic cylinder wrapped in paper. It was the paper that interested her more, apparently, because she smoothed it one-handedly and read through its contents before stuffing it into her jacket pocket.

Finally she straightened up with a sigh.

"You didn't search before," Ó Deághaidh said.

"It was such a shock, finding Stefan dead. I thought—" She made a dismissive gesture. "Never mind what I thought."

"You thought I was murdering all your friends. What is missing?"

"Nothing." She pointed toward the door with her gun. "We must go now."

"What about your friends? Have you decided to betray them then?"

"You are a stupid man. Drop the knife and—no, do not approach me. Push it toward me. Gently. Yes, just so. Now, move very slowly toward the door. Do not think to call out. I do know how to shoot a man."

Her voice was low, edged with desperation. Ó Deághaidh dropped his knife onto the floor, and nudged it toward her with his foot. When she signaled, he preceded her out the door. She was learning caution, he thought, as he watched her latch the door with a key he had not noticed before. Valerija pocketed the key. "Go. Slowly now. And keep your hands where I can see them."

He was careful not to give any cause for alarm, but as they

retraced their steps through the corridor, Ó Deághaidh reviewed all his options. She had to suspect him of murdering that man. Who was it? A friend or lover? He could not hope to talk her into letting him go. And making a disturbance was unthinkable. It would call the police upon him and his work in Montenegro. The woman had to guess that as well. He would have to escape at the first chance.

They were approaching the back door again. Ó Deághaidh stumbled and flung out his hands, grabbing the latch. As the door swung open, he let himself fall through. Almost at once, he regained his footing and spun around to grab the woman's gun. She sidestepped him and slammed the gun's butt down onto his shoulder. He gasped and fell to his knees in the mud.

"Stand up. Do not try that again," she whispered.

Ó Deághaidh lurched to his feet. He flexed his hand. Cautiously lifted his arm and winced. "I'm going to be sick," he whispered. It was not far from the truth. He retched noisily. Again, as he sensed Valerija circling around him. He might overpower her, even now, if she ventured too close. He tensed, ready to grapple her, when she made a sharp gesture.

"Stand over there," she whispered. "Quiet."

She softly drew the door to and pressed her ear against it, listening.

Ó Deághaidh held his breath. He counted several voices, all of them men. Someone coming because of the noise? No, these were men calmly discussing a matter amongst themselves in what sounded like Štokavian. Then, the murmur resolved into words.

"I saw her go back inside."

"Do you think she found Kos?"

"Must have. Ilja didn't have time to deal with the mess himself. Lazar, you and Petar search the outside. Andreas and I will take care of the room. Remember, Ilja wants us all gone before midnight."

Valerija took Ó Deághaidh's hand and led him toward the gate. Her face had gone pale and drawn. And her hands, so steady before, were trembling. "Can you run?" she whispered.

"If I must."

"Then do so."

They glided silently out the gate and into the alley, then took off in a loping run. Ignoring the dirt path down to the river, Valerija Delchev led the way into a gap between two sections of the house. They had just turned into a covered passageway when Ó Deághaidh heard shouts and a door slammed. He and Valerija dodged around the corner, into a wider lane. The sound of swift, heavy footsteps sent them pelting down its pitch-dark length. It was so dark, Ó Deághaidh nearly ran headfirst into the wooden fence at the far end. He swore and spun around.

"Stop." Valerija dragged at Ó Deághaidh's arm. "There is a gate."

She ran her hands over the slats and fumbled for the gate's latch. "Damn," she whispered. "They've locked it. They never did before."

Ó Deághaidh glanced over his shoulder. The lane was empty still. They had a few moments, no more. He leaned his good shoulder against the gate and shoved, gritting his teeth against the ache in his collarbone. The gate did not budge and he collapsed against it, shuddering. The first rush of excitement had deserted him, and he felt sick and weary.

"Can we climb over?" Valerija said.

"I might have lifted you over, but—"

"But I made that difficult when I injured you. Yes, I see. I'm sorry."

It would not do to give up yet. He examined the fence by feel once more. It was old but sturdy, built from thick planks and braced at top and bottom. One plank was missing, but the opening was too narrow for them to squeeze through. He blew out a breath. One gun and one knife against three or four men, with who knew what weapons.

Meanwhile, Valerija had made a circuit of the area. "Here," she said softly. "We can hide over here."

She drew him toward the building to their left. The fence had left a narrow gap where the chimney jutted out. They squeezed into the space—just in time, because the clatter of boots echoed down the lane. Ó Deághaidh leaned down to whisper in her ear, "Keep your gun ready. Do not shoot unless you must."

He felt the brush of her hair against his mouth as she nodded.

The footsteps slowed as their pursuer neared the fence. Ó Deághaidh could make out nothing except the man's height and bulk, and the laboring of his breath. He felt Valerija shift on her feet. She placed one hand against his chest; the other held the gun. She was breathing slowly, silently. He could smell her sandalwood perfume, stronger now. His nausea receded, overtaken by a stronger emotion. It disturbed him he would think of sex at such a time.

After what seemed an infinitely long moment, the figure moved away. Ó Deághaidh waited until the last echo of footsteps had faded and silence returned. Valerija stirred. Tilted her head up so that the warmth of her breath tickled his throat. "Not yet," Ó Deághaidh said softly.

"We must. We have to talk."

"To the police?"

She hesitated. "Eventually. But I need—I would like to ask you a few things first."

"We aren't safe here," he reminded her. "Those men might return."

"And they will watch my apartment. But I know a place where we can talk in private. Besides, you look ill."

He could not argue with that. He nodded wearily and allowed

her to guide him back along the lane, around to a wooden staircase leading to a footpath by the water's edge. Here the bank rose
steeply above their heads, and fences along the top shielded them
from view. Moonlight traced the Cetinje's waters in rippling silver, and memories from two years ago streamed back, vivid and
strong, the first he'd had in many weeks. Of the Blackwater in
Awveline City, so broad and sluggish and dark. Of a body drained
of blood, floating amongst the weeds. Some of these were true
memories, no matter what the doctors claimed. He wished them
away, nevertheless.

A half mile down the path, they came to an old stone bridge.
A flight of stairs led up to street level, into a square fronted by
several wineshops and one sprawling two-story building that
Ó Deághaidh guessed to be an inn. A nearby clock tower rang
the hour. Midnight. He would have thought it later.

A girl opened the door to the night bell. Yes, they could hire a
private room, she told Valerija in answer to her hurried questions. There were no more hot meals, but she could fetch them
wine, bread, and cold sausages.

"And bring us a pitcher of water," Valerija added, with a
glance at Aidrean Ó Deághaidh. "We are parched as well as
hungry."

Very soon, they were seated with their meal in a comfortable
room lit by two old-fashioned oil lamps. Valerija dismissed the
girl and poured Ó Deághaidh a mugful of cold water mixed with
wine. "Did I break your collarbone?" she asked as she built a
small fire. In spite of the warm night, Ó Deághaidh found himself grateful for it.

"No. Bruised, I think. What caused you to change your mind
about me?"

Valerija glanced at him with an unreadable gaze. "I'm not sure
I have. But I know now you did not kill Stefan. And I could not

leave you to Ilja and his men, any more I could leave an injured dog."

An honest answer, spoken without resentment or fear. But also without any great measure of trust. Fair enough. Ó Deághaidh gulped down half the mug of watered wine and speared one of the sausages with his fork but set that aside after no more than a few bites. He had eaten so little the past several days—his preparations for tonight had consumed the hours he normally spent in search of meals—but the grease and spices made his stomach turn over. He broke off a piece of bread to chew instead, alternating that with sips from his mug.

I would only ask that you use your best judgment, the queen had said. There had been betrayals in Éire's Court. There had been many more here, in Montenegro, if he read the signs right. To win this woman's trust, he would have to offer his own.

"Let me start," he said. "My name is Aidrean Ó Deághaidh. I'm an agent for the Queen's Constabulary in Éire. Not a spy," he added, at her narrowed eyes. "Or perhaps I am, but not for the usual reasons. The queen sent me here to investigate a matter of some delicacy."

He went on to describe how reports had come to the queen's attention, linking Anglian dissidents with unrest in the Balkans. "But she mistrusted those reports," he said. "I cannot tell you more, only that she sent me as her observer, to test their accuracy."

"And if they were true?"

"But they were not—"

"If they were?" Valerija repeated. "What then?"

Ó Deághaidh expelled a breath. "Then I was to use my best judgment on what action to take."

Valerija took up a slice of bread and crumbled it between her fingers. "So many times I've observed Éire's government take action where I thought they had no business to. Today, I find my-self wishing the opposite."

She fell silent, staring at the table with dark eyes gleaming with unshed tears. Ó Deághaidh waited, knowing that to break the silence would be to break the mood that led her to talk, even this much. It was quiet in the inn, apart from the hiss and crackle of the fire. His shoulder ached, but his earlier drowsiness had fled, leaving him alert and wonderfully clear-headed.

Abruptly, Valerija deposited the crumbs onto the platter. She released a long breath, and glanced up at him with sudden deter-mination. "My turn," she said. "His name was Stefan, the man you found dead. Stefan Kos. He is—was my cousin. Five years ago, he applied to Awveline City's university for graduate studies in physics. After three years, he took a degree and returned home to teach at our university."

Physics. And Kos had obviously used his rooms as a kind of workshop. Ó Deághaidh's skin prickled with premonition. "What was his specialty?"

"Time." She shook her head, as though remembering some-thing unpleasant. "He had a theory that one could alter how time passes, much as you can affect how particles of light travel. He was working on such a device to support that theory."

"And those who murdered him took that device. Didn't they?"

She nodded. "You must understand the device itself was harm-less. Stefan had designed it so. Just tiny alterations, to prove his theories. Except . . . Well, let me explain the second part. The complications. You see, shortly before Stefan came home from Éire, my husband and I and our friends formed a group of . . . call us concerned citizens. We wrote letters to the prince and his advisers. We distributed pamphlets and held meetings to make public our opposition to an alliance with Austria."

He thought he could see where her story led, but he did not interrupt. She was speaking now with such obvious relief, as though she had held all these secrets, the good and the dreadful, inside herself for far too long.

"Stefan joined our cause because he was family," she said, "but also because he worried as much as we did. We were not revolutionaries—far from it. But there were disagreements within our group. Some argued that the slow, safe ways were too slow. Then last summer, the elections brought those Austrian sympathizers to power. No one listened to us. No one cared. They only cared about the demon Serbs. Safety at any cost." She made a disgusted sound. "We were frustrated, all of us. Ilja Radakovic more than others. He had plans. He wanted Stefan to build a dozen of his time devices. But altered to his specifications."

"Altered how?"

"So that they made bigger disruptions—noticeable ones. Ilja insisted it would cause no lasting harm—stirring a thick soup, he called it—but doing so would make things more difficult for the government. Then the people would have to listen to us."

Ó Deághaidh shuddered. The description reminded him of his waking nightmares, when the world seemed to ripple and change shape around him. He poured a mugful of water to wash the bitter aftertaste from his mouth. "This Radakovic. Was he the man who questioned me in the cave?"

"Yes. He knew about the drop points. He intercepted your letters and made plans to kidnap you, to find out how much Éire had discovered about our group. I was there to translate. And to prove my loyalty to him."

Now the clues shifted into focus. "You believe he murdered your husband."

"I do, but I have no proof."

Just as he had no proof of the traitor in Éire. He wanted to ask her more questions about that night—about the man who died, about the knife he'd found to defend himself and whether she had provided it—but those would have to wait for later. If, he added, they *had* a later. "Tell me how your husband came to use these drop points, and not Stefan Kos."

He looked for any sign of self-consciousness in her manner, but there was none. She spoke simply, as though the answer were obvious. "It was when Stefan first arrived in Éire. All the foreign students are interviewed. Stefan met with a man—"

"His name?"

"Seán MacCailín."

Ó Deághaidh leaned back and felt the rising tension seep away. He did not recognize the name. Most likely, Kos had met with a minor official, not someone in Ó Cadhla's or De Paor's immediate circle. Or rather, Lord Ultach's, he thought, remembering that Lord De Paor had not taken over from the old lord until last year.

Valerija was watching him in return. "Do you know him?"

"Unfortunately, no. What came next for your cousin?"

"They talked a while. About Stefan's intended research, mostly, but also about Montenegro. It seems the man had visited here once. He was sympathetic about our troubles. The day before Stefan left to return home, the man visited him again, and gave him an address so they could continue their conversation, as he called it."

"Didn't your cousin wonder at that?"

She shook her head. "He was in some ways a trusting boy. But when he joined our group, he told us about this Seán MacCailín. Kiro decided to write to MacCailín himself, asking if the man knew anyone in Éire's government with influence, someone who might convince the queen to involve herself with our affairs." She smiled pensively. "I disagreed with Kiro's decision. I said the Éireann queen was no different from the Austrian king."

Ó Deághaidh would have liked to debate that point with her, but like so much else, that too would have to wait. "Did your husband tell this MacCailín about your group?"

"Yes. More than I liked, less than he wanted to. He even told this man about our impatient members. Oh, he disguised our names, and he spoke in generalities, but the matter was clear enough. I think that is why the man sent instructions, in case, he said, it became necessary to send agents to speak directly with Kiro."

So whoever he was, this mysterious Seán MacCailín knew enough about the Montenegrin situation at large, and the political conflicts in detail, to create a trap for Éire. His target could not be Ó Deághaidh himself, because the plans started long before his summons to Cill Cannig. Did MacCailín aim to discredit one of the ministers? All of them? The queen herself? And how exactly?

"Are you certain he did not send a warning about me?"

"No, I would have—" She stopped and touched her fingers to her lips. "Perhaps not. They came to a post office number. Kiro told him once how the correspondence worked. It's possible Ilja claimed the letter himself."

The pieces still did not fit together and he worried at them as he worried the bread into crumbs and then molded it back together into small neat bullets. Secret reports about Anglians in Montenegro. Rumors of civil war coming to Éire's shores. But vague and contradictory. The queen could not ignore the matter, but she could not act on mere suspicions.

And so she sends me to Montenegro. The traitor warns these revolutionaries. A scandal, surely, but not so great that it would cause the downfall of a regime. For that, it would take something far greater. . . .

"When does the Austrian delegation arrive?" he asked.

Valerija started at his question. "They meet with our prince on June first. Five days from now. A week of negotiations over troops and—"

"No. I mean when do they arrive?" He leaned forward, both hands flat on the table. "Two days from now? Three?"

"What are you talking about?"

"Let us suppose a few things," Ó Deághaidh said, ignoring her question. "Let us suppose the Austrians have no interest in the prince, only in those sympathizers and supporters in your parliament. Let us suppose, too, there are advisers to the prince who also support a connection with Austria. Let us further suppose—"

"That there will be a private meeting between those sympathizers and the Austrians days before the public one," Valerija said. "Yes. Now I understand." Her glance met his, wide and bright. "I heard talk that the Austrian prince expressed a liking for our old city and its monasteries and chapels. He wished a private tour before the grand public events."

"When?" Ó Deághaidh said urgently. "When does the prince come to Cetinje?"

"Tomorrow. No, it's past midnight. Today."

They woke the serving girl at her station by the door. Valerija thrust a handful of bills into the girl's hands, then they were out the door and running through the streets. Radakovic, Valerija told Ó Deághaidh breathlessly, had money from his uncle. He owned a boardinghouse in a well-to-do district, not far from the many embassies and consulates, and within a half mile from the palace.

"We tell the police first," she said. "It's best if they make the report to the royal guards—"

"No."

Valerija stopped in midstride. There was just enough light from a streetlamp to see that her cheeks were flushed with strong emotion. "What do you mean, no?" Her expression changed then. "I understand. You do not wish our government to discover the connection with yours."

"Not only that. Think what happens if we go to the police. It might take hours to convince them. And hours more before they can roust the guards and start a search. Meanwhile, Radakovic sets off to start a war."

"What makes you believe we can stop him alone?"

"I don't know. Listen to me, Valerija. Madame Delchev. Go to the police if you must, but tell me where Ilja Radakovic lives. Let me carry on with my orders."

She must have heard the desperation in his voice, because Valerija turned her head away. Her lips moved, as though she might be cursing him, or calculating the future in all its permutations.

"What will you do?" she said at last.

"Take him by surprise. He cannot expect me. Or, if he has gone into hiding, search his rooms for clues to his plans."

Another searching glance. An expression he could not read. Then she nodded. "Very well. We go together. This way."

It took them an hour to cross the city, keeping to side streets and the smaller lanes. Once or twice, they crossed the path of another person. A prostitute, trudging homeward. A drunken man singing with surprising vigor and beauty. Otherwise, it was as though the city were swept clean of humanity. Eventually they entered a prosperous neighborhood, with cafés and restaurants and hotels. Radakovic's boardinghouse stood on a corner, exposed. Its windows were dark; all was quiet.

Ó Deághaidh scanned all directions. No sign of any watchers posted. Very odd. He would have expected the man to take pre-

cautions in case Valerija had notified the police. The absence
made his skin go cold in premonition, in spite of the warm night.

"Which floor does he live on?" he asked.

"The ground floor."

They circled around the boardinghouse to the small courtyard between two alleyways. The rear door had been chained
shut, but a basement hatchway yielded to their efforts. Once they
gained the ground floor, Ó Deághaidh used his lockpick on the
door to Radakovic's rooms.

He pushed the door open. Within, thick curtains shut out any
light from the streetlamps. Valerija handed Ó Deághaidh the
gun. He entered first, his weapon ready, and checked each room,
while she kept watch by the door.

Empty. He signaled to Valerija. She came inside at once and
bolted the door.

"He is gone?" she asked.

"So it appears. We'll make a search."

Ó Deághaidh lit a pair of candles and they went through all
the rooms. Nothing appeared obviously missing from the
man's bedroom, and the bed had not been slept in. In the study,
Ó Deághaidh went methodically through each pigeonhole and
drawer and folder in Radakovic's desk and cabinet. There were
the accounts for the boardinghouse. Business letters. Correspondence with other political groups throughout the country—
filled with inflammatory prose, to be sure, but nothing he would
call treasonous. Notes to himself for future speeches. A few envelopes with local addresses, stuffed with bills or receipts. All so
ordinary.

"What kind of papers are you looking for?" Valerija asked.

"Letters. Coded messages. Something left over from his correspondence with Seán MacCailín. The man left in a hurry, I
would guess. Unless he destroyed the letters at once . . . Ah."

He took up a letter opener. Carefully inserted it into the first of those six ordinary envelopes. They were all made of the same thick, opaque paper, he noted. The addresses were from different towns and villages within Montenegro, but the postal marks were the same. Now that he knew what to look for, he saw the envelope had been cut open before and resealed with dabs of glue. He pointed this out to Valerija.

"That was not how he wrote to Kiro," she whispered.

"Perhaps he had several means of writing. Or perhaps he changed his methods."

A few slices and the envelope fell open to reveal a letter written in Štokavian. Ó Deághaidh scanned its contents. There was mention of the queen, a few names within Ó Breislin's department, something about requested funds—Ó Deághaidh recognized the form and style of a refusal couched in bureaucratic terms—and a reference to a mutual cause. But it was the handwriting that arrested Aidrean Ó Deághaidh's attention. Those strong vertical lines. The small tight loops. The way the writer had crossed the *T*s with a broad stroke the cut across the other letters. He had seen that same script in Cill Cannig.

Lord Alastar De Paor.

De Paor had thoroughly disguised his handwriting on the papers he inserted in Ó Deághaidh's packet of reports, but writing to Kiro Delchev, he had not bothered. Arrogance or carelessness, it didn't matter. Here was proof of the man's treason. No need to examine the rest. He would do that later, after they apprehended Radakovic. He ought to feel more triumph at the discovery, but he was left only with a mounting sense of dread.

Valerija watched, tense and expectant. "Those are MacCailín's letters," she said, when he stuffed them into his coat. It was not a question.

"Yes. But his name is not Seán MacCailín. Come, we are not yet done with our search."

One last room remained. This one turned out to be entirely given over to a long workbench overflowing with heaps of papers, metalworking tools, coils of wire, and several strange metallic boxes, which resembled those Ó Deághaidh had seen in Kos's room.

"These are Stefan's papers," Valerija said, leafing through the papers. "His workbooks and his research notes."

She handed one notebook to Ó Deághaidh. It was filled with sketches and diagrams, annotated in a combination of Latin and Štokavian. From what he could decipher, Kos's aim was to create a device capable of altering time's passage and to measure those disturbances, but in small increments, just enough to prove his theories.

In the margins, he found a series of equations in a different handwriting. Something about increasing the voltage, testing higher frequencies, followed by a series of numbers that produced an eerie sense of recognition. Where had he seen numbers like that before?

. . . a woman dressed in a hospital gown, her pale hair drifting over her face. She appeared oblivious to her surroundings, weaving her hands in patterns, her lips moving in a silent recitation. No, not entirely silent. As he drew closer, he heard her whisper, "141955329, times two, exponent 25267, add one . . ."

Prime numbers, he thought. In another lifetime, Gwen Madóc had gone mad from numbers, or so the doctors at Aonach Sanitarium told Ó Deághaidh. And in that other lifetime, Síomón Madóc had explained his theory of numbers—how they had properties beyond those used to measure and quantify.

That past no longer existed. Gwen and Síomón Madóc had founded their research institute. Kos must have read their papers and used their theories to refine his device. In his innocence, he might have shared this information with Radakovic, who saw a quite different application for the same theorems.

Ó Deághaidh sank to the floor, overcome. Now he understood why the streets around Radakovic's house were empty, why no lookouts had been posted. Radakovic had sent them all away. Ó Deághaidh knew why, too. If these calculations proved accurate, Ilja Radakovic would do far more than stir a thick soup. He would rip time to pieces. Had the man understood what that meant? Or had he cared only for his politics, no matter what the cost?

Valerija knelt beside him. "What is wrong?"

"No time," he said. "All the time. I'm sorry. I'm not making any sense."

"You are starved," she said. "You ate nothing before but a few scraps of bread."

She left his side for a few moments, returning with a paring knife and an apple, which she cut into small pieces and fed him by hand. After, she fetched water, cheese, and bread. "Eat," she insisted, when he tried to refuse. "Now, tell me what you discovered that overset you so."

In between bites and sips, he told her his suspicions. Telling it a second time did not vanquish the horror, and more than once he had to pause and collect himself. Throughout, Valerija listened, her gaze intent. When he finished, her mouth opened, closed. Then, hardly more than a whisper, "Destruction. If not that, war, which is the same thing. Us with Austria. The Prussian Alliance would join in—they always do. Then their allies and enemies. Do we go to the police now, Aidrean Ó Deághaidh?"

He shook his head.

"Stubborn man," she muttered.

He could not help smiling. "So are you. Stubborn, I mean."

She gave a smothered laugh, which broke into a sob. "If only we had our own device to turn back the time." She laid a hand upon his cheek, which nearly undid all his resolve. Ó Deághaidh felt a tremor go through his body. Valerija must have sensed it, because she drew back a step. "Come," she said softly. "We must hurry."

They exited the boarding house and once more plunged into the streets. The clocks were striking three, and the streetlamps were all extinguished. "We must go to the south end of the city," Valerija said. "Where the highway from Budva enters Cetinje. The prince intended to ride a fleet of balloons to the coast, then take motorcars north."

She took Ó Deághaidh's arm and led him, supported him, as they headed directly south along the city's main boulevard. There was no hesitation in her step, no fear at all at the danger they chased. She was like the heroines of legend, Ó Deághaidh thought, who faced the Roman invaders. But now he was hallucinating. Or simply wishing for a different past and future. Perhaps later . . . He hoped there would be a later. But first they had to find and stop Radakovic.

The city's edge came upon them before he realized it. A breeze grazed his cheek, carrying the scent of mud and ripe hay and wildflowers. He stumbled to a halt. They stood at an intersection of the highway with several smaller lanes leading to either side. His ears attuned themselves to subtleties—Valerija's quiet breathing, the silvery rill of the nearby river, his own pulse thrumming in his ears.

"We've lost him," Valerija said bitterly. "Come over here, Aidrean. Rest a moment. We must think what to do next."

She led him into a side lane, to a bench underneath sweetscented linden trees. There was something strange about her manner, but he was too tired to decipher it. No sooner did she sit beside him, than she was on her feet again. "You must be thirsty. I'll fetch you water from the fountain." Then to his astonishment, she bent and pressed a warm kiss on his lips.

The imaginary ice beneath his feet broke and divided.

"Valerija."

So much he wanted to say. Dared not say.

She kissed him a second time, her expression strangely pensive. "Wait here," she whispered. "I'll come right back."

Before he could protest, she ran toward the main road and rounded the corner. Ó Deághaidh waited, but she did not return, and it came back to him that he had seen no fountain close by. He checked his coat pocket and cursed. She must have taken the pistol when she kissed him. She meant to track down Radakovic herself. Still cursing, he staggered to his feet. "Valerija."

No answer.

Ó Deághaidh lumbered forward, swearing under his breath. As he rounded the corner, he sighted Valerija running down the road. Farther ahead, a second figure limped along the road to Budva—a tall lanky man, hatless and dressed in a flapping coat. He carried a large unwieldy box under one arm. Radakovic. It had to be.

The man's head jerked up and he spun around to face Valerija. The box tumbled to one side as he groped for something inside his coat.

A gun, Ó Deághaidh thought. *Of course he has a gun.*

Valerija paused and stared at the weapon aimed at her. "Ilja," she called out. "We know what you mean to do. We've told the police. You must not do it, Ilja. You will make a war, not end it. Don't you understand? If you—"

A sharp crack reverberated through the air. Valerija dropped to the ground and rolled to one side. With a swift sure motion, she brought her own gun to bear and fired. The distant figure staggered but did not fall. He swung his gun up just as Valerija regained her feet. Another sharp report rang out, and Valerija bent over double.

No—

The world spun and the ground tilted beneath his feet. Ó Deághaidh fought away the dizziness and stumbled to Valerija's side. His heart was leaping as he gathered her hands into his.

Blood soaked the right side her skirt. Her face seemed entirely too pale. "Valerija—"

He touched her throat. Her eyes blinked open and she gasped. "Aidrean. Ah, how it burns. One stupid bullet. Not even that. Grazed me is all. But I hit him, too. Take the gun. Go—"

She fumbled her pistol into his hands and murmured something incomprehensible. Ó Deághaidh forced himself to standing, in spite of the yammering inside his skull that said she had lied, that she was dying. *Go,* he thought he heard her say again. Then he was running down the highway.

Radakovic had vanished, but Ó Deághaidh found his trail fast enough. Less than a quarter mile down the road, bloody footprints led off to the right, into a field pocketed with holes and rocky ridges. He dodged a shot, rolled behind a boulder. Now he could hear Radakovic's uneven breathing. Definitely hurt, but still dangerous.

A flicker of motion warned him. He spun around and fired. Radakovic staggered backward and collapsed. Ó Deághaidh crept forward cautiously. Radakovic was clutching his shoulder and babbling curses. Next to him, covered with mud and grass, was the box. It was large, iron or steel, bound with copper straps. Ó Deághaidh recognized it at once as the one from Stefan Kos's drawings. Radakovic was laughing and crying and choking. "Done it. Done and done and done—"

Ó Deághaidh cuffed him with the butt of his gun and turned to the box. Its lid was open, showing circuit boards and metallic containers with fluid contents that were far heavier than he thought possible.

He swore as he snatched up the device. He could sense the electricity coursing through the wires, ungrounded, burning his palms. He had to break the circuit, but how? Off to his right he glimpsed the Cetinje River through the tall grass. He had no idea if it would stop the device from working. . . .

He hurled the box as hard as he could. It hit the water with a noisy splash and sank at once. Ó Deághaidh fell to his knees and stared at the river, his gaze fixed on the ripples marking where the box had struck. Had he destroyed the machine? *Please, oh please,* he prayed, as he had not since he was a child. *Please dear God and Mhuire and Gaia, let me be in time.*

A dull roar erupted from beneath the surface of the river. Ó Deághaidh lurched to his feet. The waters of the Cetinje were churning about, sending up gouts of spray. Then, rising up from the depths, a bubble of air broke free. With dismay, he saw it was expanding as fast as it rose. All the fields and trees beyond took on a strange distorted appearance, as though he were viewing them through a magnifying glass. He spun around and . . .

. . . *the ground vanished beneath his feet. He was plummeting through a choking darkness, arms flailing but there was nothing to catch hold of, though he could still feel the cold texture of the stable's latch pressed into his skin. He screamed, screamed until his throat closed in pain . . .*

"Aidrean."

Warm hands enclosed his. He turned his head and caught the scent of sandalwood. The ordinary world dropped away and he had the sensation of drowning in a dark, still pool of water. He tried to speak, but found his mouth would not obey his commands.

"Aidrean, can you hear me?"

. . . *the images faded and so with it the panic. He stood in a pitch-black void, made darker still by the sparks cascading all around. Soft scraps pattered over his face. It was a rainfall of paper, yellowed fragments burnt around the edges, fine parchment and cheap newssheets with writing in the margin. As he walked through it, he recognized the handwriting as his, and realized these were from all the diaries he had written and destroyed. He was walking through the memories of all his different pasts. Even as he realized this, he felt a pang deep within, as his selves joined into one. Ah, but which one? Which future lay ahead?*

"Commander Ó Deághaidh . . ."

He awoke in a room draped in white and green linens. The air smelled sharply of antiseptic, recalling another awakening, in a different hospital. A lassitude enveloped his body. His brain felt thick and unresponsive. With an effort, he turned his head and saw two figures hovering over him. One was like a shadow, thin and sharp and dressed in black. The other stood farther off—he could make out nothing but an impression of dark brown eyes and hair. The two conferred in low voices, then a door opened and shut. The scent of sandalwood lingered.

He struggled to sit up. A hand settled on his shoulder and pressed him back. "Lie still, Commander."

Ó Deághaidh's vision cleared and he recognized Lord Ó Cadhla. But a cold dread washed over him as he took in Lord Ó Cadhla's pale face, the marks of tension and great weariness—so exactly like that other interview, in that other time, when Ó Cadhla's daughter had died. Ó Deághaidh felt a tremor of the old vertigo, wondering which present and past he had tumbled into.

"What happened?" he whispered. "Where am I?"

"In a hospital. In Cetinje."

"In Cetinje. Then that means . . ."

His voice trailed away, and he tried to decide what that meant.

"They found you outside the city," Lord Ó Cadhla said. "You've been unconscious for three weeks." To Ó Deághaidh's questioning frown, he added, "The official report is that the country hereabouts suffered an earthquake. Their river has vanished underground, and a dozen or so buildings collapsed. Sixty people died, several hundred injured. But far, far fewer than if that madman had succeeded. The queen congratulates you on your success."

Ó Deághaidh closed his eyes and let his breath trickle out. Death and disaster were hardly a success. But he understood. There would have been a war otherwise, with millions dead and a continent left in ashes. "What about Lord De Paor?" he whispered.

"Arrested and awaiting trial. Madame Delchev gave me the evidence you uncovered."

"She was here, then."

"Every day, watching over you, or so they tell me. The doctors said you were babbling numbers and names constantly. They thought the explosion had deranged your mind, but Madame Delchev knew better. It was she who deciphered your gibberish and sent a telegram to the queen."

Ó Cadhla went on to tell Ó Deághaidh about a monstrous scandal exposed, involving Montenegrin collaborators and Austrian agents. The prince retained his throne, apparently, but there would be an interim council to oversee the drafting of a new constitution.

"Our queen has issued a statement of support," Ó Cadhla said. "As did Frankonia and Alba. We have all sent representatives to oversee the new elections and the transition of government." He smiled. "Though I must add I and the others are here only temporarily. Your Madame Delchev was quite firm in expressing her convictions. She and her colleagues are grateful for Éire's assistance, but they insisted on formal treaties that our presence will not be permanent. The queen agreed. I'm not certain she had much choice. It was an interesting experience, negotiating between two very strong women."

It was all too much to absorb in a few moments. Valerija. Alive and well. And overseeing the founding of a new government, just as she wished.

"As for you," Ó Cadhla said. "Madame Delchev proved both intelligent and discreet, and in the subsequent chaos, no one has thought to question your identity. For all they know, you are a migrant laborer, who had the misfortune to be on the highway when the explosion, or rather, the earthquake, took place. The queen suggests, and I agree, that you should return to Éire as soon as you are fully recovered."

"Of course."

A great weariness came over him. He would return home, his honor and reputation recovered. But he found himself strangely indifferent to his success. He probed the reasons behind that indifference, but flinched away, unwilling to explore it farther. Perhaps later, when his strength had returned. He was tired. That was all.

A warm hand pressed upon his. Lord Ó Cadhla's. "Commander Ó Deághaidh . . . We shall talk later, when you are well. But please accept my thanks for preserving this future out of so many others."

Ó Deághaidh glanced up. Ó Cadhla gave a tiny nod.

Within the week, Ó Cadhla arranged for his transfer to the local embassy, accomplished late at night under the cover of a moonless sky. The embassy chief explained that he would return to Éire as soon as his health allowed so that he might give his evidence to the queen and her ministers.

Ó Deághaidh nodded, but something in his newly subdued manner must have worried the embassy officer who reported to Ó Cadhla, because they did not hurry him on his way. He rested another week in seclusion before he set off for Éire in easy stages—by motorcar to Budva, by ship to the little-used port of Youghal, then by train to Osraighe, where a private coach carried him to Cill Cannig. There were watchers and guards for every stage, some invisible but many more making their presence known, which told Ó Deághaidh that matters were not yet settled to the queen's satisfaction.

The queen. He had no grasp of his emotions when he thought of her. He dreamed of her from time to time, but no longer as a man dreams of a woman. Instead the images were ones of state and rank, the symbolism thick enough, if he cared to examine them.

Coming home to Éire helped somewhat. He met for hours with the queen and her ministers, delivering his formal report of what transpired in Montenegro, and answering their many questions. At night, he slept with the aid of wine and a great weariness he could not shed.

A lull followed, which he did not mistake for tranquility. Then came the trials.

His own part ended the first day with his testimony, but Ó Deághaidh watched throughout the following weeks as the court conducted its meticulous examination of witnesses and evidence. This would be no private interrogation, followed by an execution or assassination in secret. Áine had apparently decided to give a clear signal to her enemies that she would punish any rebellion swiftly and without mercy.

Oh my Queen. I see the why behind what you do. But do you see the cost to yourself? To Éire in the future?

His memories of the trials themselves were fragmentary. Lord De Paor rambling on in the witness box, offering excuses and justifications. The queen's face as still as sculpted ice. The lord advocate passing sentence. Further sessions with the queen and her ministers to discuss the public's mood after De Paor's execution, and the sentencing of certain members of his staff, as more details of his activities came to light.

There would be no war, not for this generation. Or so the ministers proclaimed.

I should rejoice, Ó Deághaidh thought. *I will, later, when I recover my sense of what I have achieved, and what I have lost.*

For his part, he dutifully suffered through more ceremonies where the queen or various ministers awarded him medals. The queen herself spoke of other honors, from the obvious ones of higher rank, to more obliquely offered favors. He had refused them all as politely as he could.

So it was with some curiosity, and apprehension, that Aidrean Ó Deághaidh came for what the queen had named their final private interview. When he entered the small elegant chamber appointed for that meeting, she was already there, seated beside grand bay windows overlooking Cill Cannig's grounds. The day was a day of Éire, soft and gray and damp with the promise of rain.

Áine smiled and gestured for him to take a seat opposite her. Her steward poured tea for them both before he retired.

She allowed him a few moments to sip his tea, but her gaze was sharp and her manner that of a queen with her subject.

"Are you well, Aidrean?" she said at last.

He nodded, thinking that surely she had the reports from Doctor Loisg. Thinking as well that her face had a far, far older air, as though she too was recovering from disappointments.

"Then you are ready for a new assignment?" she asked.

He shrugged. "As you command, Your Majesty."

She smiled. It was the first smile he noticed since the days before he started for the Continent. *We have both performed our duty,* he thought. *We have both paid our price.*

"I am glad," the queen said. "You see, I spoke with Lord Ó Cadhla about the assignment, and he agrees you are the best suited. But," and her voice dropped to lower register, "let me describe the matter in full. Then you must tell me—honestly—if you agree with all your heart and not just from a sense of duty . . ."

————

High above Budva, the passenger balloon described a wide circle as it began its descent toward the landing fields. Below, the Adriatic glistened like blue satin in the April sunshine, with a darker shadow from the balloon skimming over the swells. Aidrean Ó Deághaidh checked his pocket watch, which he had adjusted for Montenegrin time. Half past noon. He would easily reach Cetinje before evening.

One hour to clear customs and collect his luggage. Two more hours winding north along the highway in the hired motorcar. The church bells were ringing half past four when he arrived at the hotel, an elegant building in the fashionable section of town, near the embassies and royal palace. Tomorrow he would meet with his new associates, but tonight was his to claim.

It was far too early for visits, he told himself.

Coward.

That I am. I have no reason not to be.

Still arguing with himself, he set off on a tour of the city, to see what had changed. A great deal, as he found. The old riverfront district had vanished along with the river. Now a greening trough ran through Centinje, its slopes covered in flowers and newly planted linden trees. There were gravel walks and stone pillars with posters advertising the elections next month, to be held according to a new constitution. So much accomplished since the previous summer.

When the clocks chimed six o'clock, Ó Deághaidh turned his steps toward the university district. He knew from reports that she had not changed her residence, and though almost a year had passed, he could find his way without any missteps. As he approached, his pace slowed as he took in the details, matching them with his memories. There it was—the same dark brick house. The same rose-colored curtains over the ground-floor windows. He climbed the steps to the porch and stopped, his hand hovering over the electric bell. It had come to this moment, and for once, he was shy. He retreated to the sidewalk and glanced up to the second floor. Her rooms were dark.

What did I expect? To find her waiting for me?

He had. A foolish thought, borne of the same foolish hope that led him to accept this post in Cetinje.

Enough. He would return to his hotel. Tomorrow, before meeting with his new colleagues at the embassy, he would send a proper letter to Madame Delchev. What he would say in that letter, he did not know. He foresaw a night spent in useless edits and revisions and second thoughts.

He turned away from the apartment building, already occupied with how to explain his presence in the city, when he saw Valerija Delchev walking toward him.

She looked just as she had a year ago, when he first sighted her in the university quarter. She had the same abstracted air. She carried the same woven basket filled with books, with more tucked beneath her arm. The only difference was that she wore dark blue, not black, and a shawl patterned in roses. Her head was bare.

Valerija had almost reached the steps, when she happened to look up. She stopped. The abstracted air vanished at once and color edged her cheeks. "Aidrean. I mean, Commander Ó Deághaidh. Good evening."

"Madame Delchev." He had to clear his throat before he could speak properly. "I . . . I came to ask if you would dine with me."

She gave a breathless laugh. "All the way from Éire?"

He ran a hand over his hair to cover his embarrassment. "In a manner, yes. I've taken a new post here with the embassy."

It took her a moment to absorb that. Then, "Are you—Is this a temporary one, or perhaps more permanent?"

"I don't know yet. I would need time to prove myself, I think."

Curiosity. A flicker of anxious doubt, which strangely reflected his own. Then her expression cleared, and she ventured a smile. "I see. Well, I would be glad to share a supper with you."

He released the breath he had not realized he held. "Well, then."

"Well, then." She accepted his proffered arm, and pressed a hand over his. "I'm glad to see you again, Aidrean Ó Deághaidh."

Together they walked beneath the blossoming trees, through the sweet-scented air and the ruddy light of sunset.

THE TIME ROADS

FEBRUARY 1914

The execution took place on the seventeenth of February, at one o'clock on a cold dank afternoon. Clouds masked the skies. Snow drizzled downward in fits and starts. It caught in the crevasses between the stones of the palace. It blew in runnels over the tiled yard and blurred the outer walls, so that the world appeared a smudged and dirty gray.

I stood on a balcony overlooking the yard. My senior guards flanked me. More guards lined the square, all of them dressed in long woolen cloaks and fur-lined hats, their rifles held across their chests. My minister of home affairs, whose responsibilities included the Anglian Dependencies, stood behind me. He and I and all these soldiers would bear witness to the death of Thomas Alan Austen, the man who had tried to assassinate me.

Nine days ago, Austen had fired a rifle from the rooftop over-looking the steps of Osraighe's cathedral. Chance alone had saved me—a remark from a companion that caught my attention and caused me to turn away. The bullet had grazed my neck and shattered the wooden doors of the cathedral. Austen had fired three more bullets and killed two of my guards, before he fled. The Garda had captured him before he could escape the city.

My half-healed wounds from that attempt ached in the cold. I had not wanted to give Austen the honor of a formal execution. My ministers, and especially Lord Ó Cadhla, had advised me otherwise. Out of respect for Lord Ó Cadhla's long service—to my father and to me—and knowing he never opposed me without reason, I had agreed.

The iron gate swung open, and four guards marched the pris-oner into the courtyard. Thomas Austen was a small, bent man, dressed in black trousers, a black smock, and black cloth slippers, already wet from the snow. He was bound with chains at his wrists and ankles, so that he could not do more than shuffle toward his death. For a moment, I almost pitied the man.

Then he lifted his gaze to mine. His eyes narrowed. His lips parted in silent laughter, turning the air silver with his breath.

My pity vanished.

You are a bold man, Thomas Austen, to look at me that way.

A guard took hold of Austen's arm and bent close to the man's ear, no doubt urging him to show respect. Austen said some-thing in reply and the guard smiled.

A dangerous man, said the reports from my Constabulary. Much loved in his homeland for his courage and his intellect. He had dedicated his life to the cause of Anglian independence.

The procession, delayed only momentarily, continued forward to the solitary wooden post at the far end of the courtyard. The post itself was a relic from my grandfather's day, when Anglia and the other Dependencies fought more vigorously against our rule. Even then, it had been reserved for political prisoners of some importance. During my father's reign, most convictions ended with imprisonment or exile. The last criminal whose death I witnessed here was Lord Alastar De Paor.

Austen vanished briefly as the guards crowded around to remove his shackles and bind him to the post. They did not want to take any chances with this prisoner—no unseemly struggles, no second attempt on the queen's life. Their task accomplished, they marched back to join their comrades by the walls, and take up their weapons in a ready stance.

I stared across the distance. Austen stared back. He'd refused his blindfold, which did not surprise me. *Have you not surrendered, even now?* I thought. *Are you plotting how to use these last moments in favor of your cause?*

A foolish question. I knew the answer.

"Guards of the firing squad, take position."

Ten guards marched in a single line across the yard, their boots crunching over the snow. The wind had died away, and the cold pressed against me, a heavy immovable weight. I suppressed a shudder, knowing that my own actions would be noted and reported as well.

On command, the guards halted and spun to face the prisoner.

"Weapons ready."

Ten rifles swung down and around.

"Fire on each count."

I heard the click of the bolt. Saw the gleam of Thomas Austen's eyes as his gaze veered away from mine and fixed itself upon those ten rifles.

"A haon."

The guns roared.

Blood spurted from the prisoner's chest. His head jerked back and he shouted, a short sharp cry. Though my pulse thrummed in my ears, I nevertheless distinctly heard the click of the bolts as the guards readied for the next shot.

"A dó."

Austen twisted away from the bullets. No, that was a trick of my expectations. It was the gunfire tearing through his already dead body that flung him against the post. For one terrible moment, Thomas Austen seemed to stand on his feet, untouched. Then slowly, oh so slowly, he collapsed, a limp and bloody sack, held upright only by the ropes binding him.

"A trí," I whispered in unison with the commander's voice.

One last crack of rifles. One last dreadful spasm.

A cloud of gun smoke hung in the air, obscuring the yard. An acrid stink drifted up to where I stood. Snow stung my cheeks, and now I did shiver, in spite of my thick woolen cloak and my fur-lined gloves. Behind me, Lord Minister Ó Duinn murmured to one of my attendants, but I continued to stare at the dark shadow that marked the post and Thomas Austen's body.

In my mind, I could still hear his last shout. And the white mist, spiraling upward to the clouds, was like the pale ghost of his breath, as though Thomas Austen continued to breathe in defiance of death. As though he continued to laugh.

But I am not rid of the man so easily, I thought.

Three hours had passed since the execution. The gray afternoon was shading into an uneasy twilight. Alone in my private offices, I sifted through reports about various matters concerning Éire and its allies. In spite of the grand fire burning in the hearth, I felt a deep ache of cold inside me. Oh, to be sure, Austen was dead, but his presence would continue to plague my kingdom. I had already received early reports of unrest from the Queen's Constabulary. Crude placards had sprouted on walls in certain public squares of Osraighe where Anglian immigrants lived. A telegraph from Londain and its outer districts spoke of clashes between protesters and the Garda. No, death had not silenced Thomas Austen. As my father said more than once, *We shall not have true peace until we settle the Anglian Matter.*

I set the papers aside and pressed my hands against my eyes. Peace. It was a will-o'-the wisp we had all pursued, I and my father and our allies, not just within Éire's borders, but throughout the world. It was for peace that I had proposed a union of nations to my ministers. *We must talk. We must rule the world together, not against one another,* I had told them. It was our last chance before we annihilated ourselves through ambition, and if all went as I planned, our first conference would take place this summer. But I did not doubt the Anglian Matter would intrude there as well.

Damn you, Thomas Austen. Damn you to hell.

I heard the tread of footsteps. My secretary appeared at the door, a sheaf of papers under one arm, and his writing case in hand. "Your Majesty—"

"Time comes to meet with my council, yes. Thank you, Coilín."

He hesitated. *Are you well enough?* was his unspoken question.

I suppressed the urge to snarl. No, I was not well. Austen's bullet had not killed me, but I had bled a great deal, and the subsequent fever had left me weak. However, I had called this meeting twelve days ago, before Thomas Austen made his attempt upon my life. My physician had argued I should abstain from my duties another month, but those same duties did not allow such a luxury.

"Are my ministers waiting for me?" I asked.

"Waiting and anxious, Your Majesty. Just as you wished."

"Good. They ought to worry. And Commander Ó Deághaidh?"

"He arrived a few hours ago, Your Majesty."

Even better.

"Then I should not keep my council waiting any longer."

With Coilín Mac Liam trailing behind me, I set off through the halls of the Royal Enclosure. My plans for this Union of Nations had begun last September, when I announced to Éire's Congress my intentions. It had cost me many favors, but I had at last persuaded a sufficient number of political factions to support me. Since then, Éire had issued invitations to the more influential rulers of Europe and Asia and the Western Continents. Today's conference was ostensibly to untangle the latest demands from our guests, but there were other, less public reasons for the gathering.

When I arrived, guards swept the doors open and announced my arrival as I passed into the conference chamber.

"Your Majesty." Lord Ó Cadhla was the first on his feet. The rest of my ministers, their secretaries and their underlings, were only moments behind.

"My lords. Honored gentlemen."

I took my seat at the head of the table, while my secretary distributed the most recent reports from my agents abroad. Lord Ó Cadhla, as minister of state, knew their contents already. Lord Ó Breislin, chief adviser for intelligence, did as well. Others scanned through these new documents with frowns, or puzzled expressions. A few smiled, but theirs were anxious smiles. A reflection of the kingdom's own mood, I knew.

At the far end of the table sat Aidrean Ó Deághaidh, now my senior commander of intelligence in Eastern Europe. I nodded in his direction. He flicked his eyes down to the papers before him and made a pretense of studying them. It had been a risk, summoning Aidrean from his post in Montenegro. I did not wish to alert any conspirators of our most recent correspondence.

(And there had been so many conspirators over the years. Madmen and opportunists. Intellectuals, such as Thomas Austen. Trusted men of my own cabinet, who proved more faithful to their ambitions than to Éire. Lord De Paor, in the Montenegro Affair, was one. And later, Lord Cleary, briefly minister of war, after Lord Mac Gioll's death.)

My steward poured a glass of watered wine for me. I drank it slowly and felt the ache from my shoulder ease. Coilín Mac Liam had taken his seat off to one side, his writing materials arranged and his pen filled with ink. When I judged that my audience had read enough of the reports, I set the goblet onto the table.

The faint chime of glass against marble brought instant silence.

"My lords," I said. "Gentlemen. As you can see, we've begun to receive suggestions from allies and friends about our proposed union."

Edged laughter met my remark. We had been deluged with various demands over the past five months. The several Mexica kingdoms each sought more representatives than the others. Frankonia insisted we address the growing problem of violence against Judaic groups throughout Europe and the Turkish States. The Prussian Alliance furiously rejected any such measure, stating that no body had the right to overstep a nation's border, unless that nation first acted outside justice and the law. Sahelia, Somalia, and Eritrea had lately reversed their earlier decisions and wished to attend the conference.

For the first two hours, we dealt with each subject, turn by turn, working out compromises where possible, and dictated the results to my secretary. A short interlude followed, with more substantial refreshments. Several murmured conversations rose up over goblets of wine or stronger spirits. Lord Ó Tíghearnaigh, my newly appointed minister of war, had collected Aidrean Ó Deághaidh and several other ministers and their aides in a corner. Judging from Aidrean's bland expression, Ó Tíghearnaigh was no doubt questioning him about his presence at this meeting.

As though I needed an excuse to consult my oldest and most trusted agent.

I summoned a servant to fill my glass with water, then took up the agenda to review the next page.

I paused, my hand gripping my glass.

The next topic concerned the security of our visitors, from kings and emperors to every member of their entourages. All three paragraphs were exactly as I had dictated them to my secretary, but on my copy there was a penciled notation in the margin: *The matter of Anglia.*

I knew the handwriting well—Lord Ó Duinn's. I lifted my gaze to find him watching me.

"A new topic?" I said.

"An old topic, Your Majesty, recently revived."

His voice was suitably nervous, but he did not flinch away from my stare.

"Very recent indeed," I said, "that you chose to introduce it to me in such a manner, and at such a time."

"Your Majesty, I did introduce it earlier. The Anglian delegation—"

"Demanded Thomas Austen's pardon. I gave them my answer with his execution."

"You did, Your Majesty, but the topic has altered itself somewhat."

His voice had risen. So had mine. Lord Ó Cadhla glanced sharply from Ó Duinn to me. Lord Ó Breislin's attention veered in our direction as well. Slowly I exhaled. However much I disliked Ó Duinn's trick—for a trick it was—a public quarrel would do neither of us any good.

"We shall discuss your topic tomorrow," I said to him. "In private."

"That is all I ask, Your Majesty."

I felt the rustle of attention settle around me, like leaves sifting into stillness after a sudden wind. Lord Ó Cadhla still watched me, as did Lord Ó Breislin. I turned my attention to the agenda and the remaining topics for the night.

It was not until midnight that Commander Ó Deághaidh was admitted by my steward to my offices, where I sat poring over the endless business of Éire.

"Sit," I told him. "I shall be done in a moment."

Aidrean nodded and took a seat by the fireplace. He carried a slim, leather-bound volume, and what appeared to be a motley collection of newspapers in Arabic script. Both newspapers and book were water stained, and the newspapers seemed especially ancient, with bits of paper and dust trailing behind as he crossed the room.

I signaled to my steward. Rian vanished through the door and returned with a flask of cold white wine, and another of water. He poured a glass for Aidrean while I scanned the most recent news from Londain. All was quiet, according to my agents. No explosions or fires or looting. The protesters had dispersed shortly after nightfall, discouraged by the sleet and the many gardaí stationed in the public squares. They could not guarantee it would remain so tomorrow.

"You are tired," Aidrean said. "We should meet another time."

"I am always tired," I said. "If I could, I would defy the dictates of science and the Church, and duplicate myself three times over."

He gave a rueful smile. "My domain is much smaller, and yet I often wish the same."

I knew what he spoke about, of course. Montenegro had recovered its independence, but Serbia continued to press for an advantage. And there was always the danger from Austria, however diminished, and the Turkish States, which were not. As senior commander for Éire's intelligence in Eastern Europe, Aidrean Ó Deághaidh oversaw a tangled network of agents, spies, informants, and other, less official observers, even while he maintained the fiction of running Éire's embassy for Montenegro.

Aidrean took only a sip from his wine before he set the glass aside and leaned back in his chair, eyes closed. I continued to skim the reports, but I was aware of his presence, as I always was. I noted the way his bones lay closer to the surface, the fine, milk-white lines, running like spiderwebs over his weathered face. He was older, so obviously older, than at our last meeting. I was sorry I had not summoned him back to Court years ago. No, to be truthful, I had. And he had politely refused.

Once I had finished, I laid a ribbon in the report to mark my place and joined Aidrean by the fire. "You mentioned troubling news."

"I did." He took up the book from the table. "Though *troubling* is far too faint a word."

He ran his fingers over the embossed lettering of the title, then pressed his thumb against the spine. A distinct click sounded, and the spine swiveled open to reveal a narrow cavity between the bound pages and the outer cover.

"The games of spies," I murmured.

"There is a reason for such a game," Aidrean replied. "But you will see in a moment."

He took a small flask from the cavity and held it up to the electric lamp.

The flask measured no more than the height and width of a man's thumb, and was filled with a clear liquid.

"A new explosive," he said. "This tiny amount could turn all of Osraighe into dust."

I stiffened. "And yet you took no precautions . . ."

"Not true. As a liquid, it's harmless. But let a few drops evaporate, then strike a match, and . . ."

He proceeded to give me the scientific details how the sub-stance worked. The liquid kept the true explosive inert, he said, which made its transportation a simple matter. Chemists in Prussia had experimented with the material, thinking to make a more effective bomb. The difficulty lay in the mechanism for striking a flame at the proper moment. "From what I understand," he said, "the substance has other, much more unusual qualities, but my sources have not proved as forthcoming on those points."

A new weapon, and the Prussians were already at work to ex-ploit its capabilities. My stomach clenched in horror. "Where did you acquire this?"

One corner of his long mouth tilted upward. "Through scraps of conversations overheard on the telephone exchange. Through visa requests from certain individuals wishing to enter Montene-gro, and others wishing to depart our borders. In short, all the usual sources."

I had not missed that inadvertent reference to *our borders*. Was that an indication of shifting loyalties? Possibly. Agents abroad were often required to pretend any number of contradictory al-legiances. Aidrean had lived ten years in Montenegro. His wife was a citizen of the country, formerly a dissident herself, and now a prominent member of the political community.

I set that suspicion to one side for today. "You believe this weapon poses a danger to my union."

"I cannot tell. I can only report its existence. The rest is for you to say."

"Hardly. But Aidrean, you are the one who requested this pri-vate meeting. Do you think then I should delay the conference? Cancel it altogether?" And then, I had to know. "Do you think I am wrong?"

It was a question spoken on impulse, borne of our former inti-macy, in the early days of my reign, when I could trust almost no one except him and Lord Ó Cadhla. I did not expect him to answer, but he nodded, his expression grave and contained, as though he were truly considering a proper response.

"You are not wrong," he said at last. "But you will find that even certain allies will oppose you. It can be a dangerous thing, wanting justice—true justice—in a world such as ours."

I had to smile, though it was a painful one. "My father spoke about the trap of idealism. I was never certain if he meant to warn me or direct me."

We were silent a while, both of us drinking our wine slowly. When Aidrean set his empty glass on the table, I refilled it. "Stay a while longer," I said. "As a favor to an old friend."

He relented, but not happily. A friend, but a troubled friend. I could accept that from him. I refilled my own glass and waited for him to speak.

"You asked me for a prediction of the future," he said at last. "That I cannot give you. But my instincts tell me that yes, those who oppose your union would use a weapon such as this one to gain their point."

Instincts. I had come to value them over the years.

"Would more guards help?" I asked. "A stronger army?" My minister of war constantly urged me to increase Éire's military. Perhaps he was right.

Aidrean shook his head. "Possibly. Or they might create the illusion of security, while nibbling away true liberty."

Not an argument I had expected from him. "You sound like one of Thomas Austen's followers."

He did not laugh, as I expected. But he did smile.

"I have no love for Thomas Austen. But there is some truth in what he and his followers say."

We spoke a while longer, about Cill Cannig and the changes in my cabinet, about his two daughters and his wife. Fifteen years had passed since my father died and I became queen. Aidrean Ó Deághaidh had served as my bodyguard and my friend in those early days, a gift I had not truly comprehended until I lost it. Later I had sent him to Montenegro. He had not only uncovered the treachery in my Court, he had undone a plot that might have plunged Europe into war.

And now? Now we were friends. A gift I deeply treasured.

And yet, I had not told him anything close to everything.

No mention of my need for an heir, that perpetual complaint from my ministers. Nor of the contentious state of Éire's Congress, which made each law, each debate, a matter for loud speeches and little action. It was this contentious state, I believed, that had led to the attempt to suborn my last favorite, and through him, Lord Cleary. Both had died by private assassination, a signal to others.

Nothing at all about Breandan Ó Cuilinn, my first true favorite, who had vanished one bright autumn day while investigating the subject of time and its fractures.

An hour later, Aidrean took his leave and departed for the suite of rooms assigned to him. Before he left, we arranged another private interview, ten days from now. He would spend the interval reacquainting himself with the Court, and conferring with the Queen's Constabulary about this new and deadly weapon. I wanted no accidents with my conference this summer.

I waited until I was certain Aidrean had crossed into the visitors' wing. Only then did I set off on my own nightly excursion, one that had become increasingly necessary over the years. With my guards trailing discreetly behind, I passed from the Royal Enclosure, through the many public rooms in the central quadrant, and into the far reaches of the palace, to a series of empty, dusty rooms, never used since a certain day twelve years before.

I paused outside the set of double doors. Here the electric lamps flickered, as though tossed by winds beyond the natural world. My heart caught in a stitch. An old habit, I told myself.

Only the past lingered inside the room before me. And yet, I came here night after night, to visit the dead.

I signaled for my guards to remain in the corridor, and passed inside alone.

No electric lamps burned here. There was only the faint glow from outside. By that uncertain light, I progressed through the empty spaces, which were interrupted here and there by old broken crates, a dust-covered worktable, a few crumbs of the past represented by discarded papers or other detritus left between two opposing time streams.

Once Breandan Ó Cuilinn had demonstrated his time machine to me in this chamber. Months after the time fractures healed, stealing my memories, I had discovered the report of its workings, which he had sent into the future.

I abandoned you.

Not that I had any choice. No, that was not correct. I had the choice—between rescuing my beloved and leaving a dozen others dead. Even if I had undone the past, I had no assurance of mending the future.

As though my thoughts had summoned it, a scrap of mist, like a scrap of white lace, floated downward from the ceiling. A moment passed. Another drifted toward me and joined with the first. And another. One by one, they gathered into a larger mass, which gradually took on the shape of a man, its form writhing in an invisible, intangible wind. Bits of the figure detached themselves and flickered off into nothing, but the shape never diminished in size. Indeed, the longer I watched, the larger it grew until it loomed over me.

I tilted my head back. The figure hovered inches away above me, its face a blank mask.

My ghost.

As with every other encounter, the face changed as I watched.

Specks and shadows and gaps whirled around until the blankness was replaced by features—features that I recognized.

Breandan Ó Cuilinn looked down at me. His lips moved rapidly, as though he urgently wished to tell me something. But when I reached upward, the ghost vanished into a whirl of dust.

The early editions of the Osraighe and Londain newspapers reported in lurid detail about Thomas Austen's execution, with altogether too many references to blood spattered over freshly fallen snow, and how the queen had fled the courtyard well before the body had been examined and wrapped in its cotton shroud. No mention of the bitter cold, or the wound Austen himself had inflicted on me. No mention of the guards who had died protecting their queen. There was one blurred and grainy photograph of a black-clad figure lying on the snow-covered ground, with soldiers stationed around. Judging by the angle and direction of the image, the photographer had been positioned on one of the surrounding rooftops, which in turn meant bribes offered and taken, and another round of investigations.

And so my mood was already dark and irritable when my secretary admitted Lord Ó Duinn for our private interview. A few steps behind came Lord Ó Cadhla. I eyed them both narrowly. "Did you conspire together, or is your appearance here, at this hour, mere happenstance?"

Lord Ó Duinn protested, but Lord Ó Cadhla merely shrugged. "The fault is mine, Your Majesty," he said. "I persuaded Lord Ó Duinn to arrange this meeting."

"Did you persuade him to use trickery as well? Never mind. I know you did. Sit, both of you. You are too old to be so troublesome," I added to Ó Cadhla.

Ó Cadhla laughed, a soft wheezing laugh that reminded me of

Lord Mac Gioll in his later years. "Would you rather I retired from Court and spent my days poking and prodding at my grand-children?"

"I would," I said. "They would not thank me, but I hardly care for their thanks."

He laughed again. "I am old. And I've abandoned the diplo-matic path for one more direct. So. Let me confess that I pro-voked and persuaded Lord Ó Duinn to request the interview, then to include me. Let me further state that you must meet with the Anglian delegation, no matter how much you dislike the idea."

A conspiracy of virtue, I thought bitterly.

We took our seats around the fireplace, which the servants had built fresh. Outside the skies were gray and sleet speckled the windows. My steward served us with coffee and tea and a selection of fresh pastries. I accepted a cup of strong coffee and waited while the others were served. Once we were alone, I nod-ded at Ó Duinn to speak.

"You knew I had already refused this delegation's demands. And you knew my reasons for doing so. Now you advise me to ignore my instincts in the matter."

"Not at all," he said. "We only suggest you might find another meeting instructive."

"How so? I've heard their petition before. What else can they demand?"

"It's not the specifics of what they demand," Ó Cadhla said. "It's a matter of hearing the intent behind their words."

A mystery, then. Ó Cadhla knew I disliked mysteries. I espe-cially disliked being maneuvered and manipulated. If this had been any other minister . . .

But it was not. Once more I reminded myself of Lord Ó Cadh-la's long service to my father and to me. He wished me to grant this interview, and he wished me to draw my own conclusions. His reasons would be good, at least by his lights.

So I quietly drank my coffee, while I considered their advice. I set aside my own prejudices as well as I could, even as I remembered past interviews and past petitions from the Anglians, all of which had ended in impossible demands. While I considered Aidrean Ó Deághaidh's words of the night before.

I have no love for Thomas Austen, but there is some truth in what he and his followers say.

"Very well," I said at last. "I shall do as you ask."

And let us hope I do not regret it.

The audience was set for three o'clock that afternoon, in the largest of my audience halls. It would be conducted with strict attention to protocol, I had told my chamberlain. If these Anglians and their fellow representatives wished me to acknowledge their status, they would certainly be reminded of mine. And so I dressed with particular care, choosing the most formal of my gowns and the crown I wore only for state occasions. Between the heavy cloth and the weight of my jewels, I felt like a stuffed doll, but one stuffed with purpose, at least.

As I entered the hall, the chamberlain pounded his staff on the tiled floor. "Her Majesty, Queen of Éire and all her Dependencies."

The size of the hall was enormous, the audience, less so. The delegation itself consisted of two dozen men, six from each District. Beyond them, standing in the alcoves to either side, or seated in the nearest rows of benches, were the usual courtiers, gossips and curiosity seekers. No doubt there would be reporters from the various newspapers, as well. After yesterday's execution of a famous Anglian dissident, today's unexpected audience with that same dissident's followers was an unexpected treat. But between the short notice and echoing expanse, their number appeared far smaller.

I took the throne and settled my gown, while the chamberlain called out the names and titles of the delegation and ordered them to come forward and make their obeisance to their queen.

"We have no queen," a voice called out.

I glanced up sharply. Silence fell over the hall at once.

So, a challenge.

I scanned the faces before me, trying to pick out who had spoken. One of the delegation, obviously. They were the usual motley collection of elderly dissidents, angry young recruits to the cause, and others who clearly had no other occupation. The chamberlain was shouting for order, but I silenced him with a gesture. "I am Queen of Éire. Do you dispute that?"

"No. But Éire is not Anglia. Nor Wight, nor Manx, nor Cymru. We are not children, nor are we unthinking beasts. You have no right to govern any of us."

Thomas Austen's words, in a tract he had published a week before he attempted to murder me. Silently, I cursed Lord Ó Cadhla and Lord Ó Duinn for persuading me into this useless audience. Out loud, I said, "Those are borrowed words, spoken with a coward's tongue. Show yourself, whoever you are."

"We are not cowards," said another voice.

A young man stepped from the midst of his fellow delegates. He was younger than the rest, his clothing of good quality, though plain in design. He was dark complected, like many Anglians from the port cities, with thick springy hair, cut close to his head. His expression was far more contained than that of his colleagues.

"Your Majesty of Éire," he said. "We are none of us cowards, whatever you believe. We are here to give voice to our people. Will you listen to us?"

Delicately and honestly spoken.

"Very well," I said. "What is your name?"

"My name is Michael Okoye."

Now I remembered the report from my secretary. Michael Okoye was the descendent of a wealthy Nri house in West Africa. Okoye's great-grandfather, Ikem Okoye, had sent three of his sons abroad to Frankonia, Anglia, and the Western Continent to oversee their growing trade concerns. I wondered how his descendant had come to join the Anglian cause.

"Tell me your petition, Mister Okoye."

Before he could answer, however, one of the older men shouldered his colleagues aside and came to the front of the crowd. "We have more than a simple petition to present," he said. "We've come with an ultimatum."

My secretary bent to whisper a reminder in my ear. This was Peter Godwin, the senior member of this delegation. I had encountered him once before, when he demanded Thomas Austen's pardon. The breath fled my body for a moment, in astonishment at his audacity. A rush of whispers echoed through the chamber.

"Tell me this ultimatum," I said softly.

"That we be given representation at this Union of Nations—a seat for each District."

Meaning, a declaration of their status as independent states.

"And if I do not grant this request?"

"Then we will ask again," he said.

"And again," said another.

"And again," Michael Okoye said. "We will continue to ask, until you admit yourself wrong to keep us as bonded servants to your empire."

"And if I never do?"

"Then we shall do more than ask," said Peter Godwin.

"They have declared war," I said to Lord Ó Duinn. "War. And you advised me to listen."

"It was necessary for you to see and hear for yourself, Your Majesty," he replied. "To understand that we cannot ignore the Anglian question any longer."

We spoke in quiet undertones, our faces fixed in expressions of polite interest as we watched the bare dirt field where the Éireann war department would present its newest aeroplanes for the queen's inspection. Ships and armies and the occasional balloon fleet had served to defend us for many years, but Lord Ó Tíghearnaigh had introduced these new machines, saying that Éire faced a new century and new enemies. If our Union of Nations did not succeed, we would need new weapons to defend ourselves.

"Now I have heard this petition, what do you advise?" I said.

Despite my effort to speak softly, my anger leaked into my voice. Lord Ó Duinn, however, did not balk. "Invite the delegation to stay," he said. "Grant them a second interview, in private, to discuss their request—"

"I cannot consider—"

"No," he said firmly. "You cannot. But I suspect Peter Godwin does not wish you to. He spoke to provoke you into tyranny—to make Thomas Austen's case for violence. If you grant them the grace of further conversation, they cannot later argue that diplomatic means had failed."

One of the new aeroplanes rumbled from its hangar onto the square field. Its nose was a rounded snub of iron gray, its wings little more than two thin wafers of steel on each side, connected by wires. Six other machines of like construction followed to form a short line before the royal grandstand. The first accelerated its motor, a deep-throated rumble that spoke of power kept in check.

"You believe they have the capacity to attack?" I asked.

"Not that. Or rather, not them alone. What I believe is—"

A roar, like that of a hunting lion, shivered the air as the first aeroplane surged forward over the track. It bumped and jolted, then gathered speed to cast up clouds of dust, so that I only saw the upper half of the plane with its pilot and companion, and two men stationed in a second row of seats. Lord Ó Tíghearnaigh was now explaining in an excited undertone how the aeroplane was equipped with guns and bombs both.

The first plane launched into the air. The second had begun its race down the concourse. A ground crew hurried between each of the remaining machines. Lord Ó Tíghearnaigh continued to speak of the advantages of aeroplanes over ordinary balloons. He had just begun to describe how they could work in parallel with our ground defenses when the air exploded.

Several things happened at once. A great wind struck me in the face. I fell to the ground amidst a chaos of broken chairs. From all around came the roar of voices, then the crackle of gunfire and yet another explosion. The air stank of diesel fuel and a strange electric scent that called up old memories, old terrors. My father calling out, *Áine! Run! Hide!*

Before I could regain my feet, a body landed atop me, driving the breath from my lungs. I slithered free, coughing and gasping for air. Another explosion rocked the viewing stand. I lurched forward and tried to brace myself. My hand came in contact with cold doughy flesh—Lord Ó Duinn. He lay sprawled in the wreckage, his eyes wide, his gaze fixed and unnatural.

A third explosion echoed from the airfield, another scorching wave rolled above us. Now I caught the scent of blood and burning human flesh. Lord Ó Duinn's body twitched. He struggled against me.

"—Majesty—"

I could barely hear the words—my ears felt muffled as though we were buried in dirt. When a man seized my wrists, I struggled to break free. He hauled me to my feet and I saw his face.

"Aidrean!" I shouted. "What has happened?"

Aidrean Ó Deághaidh shouted back, but I could not make out his words. He glanced around and signaled to someone else nearby. I was bundled away from the exhibition field and though a pair of nearby doors into a large empty building. This had to be one of the hangars for the aeroplanes. I jerked back, my thoughts tangling together the aeroplanes and explosions, but Aidrean gripped my arm tighter and half-dragged me through the doors.

"Stop!" I said.

He stopped.

My knees felt watery. I placed both hands on his chest to steady myself. Fresh blood trickled over my eyes. More injuries made themselves known to me. Bruises. A myriad of cuts and scrapes, some of them inflicted by Aidrean Ó Deághaidh as he dragged me to safety. From a distance, I heard the muffled boom of a fourth explosion.

"They promised me war," I whispered. "I should have listened."

We met in my private chambers within the hour: I, Lord Ó Duinn, Lord Ó Cadhla, Commander Ábraham of the Queen's Constabulary, and Lord Ó Breislin. My private physician hovered in the background. I had ordered him away, but he had refused, a measure of his concern. In the end, I allowed him to stay. My ministers might require his services if I could not cure my temper.

I drank down the concoction of opiates and strong coffee that he had prescribed, much against his will. Later, I might submit to his care, but not until I had dealt with this crisis. The opiates eased my throat, raw from the smoke and all the shouting I had not realized I had done.

"Arrest them all," I said to Commander Ábraham. "The entire delegation."

"On what charges?" Lord Ó Cadhla's tone was deceptively mild.

"Treason and murder, of course."

We had proof enough. Two planes destroyed, their crews torn into bits by the explosions. Another half dozen trampled in the ensuing panic.

(And yet, I remembered four explosions, not two. And Lord Ó Duinn lying dead in the wreckage.)

A soft knock sounded at the door. Coilín Mac Liam rose from his station and admitted Aidrean Ó Deághaidh into the room.

"Your Majesty," he said. "I have news to report."

All my ministers fixed their attention on him as he took a chair, refusing a glass of whiskey and taking instead a tumbler of water. He had changed his clothes, but I caught the whiff of burning ashes about his person.

"What have you found?" I asked.

"A mountain of clues, but nothing conclusive."

"How, not conclusive?" I said.

He held up hand. "Please, Your Majesty. Let me tell you what I know first. I've had but an hour to consult with the Constabulary and Lord Ó Duinn's people. However, I can say the explosives are similar to those I've encountered among certain dissidents in Eastern Europe."

He spoke with a particular emphasis that caught my attention at once. "Indeed? Then you have found a link between them?"

"Perhaps. Certain factions are known to work with each other. Before we make any assumptions, however, we must search for the motives behind today's attack. Once we know those, we shall know if such a link exists."

I leaned back in my chair. "So. Not our own Anglians?"

"Possibly. I cannot reason ahead of my information, Your Majesty."

"Nor did I ask you to."

"Not directly," he said.

I sucked in a breath. All my ministers, including Lord Ó Cadhla, went still in expectation of my forthcoming rant. Ó Deághaidh himself regarded me with a remote expression that cloaked whatever he truly thought. The same he had used in times past, when I first ordered him away from Court to investigate the Awveline murders, when I sent him to Montenegro.

He has never betrayed me. Even though I have betrayed him.

I let the air trickle from my lungs. "So. Give me your advice, Commander. What would you do in this situation?"

All around me the tension eased. Aidrean smiled, but absently, as though he had expected the question. "If I were to suggest anything, Your Majesty, I would advise you to meet with the Anglian delegation once more, and let them know you cannot properly address their concerns at the present. However, invite them to appoint several of their number to remain at Court so you might informally continue the conversation. They cannot refuse you, not without losing their own political advantage. At the same time . . ."

"I gain a hostage or two. Yes, I see."

Aidrean opened his mouth as if to respond, then shook his head. "Meanwhile, I shall continue my investigation. Unless you prefer to leave the matter entirely with the Queen's Constabulary."

That was a delicate matter.

"Lord Ó Duinn," I said. "Commander Ábraham. You will both confer with Commander Ó Deághaidh today. Include Lord Ó Cadhla or whomever else you deem necessary to the investigation. Is there anything else you would share with us?" I said to Aidrean.

"Not at the present time, Your Majesty."

Our glances met. I sensed that he had edited certain details from his report. Either he did not trust my ministers, or he did not trust me.

"What is it?" I demanded.

The bells had struck midnight. It was only in the past hour that I had successfully dismissed my physician, promising to follow his instructions for rest and solitude. I had lied.

"I cannot tell yet," Aidrean replied. "I need another week, or more, to discover the truth."

"Meanwhile?"

The question of the Anglians hovered between us.

"You should do as your conscience suggests," he said.

A useless reply, except I knew Aidrean Ó Deághaidh and I knew our history together. He would not insist. He would only hint and suggest, leaving the final decision to me.

Because I was the queen. Because I held my honor dear.

The following day, I sent word through my secretary to the Anglian delegation—a message most politely phrased and written on the finest vellum—saying that matters of state would not allow me to grant them the attention they deserved. We would certainly discuss the matter within the next month, I added. Until then, they should appoint a single representative to remain at Cill Cannig to speak for their cause.

"A hostage," Aidrean Ó Deághaidh said. He used the same word I had, the day before.

"A representative," I replied. "One of their own choosing."

We had met again over breakfast. *Discretion be damned,* I thought. News of yesterday's attack had overrun Court and beyond. The papers in Osraighe carried accounts from several witnesses. The less reputable newssheets also displayed lurid photographs of bodies among the wreckage. Soon enough the reports would spread to the Continent.

Nine pilots and their crew murdered. A dozen more in grave condition. The stink of blood and burning gasoline forever imprinted on my memory.

And yet, the blood of Thomas Austen does not trouble you.

"I will not arrest them without proof," I continued. "But I cannot ignore their threat."

He tilted his hand to one side. "Agreed. I would only mention that an indefinite invitation is little better than an indefinite arrest."

I smiled, somewhat wearily. "Your absence from Court has made you blunt. Not that Lord Ó Cadhla and Lord Ó Breislin are gentle with me."

"We are blunt because we love you."

My breath stilled within me. I knew what he meant, but it had been many years since anyone had used the word *love* in my presence.

"Tell me the latest news," I said.

The faint lines etched across his face deepened. "Several details have emerged since we last spoke. Or rather, details that contradict details several times over, all of them from reliable witnesses . . ." He stopped and chafed one hand inside the other—a sure signal of his troubled mind. "It's a matter of time. Of time fractures."

Oh, oh, and now the cold did flow through my body. Time fractures. I hated the day I first heard mention of them. Time fractures had lured Breandan Ó Cuilinn into a fate unknown. They had murdered a dozen or more students from Awveline University, then restored them to life once the fractures healed. Aidrean Ó Deághaidh had spent nearly two years trapped in madness because of them.

"How many explosions did you count yesterday?" I asked.

"Six."

"I counted four."

"The official reports, what I can confirm, have the number at three."

"And the dead?"

"Nine or thirteen, depending on which witnesses you believe." There came the barest hesitation before he added, "One man claims a hundred died."

The catch in his voice warned me there was more than a simple anomaly of numbers. "What else? Tell me, Aidrean. What else did that report say?"

Reluctantly, his lifted his gaze to mine. "It was a single report, from a member of the ground crew. He insists that all ten planes were destroyed. He also claims that a dozen more explosions crushed the reviewing stands and turned them into dust and ashes. He says . . . He says he saw you die."

Now I understood his hesitation.

"That vial you showed me," I whispered.

"Might be connected, yes. We shall have to conduct experiments."

"Do it," I said. "Once we know, we can proceed with our investigation."

The Queen's Constabulary chose a remote gorge to the south-west for their experiment, miles away from any farms or villages. Little grew on the rocky slopes, and near the midpoint, the gorge narrowed so that its cliffs loomed directly over the floor. A crude means to contain the blast, Aidrean told me later, as he recounted the many details and emotions absent from the Constabulary's dry account.

Commander Ábraham himself directed the operation, with

Aidrean at his side. That afternoon, they selected the site for the experiment, and the men cleared a path from the edge of the gorge through the underbrush and into the trees. Dusk had fallen before they had finished, and the first stars had popped into view against the violet sky.

Aidrean added a single droplet of the liquid to cotton wadding, then inserted the material in a sealed metal tube, from which protruded a length of slow-burning cord. He handed the device to another of Ábraham's agents, then took his position a half mile away at the observation post, where the gorge veered west and he and the commander had a clear view of the target site. A freezing rain had fallen earlier in the day. The air was brittle with cold, and laden with the scent of pine and snow.

He gave the signal, a flash from a lantern. The agent struck a match to light the cord, then hurled the device over the side of the cliff. From his observation point, Aidrean saw the bright speck of the burning cord arcing through the darkness, the jerk and jump from the agent's lantern as he sprinted away from the cliff. Both vanished from sight, and for one moment, Aidrean was convinced, he told me, that their experiment had failed.

Then a white flash illuminated the night.

The air went taut. The stars went dark. Reappeared.

Soft exclamations broke out amongst the other agents. From below came the faint rill of the stream, and farther on, the yip of a hunting fox, as though nothing had touched the gorge. Still Aidrean waited, counting softly to himself. *A haon, a dó, a trí . . .*

He had just reached a thousand when an explosion split the darkness and rocked the earth.

Time, time, time. Time was an illusion, according to certain modern philosophers.

Those from the older traditions spoke of the time roads, which allowed the adept to travel into the future or the past. The modern world called those beliefs mysticism, but there were elements of science that those in the past would have called fantasy.

"They have found a way to send their weapons into the future," I said. "But who has that ability? And why attack us?"

"I suspect the Serbian contingent," Ó Deághaidh said. "But I cannot be certain."

"Them or the Austrians," Ó Breislin added. "Neither has forgiven us for the Montenegro affair."

"Do not forget the wider world," Ó Cadhla said softly. "Too often, we forget the nations beyond our borders and that of Europe. I doubt the Mexica nations are involved, but there are the Turkish States and the Russian principalities, none of them peaceful."

No one mentioned the Anglians, but they did not need to.

"Finding the guilty will be your responsibility," I told the chief of the Queen's Constabulary. "Commander Ó Deághaidh will serve as your liaison and adviser. Consider this affair as one of extreme political delicacy, but do not hesitate to act if you must. I want no accidents at my conference this summer. Meanwhile, I shall conduct an investigation of my own."

Twelve hours later, I waited anxiously in the smallest and most richly appointed of my audience chambers. My father and grandfather had preferred this chamber for highly honored guests, or the most delicate negotiations. Both terms applied to today's interview, I thought. Gwen and Síomón Madóc had become famous in academia for their theories involving mathematics and time. Twelve years ago, they had founded a research institute to investigate the practical and arcane applications of their discoveries. They were ambitious, though not in the usual fashion—that much I knew from my reports from the Queen's Constabulary.

But I had other memories to draw upon. A series of murders in Awveline City, involving graduate students in the mathematics department. A past erased and rewritten, with those dead come alive and other events altered beyond recognition.

While I waited, I adjusted the curtains, examined the rows of carafes with water and tea. A late winter snowfall hushed against the windowpanes. The new mechanical clock on the mantelpiece ticked loudly and incessantly. *Time, time, time,* it said. *Time was not the immutable property you once thought it to be.*

A discreet knock sounded at my door. I spun around, the skirts of my gown hissing.

"Doctor Síomón Madóc."

The photographs provided by the Constabulary proved misleading, I thought, as I clasped his hand and gestured toward the chairs. The gray and white image had shown a long bony face, the hair cut close except for a few curling wisps over his black doctoral robes. They had revealed nothing of his height, or how his gaze alternated between distracted and keenly observant. Today, he wore a gray suit of an elegant cut.

He bowed over my hand and took the designated seat.

"Doctor Gwen Madóc."

Gwen Madóc had the same spare features as her brother, the same pale blonde hair. But here the photographs were true, perhaps because these had been obtained when the subject was unaware. Her blue eyes met mine in an unflinching gaze, before she sank into a curtsy. Like her brother, she wore the kind of clothing one expected from a member of a wealthy, privileged family.

"Your Majesty. You have a problem with time fractures," she said in a low voice.

My breath stilled. Not a question. A direct statement.

"Yes. How did you know?"

She shrugged. "It's a question of probability and our special-ized knowledge."

Indeed. Yet she had spoken with more certainty than a simple guess would have indicated. I would have to take care with these two. To my secretary, who hovered in the background, I said, "You may go, Coilín. I shall ring when I need you."

My steward poured tea, and retired. Brother and sister sipped politely while I considered once more how to explain the matter. But it was Gwen Madóc who broke the silence first. "You wished for a consultation, Your Majesty. We are willing to offer whatever assistance we can, but I must warn you that we are scientists, not magicians. We cannot scribble an equation and undo the past."

"I would not expect it," I said. "I was hoping to undo the future."

That arrested her attention, and her brother's, too.

"What has happened?" she demanded.

I told them, giving as much details as I dared. The explosions. The confusion. The contradiction between my memories and the later reports of those who had survived. The even more un-settling reports from those who had seemingly died, yet never-theless reappeared alive and untouched.

Síomón closed his eyes and listened, his mouth drawn into a thin line. Gwen let her gaze drift upward to the ceiling with its patterns etched in plaster and paint. When I mentioned the dis-crepancies between one report and the next, her brother twitched, but she did not.

"You believe they have achieved mastery of time?" Gwen asked.

"I don't know," I said. "I only know they threaten us all—Éire, Anglia, and everyone throughout the world—with chaos."

"And what do you wish from us?"

I had spent much of the past day considering how to phrase the request. What I wanted, after all, was such a nebulous thing.

"I want the opportunity for peace," I said softly. "Not just for myself and my queendom, but for the world. I told you I wanted to change the future, but not with weapons or armies. For that I must know which decisions are the right ones. The best ones. That is my wish."

Wish. A word chosen from dreams and intentions both, but Gwen Madóc did not smile at my words. "You need us to investigate the future," she said. "To see where the time roads lead."

"Yes," I said. "But all of them, you understand."

She held out a hand. I clasped hers in mine, wondering at her strong grip, the chilled flesh, the strange intent gaze she lifted to mine.

"I understand," she said. "More than most."

I gave them the same suite of rooms that Breandan Ó Cuilinn had once occupied, twelve years ago. And like that previous, that once innocent time, I never questioned their demands. They brought truckloads of their own equipment. I supplied them with clerks, equipment, reams of paper, and the newest mechanical calculators for their research. Aidrean Ó Deághaidh did not approve of their presence—there was a curious tension between him and Síomón Madóc—but he never openly objected, and after a few days, even that first tension had vanished.

"What do you think?" I asked him.

"I don't know."

"You always know."

His mouth flickered into an all-too-brief smile. The crease remained even after the humor had left his face. It made me think of shadows, and a time when I had once trusted, and loved, and laughed.

———

Three weeks passed in a strange and oppressive calm. Throughout the day, I conducted all my ordinary duties as queen. I continued with the plans for my Union of Nations, with over thirty
countries to attend our first session in August, which was to be
held in a new hall outside Osraighe. Over dinner and through
the evening, I met with Commander Ábraham from the Queen's
Constabulary, or with Aidrean Ó Deághaidh and Lord Ó Duinn,
whose investigations had proved frustrating.

"My agents have kept watch over the members of the delegation," Ó Duinn replied when I asked. "Without exception, they
have all returned to their ordinary lives. Merchants. Professors.
Booksellers. Physicians. Unless they have constructed a series of
secret tunnels underneath the streets of Londain, they conduct
their daily affairs in public and remain at home during the night."

"We've considered the possibility of their passing messages to
each other," Aidrean said. "Our people have intercepted all their
letters, but the contents have proved annoyingly mundane. The
Constabulary has assigned a cipher team to examine them, just
in case."

"What about our guest?" I said. "Has the great Peter Godwin
resigned himself to his quarters?" In the days immediately after
the disaster on the airfield, I had dismissed my so-called guest
from my thoughts, but now I thought it curious that Godwin had
not inundated me with demands.

Ó Duinn glanced up from his sheaf of notes. "I thought I had
mentioned in my reports—No, Godwin returned to the Dependencies along with the others. It is Michael Okoye who remained
behind. He's a quiet young man. He spends his days writing—
letters, poetry, for the most part. They tell me he has a talent in
that direction."

I gave an exhalation of surprise. "Okoye. I would not have
expected—Why did they choose him, do you suppose?"

"I suppose nothing, Your Majesty," Aidrean said. "Not even

that Godwin and his associates are guilty. We know of a dozen organizations outside the Districts who are addicted to violence."

"Not to mention Thomas Austen's more radical followers," Ó Duinn added. "And they would have nothing to do with anything as diplomatic as petitions or delegations. The puzzling thing is that none have the funds or the connections to create such a device. Or so we believe."

A complicated set of puzzles, I agreed. Letters that meant nothing. Dissidents who seem to have given over their activities. And a young man writing poetry while he waited for release from his richly appointed captivity.

My meetings with Síomón and Gwen Madóc were less fraught, but ultimately just as frustrating. They had mapped the time fractures around the airfield and discovered key differences between them and the ones Breandan Ó Cuilinn had described in his research.

Accidental is the word Síomón used to describe the older fractures. Just as there were faults in the Earth's crust, there were natural cracks in the fabric of time. The causes for the original fractures were yet unknown, but Gwen had a theory connecting the fractures with upheavals in the far, far past. "As the universe expanded, worlds might have replicated themselves, much as cells do, but as they separated, they weakened the fabric of time."

"But these are different," I said.

"Very much so," Gwen said. "The term I would apply here is *deliberate*."

"How can you tell?"

"We've measured the patterns of activity. Electrical and radioactive readings generally signal the presence of time fractures. We compare those readings with ones from our own devices.

Those around the airfield and the experiment your Constabulary conducted are far too regular, compared to the accidental ones."

"But why?" I said.

I later said the same to Aidrean Ó Deághaidh.

"Perhaps it was meant to frighten us," I said.

"Perhaps it was an experiment," he replied.

The second attack came an hour past midnight, on a cold clear March night.

My secretary roused me from sleep. Aidrean Ó Deághaidh was only a few steps behind. He delivered his report while I drank the strong tea my steward provided. "A single attack using three devices," Aidrean was saying. "Two others we cannot confirm. You understand the difficulty."

"I understand." I thrust the mug back into my steward's hands. "More tea for us both. And water." To Aidrean, I said, "Continue. And tell me everything, even the uncertainties."

The account was chilling. Three more devices had been set in the harbor district of Loch Garman, a port city on the Éireann Sea. The explosions had killed two dozen dockworkers and sailors. Several dozen more had been more gravely injured by falling debris and the fires that broke out in the warehouses, and on board the ships closest to the explosion.

"We have also received a message," Aidrean said.

My heart paused, then stumbled on at a faster pace.

"From whom?" I demanded. "The Anglians?"

He hesitated and glanced around my bedchamber. With a gesture, I dismissed my maids and secretary and steward. Once they had gone, I repeated, "Tell me. What did the message say?"

Aidrean blew out a breath. He was shaken—truly shaken—a thing I had believed to be impossible. "The reports are incomplete.

However, this much I know. An officer discovered a letter nailed to the door of the main Garda station in Osraighe." He paused and licked his lips. "The letter was addressed to you."

"Ah." I found my own breath not so steady.

"It accused you of tyranny. It said there could be no true Union of Nations, while you held other nations in bondage. It then said that Éire herself would pay in blood and fire and tears that night for your actions. We telegraphed all the chief stations throughout the kingdom, but we were too late. . . ."

He rubbed a hand over his eyes.

"You had no way to know," I said.

"I did, and I did not," he replied. "We knew about these new devices. We had word of disaffected groups throughout Éire and all four Districts. We had spies wherever we could place them. But Áine . . . Your Majesty. We cannot police every citizen of Éire and its Dependencies. And to speak honestly, I should not want to hear you give such an order. I do not want to witness here what I have in Austria and the Prussian Alliance, where safety *has* become an excuse for tyranny."

He smiled, a faint and pensive smile. "Perhaps I am no longer suited for your service."

"You are," I said softly. "Because you are honest with me."

That smile flickered into life again, only to fade just as quickly. The electric light was not kind to his features—the angles of his face seemed thinner and sharper, the shadows deeper, and the impression of the flesh worn away to bones was even stronger than before. He had come to me old; the past month had made him older still. Older and more weary.

When have I not seen him so?

Not since our first interview, fifteen years ago.

This was no moment for such memories. "Tell me about these other explosions. Or rather, these ghosts of explosions. Were they failed attempts, do you think?"

I had to wait a long moment before he answered. When he did speak at last, his tone was curiously hesitant. "I don't know. The reports came from Osraighe. Several were quite specific—they listed the buildings destroyed, the names of the dead and wounded. Even more convincing, the reports gave details only a genuine witness would think to include. How they tried to call for help, but could hear nothing because the explosion had left them deaf and confused. The gardaí taking notes commented that their anger was most convincing. And yet, when our people dispatched forces to the site, they found no destruction, no one harmed— nothing out of the ordinary. My agents believe the reports to be deliberate mischief, an attempt by the rebels to sow further confusion."

"But you do not."

"I do not. I visited the site myself. It reminded me . . ." His gaze took on a diffuse quality. "It reminded me of the aftermath of that device in Montenegro. The explosion itself was terrible enough, but what truly frightened me was how I felt myself unanchored from time."

He did not speak of that other, even earlier episode, when his memories had wandered through a past that no longer existed. We had all become unanchored, if only temporarily, while history altered its shape as the time fractures healed.

"There is another difficulty," Aidrean said. "Peter Godwin has vanished. I telegraphed our agents in Londain to obtain a statement from him. He was last sighted entering a trolley car bound for the north end of the city. This was yesterday morning."

The anger and fright had leached away by now, and I had a clear picture of what I might do. "Arrest Michael Okoye. He must know Godwin's plans. Put him in one of the cells in the palace, not the ordinary prison. You and I shall question him together."

"He might be innocent," Aidrean said.

"He might be." But my thoughts were on Éire and not my unwilling guest. "Send word to my ministers and your chief agents," I said. "We shall meet early in the morning to plan our course. Meanwhile, I must see where this phantom attack took place. Then I shall go to the hospital in Loch Garman to visit the wounded. No, do not argue, Aidrean. I cannot have the Anglians say I hid in safety while my people died."

I sent him away while I hurriedly dressed, but as soon as he had issued the necessary orders to his people, Aidrean returned, saying he must and would accompany me.

"You have never given over your post as my personal guard," I said.

He made an impatient gesture with one hand. "It is my duty. Just as it is my duty to insist you remain at Cill Cannig, Your Majesty. It's possible the Anglians set those devices in Osraighe as a trap. Your death would make a gift of confusion to our enemies."

"I must," I repeated. "I must go, Commander."

He gave over arguing, but I could sense his reluctance all through the ride from Cill Cannig to Osraighe. Perhaps he knew me too well to continue his objections. Or perhaps we had once more resumed our roles as queen and minion, and not friend and friend.

The church bells were ringing two o'clock when we arrived at our destination. A dozen guards stood watch in the square. My own took their positions around me as I walked the circuit. Our footsteps echoed from the paving stones, and the air continued to vibrate from the clangor of bells, but the night was otherwise quiet and still. The sharp cold of winter had softened with the approach of spring, and even in this city square, there came the hint of green growing things. A full moon shone overhead, casting shadows ahead of me.

I knew the square well—it was one of the wealthier districts inhabited by the directors of Éire's banking concerns, certain influential members of Éire's Congress, and various heads of the great merchant and trade houses. With one terrible weapon, the Anglian rebels could destroy much of Éire's economy and government.

At the northern edge of the square, I paused. Why had this attack failed? Or were these reports, and even my commander's impressions, merely the product of terror itself?

I turned back toward Aidrean . . .

. . . the ground underneath me tilted. I fell backward into a deep pit. My guards had vanished. Torn bodies surrounded me, the earth was soaked in their blood. I tried to scrabble upward through the mass of dead, but the flesh dissolved into a mist between my fingers . . .

I staggered backward. Aidrean Ó Deághaidh caught and steadied me. My vision had blurred and it seemed the stars and moon had shifted in the sky. "Aidrean," I whispered. "Did you see?"

"I did. Look again, Your Majesty. Look."

I looked.

And saw a quiet moonlit square untouched by violence.

But in the air, I felt the breath and whisper of the future.

We proceeded to Loch Garman in the motorcar. Within a few miles of the coast, I could see the blood-red glimmer of the fires. By the time we reached the city walls, the air was thick with smoke and ashes. We passed through broad avenues lined by dark houses, then looped around King's Street to the harbor itself. As we approached the site where the device had exploded, we passed squads of gardaí, wagons carrying away debris, and others transporting the injured to hospitals. Hundreds of lanterns illuminated the harbor walls, casting an uncanny light over the wrecked ships and shattered buildings, which continued to burn.

Osraighe's vision made real, I thought.

"Have you seen enough?" Aidrean asked me.

"Not yet," I replied, though a heavy knot had lodged beneath my heart. "Take me to the hospital, please."

My visit was a brief one—long enough to walk the corridors of two wards. The light here was dim, except for a few shaded lanterns, and the nurses spoke in whispers. I paused by this bed and that one. One man lay awake and weeping. Two women, mother and daughter, lay in beds next to each other, hands clasped. The gardaí had discovered more victims in the ruined buildings, a surgeon's aide told me in hushed tones. Fifty dead, and the morning might see more. I could not speak any words of comfort, so I said nothing at all. Throughout, Aidrean paced behind me, like a shadow in the moonlight.

We returned to Cill Cannig in the rising dawn. Outside the Royal Residence, we separated—he to gather the necessary reports for the Council, and I to scrub the scent of blood and ashes from my skin, while I considered how to meet this newest disaster.

The bells were ringing seven o'clock when I sat down with the men who acted as my closest advisers. Lord Ó Duinn and Lord Ó Tíghearnaigh. Lord Ó Cadhla. Lord Ó Breislin. Commander Ábraham, Chief of the Queen's Constabulary. To their number I had added Lord Ó Luain, minister of finance, and the leaders of the two most influential factions in Congress. Lord Ó Bruicléigh had recently been elected as chief speaker. Lord Ó Rothláin, a wealthy industrialist, represented the opposition, though there were times I thought them both more in opposition to me than each other. Indeed, I had debated whether to include them. It was only the words of my mother about secrecy that finally convinced me to do so.

Secrecy is an insidious habit, she had told me more than once. *Our Court is stitched and sewn from the cloth of intrigue. But you must learn to recognize when discretion is necessary, and when it has become a sickness.*

But I would have to act carefully. Oh so carefully. I did not wish another Lord De Paor.

Síomón and Gwen Madóc were the next to arrive. Both wore dark, rumpled clothing, with the sleeves rolled up to their elbows, exposing curious scars, like silvery freckles, over their hands and arms. I had the impression they had worked through the night, and only reluctantly consented to break off their research at my secretary's insistence. They circled the table to take seats at the far end.

A murmur of surprise rippled around the room at their appearance. I caught a flash of outright eagerness on Ó Tíghearnaigh's face—as though he had sighted an enemy and wished to engage. Ó Breislin observed them with an air of expectation. Ó Cadhla glanced in my direction. His expression was closed, but I knew he had received an early report of the crisis through the Queen's Constabulary. The rest had heard enough rumors to be frightened and suspicious.

They will soon be more frightened, I thought.

Aidrean Ó Deághaidh hurried through the door, followed by three of his chief aides, each of them carrying stacks of paper. They proceeded to distribute the papers to all those present, while Aidrean took the remaining open seat at my right hand side. (Another, quite obvious signal to those who attended.)

"Your Majesty," he said. "I have grave news to report."

He gave a summary of the night's events in that flat tone I had come to associate with terrible news. The number of dead. The property destroyed. The probable effect on trade and international reputation.

"And further is the matter of future devices."

That provoked a sudden intake of breath around the table.

"What do you mean?" Lord Ó Duinn said.

"That our enemies have planted devices set to explode in future days," Ó Deághaidh replied. "I cannot tell if those explosion are inevitable, or if we can prevent them by our actions. The only fact I can report with certainty is that they are destined to destroy."

"Where?" Lord Ó Bruicléigh demanded.

"In Osraighe," Ó Deághaidh said. "We have identified three sites."

He went on to name them. The square in Osraighe, which I had visited. A marketplace frequented by more ordinary citizens. Then finally the site north of the city where I had planned to hold my first gathering for the Union of Nations.

Of course, I thought. *Of course they would strike there.*

Aidrean's announcement produced a rustle throughout the chamber. Síomón Madóc straightened up in his chair, but Gwen was nodding, as though she just received confirmation of a theory. "We shall have to inspect the area, of course," she said. "But from what you say, the effects are similar enough to what we observed in the airfield."

More murmuring, more stares, especially among the members of Congress. Ó Duinn was shaking his head—he had disagreed on making public what we had discovered so far. Ó Cadhla had tented his fingers and continued his silent observation.

"You told us the airfield was an accident," Ó Rothláin said. "A fuel tank . . ."

"We lied," I said. "Those were my orders, my lord."

"A matter of national security," Ó Bruicléigh muttered.

"Just so." I turned to Síomón Madóc. "You said the patterns of time fractures at the airfield were too regular to be a natural occurrence. You've seen the reports from the Constabulary's experiments as well. Is such a thing possible—to create a disaster in the future?"

Síomón glanced at his sister, who shrugged. "We have only theories, no conclusions, Your Majesty."

"What experiments?" Ó Tíghearnaigh demanded. "Does that mean you can send a man, or several men, properly armed, into the future?"

"No." Gwen Madóc regarded Ó Tíghearnaigh with narrowed eyes. "No, we cannot."

He paid her no attention, and turned to Lord Ó Cadhla. "If we could pinpoint when the next attacks would occur, we could arrest the criminals before they act. . . ."

"Except we would then outrage our citizens," Lord Ó Rothláin said. "We cannot arrest a man if he's committed no crime."

"What if we sent our soldiers to the moment before the attack took place?" Lord Ó Tíghearnaigh said. "We would have the evidence . . ."

"Impossible," Gwen said. "We cannot predict the future."

"But you can breach the walls of time," the war minister said.

At that, I heard a definite hesitation, before Gwen gave a noncommittal reply.

I shall have to question her and her brother later.

An argument broke out—noisy and useless—over the possibilities of time travel. Ó Tíghearnaigh demanded to know if Madóc could predict the outcome of future battles. Ó Breislin wished to learn which allies we might trust, and which we ought to take action against, before they acted against us. I allowed the debate to continue another few minutes before I lifted a hand for silence.

"Enough. We cannot take action before we know more. You," I said to Gwen Madóc, "shall go with your brother and Commander Ábraham to inspect the sites in Loch Garman and Osraighe. And you," I said to Aidrean, "will question our Anglian guest while I observe."

The prison was an artifact of Éire's earliest days, when the old kings had imprisoned their highborn enemies in Cill Cannig itself, holding them for later ransom, or more often, execution. War and rebellion, and the passage of centuries, had altered that ancient fortress into a palace, but the original prison remained. As Aidrean and I left behind the modern corridors with their electric lights, and entered the old stone passageways lit by oil lamps, I caught a whiff and whisper of those olden days.

We passed cell after dark and empty cell. Our footsteps echoed over the worn stone, shadows from the lamps rippled over the rough walls, and the air had a stale, metallic scent. These days, the cells were seldom occupied, and then only by political prisoners of high rank. I could count only a dozen instances in the past hundred years, and only two from my own reign. Lord Alastar De Paor had waited for his trial in this one, a windowless cage of stone. He had cursed and railed against his arrest, they told me, until the final days when he crouched on the floor and wept. Six years later, Lord Nesbit had spent a single night, before his release and eventual assassination.

The senior warden waited for us at the end of the passageway, keys in hand.

"Your Majesty. Commander Ó Deághaidh."

"How is our friend?" I asked.

"Well enough. Curious. We've said nothing, as you wished."

The cell where they had put Michael Okoye was larger than the others, with a small vent in the outer wall to let in fresh air and sunlight, but it was nevertheless a bare bleak room, with its walls of gray stone, the dented metal washbasin, and the chamber pot tucked into one corner. The air was chilled, more like winter than spring.

Michael Okoye sat on the cot, his gaze pinned on the vent, which was covered with a network of iron bars. Though they must have roused him from his bed, he was dressed in a fine dark suit and stiff white shirt. His manner was still and contained, his expression remote, as though he had wiped away all emotion, all expectation. He did not acknowledge our presence.

Aidrean Ó Deághaidh spoke first. "Mister Okoye. I have come to ask you some questions."

Okoye glanced from him to me. "Why am I here?"

"Because your delegation chose you," I said.

"No. I chose myself. Now tell me. Why am I in this cell?"

His voice was cool and soft, the vowels faintly rounded as was usual for the Anglian tongue. I caught a hint of anger in those few words, however much he had tried to hide it, and I exchanged a glance with Aidrean Ó Deághaidh. He too had heard something in Okoye's tone. He motioned for the warden to unlock the cell door.

"We shall be comfortable enough," he told the man. "Lock the door behind me, and leave us until we send for you. Her Majesty wishes to observe."

A bench with pillows was fetched. I took my seat and the warden left us.

Okoye watched these preparations impassively. He had spent three weeks waiting for an audience with me. It seemed he was willing to wait longer.

Aidrean did not begin his questions at once. He sat on a wooden stool, which I had not noticed before, and leaned against the wall, studying Okoye with a pleasant smile. Okoye met his gaze steadily, even as the silence extended to a quarter of an hour and beyond, and I felt myself grow invisible to the two men inside the cell.

Then, "How old are you, Mister Okoye?"

Michael Okoye drew a quick breath, startled against his will. "Surely, you know everything about me, Commander. Éire has spies enough in our country."

"Please answer the question, Mister Okoye."

"First tell me why you have arrested me. I've committed no crime—"

"Answer the question, or I shall charge you with treason."

Aidrean Ó Deághaidh spoke mildly, and the pleasant smile never left his face. I had not witnessed this aspect of his character before.

Okoye remained silent a moment longer, then said, "Twenty-six."

Younger than I had guessed.

"Where were you born?"

"If I answer, will you tell me why—?"

"Where were you born, Mister Okoye?"

"In Londain," Okoye said with a sigh. "Why must you ask me these questions, when surely you have the answers already?"

Because ink and paper are only the outermost details, I thought. *Because Aidrean Ó Deághaidh will learn more about your character from the timbre of your voice, the silences and hesitations, the almost infinitesimal changes in the direction of your gaze, and the tension in your mouth. I know this because I have lived my entire life in Court, reading the character of men and women as Aidrean Ó Deághaidh now reads yours.*

Aidrean merely shrugged and asked another question—this one concerning the number of siblings and their names. A dozen more seemingly irrelevant questions followed. From them I learned that Michael Okoye was the second oldest of five children. He had three brothers and one sister, the youngest. From twelve to sixteen, he lived with his father's relatives in the Nri Republic, where he perfected his knowledge of the Igbo language, as well as learning the family business—a trade consortium his great-grandfather had founded.

Behind Okoye's answers, I heard the squabbling of brothers and sisters, and affection, too. I saw a large family immersed in duty to an even larger family that extended from Africa to Éire to the Western Continent. I saw a young man with a restless curiosity who was adept at languages and poetry, as well as the far different world of trade.

I also saw a young man with a passion for justice. Such a passion must have led him to join the cause for Anglian liberty, and from there to Peter Godwin's useless and dangerous faction.

"You attended Awveline University," Aidrean Ó Deághaidh said. "And graduated with honors, with degrees in economics and philosophy. An interesting mix."

"A compromise," Michael said. "My father wished me to be competent in our business, and I wished for an education beyond goods and freight and currencies. As long as I satisfied his demands, he agreed to indulge mine."

"I can understand," Aidrean said. "It was for that reason I studied mathematics, and for the same reason I gave over those studies." He glanced around the cell, as though searching for a few last, almost forgotten clues, then abruptly stood. "Thank you, Mister Okoye."

Michael Okoye blinked. "You have nothing more to ask?"

"None for today."

"When will you release me, then?"

Aidrean Ó Deághaidh shook his head. Already the warden had appeared—I suspected the man had kept watch from a hidden alcove for just this moment—and was unlocking the cell door. Michael Okoye stood as though to insist on an answer, when his gaze snapped toward me and he stiffened, suddenly aware of my presence once more. Before he had recovered himself, Aidrean Ó Deághaidh exited the cell and the door rang shut.

"He could be innocent," Aidrean said, once we had left the prison wing.

"Are you certain?"

"No." He paused and glanced around. Guards were stationed behind us and at the next intersection. In a lower voice, he said, "I am not certain about him or about what we do."

"What do you mean? They have murdered a dozen people or more."

"They, yes. But—" He broke off. "My apologies, Your Majesty."

"Apologies be damned, Aidrean. Do you believe I should release the man?"

He shook his head. "There is no one clear answer to that question. Is he guilty? My instincts tell me he has committed no crime. His family, too, has enough influence in the Nri Republic to cause you difficulties. And yet, my instincts also tell me that he and I might have a useful conversation or two."

"About mathematics and philosophy?"

I meant to speak lightly, but I knew at once I had struck the wrong note. Aidrean Ó Deághaidh bowed in reply, his face now carefully blank. I drew a breath, ready to apologize, but this was too public a place. At the next intersection we parted, he to speak with Commander Ábraham and I to speak in private with Lords Ó Cadhla and Ó Duinn.

But as I passed into the Royal Enclosure, my steps turned of their own accord to the family's chapel. Even at this late hour, a priest came to meet me as I approached the altar rail. She offered me a sip of red wine and a thin wafer, the reminder of Christ and Gaia, then withdrew to let me pray.

God and Mhuire and blessed Gaia, please give me guidance. . . .

The formal words of the prayer died away in my thoughts.

God and Gaia would not take this burden of the Anglians from me, no matter how much I wished it. My ancestors had gone to war against these people to win our own liberty. We'd set soldiers in their land and spies in their houses, taken their freedom as payment for ours. Three thousand had died when my grandfather had put down the last rebellion, three hundred since I took the crown, in riots and battles with the Garda. My father had hoped to free the Districts. His reign had ended—abruptly—before he could see his wish made true. I had attempted to do what I could, but the times and the press of other business had prevented me.

You will be queen, my father had told me, ten days before he died. *The guilt of your past, and your people, is yours.*

I am convinced that none of us slept in the days that followed. At Aidrean Ó Deághaidh's suggestion, the Queen's Constabulary offered a reward of a million pounds for information concerning the tragedy in Loch Garman. And Ó Deághaidh himself worked with Lord Ó Duinn's people and those from the Constabulary to review all recent reports concerning disaffected groups in the Districts and Éire itself, searching for patterns to past activities that they might predict future attacks. He and I held daily meetings with Gwen and Síomón Madóc to discuss other patterns—patterns of time and its fractures.

Late in the afternoon of the third day, Aidrean came to me requesting an immediate private interview. From his face alone, I knew at once he had difficult news.

"Peter Godwin is dead," he said, once we were alone.

"Dead? How? When?"

"Murdered. His body was discovered in the Thames, early this morning, by a fisherman and his son."

I asked for more details, knowing they would be ugly.

According to the Constabulary examiner, Peter Godwin had been strangled with a rough cord, which had left burn marks around his neck. His face and arms were badly bruised, and several teeth were missing, indicating he had fought his captors. Those captors had fastened weights around Godwin's body to prevent it from floating, but they evidently had not tied the ropes securely enough, because the body was discovered in the mud flats near the estuary. The gardaí had discovered the ropes and weights themselves further upstream.

"A quarrel within the conspiracy?" I asked.

"We don't know yet. The examiner believes he died before Loch Garman."

I sighed. With every new detail uncovered, the questions grew. "What of the Constabulary's reward? Do we have news there?"

"None so far. Our friends, or so Lord Ó Duinn calls them, have inundated the Constabulary with their sightings of suspicious characters, both in Osraighe and in Loch Garman. A dozen have claimed responsibility for the attack themselves, with the understanding they would only betray their comrades in exchange for the reward and immunity from prosecution. Others have accused their neighbors, or the overseer in the shop where they work, or sometimes a cousin or uncle whom they've never quite trusted."

"They've seen nothing, then."

He shrugged. "That I cannot say for certain. We've reviewed the claims, even the more unusual ones, because there is always the chance for truth amongst the chaff." He paused and glanced out the window, where the sun was slanting down toward the horizon. Rags of clouds hung low in the skies, dull brown and stained crimson from the approaching sunset. Aidrean shook his head and rubbed a hand over his eyes.

"You should sleep," I said, on impulse.

He smiled at me. "As should you."

"I shall," I said. "Once my kingdom is safe."

"As will I." He shuffled his papers together, but did not make a move to depart. "Ábraham believes we ought to declare a national crisis," he said softly. "He claims that would grant us the freedom to search as we must, without provoking an outcry. Ó Tíghearnaigh insists our only course is to increase our armies and begin the manufacture of weapons." Aidrean allowed himself a smile. "He mentioned your scientists, and not in a complimentary fashion. He suspects they could provide us with extraordinary weapons from the future, if only they wished to."

I had suspected much the same. "Lord Ó Cadhla believes the situation is more complex than Ó Tíghearnaigh states."

He laughed. "That would be an understatement." But the humor drained from his face all too quickly. There was a curious hesitation about his manner, then he said, "I spoke with Michael Okoye this morning, before I heard the news of Peter Godwin."

"And was your conversation productive?"

"Indirectly. We talked of poetry. He favors the metaphysical poets of the seventeenth century. Outside Thomas Austen, there were few connected with the Anglian cause who shared his interest. Except for one. A man named Daniel Strong, who, as it happens, is Peter Godwin's nephew."

More answers, provoking more questions.

"And what does this *signify*?" I asked.

"Nothing yet. I've sent a telegraph to our agents in Londain to question Strong. Apparently he quarreled with Godwin six months ago and has broken all connection with the other members of the delegation. More than that, I cannot say."

"And what about Okoye?"

"I want to talk with him tomorrow. Innocent or not, I suspect he might be in danger if he leaves Cill Cannig. I would like to persuade him to remain here, until we discover who murdered Godwin."

"Remain as prisoner or guest?" I waved my hand to cut off his reply. "No, I know your answer. You leave the decision to me and my honor."

Aidrean opened his mouth as if to reply, but he only shook his head. "I must go to Osraighe," he said. "The chief of the Garda station says a witness has come forward with information about the message we received. Shall I come to you afterward, Your Majesty?"

"Yes," I said softly. "No. Unless the news proves important, truly important, let it wait until morning. I want you to make an early end to your day."

He smiled again, but did not make any promises.

We had finished our business. Aidrean tucked the papers back into the leather case and stood, wincing as he did so. The late afternoon sunlight threw the lines in his face into sharp relief, and a shock of white and silver stood out against his dark hair. He was forty-nine, almost fifty, I reminded myself. No longer the indefatigable guardian of my early reign.

I should send him home, home to Montenegro, to Valerija Delchev and their children.

As he turned to go, I said, "And Aidrean, I will keep in mind what you say about Okoye. I promise."

I dined early and alone, in my private suite, by candlelight. I had two more interviews scheduled in the evening, three if Aidrean Ó Deághaidh brought news from Osraighe. I needed this interlude to myself, without the constant press of demands and inquiries, the need for diplomatic conversation, even with my most trusted advisers. Without, I thought, the cold bright light of electric lamps, and their reminder of the implacable future.

Twilight was falling. I stirred the fire, recalling as I did so the chill air in Michael Okoye's cell. Aidrean believed him innocent, but useful. Ó Cadhla remained carefully neutral on the subject, but my minister of war had stated more than once his conviction that we could not trust the Anglians, any Anglians. My own impressions were deeply suspect, but I began to think we had, all of us, viewed him as a playing piece—a symbol and not a man.

The coals flared into bright flames. I replaced the poker and turned back toward my neglected dinner. The window beyond showed the dark blue of the approaching night, with the lights of Osraighe glimmering on the horizon.

And then the night exploded in bright flames.

Moments later, a dull boom made the window glass shudder.

I fell back a dozen steps before the strength deserted me and I dropped to my knees. A second explosion, and second burst of light flared upward into the twilit sky. The glass rattled but held. I stared, breathless and trembling, at the blood-bright horizon. *What have they done?*

But I knew what they—whoever they were—had done. They had warned us clearly enough with Loch Garman.

I staggered to my feet and ran into the next room. "Send runners for my secretary and Commander Ó Deághaidh," I ordered the maids. "Tell him I wish to hear the reports myself as they come."

"At once, Your Majesty."

My servants scattered to obey. I returned to my sitting room to drink down a glass of water. My throat had gone dry and I was shivering—from shock, I told myself. Shock and rage at this sense of being flung into chaos.

Word came back through my secretary that Commander Ó Deághaidh had not yet returned to Cill Cannig, but that Commander Ábraham had received the first reports from Osraighe, and did I wish to summon my advisers?

"Of course," I replied sharply. "Send word to my cabinet and both Doctors Madóc. No, wait." I reconsidered the urge to have my mathematical advisers present just yet. "If they are at work, do not disturb them, but give them notice we shall require their presence by morning."

Within the hour, we had gathered in a small audience chamber, within the Royal Residence. Ó Duinn and I had arrived first, with my other ministers appearing soon after. Commander Ábraham was the last, accompanied by my secretary.

"Your Majesty," he said. "I have a tragedy to report."

"We are aware of the tragedy—"

"You are not—" He broke off. With obvious effort, he said, "Your Majesty, let me give my report and you will understand. Please."

His face was pale, the color of the dead, I thought. Silently, I motioned him to sit at the table. My steward had already poured a glass of water mixed with crush mint. I waited until Ábraham had drunk one tumbler before I spoke.

"You say we have a tragedy. What more have you learned?"

"More than I ever wished to," he replied.

I listened, numb, as he recounted the main points. Three devices had exploded in Osraighe, Galway, and Belfast, each one twice as murderous as those that had destroyed Loch Garman's harbor district. Two hundred instantly dead. Six hundred wounded. The Garda and hospitals were searching for others buried in the rubble. The count would rise before morning.

"And there is more," Ábraham was saying. "The device in Osraighe destroyed the main Garda station. Commander Ó Deághaidh had left only moments before it exploded. We have not yet recovered his . . . we have not yet found him, Your Majesty."

A silence, as cold as winter, fell in the room.

"He is dead?"

I heard my voice as something alien and unfamiliar, disconnected from myself.

"We do not know. I have set all the gardaí—all those who survived—to search the rubble. And, Your Majesty, there is more to report."

No more, no more, I thought, but the part of me that still acted as queen motioned for him to continue. I listened with growing dread as Ábraham went on to tell of other explosions in Frankonia, Catalonia, Egypt, and Gujarat, which had taken place a few hours before the one in Osraighe. These were the act of a fascist network, he said, which his agents suspected had ties to certain rising factions in the Prussian government.

"And to our own rebels?" I asked.

"So we believe," Ó Duinn said. "Commander Ó Deághaidh spoke with me by telephone from Osraighe. A witness had come forward to give evidence about a man named Daniel Strong. The man claimed Strong had boasted he would do what Thomas Austen could not."

Thomas Austen had wanted me dead. This Daniel Strong aimed to destroy Éire.

"There is more," Lord Ó Cadhla said. "The Papal States, Catalonia, Poland, and Russia have telegraphed to say they must withdraw from our Union of Nations, and both the Chinese and Japanese empires have expressed grave concerns. No doubt I will find more messages before the night ends."

The implication was clear. Whoever had organized these attacks had chosen our oldest allies. Even such a tentative connection as my Union might prove too dangerous. I pressed my hands against my eyes. "I cannot. I cannot give up on my Union. Not yet."

But a chill had settled over me as I recalled the vision I'd had in Osraighe. The rebels, or their allies, had planted their devices at different moments in the future. Tomorrow might bring news that the hall for my Union lay in ruins. Or that fire had gutted Éire's Congress and banks. And what if they could not undo the future attacks, even if we acquiesced to their demands?

"Send word to evacuate Osraighe," I said softly.

"We don't want to cause panic—"

"We have no choice," I snapped. "They have laid traps for us. Even if we could discover the *where*, we cannot know *when*. Even if we knew *when*, we do not know how. Not yet."

"What of our prisoner?" Ó Tíghearnaigh said. "With proper persuasion he might recall enough to lead us to the rebels."

"No. No torture," I said. "Whatever you call it."

We settled into an uneasy and angry silence. Lord Ó Tíghearnaigh drank a second glass of whiskey. Lord Ó Duinn reviewed the collection of papers in his hands, as if hoping to discover clues on how to proceed. Lord Ó Cadhla had an air of resignation utterly foreign to all my memories of him. It was in this moment that Lord Ó Breislin arrived. He wore an expression far more hopeful than I thought possible

"I would be grateful for some good news," I told him.

Ó Breislin took a seat and poured a glass of whiskey. "None, except that Commander Ó Deághaidh has been found. Found and found alive. Is that enough?"

My heart leapt. "He lives?"

"He does. The Garda discovered him half buried in the rubble of the station. His leg is shattered, and he has lost a dangerous quantity of blood. Even so, the doctors tell me he did not succumb gently to their care. They had to forcibly administer a sleep draught before they could properly attend to his injuries."

Aidrean alive. I whispered a silent prayer of thanks to God and Mhuire and Gaia.

———

After that, there was nothing left for us to discuss. Commander Ábraham departed to keep watch with his agents for further news. My ministers and I agreed to meet early the next morning to discuss how to evacuate Osraighe. It was near ten o'clock when I retired to my bedroom and undressed. I lay down and closed my eyes, never expecting to find sleep . . .

. . . and woke at midnight, breathless and on edge.

At first I saw nothing, heard nothing except the fading chimes from the nearby clock tower. The moon had set and the palace lay in a smothering darkness, without stars or lamplight to relieve it.

Then I heard it—a faint exhalation, as though someone stood quite close to me.

Assassins.

I lunged from bed, shouting for my guards. My legs tangled in the linens and I landed with a thump on the floor. A wet gurgling noise sounded behind me. I scrambled away on hands and knees until I came to my wardrobe, then the wall of my bedchamber. I eased up to standing and turned to face the intruder.

Nothing. Only fluttering shadows.

Then came another audible gasp. I could not fix on where it came from. Where were my guards? Taking care to move as silently as I could, I crept toward the door and found the switch for the electric lamps. With a snap, light flooded my bedroom.

A man crouched at the foot of my bed, his head bent over his chest, and one hand clutching at the bedcovers, the other splayed against the carpet. Pale blond hair, so pale it appeared silver, tumbled over his face. His clothes were covered in dust, and a faint acrid cloud drifted around him.

Then he lifted his face and I cried out, or tried to, but panic clamped my throat shut.

Breandan Ó Cuilinn stared back at me. Oh, but a strangely altered Breandan, his face scored and seamed with age, his hair an unkempt tangle of silver and gray. Only his eyes were the same, that bright and vivid gaze that pinned my heart even after the absence of twelve years.

"Breandan," I whispered.

His eyes stretched wide. "Áine. I . . . Have I found you at last? I thought—"

A spasm took him and his mouth twisted in agony.

Oh, my love. What have you done?

Breandan coughed, a harsh, bubbling cough that shook his body. Once more he lifted his head—I could see the effort it took—and stared at me. His eyes were dark now, with only a rim of blue around the pupil. His gaze flickered from me then away, to some point in the far distance. Then slowly, so slowly, all the brilliance faded away, and his eyes turned blank, as though a veil had fallen over them. Even as he reached toward me, his body collapsed into a heap.

"Your Majesty!"

The door latch rattled. I started. Of course, my guards. I glanced toward Breandan. For a moment, my vision wavered—I thought I could see the pattern of the carpet through his body—then, I blinked and the impression disappeared.

"Your Majesty!"

I must know what has happened first.

"It was nothing," I called out. "A nightmare."

From the other side came a muttering. I waited until I heard their footsteps withdraw, then closed my eyes and leaned against the door's solid expanse, shivering.

I cannot believe he came to me, only to die.

Fragments of lessons from years ago, from a tutor who had schooled me and my siblings in philosophy. *Mankind's arrogance shows itself in the belief that all our acts are deliberate,* he told us. *However much we plot our lives, we too are overtaken by chance, by misfortune, by the errant path of a great storm.*

It took me many long moments before I expelled a breath and hurried to Breandan's side. He was so still, so unnaturally still. My throat drew tight as I fumbled to find the pulse at his neck. No success, and when I attempted to find the one at his wrist, his arm was heavy and lifeless, the skin already cooling to my touch.

I rocked back on my heels. Stared down at my ghost, now become flesh.

He had changed, utterly changed. The gold of his hair was entirely silver now, and thinned to almost nothing over his skull, and the faint lines around his eyes and mouth cut much deeper now. His clothing too was strange—ill fitting and worn, the cut and cloth like nothing I had seen before. I had to shift and rearrange all the images from my memory, which had fixed Breandan Ó Cuilinn as I knew him, all those years ago.

Where have you been? Why—How did you come back to me?

Underneath those thoughts was the idea that he had spent the past twelve years trapped in the cracks and fissures of time itself. No, impossible. The peculiar clothing itself was proof that Breandan Ó Cuilinn had launched himself—if not into the future, then into a different time altogether. But where? And when?

I hesitated a moment, then felt inside one jacket pocket, then another.

The results were odd—odd and mundane and unsettling, all at once. A wad of paper currency, which I tossed to one side. The torn token from a streetcar. A pocket watch. My heart gave an uncomfortable lurch at the sight of the watch, which I recognized at once from our days together, but I continued to search albeit with unsteady hands. I found a packet of cigarettes, mostly empty, the stub of a pencil, a much-folded clipping from a newspaper with the date of February 1, 1943.

1943?

I read through the article, growing colder and colder. A new curfew had been enacted by the government. Citizens without the necessary papers would be fined and imprisoned for the week. Repeated offenses meant transportation to the eastern front. Manufactories would issue proper identification cards to those laborers working the night shift.

No, no, no. This was impossible. I thrust away the newspaper clipping and unfolded the crumpled wad of paper currency. There were six banknotes in various small denominations. All bore the portrait of a thickset man in military dress against a patterned background on one side. On the other was an eagle drawn in stark black lines, its wings outspread, and the words *Empire of Prussia* engraved in Éireann and German.

The bills fell from my hands. I covered my face, not to weep, because I was beyond grief now. Éire lost. Its borders overrun and its people conquered. My Union no more, or perhaps it never came to be.

Is that why you came back, my love? To warn me?

The breath fled my body. A warning. Yes, yes. Oh please let that be true. Only how to find out the message?

Hurriedly, I reexamined the other objects. The equations meant nothing to me. The cigarette packet contained only a few cigarettes, several of them broken. If I were any sort of spy, I thought bitterly, I could read these puzzle pieces myself. That Éire faced disaster was obvious enough, but what had taken place in our future . . .

I stood—unsteadily—and wrapped myself in a robe. On impulse, I dragged a blanket from my bed to cover Breandan's body and switched off the electric light. My dressing room was dark and empty, but as I expected, a lamp was lit in the sitting room beyond, and a sleepy maidservant kept watch. "Your Majesty," she said, rising to her feet.

"Have the kitchen brew me a pot of tisane," I told her. "And

send a runner to fetch Doctor Gwen Madóc to me. Tell her . . .
tell her I want her advice about a mathematical problem."

Soon enough, the tisane arrived. At my request, the maid
built up the fire, then retired to her bed. The moment she had
gone, I returned to my bedchamber to lock the door, then paced
the sitting room for the next quarter hour. I had just determined
to send a second runner, when the first man arrived with Gwen
Madóc close behind.

"Your Majesty."

"Doctor Madóc. Thank you for indulging me."

I poured her a cup of tisane and one for myself. Her eyes narrowed as she scanned the room, taking in the state of my dress,
the newly built fire, and the tray with cups and a silver pot. However, she kept silent until the runner had withdrawn and we
were alone.

"I cannot change the past," she said immediately. "I cannot
bring the dead of Osraighe and Belfast back to life. Nor can I
undo your Commander Ó Deághaidh's injuries."

"I did not ask you to," I replied. "Sit. Drink your tea and listen."

She sat, but ignored the cup of tisane. I took the seat opposite
her and sipped, observing the marks of exhaustion, the tense lines
of her mouth, or perhaps it was more impatience. Judging from
the state of her dress, I had once more interrupted her work.

I took another sip, then set my cup aside. "Four days ago, Lord
Ó Tíghearnaigh asked if you could breach the walls of time. You
denied that. You were lying."

Gwen started up, her cheeks flushed. I held up a hand to fore-
stall her protests.

"You lied because you know the dangers."

"I lied because—" She broke off and swore under her breath.
"Your Lord Ó Tíghearnaigh believes science is nothing but a
weapon. He wants us to transport his armies into the past and

the future. But I told the truth when I said we could not send a man to any exact moment in time. Our work . . ."

"Is incomplete. I understand that. Tell me what you have accomplished."

Still she hesitated.

So and so. I would have to offer her my trust, before she could do the same for me. I stood. "Come. Come, and I will show you the reason for my questions."

We traversed the darkened dressing room. I unlocked my bedroom door and switched on the electric light. As I stepped to one side, Gwen entered the room. I knew the moment she sighted Breandan's body underneath the blanket, because she went still as a hunting dog.

"What has happened here?" she whispered.

"A visitation from the future," I said. I pulled away the blanket and knelt at Breandan's side. "This man was Doctor Breandan Ó Cuilinn."

She hissed. She would know the name and his history, of course. Ó Cuilinn had lectured in mathematics at Awveline University during the same years her brother had attended for his graduate studies. Murder and the vanishment of time lines had obliterated much of his work, but I had no doubt that brother and sister had made it their business to read what papers remained.

"He materialized not more than an hour ago," I said. "He was dying even then, and could not speak more than a few words. I believe he had a message for me."

Her pale face had gone paper white. "You are certain of his purpose?"

"I am."

Her gaze flickered from Breandan's body to my face, then back. "Have you searched him?"

Cold, so cold, and yet, I understood her manner, better than I had anyone else. I pointed to the small heap on the floor, the coins and scraps of paper and the currency bills. Gwen seemed to find the latter more intriguing than the first. "He *has* traveled the time roads," she said softly.

She then proceeded to search Breandan's clothing more thoroughly. She tugged the jacket loose enough to examine the second outer pocket, which yielded only more scribbled equations and a matchbox. An inner pocket, however, held a wallet with more banknotes and an identification card bearing the name Breandan Ó Corráin, citizen of the regional district of Osraighe. I recognized the street name as one on the western edge of the city, less than a mile from Cill Cannig.

Twelve years spent in the alien land of the future. How had he survived? I could only guess that the war and its aftermath had offered the necessary chaos for him to create a new name and identity. He must have resumed work almost at once to create a new time machine. . . .

"You see why I asked you to come," I said. "Perhaps I cannot save my dead. But perhaps I can save those who come after me. If I could speak with Breandan, I might learn what I need to make the right decisions. Will you show me the time roads?"

The quiet of a soft Éireann night filled the room.

"I can promise nothing."

"I know that. But if we do not act, we say that he gave his life for nothing."

She glanced from me to Breandan's face and back. "Let us go to the laboratory and I shall do what I can."

We would need to wear inconspicuous clothing, Gwen told me. There could be no certainty as to what qualified as inconspicuous, I thought. In the end, I chose a plain costume of dark trousers, low boots, and a dark woolen jumper. Gwen herself wore her usual working clothes of trousers and shirt, which were equally plain. My wardrobe provided us both with long drab coats of wool. If we could avoid direct confrontation, we might pass as men.

With the door to my bedroom locked, and the key in my pocket, we exited my apartments. I gave orders to the guards to admit no one, not my ministers, not even the chief of the Queen's Constabulary. With one guard to follow, we hurried through the corridors of Cill Cannig, across the great public halls, and into the wing I had once assigned to Breandan Ó Cuilinn. My guard took his post outside, while I continued alone with Gwen.

Most of the laboratory was dark. One lamp illuminated the far end, and I recognized Síomón Madóc bent over his desk, with several open books scattered about and a calculator machine to his right. His head jerked up at our approach, and he gave an exclamation of surprise and displeasure. "Gwen . . ."

"She comes with my permission, Síomón. I will tell you about it later."

He shrugged and returned to his work, already dismissing us from his attention as we passed by his desk, to the end of the laboratory itself, where more crates partially obscured a plain wooden door. A storage closet or something like, I thought.

Gwen slid between the crates and unlocked the door. I followed, only to stop in surprise on the threshold.

"You have made more progress than I expected," I said softly.

The room measured the width of my outstretched arms, and was twice as tall. Thin glass tubes, encased in metal webbing, crisscrossed the walls to either side and the ceiling overhead, and thick wires nested in between, leading down to a row of electrical plugs, obviously of a custom design. The wall opposite the door was covered in a strange black metal, which gleamed softly in the shadows, and off to the left, I noticed how the tubes angled around a small square of panels and dials.

"We began work on a similar device several years ago," Gwen

said. "When you asked for our assistance, we transported the existing machine here, and used the latest measurements to refine our model. Excuse me, please."

She brushed her hand over the dials. I heard a faint hiss, as if a monster had drawn a breath. Light poured out of a flat disc overhead. The door slid shut and I heard the click of bolts. A silvery gleam traveled along the length of the glass tubes around us, like liquid starlight, and the cables and outlets gave off a strong odor of chemicals.

"You have used this machine yourself?"

Gwen must have caught the hint of panic in my voice, because a fleeting smile crossed her face. "I have," she said. "But until recently, only to visit the past. It's been just a week since we made any successful journeys into the future."

She twisted a knob. A rectangular panel clicked open from the wall. Gwen tilted the panel downward to reveal a tray that resembled a typewriter, with several extra rows of keys marked with mathematical symbols. She tapped the keys. Several other panels slid open. One narrow slot disgorged a slip of paper, which fell into a bucket at Gwen's side. She glanced down, tapped a few more keys, and consulted the next slip.

"We shall not have long," she said. "The time fractures have different properties for those traveling ahead. The disturbances are less extreme, but they are nevertheless present. My brother and I have not yet worked out all the permutations."

She tapped a long and complicated sequence, using more of the symbol keys than before. Then, unexpectedly, she slid the tray back into its slot.

"Now," she said. "Quickly."

She took me by the hand and led me through an opening that had abruptly appeared opposite the door. I was too surprised to resist. It was impossible, this corridor stretching onward and into shadows and then into an infinity beyond. There was no space for it to exist behind the machine, or anywhere in Cill Cannig. But I had asked for the impossible.

A dozen steps and darkness closed around us. I glanced back and saw only a blurred square of light. Gwen whispered urgently that we could not hesitate. Her words were hard to make out but her intent was clear enough. We hurried on into a thick mist. Within moments I no longer sensed the walls of a corridor around us. My boots trod soundlessly on a smooth road that arrowed straight ahead. My breath came short, but I heard nothing beyond the thrumming of my pulse, and even that had an odd unnatural quality to it. When Gwen spoke again, her lips moved soundlessly. She shook her head and frowned. For the first time, she seemed anxious.

The darkness eased.

Pinpricks of light appeared overhead. If I stared directly at them, they shifted. Jumped. Their halos blurred. I dropped my gaze back to the road. It tilted oddly beneath me and my stomach lurched. I blinked. Saw the road divide into a dozen, a hundred, a myriad of separate paths spinning off in all directions, to other pasts and other futures. I must have made a sound, because Gwen gripped my hand tightly. She spoke, but the words ran together and swirled around like the waters of two rivers when they meet.

Sound stopped. Started.

We were running. No, walking but the mists streamed past us, making our passage seem much swifter. The stars overhead had become streaks that spiraled down to the horizon, to the point where the road vanished from sight. Gwen was murmuring to herself. I heard her clearly now. She recited a stream of numbers.

"353665707. Times two. 25814. Minus 1. 353665707*225814+1. 1958349*231415−1. 1958349*231415+1. Yes. There. There it is. The future, Your Majesty."

My attention snapped back to the road. The stars had stilled. An indigo band marked the division between ground and sky. And there, where Gwen pointed, a bright liquid flare of true sunlight. We ran. We ran without hesitation toward the sun-bright disc. I believe I was laughing, though partly in terror. And when Gwen herself loosed my hand and leapt into its heart, I followed.

For many long moments, I was aware of nothing more than an overpowering giddiness. I crouched with hands splayed against icy cobblestones, spewing water and tisane. My stomach knotted into a fist-sized lump and heaved itself against my ribs, though I had nothing left to give. Snow was falling in steady streamers, and a bone-deep cold penetrated my clothes.

Gwen Madóc pressed a hand against my shoulder. "Your Majesty. My friend. We must hurry. We have an hour, if that, before the time fractures undo our passage back."

She helped me to my feet. I staggered, then clutched at her arms. My head was swimming and I wanted nothing more than a shot glass of whiskey. "Where are we?" I croaked.

"Cill Canning," she replied softly. "But the when is more important. I told the truth that we could not send ourselves to one particular moment, past or future. The most I know is that this is the winter of 1943. January or possibly February."

I wiped the snow from my eyes and stared at our surroundings.

We had not traveled more than a dozen yards, if that, from where Gwen and Síomón Madóc's machine had stood. Everything else, however, had been transformed beyond knowing. Cill Cannig had vanished. In its place was a ruin of walls. A few hundred yards away stood a large stone building with electric lamps burning in two or three of the ground-floor windows. By their faint light, I could see the ground between was taken up with rubble and trash, now vanishing under the snow, and a strange sour scent filled the air—not poison, not exactly, but the smell made me think of slaughterhouses and those laboratories dedicated to breaking down flesh and analyzing its properties.

"We must hurry," Gwen said. "We cannot have anyone find us here."

She dragged me down a lane filled with more rubble, more trash. We exited the palace grounds, leaving behind even the electric lights, and plunging into a maze of lanes bounded by tall wooden buildings. The fields and farmland I remembered were gone, replaced by ugly warehouses.

The snow was falling faster now. I had to tuck my hands under my arms and bend my head to watch my footing. Moonlight broke through the clouds from time to time, but our progress was slow. More than once, we dodged into alleyways or courtyards to avoid the patrols that kept watch. I heard muttered conversations in German and Éireann. The patrols had no dogs, and I had the impression the cold discouraged them from making a thorough search. Even so, my pulse thrummed hard and fast, and I had to bite down to keep my teeth from clattering together.

We had just reached the old outer walls of Osraighe when a mechanical grinding broke the silence. Then came the booming noise of a bell directly overhead. *A naoi, a deich, a haon deág . . .* The midnight hour was striking.

"The doorway will close before the bells mark the next hour," Gwen told me. "We must not be late. Are you afraid?"

Do you wish to go back now? was her second, implied question.

"I am terrified," I told her. "Let us go."

We hurried as quickly as the deepening snow allowed, but nearly half an hour longer passed before we found the address in Breandan's papers. The building was an older brick and timber structure, tall and narrow, that dated from the mid sixteenth century, with a chimney that spiraled up from the slate rooftop. This had once been a prosperous neighborhood three hundred years ago. Since then the nobles had sold their homes to wealthier merchants, whose descendants had rented to the rising working class. Now? Between the late hour and the darkness, I could not tell.

A narrow porch gave us some protection from the snow and wind. The door itself was a massive thing, fashioned from heavy iron that was giving way to the inevitable rust. Gwen pointed to a metal grate set into the left-hand side of the door. She wiped away the snow and uncovered a series of plaques with names, and a button next to each.

Ó Corráin, Breandan, read one.

Gwen stopped me before I could press the button.

"Remember what I told you," she said. "There are no guarantees in what we do. I know. I tried more than once to alter the past. You might find that you cannot undo the future."

"I know I might fail," I said quietly. "But I must try. I *must.*"

She nodded and stood aside. I stabbed the button—a harsh buzzer reverberated, making us both jump with sudden panic. I glanced over my shoulder, certain we would be discovered. Gwen counting under her breath to a hundred, then rang the bell six times quickly.

"Who is there?"

A tinny voice emanated from the metal grill.

I recognized him at once. "Breandan. Breandan Ó Cuilinn."

There was a pause. "You've misread the sign. My name is Breandan Ó Corráin."

Even with the distortion I could hear the alarm in his voice. Hurriedly, I said, "I have not misread the sign, Doctor Ó Cuilinn. I came to say I received your message. I have some questions . . ."

"I sent no message." But now the voice was uncertain.

"You did," I said. "Or you will try to. Please, listen. Just a moment." And then, because memory itself flooded me, I could not keep the anguish from my voice. "You told me you would prove your device. Your golden octopus. Do you remember that day, Breandan? You set your own journal into the octopus and launched it into the future. And then, and then . . . you followed."

By now I was weeping, my tears frozen into specks of ice. I rubbed my knuckles over my eyes and glared at the silent metal grating, as if by glaring alone, I could force it to produce Breandan Ó Cuilinn. Next to me, Gwen shifted from foot to foot. In a moment she would flee, I could tell it. My own flesh felt unnaturally heavy from the cold.

"Áine. Wait."

A dozen, two dozen heartbeats, echoed in my ears. Then the door opened.

It was him—the face I had seen in my bedchambers not three hours before, but alive, his cheeks flushed with emotion and his gazed fixed on me, as if he thought I might vanish from before his eyes.

Then he saw Gwen and flinched back. "Who are you?"

"A friend," she said quickly. "A fellow traveler of the time roads. You exchanged letters with me one summer, Doctor Ó Cuilinn. My name is Gwen Madóc."

Another jolt of amazement and recognition. Then he glanced up and down the street. "We cannot talk here," he said. "Come inside."

He led us up a flight of stairs to a landing with three doors. The air here was chill, and the plaster walls chipped and discolored. Wood smoke and urine and the scent of stale cabbage made for a noxious combination of scents. Breandan unlocked the door to the left and ushered us inside.

We came into an entryway, which was little more than a cupboard, hung with several coats that smelled of mud and smoke.

There were no lamps here, and the only light spilled through a half-open door ahead. A man's boots had been flung into one corner. A faint electric scent, which called up memories from years ago, drifted from the rooms beyond.

Gwen passed me and went into the main apartment. I followed with Breandan.

More memories, but transplanted into this cramped and shabby setting. What had once been the parlor or sitting room was given over entirely to an enormous worktable covered with trays of wire, screws, batteries, and strange glass tubes. Various tools were scattered about, and in one corner stood a metal cage that reminded me of Gwen Madóc's own metal monster, but on a much smaller scale. An electric lamp hung over the table. The windows themselves were papered over thickly.

Breandan came into the room, still with that frightened wondering expression. "Áine. You . . . how did you find me?"

I touched his cheek. "Because you found me first. Let me explain." I needed a few moments to do so, however. I rubbed my cold-numbed hands together and paced around the room, finding it easier to speak when I did not look at Breandan directly. "For me, the year is 1914. You came to me at midnight, on March twenty-ninth."

"Yes, to warn you. There is a plot against Éire. Lord Ó Tíghearnaigh—"

"Ó Tíghearnaigh?"

"It started with another man. I can't remember his name. There were bribes, monies offered in exchange for more favorable trade agreements with the Prussian Alliance. Lord Ó Tíghearnaigh entered the scheme later, on the promise that he—"

"Enough," Gwen said sharply. "We must return to Cill Cannig, Your Majesty."

From outside, I heard the quarter bells ringing. Once, twice. We had half an hour, or less, before the time roads closed to us.

"One moment," I said to Gwen. "Breandan. You must not return to the past. If you do, you will die. You already have."

"But Áine, I must tell you more."

I shook my head. "I have Ó Tíghearnaigh's name. I will find out his accomplice. But you—you must not attempt to come back in time. Promise me, Breandan."

He seized me in an embrace. "I love you," he whispered in my ear. "I will always love you. Go, my love. Go, before you too are caught in the web of time."

He pressed his lips against mine in one last, long passionate kiss. Then, with a laugh, he caught up a book from the worktable and pressed it into my hands. "My last message, my love. Farewell."

I remembered only fragments of our journey back to the Éire of 1914. We hurried through the lanes to Cill Cannig's ruins. There, in that same courtyard where we had emerged, the air had already taken on an iridescent quality. Then a man's voice called out from the shadows. Gwen tightened her grip on my wrist and hurled us into the maelstrom.

Again the blackness. Again the stars blurred and jumped. Again the thousand and more paths radiating outward from each step. A numbness overtook me, until I knew nothing except Gwen's cold hand clasping mine, and the book Breandan had thrust at me in those last moments, which I held against my chest.

The stars spun around, and down toward the horizon, to a speck of gold, which seemed much smaller than the golden disc of the future. Gwen was reciting her numbers again, but with longer pauses in between. The numbers were growing smaller—from six digits, to five. I recognized a prime number from the mathematical studies of my childhood. The light marking our destination wavered, but Gwen did not deviate from the road, nor did she stop her recitation of ever smaller and smaller numbers.

. . . *Forty-one. Thirty-seven. Thirty-one. Twenty-nine. Nineteen. Seventeen. Thirteen. Seven. Three* . . .

Zero.

We tumbled into the time machine, skidding over the smooth floor until we crashed against the far wall. Bruised and dizzied, I lay gasping for breath. My skin prickled in the unexpected warmth. My heart thudded against my ribs. My thoughts tumbled even faster than my body had.

Gwen had loosed her grip on my hand. Dimly I heard her stumble to her feet. I rolled over onto my hands and knees. A stitch caught beneath my ribs and I bit back a groan. Already the images from Éire's future had blurred in my memory. It would be all too simple to believe them a fantasy. And what, after all, had we accomplished?

My companion was now hunched over her keyboard, tapping out a new command sequence. Her gaze skipped from me to a point beyond. I followed the direction of her glance and saw a book lying a few feet away, surrounded by a spattering of melting snow. *Breandan's gift.* I snatched it up.

The cover was plain black cardboard, worn around the edges with handling, and with a crack running diagonally across the title—*A History of the Modern World, Volume III*—printed in thick square letters.

The author's name was printed along the bottom edge of the cover. I could just make out the title of professor and a few letters of the surname. My hands still shaking, I opened the book and leafed through several blank pages until I came to one with the title repeated, then in smaller print, *Herr Professor Edward James White, Professor of Anglian Histories, Second Edition, Copyright 1939.*

My breath deserted me in that moment. This, this was more than a last message. This was a roadmap to the future.

I closed my eyes. No. This was a record of one future. Remember all those other roads, leading to other futures, I told myself. They might all be true, a set of parallels, or they might each represent potential futures, with only one remaining in the end. It didn't matter which. It only meant that changing one moment now did not necessarily create the future I desired.

Gwen had finished with her manipulation of the equipment. Now she eyed me with a strange intent expression. "Think carefully what you do."

I nodded. "I will. I promise."

Her brother had vanished from the outer laboratory. Gwen sat down at the nearest worktable and switched on one of the electric lamps. She had already dismissed my presence from her thoughts and was writing in a journal. I tucked Breandan's book underneath my arm and continued on to the outer doors, where my guard waited. We stared at each other, and I was conscious of my wind-blown hair and the mud stains on my coat. Then his gaze went blank and proper. Oh, there would be rumors, I knew. But not yet. Not until I had a chance to act.

Once I gained my apartments, I dismissed my escort and passed alone through the darkened rooms to my bedchamber door. I slipped the key from my pocket and let myself inside.

A turn of the switch flooded the room with cold light. I saw my rumpled bedclothes. Saw a shadow on the carpet, like that of a blanket hurriedly cast over a figure. Even as I fixed my gaze upon it, the image faded.

My breath trickled out. I drew another, and another.

He lives. Yes, he lives. Now I must see to the rest.

I spent the rest of the night reading and taking notes. By sunrise, I had the shape of a plan. Oh, but I would need all the caution and cleverness I possessed. Each decision I made would undo snippets of the future, but once undone, they might cause other and greater difficulties. More than once, I wished for my own machine to calculate the probabilities for each decision and its outcome. More than once, I wished for Aidrean Ó Deághaidh's counsel.

My first interview took place at seven o'clock, with Commander Ábraham of the Queen's Constabulary.

"I have received vital information," I told him, "concerning certain radical factions in Éire and across the Continent. Here are the names of their leaders, and where you might find them."

I handed him a sheet of paper with the names of Daniel Strong and his associates, the specifics gleaned from White's chapters on Éire's civil war. I included the method they had used to communicate their plans—a code based on the metaphysical poets of the seventeenth century—as well as the observation that Michael Okoye himself was not a part of their conspiracy.

Ábraham stared at the sheet. His lips moved, and I thought I saw recognition on his face, as though these names were not unknown to him. "What do you wish me to do, Your Majesty?"

"Detain our own citizens on suspicion of treason," I said. "While you have them in custody, take measures to contain the devices they have planted in Osraighe and other cities throughout Éire. Here is the list of suspected sites. The devices are not visible yet, but you understand the means they've used. Secure them as you would any ordinary bomb. Lord Ó Cadhla will have responsibility for the ones outside our borders. You understand?"

"Oh, yes, Your Majesty," he breathed. "I understand. Where—"

"From a number of sources," I replied. "They wish to remain anonymous."

Not that I thought he would believe me if I told him the truth—that my source was a book written in the future, which foretold my assassination this summer, and which told how, if we did not act, our cities would be turned to dust and Europe would be overrun by hordes of soldiers from the Prussian Alliance. Perhaps something of my own horror showed on my face, because Commander Ábraham did not question me further. "I will do as you command, Your Majesty."

Lord Ó Cadhla arrived when the clocks were striking half past nine. "I've heard a number of interesting rumors, Your Majesty."

"No doubt you have, my lord. The truth is even more unsettling."

He glanced around the audience chamber. I had locked away Breandan's history book in my private safe box long before I emerged from my bedchamber, but I knew at least one guard had noted its presence the night before.

"We have traitors in our Congress," I said. "Traitors across Europe. If we do nothing, Prussia will lay claim to the Continent, and from there, all of Africa and western Asia. Here is the report I have received from my spies."

I gave him a duplicate of the sheet I had given Commander Ábraham. To that, I added a second sheet with details about further attacks planned in Frankonia, Austria, Catalonia, and Serbia. To these, I had added their probable dates, all of them within the next five days.

His reaction was less pronounced, but nevertheless I could tell the surprise and shock went deep.

"There is more," I told him. "We must prevent an outbreak of war with the Nri Republic. They have a great deal of influence in Africa and Western Europe. I have word that radicals would like to assassinate Michael Okoye and lay the blame on us. They would do the same with the other members of the delegation. My proposal is this: we set a guard on the delegation, an obtrusive one. We also keep Mister Okoye in our prison another day or two. By then, we shall have taken the assassins into custody. I have further plans at work to make even this temporary delay more palatable."

Lord Ó Cadhla offered me a grim smile. "You do? And would you share these plans with me?"

"No. I am sorry, my friend, but I cannot. But I should be happy to explain my reasons afterward."

A lie, and he knew it. I could not tell him everything that had taken place this past night without betraying Gwen Madóc and her time machine. Nor the book that laid out all the dangers, including Lord Ó Cadhla's execution by radicals when he protested the military law advanced by Lord Ó Tíghearnaigh and his generals.

Two obstacles dealt with. The most difficult yet to come.

I had arranged for this meeting to take place at two o'clock, in an audience chamber situated in a remote wing of Cill Cannig. A little-used corridor led from here to the prison, but few knew about the connection. If this interview went badly—and I had no way to predict its outcome—I should want it.

Lord Ó Tíghearnaigh was the first to arrive. My steward was in attendance and offered us both a selection of wines and stronger spirits. Ó Tíghearnaigh accepted a glass of wine and had just taken his seat when my steward announced Lord Ó Rothláin's arrival.

"My lords," I said to them. "Please sit. I have a few questions for you."

My questions were more like statements. I wanted to know when they had first conspired to secret meetings with the Prussian agents, and when those meetings had turned from simple bribery to treason itself.

"Impossible," Lord Ó Tíghearnaigh breathed.

Lord Ó Rothláin regarded me with a cold stare. "You have no right to accuse us without evidence."

"But I have evidence, which Commander Ábraham's people have extracted from your private quarters. He acted with Lord Ó Duinn's permission, and mine. If you wish the Congress to hear your complaints, I am happy to agree."

I met their gazes with a smile. Lord Ó Rothláin shrugged, but Lord Ó Tíghearnaigh twitched nervously. If I were to believe the account from Breandan's history book, Ó Tíghearnaigh had resisted Ó Rothláin's bribes at first. It was only the last few months that he had succumbed to his own desires for a greater and grander army.

"Here is my proposal," I told them. "I wish to include Anglia, Manx, Wight, and Cymru in my Union of Nations. Further, I wish to make provisions for their representation in our Congress."

"You wish to grant the radicals their demands," Ó Rothláin said.

"Perhaps. Perhaps they have the right of it. What about you, my lord? Did you make these ghastly devices available to the Anglian radicals because you believe in their cause? Or because you think to win favors with the Prussians?"

"It's a lie," Ó Tíghearnaigh burst out. "I never meant—"

"Shut up, you fool."

If I had not already known which one had suborned the other, I would have now.

"I have the evidence to execute you both," I said. "Or I could call a trial for you and all your family and associates. Or . . . I might offer you clemency. Support my proposal for the Dependencies, and I promise not to prosecute you."

We argued for the remainder of that day and into the night. In the end, in the face of evidence, Lord Ó Rothláin agreed to persuade his faction to vote in favor of my plans. Lord Ó Tíghearnaigh proved less tractable, but in the end, he consented not to oppose me. On Tuesday morning, at ten o'clock, the Congress of Éire met to consider the matter of our Dependencies. Once, only once, that morning I dared to open my history book. The ink had blurred and the text shifted from one prophecy to another.

As the members of my Council and my Congress filed out of the chamber, I leaned back and closed my eyes. Victory. I hardly dared to admit the word, even in the silence of my thoughts. A temporary victory, I amended. Once the terror of these past few attacks had faded, these same congressmen would attempt to nibble away at my provisions for Anglia and its sister districts.

Gradually their footsteps receded and I was left in the silence of an empty room. I opened my eyes to the uncertain sunlight of a late March afternoon. Shadows flickered over the windows, as clouds drifted past the face of the sun, and there was a hint of rain in the air. I smiled. When was there ever not?

I stood—with amazing ease. I had expected to be utterly drained. So much accomplished in this morning, and yet so much more remained to be done. I was not fool enough to think we were finished with the future. It came to us step by step, fed by our desires and our ignorance. Even with Breándan's gift, I could not control all the possible paths.

Coilín waited for me outside the chamber. "Your Majesty. Commander Ábraham reports the Garda has arrested Strong and his associates, and they shall have all the devices from Osraighe secured before nightfall. He has notified the other nations as well, so that they can take measures."

"And our friends in Anglia and Wight and the rest of the Districts?"

"Watched and guarded, Your Majesty. There shall be no more accidents. Lord Ó Duinn himself has promised it."

I resisted the urge to retreat to my private apartments to consult my history book. I had two more necessary tasks to accomplish, before I could grant myself the solitude and sleep I craved.

To Coilín, I said, "I shall require an official copy of the proclamation, concerning my Union, as well as unofficial copies of the proposed amendments with regard to the Dependencies. Send for a motorcar, and have the copies ready when I return."

The hospital where the victims from Sunday's attack lay on the northwest edge of the city. The chief surgeon himself met me at the front doors, having received word from my secretary to expect me. They had placed Aidrean Ó Deághaidh in one of the private wards, he explained, as he escorted me through the corridors. The commander had slept only fretfully these past two days, in spite of the laudanum.

"He escaped the blast itself, but a section of the stone wall crushed the knee. We were able to avoid amputation, but barely. Even so, I fear he will never recover full use of his leg. The worst danger now, of course, is infection. He must sleep before he can heal, Your Majesty."

We had just arrived at Aidrean's room. "A quarter hour is all I ask," I said. "No longer."

The man withdrew. I entered alone and shut the door behind me.

The air was heavy with the scents of soap and antiseptic. A whispery breeze from a half-open window, however, brought with it a trace of damp earth, and the first ripe scent of the approaching spring.

Aidrean lay motionless on his bed. Bandages swathed his head and half his face. One leg had been braced and splinted. As I moved toward him, I took in more details of his injuries. The purpling bruises, the swollen jaw. The one hand lying limp by his side, encased in bandages almost to the fingertips. His dark complexion was gray in the sunlight, and he breathed unsteadily.

Oh, my friend.

As I approached his side, his eyes fluttered open.

"My Queen."

His voice was hardly more than a whisper. I gathered his hand loosely in both of mine. "My friend. I have come with good news. And a request."

He listened quietly as I recounted everything from the past day. About Breandan Ó Cuilinn, dead and alive. About my strange journey into the future, the book of history that foretold Éire's destruction and the rise of the Prussian dictatorship. The actions we had taken to undo that future. To everyone else I had lied, but to Aidrean Ó Deághaidh I could do nothing but tell him the truth.

"They shall demand you open the time roads," he said, when I described the outcome of my conference with Congress and Council. "Ó Tíghearnaigh . . ."

"Ó Tíghearnaigh and Ó Rothláin are aware I shall keep a watch on them. No one except you and I and Gwen Madóc know about Doctor Ó Cuilinn's book—not even Lord Ó Cadhla. For all they can tell, I have my own company of secret spies."

Aidrean laughed softly. "My Queen, you are . . ."

"Incomparable," I said with a smile. "But I promised to keep this visit to a quarter hour, and I must ask you now my great favor." I hesitated. "What I ask is not fair, but I have never treated you fairly."

His fingers curled around my hands. "We are both servants of Éire. What is this favor?"

I gave myself a few moments, considering how to best phrase my thoughts. "The surgeons tell me your leg is badly injured, and you will need many months to recover. That is one thing. Another is that we have evaded immediate disaster, but we must be vigilant. We have not cured the sickness and hatred and violence, we have only temporarily bandaged the wounds. So. I want you to return to Cetinje and your family. Let a few months pass, then apply to me to relinquish your post as chief of the embassy. You will remain in Cetinje, however. You have friends there already. From time to time, you might visit other cities to consult physicians about your health. Along the way, you will make new friends."

"A spy, then?"

I heard the faint edge to his words. I smiled. "I told you this was a great favor. No, I don't want a spy, but I do want you to be my trusted eyes and ears. Listen to what people say in the markets and cafés and in the streets. Watch for the danger signals. I shall never have a book from the future again. Will you do this for me? For Éire?"

He sighed and stared upward at the ceiling. I waited patiently as the clock ticked onward through the minutes. "I will do as you ask," he said at last. "I . . . I've grown accustomed to the sunlight in Montenegro. And I would like to spend more time with Valerija and my daughters." The tension in his mouth eased into an almost smile. "I might even take up mathematics again."

The sun was slanting behind the rooftops of Cill Cannig when I returned. My secretary waited for me with a sheaf of papers, wrapped in a leather case and tied with ribbons. "The proclamation and the transcripts you requested, Your Majesty."

"Thank you, Coilín." I took the papers from his hands. "Where is Mister Okoye?"

"In the south orchard. The Constabulary made a search before he entered the grounds. He is safe, Your Majesty."

I nodded and continued around the palace, down the flight of flagstone steps and through a wrought iron gate. Beyond the formal gardens, past the newly greening lawns, another gate brought me into the orchard my great-great-grandmother had commissioned, when she first assumed the throne. Apple trees stood in rows, their bare branches like stiff gray brushstrokes, but I could see the knobs where leaves would bloom within the next month.

I picked my way down the stone path between the trees. Okoye was not in sight, but I suspected where he'd gone. When I came to the next fork, I took the one that curved away to the left, between the trees, and down to a pool of water bordered by flat limestone boulders from Éire's north. Birch and pine saplings blanketed the grounds. A rich ripe scent met me as I entered the green-lit copse. Here it was nearly twilight, but high above the skies were alight with the setting sun, and the pale walls of Cill Cannig were visible through the trees.

Just as I had guessed, Michael Okoye stood at the water's edge, gazing at the dark expanse.

"Mister Okoye."

He spun around.

So much had transpired in the six weeks since Thomas Alan Austen had died in the snow-drifted courtyard—murder and terror and a world tipping over into chaos.

"I have news," I said. "And a request."

His mouth twitched into a bitter smile. "You have demanded a great deal from me already. Why should I agree to more?"

"Because it concerns your homeland. Because it concerns Peter Godwin, who is dead."

I motioned toward a stone bench, set underneath an elderly apple tree. Michael Okoye stiffened at the mention of Godwin. When I pointed again, he sat down with obvious reluctance and clasped his hands together tightly. "When did he die?" he asked.

"Four days ago. We believe it was nationalist radicals from Prussia. They wished to implicate the Anglian cause in the attack on Osraighe. The attack is why I had you arrested. Mister Godwin's death is why I did not release you until today."

He laughed soundlessly. "And I should be grateful for that?"

"No." I took the seat beside him and untied the ribbons around the leather case. "My request has nothing to do with gratitude, only with the security of our nations. Here . . ." I laid the proclamation out before him with all its seals and signatures. "Anglia, Manx, Wight, and Cymru will each have a seat in the Union of Nations. And with these . . ." I spread out the record of the morning's session. ". . . my Congress has agreed that each District shall have the right to elect representatives to Éire's Congress."

Quite a long time passed as Michael Okoye stared at the papers.

"And what is your request?" he said at last.

"It comes in two parts. That you present my proclamation to your fellow delegates and all the Districts. Once you have done so, I would like you to return to Cill Cannig, this time as my guest—my true guest. You understand," I added, "that each District will have its own representative, and the others are not obligated to align themselves with Anglia's wishes."

Another laugh, just as silent, but this time colored with genuine amusement. "Yes, I know what you mean. There are times I believe Anglia would like to rule over the Districts, as much as Éire rules over them." Then the humor leaked away and he stared pensively across the water. "But why ask *me* to come back? Why not one of the others?"

From a distance came the trill of birdsong, and the whisper of a breeze amongst the trees. Though I knew my guards stood watch around this dell, I had the sense of a strange and special intimacy that I might never capture again. *Honesty for honesty,* I told myself. *Trust for trust.*

"Because I have a need for hard truths," I said, "however much I dislike them. Because I believe you have a sense of justice. Whatever representatives Anglia and the other districts elect, I should like to have your advice in days to come."

He shook his head, but I knew this was not an answer. For the second time within the hour, I waited patiently as the sun ticked down behind the trees and the air shimmered gold and crimson with the dying sunset.

"I will," he said quietly. "Not for your sake, or mine, but for those who come after us. I cannot say when yet—I must deliver your message to the Districts and speak with my friends first. After that, I must make arrangements with my family. But yes, before the year is over, I shall return. I promise."

Two promises given. Two candles lit for the future.

I returned at last to my bedchamber. My maids undressed me and helped me into a nightgown and wrapper. They laid out a supper of hot soup and warm bread, built up the fire, then left me to the solitude I so badly needed.

Aidrean would remain in Éire another two months, according to the surgeons. Michael Okoye would depart within a few days, carrying my offering of representation to his people. Soon Gwen and Síomón Madóc would dismantle their laboratory and return to their institute. In the next month or so, I would send a letter to Gwen and ask that she write to me from time to time about her experiments, but I would not depend on her answering. She and her brother were justly dubious about allowing me, and through me the kingdom of Éire, to know what possibilities they discovered.

I finished my supper and set the dishes aside. Sleep called out to me, but I was not yet done with the day. From the safe box behind my bed, I took out the history book Breandan had thrust into my hands in those last frantic moments. My pulse leapt as I confirmed that the paragraphs describing my assassination had vanished. So too Michael Okoye's death. The Prussian Empire did not overrun Frankonia's borders.

Neither did I know what events replaced those. The ink had blurred, the pages had turned blank or were missing. Whatever dangers lay ahead, I had no road map to avoid them.

But I remembered Michael Okoye's promise. To myself, I made a vow.

We shall have our tomorrow. I swear it.